DROWNING TUCSON

DROWNING TUCSON

A NOVEL

Aaron Michael Morales

COFFEE HOUSE PRESS
MINNEAPOLIS 2010

COFFEE HOUSE PRESS books are available to the trade through our primary distributor, Consortium Book Sales & Distribution, www.cbsd.com or (800) 283-3572. For personal orders, catalogs, or other information, write to: info@coffeehousepress.org.

Coffee House Press is a nonprofit literary publishing house. Support from private foundations, corporate giving programs, government programs, and generous individuals helps make the publication of our books possible. We gratefully acknowledge their support in detail in the back of this book. To you and our many readers around the world, we send our thanks for your continuing support.

Good books are brewing at coffeehousepress.org.

LIBRARY OF CONGRESS CIP INFORMATION

Morales, Aaron Michael.
Drowning Tucson / by Aaron Michael Morales.
p. cm.
ISBN 978-1-56689-240-7 (alk. paper)
1. Tucson (Ariz.)—Fiction. 2. Inner cities—Fiction.
3. Street life—Fiction. 4. Urban poor—Fiction.
5. Poor families—Fiction. 6. Gangs—Fiction.
7. Violence—Fiction.
I. Title.
PS3613.066D76 2010
813'.6—DC22
2010000380

PRINTED IN CANADA
1 3 5 7 9 8 6 4 2
FIRST EDITION | FIRST PRINTING

ACKNOWLEDGMENTS

The author would like to thank the following people: Francisco Aragón, Fred Arroyo, Anitra Budd, Paloma Martinez-Cruz, Scott Heim, Patricia Henley, Chris Fischbach, Rachel Wedding McClelland, Howard McMillan, Patricia Moosbrugger, the entire Morales clan, Carlos Murillo, Paul Martinez Pompa, Erin Pringle, the Rose family, Benjamin Alire Sáenz, Leslie Marmon Silko, Sharon Solwitz, Luis Alberto Urrea, and Helena María Viramontes.

Portions of *Drowning Tucson* originally appeared in *Another Chicago Magazine*, MAKE: *A Chicago Literary Magazine*, PALABRA: *A Magazine of Chicano & Latino Literary Art*, *Passages North*, and in a chapbook of short fiction titled *From Here You Can Almost See the End of the Desert* (Momotombo Press, 2008).

For Elizabeth

TABLES OF CONTENTS

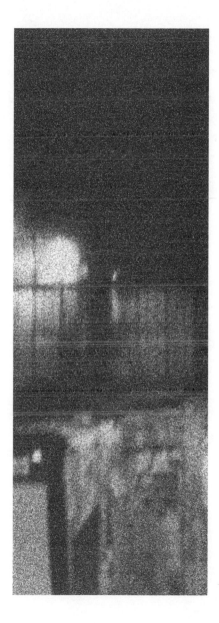

TORCHY'S

THERE'S THE GODDAM SPICS I WAS TELLING YOU ABOUT. Hanging out next to Torchy's. If they aren't sticking up poor Torchy, they're laying some girl behind the place. Nothing but trouble. You'll learn. Officer Loudermilk's new partner nodded, making notes. Torchy's. Spics. He listened to Loudermilk. Yep, you'll see. Get a chance to meet em soon enough. Especially them fuckin Nuñezes. This is their favorite hangout. This and Reid Park. Nuñez. Reid Park. Torchy's. He wrote fast. Officer Loudermilk pulled the cruiser up next to the liquor store, flipped on his cherries. What you boys up to? They cuffed their cigarettes, choked back their smoke. Nothin. Just waitin on the school bus—which was a lie. School was within walking distance. They were waiting on Felipe to show up. Well, you'd better get moving. I'll be back in fifteen minutes and if you're still here, I'm taking all of you in to juvey for truancy. He rolled the window up and drove off. The kids waited until he turned the corner, then they flipped him off. Fuck you, Loudermilk. Yeah, and your punkass wife. Trying to one up each other. And your mom, with her stank fifty-husband-havin ass. Hahaha. Fuckin pigs. They leaned back against the wall and puffed their cigarettes, waiting on Felipe to show so they could rib him a few more times before he was made into a King and became off-limits, unless you wanted to get the shit kicked out of you.

A few of them scraped paint off the walls of the liquor store. It came off in big flakes, and sometimes a sharp point stabbed the flesh beneath their nails and hurt like hell. Felipe's best friend, Ricardo, used his house key to carve his name into a poster advertising Mexican beer. La cerveza mas fina. They always made Mexico look so pretty. You think he'll show, Ricardo? You damn right he'll show. Felipe aint no bitch. He'd take you and Loudermilk at the same time. He talked his friend up, but even he was worried about whether or not Felipe was going to show. Today Felipe was going to get his ass kicked worse than he ever had. For him, becoming a King was going to be harder than it had been for his brothers because he was the last one. The last Nuñez. The one who had to continue the dynasty. Nuñez. That's no small shit around here.

Ricardo was glad they were friends. He liked Felipe because he was different from the others. His conversations were about more than bitches and drugs. If you got him alone, he would surprise you with his ability to carry on an intelligent conversation. He told good jokes. Said smart things. He didn't judge Ricardo for wearing the same pair of jeans for the past two years. Plus Ricardo knew something the others didn't. Felipe, for all of his toughness, loved books—especially their smell. When he wasn't hanging out with the Kings and his brothers, or sitting beside Torchy's watching his friends breakdance on a flattened refrigerator box, he hid in his bedroom reading Dickens and Hardy. On their walks to and from school, they talked about how they wanted to save up money and one day go to London to see if the city was still as crazy as Dickens made it sound.

Unlike the rest of the guys standing next to Torchy's waiting to see how scared Felipe was, Ricardo wanted to talk with Felipe so he could tell him it was going to be all right. He wished the other guys weren't there so he could go up to his friend and give him a hug and say I'm here for you man, if you need a place to go or someone to talk with. He was scared for Felipe. Although Ricardo had never been beaten himself, he'd seen the way people were inducted into the gang plenty of times. On rare occasions a person or two had almost fought his way out—the bigger and older ones—but they always fell to the sheer number of men beating them. A hard enough blow to the kidneys, a well-placed kick to the stomach, and the guy just dropped and folded into a tight knot, waiting for the punches and kicks to stop. Even though he wasn't in a gang, he knew how these things worked. The more they liked you and the more respect they had for you, the worse the beating.

While his friends waited for him outside Torchy's, Felipe kissed his mother goodbye and pulled on his backpack. On his way out the door his brothers waved and told him see you after school. He was nervous about the beating he was going to get, but he didn't want his mother to notice and do that huggy thing where she never let go of him, as if she were never going to see him again. Every morning before school the same thing. Hug your mother, Felipe. Give an old woman a hug and don't be so mean. He stood beside her while she sat in her rocking chair, leaning down and immediately trying to pull away as soon as her arms were around his neck. It bothered him the way she held on a little too long. Like she loved him more than a mother should. But today he let her hug him longer than usual, and then he kissed her goodbye and closed the door behind him and left her sitting in her rocking chair where she stayed every day since her husband had died three years earlier. The fear he had been suppressing all morning came crashing down when he walked through the front yard and out the gate to meet his friends. He was afraid of the asskicking planned for this afternoon, but that's what it takes to be a King. Especially being the last Nuñez brother. All of them were Kings. Even his dad had been one, though he had gone into retirement by getting married and having four sons. Felipe kept repeating to himself, just play it cool. You let the others see you're scared and you'll only make it worse. But he was scared. Not of a few punches. His brothers had been abusing him since he was two years old, took turns punching him or smothering him with a pillow. So that wasn't it. Besides, punches and kicks stopped hurting after a while. He was scared it would be worse than that. A royal beating. That's the life here. He understood that much. You take your raps and keep going. He didn't feel sorry for himself. It was much more than that. He was at a crossroads. Soon he had to make a decision. Though his path had been chosen for him before he was born, he tried to understand the consequences in his adolescent sort of way. There were certainly benefits for joining the Kings. He'd have the respect—or at least the fear—of all his peers. He'd get the chance to lay girls he had only dreamed of. There would always be money, booze, drugs. And while these things were nice, Felipe knew there was a price. That's what bothered him the most.

Knowing his life would improve but living with the fear of prison or death. He didn't want to be found in the desert with a bullet in his head, or locked in the trunk of a car in the Tucson Mall parking lot. He wanted something else. To be a man in a different way.

The night before, he had lain awake listening to the sound of the swamp cooler switching on periodically, its engine vibrating the ceiling, and it took him a long time to find a rhythm to the motor's whirring, a regularity to the intervals when the sound would cease and he could doze off. When he finally slept, his dreams were short, violent snatches of being chased by cops, beating groups of rival gang members, the sounds of weeping mothers and girlfriends mourning the loss of their men. It seemed the whole city wept, like it was drowning in tears over the blood shed on its streets every day. Felipe woke with the sound of wailing in his ears and lay awake the rest of the night trying to erase the terrible images from his mind.

After he hugged his mother goodbye, he walked toward Country Club Road, wondering why he was more ashamed and scared than proud. Although it was his fifteenth birthday, he didn't feel any wiser. He had been looking forward to this day forever. He was supposed to gain some sort of knowledge about life, but he only felt confused. And lonely. His friends waiting for him at Torchy's could never understand the pressure he was under. Even Ricardo could not know how Felipe was torn between his destiny as a Nuñez and his desire to leave this neighborhood to seek an entirely different life.

His friends were only waiting so they could make fun of him one last time. He knew they were actually terrified of him. They were probably jealous too, though Felipe thought he had a better reason to be jealous than they. At least they had a choice in their futures. If the Kings didn't pick one of them, they could fade into anonymity. But he had been chosen. He had never specifically been told there were no other options. He simply became aware of the fact as he grew older. It was his arranged marriage.

His brothers had sculpted him into a petty criminal before he was old enough to realize what they were doing. When he was six, they'd babysat him every Friday while their parents worked late. Instead of playing with Felipe in the backyard or reading him books, they walked him over to Food Giant, plopped him into a shopping cart, and toured around the grocery store, filling his pants and shirt with cigarettes and candy and beef jerky. They bought a gallon of milk, then wheeled him out of the store, laughing about how they'd pulled another one over on the gringos. It was always pulling one over on the gringos. It would be another two years before Felipe understood what gringos were. He thought they were some kind of monster when he was a boy. He couldn't understand why every night when he asked his mother to tuck him in and pray the gringos don't get me mommy, she'd laugh and sign the cross above him. If it was so funny and they were so harmless, then why were his brothers and their friends always talking about getting them? Every Friday they'd go back to Food Giant and fill Felipe's clothes and get the gringos, and Felipe grew so used to their game that for years he had to check himself when he went grocery shopping with his mother. His hands would grow itchy. His pockets felt twice their size, taunting him to stuff them full when no one was looking.

It didn't take long for his brothers to tire of that game. There were other ways to get gringos. Other ways to groom their youngest brother for greatness. The Food Giant jobs were fun, but they were too easy. After all, if a six-year-old boy could get away with stealing cigarettes week after week, then the gringos had bigger problems than the Nuñezes.

The day after Felipe's eleventh birthday, he pulled his first real job. It was the one that finally earned him respect and credibility with the Kings. He was sitting at the park watching his brothers play ball with their friends, smoking cigarette butts he found lying along the edges of the basketball court. When it began to get dark, they sat on a picnic table passing a joint between them, watching the occasional drunk stumble past with a brown bag clutched in his fist. They made bets on which ones would fall over and which ones would actually sit down before passing out. The bet with the highest odds was guessing which drunk would actually puke. Most of them pissed themselves, a few even smelled like they had just shit their pants, but puking was something these guys just didn't seem capable of doing. They didn't waste liquor.

A drunk gringo stumbled toward them in a dirty, grease-stained trenchcoat. Felipe's two oldest brothers, Chuy and Rogelio, bet their friends the guy would pass out standing. Five bucks. Five bucks? How bout I get Marcela to suck you off instead? Okay. Everyone watched as the drunk drew closer, stopped, teetered, found his footing, then bee-lined for a metal trashbarrel and hugged it as he vomited into the container. They all thought the same thing. FUCK. I knew I should've bet this one was a puker. The boys laughed and Chuy told them if I get that bad, just kill me. Just give me a kick in the head. His best friend, Peanut, said why don't we get a little practice on him? The drunk was slumped against the trashbarrel, breathing heavily and cradling his paper bag. Felipe laughed, trying to sound tough. Kick his ass. They all laughed at him. Talkin like a big man. Like a real vato. Peanut said why don't we let Felipe do it? He needs to take things up a notch. Show his Nuñez blood. If Peanut hadn't said that last line, Felipe's brothers might have laughed it off. But once he mentioned their name, they were obligated to make their little brother go through with it.

Felipe looked at his brothers. They were silent for too long. Usually they'd snap right back with a smartass comment or something, but they weren't talking. They were trying to decide between the danger of sending their baby brother to beat a grown man—what if the guy's not that drunk and he hurts Felipe?—and the necessity of upholding the family name. Felipe knew it was decided before his brother Rogelio elbowed him in the ribs and told him go roll that fuckin bum. Just go up and blast him upside the head and check his pockets. Before he could think of an excuse, Felipe was being cheered on by the guys, and Peanut was pointing to the crown tattooed on the back of his neck, nodding to Felipe and looking genuinely proud of him as he stood up and walked quickly over to the drunk before he could chicken out. When he was still more than twenty feet away, he could smell the liquor pouring off the guy and knew he was probably blacked out already, or at least too wasted to fight back, so he ran straight at the man, the cheers of the guys behind him propelling him faster, and he kicked him dead in the side of his skull and the man's eyes shot open, confused, full of pain and surprise, and for a moment Felipe thought fuck, I'm dead, he was faking all along, not realizing he was still kicking the guy in the side of the head until he heard the man grunt and saw him fall over onto his side, spilling his beer on the ground around him, and Felipe's foot hurt like hell, but he ignored it and punched the guy in the stomach, then shuffled through the stinking-drunk gringo's pockets, only finding a dollar and some change and a crumpled pack of Merits, happy the man had been too far gone to fight back or even see him coming and pleased with himself because he knew he had made his brothers proud, their whoops and yells of approval making him feel twice his size.

All the way home, his brothers congratulated him on how he'd rolled the fuckin gringo like a Nuñez. Just like a real goddam vato. They took turns rustling his hair and slapping him on the back. You're one of us now. At the time Felipe wasn't sure what that meant. One of who? A Nuñez? A King? But as the years passed and he grew closer to his brothers and their friends, he realized he was both.

The day in the park had been a test for Felipe. Peanut had wanted to see if the little guy had the same craziness in him as his brothers. He also wanted to know whether or not Felipe would take orders. Kicking some drunk's ass was only a start. A baby step. Felipe knew this too. So he wasn't surprised when their neighbor, Señor Gutierrez, went on vacation and the Kings decided to poke around in his house a bit. Since it was summer, Felipe was left alone all day with his brothers. The Kings gathered at the Nuñez house and snuck down the alley toward Señor Gutierrez's backyard.

Behind the back wall someone said okay Felipe, you're the first one in. Climb through that back window—break it if you have to—then go around and unlock the back door. We'll take care of the rest. They lifted him over the wall, giving him words of encouragement, and he ran to the house, stopping only to pick up a stone and throw it through the old man's bedroom window, then feeling around for the latch. He unlocked the window and climbed inside. The house was cool. It felt quiet and holy, like a church, and he immediately regretted breaking in. He suddenly realized this wasn't a gringo's house they were messing with. It belonged to Gutierrez, the poor man everyone in the neighborhood liked. He wanted to run out the front door, circle around, and tell the guys some bullshit about how there was an alarm or he'd heard a dog growling. Besides, there isn't shit here to steal anyways.

He looked out the window and saw them waving and gesturing impatiently. A couple had already jumped the wall and were walking toward the house. Felipe turned around and passed through the room—trying to ignore the old man's neatly made bed and the photos of his dead wife and son on the nightstand—and into the kitchen where he unlocked the back door and let them in and considered yelling why are we messin with old Gutierrez? But he'd already been pushed out of the way by the guys surging through the back door. In all, they spent less than ten minutes ransacking the house, and when they met back at the Nuñez's house their take was a VCR—the TV was a console and too heavy to get out in a hurry—eight cassettes, a gold-plated Seiko watch, and a jar full of quarters. Not much of a haul, someone said. But for Felipe it was too much.

Stealing from a store or slashing tires or pouring sugar into a gas tank was easy. It was easier still to kick some drunk's ass and take his money. But Gutierrez was a friend of the family. They were stealing from a person they knew actually needed the things they were taking. He wasn't a drunk. He wasn't a bitter burned-out shell, like most of the old people in the neighborhood. He was kind and cheerful and all the kids on the block knew this. They knew he gave out the best candy every Halloween. They knew if their school was having a fundraiser, Gutierrez was guaranteed to buy something from them. Even back when Rogelio played soccer for the AYSO, Gutierrez had donated money to the team for uniforms.

Felipe didn't like the guilt he was feeling. He had no desire to hear the Kings applaud him for his performance and his balls. But it was a step in the right direction. Felipe was moving up, and he knew it.

And so did all of his peers. The ones waiting outside Torchy's, smoking cigarettes, checking out the bitches, whistling at the young mommys on their morning walks. Felipe didn't want to see them. He didn't want to hear their questions about his big day. He wanted to walk right past Torchy's and Food Giant and the El Campo tire store where men lazed about on stacks of tires, waiting for customers, their hair held up in black hairnets and cigarettes flapping in their mouths. He could go south to

Interstate 10 and maybe over to Benson and then to Las Cruces or El Paso, wandering the desert in search of a different life. But he was too scared. He had no idea what was out there. Here at least he knew what was expected.

He was jealous of his friends. They could commit a crime and everyone would consider them men. Or, if all else failed, any of them could find a willing girl and take her behind Torchy's and throw her on the mattress by the dumpster, climb on top of her, and lay her good while she squirmed beneath him, feigning interest but really reading the posters stapled to the building advertising Mexican beer or pork rinds, silently translating the Spanish to English and back to Spanish until the boy above her was finished. If he forgot, she'd remind him to give her a hickey so he could prove he'd slept with her. She'd scratch his back a little or grab his arm enough to leave a bruise for him to show off to his friends. But being a Nuñez meant there were no other options. Just bite the bullet, take your lumps, and carry on. It was that simple.

Ricardo saw him round the corner first. Hey, Felipe. The rest of the guys stood and yelled here comes Mister-the-King himself. Takin names and smackin bitches. Felipe smiled, but he wanted to tell them all to fuck off. Get your little asses off the wall and go to school. It made him sick the way they sucked up to him. Especially because he knew they all talked shit behind his back and were probably bursting with anticipation for the after-school initiation. All except Ricardo. He was the only one who knew Felipe's secret—that he didn't want to be in a gang. That he didn't want to spend his life pretending to hate cops when really he was afraid of them. If Felipe joined the Kings, he would be one forever. Until he died, or went to prison, or got married and found a job fixing cars or working in a restaurant.

His friends gathered around him. Hey, Felipe, you bring your helmet for after school? They laughed. Lit more cigarettes. We thought maybe you had some last words. Yeah, you know, maybe you should pray for your soul during lunch. They joked the rest of the way to school and Ricardo occasionally patted Felipe on the shoulder, when no one was looking.

———

Señora Nuñez sat in her rocking chair thinking of her son. Ever since she had whispered I love you in his ear when he hugged her goodbye, she had been praying the rosary on his behalf. Why are men so foolish? Why do they hurt themselves and each other when there are people at home who love them? For years she had been asking herself these questions, and she had never received an answer. So she succumbed to her belief that men are only capable of loving behind closed doors, and she petitioned the Blessed Virgin to pray for her sons.

She was glad this was the last time she would have to worry over a child. Her heart was tired and could take no more sorrow. Many years before, when her oldest son was still a boy, she had realized the trials of motherhood. Sure, there was great joy in creating children and raising them. There was the pride of first footsteps, first words, and the first day of school. But she never anticipated the sadness of watching her boys grow into men.

Even before her sons were old enough to make foolish decisions, she had learned to hide her pain and make her boys tough. Like the time Chuy had gotten his first paper route. He had been so excited when he finished wrapping the newspapers and stuffing them into the bags tied to his bike handlebars for the first time. She'd waved from the door and smiled as her son wobbled down the driveway, weaving back and forth before he finally straightened his bike and pedaled into the darkness. She was still beaming and holding her bathrobe closed when she heard the sound of Chuy's bike crashing and the horrible shrieks that pierced her heart and sent her running across the street, her robe blowing open as she ran, ignoring the fact that her naked body had grown cold, exposed to the morning air, not caring that anyone looking out his window could see her breasts bouncing under the streetlamps as she dashed frantically to her son's side and pulled him from the row of cactus where he had landed.

She carried Chuy back home and laid him on the couch, holding back tears so her other sons, who stood in the living room, awakened by the noise and rubbing their eyes, wouldn't have to see their mother's sadness. Chuy lay there, trickling blood from hundreds of punctures. She ordered her sons to help her tear the needles from his flesh, and for the rest of the morning, Señora Nuñez and her boys worked in silence, removing every spine from Chuy's arms and scalp and stomach. Had she known motherhood could be so painful, she might not have had four sons.

They were so sweet when they were young. Back when they needed her. She missed the way her sons used to come to her when something was wrong, as if she were the only person in the world who could fix their problems. But the older they grew, the colder they became. They cut themselves off from her. And now she had no idea whether or not they were sad or happy. Their faces were simply hard masks.

She didn't understand how babies could grow to be such hate-filled creatures. One by one, as her three eldest sons turned into men, she watched them come into the house covered in cuts and bruises, mumbling curses. She knew they had joined that stupid gang, the one her husband used to be in. He had warned them about joining the Kings, had told them time and again how he would beat them senseless if he ever got word of them running around with those thugs, but he worked such long hours there was no way he could enforce the rules. She tried to do it for him, but she could never bring herself to punish her sons when they came home late, smelling like marijuana and alcohol. Instead, she nursed their wounds and helped them get cleaned up and into bed before their father came home.

For years she took solace in her youngest boy. She longed for him to become a respectable man, the kind of man she had wanted her other sons to become. At night, while her husband and sons slept, she snuck into the boys' room and lifted Felipe out of his crib and carried him into the living room to rock him. She sang him songs and told him stories. She loved that he smelled like a man. Even when he was young enough to breastfeed, his body had the scent of a hard day's work. She took it as a sign—he was the one who was going to go to college and meet a nice girl and get married and make her lots of grandbabies. So, when her husband came home angry and beat the boys because they had probably done something bad while he was away, she grabbed Felipe and carried him into her bedroom, snuggling with him on the bed until his father's rage had passed. More than once, when he actually chased after Felipe with a belt, she had stepped between them and told her husband he would have to beat her to get to her baby. Eventually he forgot about Felipe and focused all of his attention on his other sons.

More than anything, she hoped Felipe would come home today the same as when he left. She wasn't sure if she could handle seeing another one of her sons come home with the look in his eyes that said I'm a man now and I understand my burden is to become hard so I can handle the pain of living among other men. But she understood Felipe needed to make this decision on his own.

While she sat worrying about losing her last son, Chuy and Rogelio and David walked past and told her bye. Got to get to work, Mom. Got to help Peanut with his car. They always had something to do. Anything but stay home and keep their mother company. But that's okay. I'll just sit here and wait on Felipe. The house is clean and in a couple hours I'll put his cake in the oven so it will be ready by the time he comes home. I hope he likes it. It's his favorite. The yellow cake with chocolate icing. She was proud of her son. She rocked in her chair and waited.

In the lunchroom at Mansfield Junior High the students were unusually calm. They talked quietly and looked around nervously. Once in a while Felipe heard his name whispered, but he ignored it. He sat next to Ricardo and picked the meat from his sloppy joe. It was stringy and stained his fingers a rusty color. His appetite was gone.

They went outside to walk around for the rest of the lunch period. Some black guys were playing ball in front of a group of white girls, and one of Felipe's friends commented on how the niggers get all the good pussy these days. Between them and the Kings, we only get scraps. What's wrong with those bitches anyway? Felipe rolled his eyes. He wasn't in the mood. All morning he had been going over his options.

He could run. That would solve one problem. But earlier in the day another problem arose when Lavinía slipped him a note telling him how proud she was of him for becoming a King. How she had been eying him ever since she moved to 25th Street seven years earlier. She and her friends, Helena and the two Rosas, had talked about him many times and decided she and Felipe were a perfect match. He had everything she was looking for. He was handsome. He was intelligent. People looked up to him. If the note was supposed to help, it didn't. Now he wasn't sure what to do. Lavinía had told him outright that she wanted him, and that was hard to turn down. She was fine. Beautiful brown hair. Nice rack. The works. Now here she was telling him that after he became a King she would be proud to be his girlfriend. He ignored his friends rambling about all the different bitches at Mansfield they wanted to screw and thought about Lavinía and how much he'd like to give her a book he'd stolen from the school library. The librarian let him steal books because he took good ones. Not the usual horror or romance novels the other kids tried to lift. If he gave her *Wuthering Heights,* maybe she'd invite him over one day after school and they could talk about it on the couch while he rubbed her arm or her hair and leaned forward as she was in the middle of a sentence to surprise her with a kiss. After that she would give herself to him and they would make love and snuggle until it was time for him to go home for dinner.

He stopped walking when he reached the fence at the far end of the schoolyard and told his friends to go on without him. You sure, Felipe? Yeah. You too, Ricardo. I need to be alone. They left and he stood looking at the brush on the other side of the fence, thinking of Lavinía and his mother and his brothers and all the things everyone expected of him, growing angry, frustrated. He jumped over the fence and ran, ignoring his friends, who yelled after him. If he had turned around he might have seen Ricardo smiling and nodding his head. But he didn't.

He ran as fast as he could, leaping over cactus and weaving around other, spidery plants until he made it to the nearest alley, where he turned and ran more, ignoring the pain in his chest and shins and the pounding in his temples, trying desperately to think of a place to go and scared that if he stopped he would break into tears over his foolishness and feel like a helpless little boy, so he kept going, running until he found himself exhausted and standing in an unfamiliar part of the city.

Stone Avenue was dotted with empty buildings. Hotels with their signs bashed or burned out, a few strip joints, stores that reminded him of Old West watering holes. Felipe wandered around trying to catch his breath, looking in windows and checking doors to see if any were unlocked. None were. He stopped at a pastel blue building with a sign that said The S ank Club. There was a bright outline of paint where the W had fallen off. Looking for a place to rest, he walked behind the building and found a cove where deliveries were only accepted between the hours of 2 and 4 p.m. It was shady and cool. He found some old cardboard boxes and spread them out, then he lay down on them and slept for the rest of the afternoon.

When Felipe woke hours later, the sun had already gone down. He lay still with his eyes open, trying to remember the route he had taken to end up in this deserted part of the city.

When he finally rose and walked to the front of the building, he was startled to find the street alive with activity. Cars cruised by playing music loudly, their drivers sunk down in their seats with only their foreheads visible above their opened windows. The hotels, which had looked abandoned earlier, were lit up against the desert sky.

The walls of the Swank Club shook with the deep bass of dance music. Felipe tried to see inside, but the windows were blacked out. He didn't understand why a bar wouldn't want anyone to see in, so he walked to the front door and pulled it open. When his eyes adjusted to the smoke and lights, he saw a woman lying on her back in the middle of the bar, twirling her bra above her head. She got to her knees and began pulling at her panties, revealing a little patch of hair, and Felipe couldn't believe his luck. A naked woman, with great tits, right there in front of him. Close enough that he only had to take a few steps and he could reach out and feel her soft skin.

Is this some kind of joke? Felipe looked to his left, directly at the chest of a huge man looming over him. A joke? What do you mean? The bouncer's arms were so thick he couldn't cross them over his chest. He just rested them on top of his gut and stared down at Felipe. You got ID? You know you have to be an adult to come in here, and I'm guessing, little man, that you aren't exactly full-grown yet. Felipe shook his head. He was mortified. Everyone in the place is probably looking right at me thinking look at this dumbass kid trying to sneak in here. He turned to leave, and the bouncer stopped him. Hey, little man. Consider that a freebie. Now you know what you have to look forward to. He smiled, see you in a few years, then he pushed the door open for Felipe to leave.

If that's what I have to look forward to, I can wait. He wasn't thinking about the naked woman. He was thinking about the lonely-looking man he'd seen just as the bouncer kicked him out. The old man was crouched in his chair at the foot of a stage, where another dancer was shedding her clothes. His back was an exhausted curve, his hair badly brushed over his balding scalp. The man's arm was extended toward her, a dollar bill folded between his fingers for her to grab whenever she became desperate enough to approach him. They seemed to both be there because of an obligation and not because they had chosen to show up. Felipe always figured if you went to a tittie bar, you would be excited. Maybe there was a small chance you could even score with a stripper. But this guy was sitting there like he was being forced to sit through a midnight mass. Damn, the stripper's tits were real nice, though. They looked real firm, and he wished he could've touched them just once. Still, it hadn't been a total loss.

He walked to the street and sat down on the curb to smoke a cigarette and watch traffic. If Ricardo knew he'd been in a strip joint, even if it had only been for a moment, he'd be so jealous.

He hadn't noticed it before, but there were women everywhere. They were walking down the street in pairs, laughing and flicking cigarettes onto the pavement. A few leaned against lampposts or lounged in the doorways of bars or under the awnings of hotel lobbies, playing with their hair or checking their makeup in compact mirrors. Felipe couldn't believe the way the women in this part of town dressed. Miniskirts. Go-go boots with tall, see-through heels. They barely had anything on, and there were so many of them.

A woman sat down beside him and introduced herself. I'm Rainbow. Her lips puckered with the words, mesmerizing him. He liked the way her toes poked out of her shoes. They were tiny, and the nails were painted metallic blue to match her top. She put her hand on his knee, and he hoped the fuzz on his lip was dark enough that she'd mistake it for a mustache. I'm Felipe. She said his name back to him slowly, puckering her lips again. You got a cigarette? He had one out before she had finished asking the question. They smoked a while in silence, and he looked at her long legs sticking out into the road. Rainbow finally broke the pause by asking if he was lonely tonight. Yeah. I'm lonely. Don't really know anyone here, and I have nowhere to go. Her thin hand crept higher up his leg. Do you want a girlfriend tonight? You know, some company? He nodded his head and swallowed, and Rainbow flipped her cigarette out into the street. She stood up and pulled Felipe to his feet. Follow me. I have somewhere we can go.

They walked across the street holding hands, and most of the women they passed whistled and said you go girl. Felipe blushed, thinking they were making fun of him, a little embarrassed at all the attention being drawn to him, but he was also proud he had gotten a hot girl so easily. Already he had forgotten the shame he had felt for being kicked out of the Swank.

Rainbow stopped outside the office of the No-Tel Motel and told him to wait. She went in and came back out a moment later with a room key twirling around her finger. This way, cowboy. He really liked her. Not only was she sexy, she also made him feel good, the way she approached him and talked to him on the same level, as if they were equals.

In the hotel room, Rainbow spoke in a whisper. She went immediately to the bed, clicked on the lamp, and asked him for a cigarette. He handed her his whole pack. You can have as many as you want. Thank you, sweetie. He felt himself blushing but figured the room was dim enough to cover his redness. He sat down on the edge of the bed, giving Rainbow her space, not wanting to rush anything, and asked if she wanted to watch TV or something. She laughed. If you want. It's your dime. Now that they were in a hotel room together, he noticed Rainbow smelled liked overripe berries. Almost too sweet.

I'll tell you what. You figure out what you want, she flipped her ash, and I'll get ready. In his line of peripheral vision, he saw her legs open, and he turned to get a better look. She had her head on the pillow, turned away from the lamp, her cigarette in her left hand and her right hand holding her skirt up to her waist. She was naked beneath it. Felipe's mouth dropped open, and the smoke he forgot to inhale rolled out of his mouth and drifted up into his eyes. They burned, but he didn't close them. He couldn't believe what he was seeing, this chick fingering herself and we just met. A man could get used to this.

She licked her lips. Took a drag off her cigarette. So, what would you like? You want me to blow you? Fifty bucks. You want anal? Two hundred. If you just want to watch, thirty bucks. If you want something freaky, the price goes up.

The bitch. He already had his dick halfway out of his pants, and he didn't have more than ten bucks in his pocket. And some change. He never imagined they charged so much. But he was all worked up now so he thought fuck it. Enjoy it while it lasts.

He walked toward her with his joint in his hand and smiled. He touched her leg. She was so soft. He closed his eyes.

Well? What'll it be? I need to see money before we can get down to it. You do have money?

He nodded, hoping that would be enough for her to continue. Felt her breath on his chest. She smelled too good. Almost nauseating with her sweetness.

Show me. Show me your money and we'll talk. She grabbed his ass and pulled him to her. Where is it?

He felt her wonderful tits against his stomach as he stood next to her. His pants had slid down to his knees, and he bent over to pull them up so he could dig in the pockets for his money. He fumbled around, trying not to break contact with this beautiful woman. He found the change and began to pull it out when she surprised him by grabbing his cock and stroking it, and he dropped the change on the floor where it jingled against the linoleum, and Rainbow stopped stroking and looked down, then back at him, is this supposed to be funny? flinging his cock from her hand as if she had accidentally picked up a roach, tell me you have money, and he watched as she seemed to transform in front of him, pulling her skirt down and grabbing her purse before he realized he'd fucked up big, you think these goddam hotel rooms pay for themselves, I mean WHATTHAFUCK, and she opened her purse and pulled out a can of mace and sprayed it into his eyes and he screamed and tore at his face, scratching his eyes and cheeks while Rainbow gathered her things and told him beat it, you fuck, before you get in deeper shit, kicking and punching him and hitting him with her bag, I shoulda known a little fuckin punk kid like you, cursing and punching him the whole time she pulled him to the door and threw him out on the pavement, kicking him in the ass as hard as she could for good measure, shouting DON'T bring your little cock back to Miracle Mile if you can't afford it, and she slammed the door behind him.

Felipe lay on the ground, writhing in pain. His crotch was sore. His eyes were burning. His ass still felt the intense stab from her kick. All he could do was roll in front of the hotel room, too sore to pull his pants back up.

When the pain finally subsided to a dull ache, he fastened his jeans and stumbled down the street humiliated, ignoring the women jeering at him and the cars honking and the obnoxious lights everywhere. The sting from the mace still blurred his vision, so he walked away from the sounds of the women yelling and laughing, extending his hands in front of him to avoid bumping into anything and taking careful steps to be sure he was on the sidewalk and not wandering into traffic.

Eventually the sounds of Miracle Mile faded away, and his vision improved. He still had no idea where he was, but he knew he wanted to hide. The name Nuñez meant nothing on Miracle Mile. He only knew the Kings and 24th Street, but he had failed there, too. He had run away like a coward, and they would never take him back. They couldn't. It was his destiny, and he had turned his back on it.

Lightning flashed across the sky. I just need to find a place to lie down where no one will find me. He walked faster, feeling an occasional drop of rain splashing on his arms. He saw an overpass ahead, and he ran to it as the rain began to fall harder. He scaled the cement slope leading up to the overpass and when he reached the top, he wedged his body between the cement beneath him and the warm road above, feeling safe for the first time that day. For now he was protected from the rain, and at least that was something.

⁓

Across Tucson animals scurried into hiding beneath wastebins. They ran into the doorways of homes. By the time the flashflood broke, the animals carried on in such a way—trying to claw their way through the walls of homes, overflowing from beneath the lids of dumpsters, packing themselves into the wheel wells of cars—that five minutes later not one could be seen roaming the streets. Mothers plucked up their children from their beds and rocked them silently, shushing them, more nervous than the confused children who seemed to know that now was not the time to question their mothers' motives. The walls of houses shook, fighting against the storm's wrath. It sounded as if all the oceans of the world had been lifted above this city in the middle of the desert and been dropped at once. Trailers were lifted from their foundations on the outskirts of town. Gullies and washes overflowed. Cars were swept away. By the time the storm had ceased thirty minutes later, the sides of hills had been sloughed off and semis lay overturned on the highway.

And then it was over. There was mud in the streets one minute, and the next minute the desert had opened its mouth and sucked up every last drop of moisture. There was no water to show for it. People told themselves that semis always overturn and drift down the road, and that occasionally homes leave their foundations in search of a place to fall on their sides and expire.

Señora Nuñez sat in her rocking chair listening to the storm, wondering if her son was safe. She lit candles to the Virgin and prayed for his swift return. Then she crossed herself and crawled back to bed on her knees.

———

Felipe awoke the next morning more tired than when he had fallen asleep. His eyes were dry and scratchy from the mace. His body ached all over. The cement beneath him and the cool shade of the overpass made him think it was cooler outside than it actually was. He lay there, registering his various wounds. Nothing serious. A couple of scratches and some soreness. The worst damage had been done to his ego, but he didn't have time to think about that now. His stomach felt like it was digesting itself, and he needed to eat. He hadn't had a meal since breakfast the morning before. Chorizo and eggs sounded good. All he had to do was find a taqueria and he'd be set. Then he remembered he had dropped his money on the hotel floor right before Rainbow attacked him. Slut. She could've at least let me grab my change before hauling off and kicking my ass like that. If the boys only knew he'd gotten beat up by a woman. Hey, I got caught with my cock in my hand.

Now that he was fully awake, he realized he had some decisions to make. He had no ID, so he couldn't get work. He had no money, so he couldn't eat. He was beaten before he had even started. It was bad planning, taking off from school like an idiot. He knew he had no choice but to go home. That terrified him more than anything. If he had never expressed interest in the Kings, then they wouldn't have cared if he decided not to join them. But they had let him into their circle. He had shared in the benefits and now he had to do his time. Goddam, and I went along without even questioning it. He didn't want to think about it, so he began walking north until he came to a street he recognized. Still unsure of exactly where he was, Felipe stopped at a 7-Eleven and asked for directions back to Reid Park. On his way out, he swiped a bag of chips and a pack of Parliaments.

Three hours later the pack was half gone, but he was only a couple miles from home, so instead of smoking he slowed his pace and thought of excuses to tell the Kings when they came looking for him.

Guys. I'm sorry. I got sunstroke or something and went out of my head.

Jesus, that was lame.

There was a rumor that you had been rounded up and arrested.

Nope. If that were true, he would have gotten a call from home or one of his brothers would have picked him up. He was so consumed with excuses he didn't notice a school bus drive by full of kids from Mansfield. They pointed, unable to believe he was back.

Okay, Peanut. Rogelio. Chuy. David. You have to believe me. I thought instead of the usual assbeating, I would sneak onto someone else's turf—the Crips or something—and I was gonna off one of those niggers and tag him. You know, let those bastards know the Kings are here to stay and you cannot fuck with us. It could work, except that he had done nothing. He had nothing to show for his night away except some bruises.

Then he thought about his mother and how maybe he could just go home and she'd step in between him and his brothers like she'd done with his father and she'd let him sleep with her in her bed where he could hide, except that wouldn't work because he'd eventually have to go to the bathroom or something and so he'd have to leave her side, and they'd be waiting to drag him out the back door, or the food would run out so his mother would have to go to Food Giant, and if he went with her they'd pick him off, holding her at a distance while they punished him for backing down.

GODDAMMIT. Why can't I just tell them the truth? How about, FUCK Peanut and the Kings? Okay? I was scared. This isn't for me. I just want to be normal. Lay girls. Buy a car. Flip burgers. I don't want to be scared the rest of my life. That's not how a man lives. I want to do things I can be proud of one day. I don't want that stupid tattoo on my neck that proves I'm stone cold. Just leave me alone.

Hey, Felipe. Ricardo ran up to him. Man, why'd you come back? We all thought you were gone for good, and I was so happy for you. I thought you'd finally figured shit out, and now you're back and everybody knows. And the Kings are pissed royal.

I know.

You should've stayed gone. You know you disrespected your brothers and everything. Hurry up and leave, man. It's not too late.

I can't.

Felipe was too tired. He couldn't run because there was nowhere to go. 24th Street was engrained in him. He hugged Ricardo and asked will you just keep me company?

Together they walked past the park and toward Torchy's, where a crowd of people stood waiting. Ricardo walked beside him, trying to stay strong for his best friend.

They walked in silence for the last few steps that separated them from the group, and right before Felipe stepped forward, Ricardo grabbed his hand and held it, just for a second. Then he let it drop and took a step back. The crowd closed in.

Felipe stood with his back straight and his hands at his sides, facing his brothers. He knew they had to throw the first punches. That's how it worked. Another test for the Nuñez boys. No one spoke. Felipe scanned the crowd and saw Helena and the two Rosas hugging Lavinía while she lowered her head and cried, unable to watch. He looked each person in the eyes, standing his ground, and spoke two words. I'm ready.

Chuy was the first to throw a punch. Felipe didn't flinch. It landed on his forehead, splitting the skin open above his right eyebrow. Blood drained down into his eye, but he made no move to wipe it away. Rogelio was next. His fist came at Felipe, as large as a cement block, and knocked his jaw loose. When Davíd blasted him in the ear, he heard it more than he felt it. Already he could feel his head swollen with blood, and this was just the beginning. That's how it worked.

Felipe's knees buckled beneath him and his body began to fall to the ground, but someone caught him from behind and held him upright as a flurry of fists pummeled his face, breaking his nose and popping teeth out of his mouth, but Felipe didn't cry out, he only waited for it to be over, thinking how nice it would be to crawl into bed and tell his mom it's going to be okay, just bring me a cold washcloth and lay it on my face, and then he felt the sharp sting of someone punching him in the kidneys and he lost his breath, unable to regain it because he was being kicked in the stomach and in the balls and his legs went out from under him but he didn't fall—how come I'm not falling?—because the crowd had pushed in so tightly around him that there was nowhere for him to collapse, and everyone wanted a shot at this pussy who'd dared to disrespect them, dared to turn his back on the Kings when they had let him in and shown him the ropes and trusted him, only for him to turn around and shove it back in their faces, knowing damn well this wouldn't fly in their neighborhood, even if you are a Nuñez, *especially since* you are a Nuñez, and so many people were beating him from so many different directions that he could no longer discern one blow from the next, nor did he realize he had finally crumpled to the ground where they continued to kick his limp body and stomp on him, yelling and cursing this boy beneath them, who was never going to be a man, despite his courage to stand up to them and take his punishment, which was only supposed to be an assbeating, but had turned into a swarm of people taking their fear and rage out on the bravest man who had ever walked 24th Street, and Felipe opened his eyes and through his blurry red vision tried to decipher the mass of limbs that continued to bludgeon him, but he could see nothing, could only hear the weeping of Lavinía and her friends, and Ricardo watched in horror as the men who beat Felipe came away with bloodied hands, and he tried to plead with them to stop, he's had enough, but saw that they were not giving up, that they were so far away from satisfying their rage that he could do nothing to the mob as they kicked Felipe into a pulpy mass, and he knew they would keep kicking and punching in the general area where Felipe once lay, even though they were beating their own hands and feet into bloody stumps, completely unaware that they had begun beating each other, and Ricardo knew they would never stop because this was not a man in front of them, he was less than that, a coward, not worthy of his body lying on the ground in pieces, not worthy of the dirt mixing with his blood and turning into rusty mud, not worthy of the street they were smearing him into, the street Felipe, the last of the Nuñez brothers, had grown up on, the street where his mother, Señora Carmen Nuñez, who wanted nothing more than to turn her boys into respectable men, sat in solitude waiting for the door to open, wondering whether her youngest son would return home with a look of pride in his eyes or hanging his head in shame.

EASTER SUNDAY

 THE GRASS IN REID PARK WAS COVERED WITH EGGS. Bright dots by the thousands. Up in trees. Sitting in the seats of swingsets. In clumps of brush. A mob of children stood behind a long line of police caution tape, waiting for the sound of the horn so they could break the strip and rush after the eggs.

Alright. Fuck the ones sitting out in the open, Davey. Run right through em and head for the trees.

Yes, sir.

I mean it. Last year the golden egg was hidden at the top of the rocket slide. Kid won five hundred bucks and a family pass to Justin's Water World. We *need* that egg.

The whole time he was talking to his son, Davey's father was thinking man, if Davey gets that egg, I'll be in heaven. Five hundred to take down to the Mile, where I can get the finest piece on the strip, and when Rogelio Nuñez goes waving his fifty around like he does every night at the bar after work, I'll pull out a nice crisp c-note and show that fuckstick up once and for all. No more of his talk about his bitch and her fat mooseknuckle of a puss bunched up in her acid-washed jeans. I've seen her come into the shop on our lunch break, and he's got nothing to brag about. Hell, I'd be in the bar getting drunk too, fucking that. Damn Mexicans. He should be mailing that fifty to his family back in Meh-hee-co.

He grabbed his son's ear, jerking his head hard, and Davey heard a pop and felt the cartilage tear and the sting spread through his head like a web. He bit his tongue to draw his attention away from the worse pain.

You hear me, boy? You're bigger than the rest of those beaners.

Yes, sir.

Just run over the top of em and find the golden fuckin egg and everything will be fine. Now get in there. He knocked his son on the head with his silver-and-turquoise wedding ring.

Davey walked to the rope where the rest of the kids were waiting for the horn to blow so the hunt could begin. He was taller than most of them and felt stupid. The other parents were giving him disgusted looks, making no secret about their disapproval of such a large boy among their children. Heads shaking. Grimaces. And standing in front of them was his dad, loudly telling the others how his son was gonna get that golden fuckin egg this year. Yep, Davey's got it, he gloated, adjusting his ballsack in his tight jeans.

Davey kicked at a clump of grass. I hate him. Always messin with me. Pullin my hair and rappin me on the head with that stupid ring. He wanted to punch the kid next to him. His head still hurt.

The kids were getting antsy waiting on the horn. They bobbed up and down and nudged each other, plotting their attack.

I'm getting all the blue ones. Blue's my favorite.

Red's mine.

Davey thought just the golden egg for me. He was ten years old. Right at the cutoff for being too old for the egg hunt or caring about the other stupid eggs.

It's not like anyone's going to card you his father said during their walk to the park. But he had folded his son's birth certificate into his back pocket anyway. Just in case. They aren't keeping us out. Let those sonsabitches try. The entire walk his dad threatened the sonsabitches. Dared them to question his son's age. Davey spent the whole time thinking of how badly he wanted the new He-Man toy—Castle Grayskull.

And now, waiting on the horn to blow, he thought about how he hadn't peed before they left the house, he hadn't had the time, with his dad dragging him out of bed and into the bathroom, where he splashed cold water on Davey's face then told him you have exactly two minutes to meet me outside, and Davey picked up a shirt off the floor and shook it and turned it right-side-out and stumbled to the front yard, where his dad stood beneath the palm tree and said you got sixty seconds to get from this tree to that saguaro in front of the Colón house. Sixty seconds. Go. Davey ran, his head still blurry from waking only three minutes earlier, and wondered why every year his dad did the same thing. No Easter basket. No good morning, just run, Davey. Faster. I can't believe you let those little wetback mo-ha-dohs outrun you. We own them. And Davey waited on the horn and felt his bladder bulging beneath his belt, taunting him, forcing him to thrust his hand into his pocket and pinch the tip of his wiener, and the pain kept him from peeing for now, but he looked over his shoulder anyway and considered going back to his dad, who was still going on about the golden fuckin egg, to ask if he could go potty real quick. But he knew better.

So he crossed his legs and rocked back and forth and wondered when they were going to blow the stupid horn. Don't think of pee or the golden fuckin egg. Something to make the dumb horn blow—little boy blue, come blow your horn—and back and forth, pinching his wiener and looking around and loosening his belt a notch to let his bladder expand a little so he'd be able to run. Blow your horn, dang you. Dad can take the money, I want the prize. A brand-new mountain bike this year. I'll ride all over the place. Learn how to jump ramps like the big kids and maybe race professionally when I grow up like those guys in *BMX Magazine,* especially if it's a cool bike like a Mongoose or a Diamondback or—

The horn blew and the kids ran frantically, stampeding, defying gravity by scooping up eggs as they went, bent over and never running upright, and as Davey watched the kids get farther away from him, the eggs disappeared, the ground turning green again as if a plague of locusts were attacking a field of wheat, like they told him about in Sunday school to illustrate God's wrath.

GODDAMMIT, BOY. Get your ASS in there and GET THAT EGG.

Davey let go of his wiener and broke into a run—ignoring the pain in his bladder—and heard another parent calling his dad an asshole and why don't you just leave the poor kid alone, you jerk. He lowered his head and ran straight toward the middle of the group, where the kids were still bunched together and running for the trees. He passed children with big smiles on their faces, happy with the three or four eggs they'd managed to get their hands on. A few of them had been tripped or knocked over and sat on the ground looking as if they weren't sure whether or not they should cry or keep going, there were still so many eggs.

By the time he got to the trees, they were full of kids who weren't afraid of climbing, and smaller ones looked up the trunks at the brave kids and lowered their heads and kept going toward the pond, the cutoff point for the hunt, scattering, looking in bushes, under rocks, sometimes pushing the smallest kids over and stealing their eggs, and the parents shouted words of encouragement that sounded like a crackling roar as the trees broke the sound apart while Davey ran past several eggs mashed into the grass by the mob of children now spread all over the park, searching for the better-hidden eggs or giving up and walking back toward their parents or the playground, but he pushed on, knowing the golden egg wouldn't be out in plain view, heading toward a row of bushes that lined the bank of the stream spilling out of the pond, where a small girl crouched beneath a bush and then emerged with a glittering egg in her hand.

He stopped running and looked at the girl. She looked back at him, clutching the golden fuckin egg in her fist. He took a step toward her. None of the others had noticed her. None of them saw the two children staring each other down, sizing each other up. Give me the egg. He took another step toward her.

No. It's mine. It's my egg cause I found it.

He took another step and saw the girl's body tense up as if she were about to break into a run. Give it. Gimme the golden fuckin egg. Please. I need it.

The girl smiled at him. He started to smile back. She's actually going to give it to me.

But then she started laughing and put one hand over her mouth and pointed the other—the one with the egg—at his crotch. At the cold wet stain he hadn't noticed while he was running. The left leg of his jeans was saturated and sticking to him. He felt more pee seep into his underwear and embarrassment rush into his cheeks. Still, at least no one else saw, if anyone else sees I'll just die, and the girl bowed her head laughing. Davey walked up to her, ignoring his pee-squishy shoes, and grabbed the hand with the egg. Get the egg. Gotta get the egg. She stopped laughing and jerked her hand away, backing into the bushes. He followed her, ignoring the branches scratching his face and arms, grabbing at her leg. She fell backwards and tried to scoot away, still clutching her hand to her chest, trying to scream for her mommy. Shut up. Just shut up and give me the egg and pretend you never found it.

NO. She squirmed, kicking at his hand. He ignored the pain, thinking of his dad back there telling the other parents how Davey's got this one in the bag, the golden fuckin egg, probably dancing around and scratching his nuts.

The girl's hand touched water, and she stopped moving. He knew she was trapped, but she didn't stop kicking, wouldn't hand over the egg.

He crawled through the bush, holding her leg down and trying to block her other foot from kicking his face. The girl turned to look for an escape but he pinned her down and lay on top of her, trying to wrestle the egg from her hand. It's mine. If she'd just stop screaming and give it to me. He pushed her head into the stream then pulled it out again. She spat up water but didn't let go of the egg. Just gimme it. Pushed her head under again. Gimme. Dunked her head again and held her down, ignoring her kicking and her hands scratching and punching at his neck and face, listening to her screams bubbling up through the water and pulling her hair harder and harder and wishing he'd gone pee before he left the house instead of wetting his pants like a baby, thinking Dad's gonna beat me when he sees my pants, especially if I don't come back with the egg, and then the girl finally stopped kicking and lay still and Davey thought good, she's going to give up and maybe we can be friends. I'll let her ride my bike and when I get too big for it, I can sell it to her for cheap and then maybe she'll be my girlfriend, and he held her head underwater a little longer while he felt around her body with his other hand, looking for the egg, and when he located it he felt a calmness in his heart and he rubbed the egg's sparkling surface with his thumb and crawled off the girl and crouched beneath the bushes to catch his breath and to think of a reason for having wet pants so he could bring the egg to his dad.

He watched the water running through the girl's hair, thinking how pretty her hair looked all spread out in the stream like that. Like seaweed. Then, when he caught his breath, he scrambled out of the bush and started walking toward his dad, imagining how much fun it's gonna be to jump the ramp on my first try and with all the kids watching.

LOVEBOAT

MANNY CAME FOR THE TITS, BUT NOW HE DIDN'T notice them jiggling in his face. He was looking for Vinnie and thinking of the men lining the stage and the way they whooped and yelled and slapped each other's backs and winked at the topless waitresses walking by, obviously not of the same ilk as the girls deemed worthy of baring not just their breasts but also their neatly shorn crotches in front of the hardworking men who came to the Loveboat at each day's end. The waitresses didn't mind getting less attention than the girls on stage, because lord knows we get our share of ass-grabbin and titty-pinchin from the airmen who come across the street from Davis-Monthan Air Force Base at the end of each day in stumbling groups yelling gonna see us some tits tonight and man, the pussy up in this bitch be finuh than hell, and laughing and bellying up to the bar before the lights dimmed and the first stripper took the stage in her ten-inch black leather stiletto go-go boots, with a hyena tattooed on her left ass cheek that laughed at everyone who wanted to touch it.

The DJ—a man with a smug face who loved his job, had even called all of his buddies up the day he landed the Loveboat gig and gloated about how he gets paid to look at naked chicks all night long—told everyone give it up for Desire, and they did, raising their beers in the air and whistling smoky ear-piercing whistles and juggling their dice in anticipation, nodding and grinning and ordering a few spare drinks to hold them over until her set was finished. They did not want to miss a thing. Not even one bead of the sweat dripping between her jugs or along the small of her back, teasing them, dancing on the edge of her thong, threatening at any moment to dive into the miraculous cavern between her ass cheeks.

By the time Manny had arrived, the Loveboat was already filled with airmen and the stench of testosterone, that overwhelming scent of sweat and smoke and alcohol seeping from a billion pores. Excitement crept down between his legs. He watched Desire hanging upside-down from a brass pole in the middle of the stage with her legs wrapped around it and her hair brushing the ground and her tits covering the bottom half of her face. He made his way to an open spot at the front and center of the stage and sat down, making sure to look directly at the stripper jiggling and slapping her cheeks while she bent over and then ran her middle finger up the length of her crack. The chair next to him was open, so he placed his jacket on the seat to reserve it for Vinnie.

When the waitress came, Manny told her get me a Dos Equis and gave her a slap on the ass, then looked around to see who saw him do it. Another patron in a leather bomber jacket made eye contact with Manny and winked and nodded—the universal look that said we're paying customers here and we gotta let em know who's boss.

Manny settled into his seat, laying his head back for a moment, closing his eyes and breathing deeply to regulate his excitable heart. The shouting and laughing sounded more like the men were at a boxing match than a place where they came to admire young, tight, naked women. Boy was Vinnie missing out. Earlier Manny had heard him ribbing some guy at the base, telling him be sure to come out to the Boat tonight, wouldn't want anyone to get the wrong idea if you keep turning down invitations. Manny hadn't exactly been invited, but he was sure Vinnie knew him well enough that if he said hi or offered him a beer he'd probably stop and talk to him.

A man behind him talked about how I fucked Yolanda and she's a freak, man, lets me do all typa crazy shit, the other guy not believing him, saying man, you aint got to fuckin lie about that bitch, and laughing and giving each other some dap then silence while they drank from their beers. To Manny's left, two black airmen said we've got to find us some hoes, ya know, new tail, not this old airbase pussy running around here on the weekends. Yeah, I'm tired of useless bitches like Vicki pushin her babies down Kolb, hopin to find a daddy for them kids, all used up and lookin for a joint to smoke. Yeah, we can bounce, but first let's get an eyeful of some of this prime college ass.

Manny covered a smirk with his beer. What do these Air Force punks know about women? Thinking they have them all figured out when they're just kids themselves. He saw guys like these every day in his office, re-class pilots from other branches of the service who'd seen *Top Gun* one time too many in high school. Didn't they even know the *Top Gun* pilots were Navy? These chumps parading around as grown men when they're kids, really, with dreams of showing up in a club like this one and making girls swoon as soon as they see the flashy wings on their bomber jackets. He knew most of them didn't understand that even during peacetime a good soldier tries to move up in rank. As he had done. With rank comes respect—and women, if that's the only reason these jokers wear the uniform. A couple flyovers in Honduras, a few classified missions near the Philippines, and they might be able to land a nice commissioned officer post.

Like Vinnie. Now he does the Air Force uniform proud. Ever since his arrival at the base a couple months before, he'd turned heads with the way he made the dull brass on his uniform shine. People often wondered whether he went straight home after work and polished those wings until he passed out. Although he was a first sergeant for a separate company, Manny still admired him from afar, envying the way he managed to look relaxed and formal when he walked, his perfect posture, the way his shoes shone. Immaculate. He wondered how Vinnie would look under the colorful lighting of the Loveboat.

Manny saw the club lights from beneath his closed eyelids every time they passed over his face. After he acclimated himself to the place, he felt ready to look at Desire again, knowing he only had a couple hours before he should get home to Stella and his two boys, thinking at least she thinks I'm out with my officers having dinner, planning promotions and field tests for new planes, which usually means a few drinks afterwards. Even though he knew he would reek of stripper—the distinct flowery smell that wouldn't wash off completely for days—Stella would ignore it when he crawled into bed and pretended to be exhausted whispering baby, you'd think I'd get used to dealing with it, but with defense cuts and people always coming into my office to see if their jobs are in danger, the stress is wearing me out, keeping his back to her while she rubbed her foot against his calf and her ass against his back, thinking she was turning him on, Manny closing his eyes and trying to feel sorry for his naked wife behind him, who had been home alone all day getting the house in order and shopping and picking up the kids and making the bed and changing into some sexy clothes she thought he liked, and she persisted, as she always did, slowly sliding her hand across his back and over his chest and down his stomach, rubbing lightly back and forth, and then she would twirl a little tuft of his pubes between her fingers and search around for his cock until she found it resting on his left thigh and she would wiggle it a little bit and giggle in his ear and play with the head, rolling it between her fingers until she felt the slightest reaction, the dimmest pulse of blood, and then she would be reaffirmed and whisper I love you, Manny, and giggle some more as he grew in her hand and he, still trying to ignore her, could not stop his body from reacting to her skillful taunting, growing harder while she coaxed him over onto his back and climbed on top of him, telling him I want you, Manny, I've missed you, maneuvering her hips above him to where she could grab his shaft and hold it upright while she slowly eased herself down onto him, a little at a time until he was fully inside her, and she would groan and throw her head back and bob slowly, slowly, talking real sweet to him and smiling until they got into a nice rhythm and he would grab her hips and shove her down on him harder and speed up, doing this out of frustration and necessity, which Stella always misinterpreted as desire, until they were one organism moving and bouncing on the bed, everything around them falling into their rhythm—the bed, the clock, the swamp cooler clicking on and off—and his wife writhing on top of him and scratching his sides and leaning down to bite him on his shoulders and neck and ears over and over and over. But that would be later.

Now Manny spotted Vinnie laughing with a few guys on the other side of the stage and decided he was ready to watch Desire thrust her tits at him, grabbing them by the nipples and swinging them around like two soggy yams covered in silver glitter. He was pleased that so many of the airmen came out tonight because it made him feel more anonymous. Helped his uniform blend in. Although it wouldn't be so terrible if someone did notice him, since he only came here two or three times a year. He pretended to be looking for a friend, glancing across the room at Vinnie and his sharp-lined face. He had a smile that only showed his top row of teeth and made him look prestigious. Not an overly toothy smile, which could make guys look ignorant. He had one of those laughs that made Manny want to hear what had been so funny. Apparently Manny wasn't alone. A group of men surrounding Vinnie seemed to be digesting every word he said, waiting for his punchlines, laughing in all the appropriate places. The men looked at the dancer on stage occasionally, but seemed more engrossed in Vinnie's conversation. So Manny's staring went unnoticed.

The next time he looked up at the stage, Desire ripped off her breakaway thong and a gasp went through the crowd. The room filled with the raging sex drive of hundreds of men wishing out loud if I could just get that bitch alone for ten minutes, wanting to touch her, to smell her, to taste her, to shout damn, woman, just gimme one lick. Manny could feel the weight of all the men longing, needing to relieve the tension. Most of the men from the airbase were privates, fresh out of basic, a few of them even virgins. They were easy enough to spot since they still tried to cover their erections with beer bottles or packs of cigarettes or by standing really close to the chairs in front of them.

Everyone on the base knew about the Loveboat, even if they had never been inside. The enormous ship with the crude cement figurehead of a nude woman was out of place on the tiny plot of desert right across from the base, as if many years earlier, when the land was covered in water and the mountains were islands, some Spaniard ran aground, ending his quest to map the ends of the world. The enormous naked torso taunted everyone leaving the gates of the base. It made mothers blush and cover their children's eyes—though most kids still managed to peek. It caused fights between lovers when a woman noticed the slightest pause in conversation and turned to find her man's gaze directed at the enormous cement breasts. If it was dark enough outside, the club's lights passed through the portholes on the sides of the boat and it looked as if oars were flapping through the air. On cloudy nights, the colossal naked woman appeared to emerge from the darkness with a vessel of lust in tow.

The pirate theme inside the bar amused most of the soldiers. They often talked before and after PT about the grand finale each night, when the entire bar lit up with swirling blue spotlights and the whole cast of dancers reappeared in mermaid outfits, flopping around the stage, touching each other while the men lifted their drinks and swayed and sang yo, ho, ho, and a bottle o' rum. When they finished, the lights came up and the men scurried out the door to meet their girls or to find a piece out on Miracle Mile.

But it was still early in the evening, and Manny was happy. Instead of sitting at his desk all day and then returning home to his wife, he was doing exactly what he heard most other men on the base talking about every Monday when they came to work smelling vaguely of alcohol and bragging about bagging yet another female from off-post. He fit in here, where all the men in the area hung out—bikers, lawyers, military men, bankers, teachers, politicians—men of all rank and stature. At that moment they were men together, all wanting the same thing—a piece of Desire. But when her set was finished, she was forgotten and they shouted and cheered for Peaches, a waifish blonde girl in a sheer pink teddy who came out with a pacifier on a cord around her neck and a baby doll under her arm, and the men slapped their foreheads and said goddam look at THAT piece, and after more drinks they got up the nerve to yell at Peaches instead of each other, will you marry my boy over here? he's cryin over yo sweet ass, and they ordered more rounds of drinks from the waitresses and slapped them on their asses, asking can you hook us up with Peaches? does she have a boyfriend? until they were quieted by Peaches removing her teddy and twirling it over her head, using it to wipe the brass pole, which she promptly wrapped her legs around.

After the initial shock of her angelic nude body wore off, they resumed talking to one another about gettin an eightball cause I'm jonesin and maybe a sack of weed since our next piss test aint for five more weeks.

Manny ignored their comments, even though they were soldiers of lesser rank and he could get them discharged if all their talk was true, but that's what MPs are for. He was glad to be around them, happy knowing that each of them was dying to get off, happier still that the few soldiers who noticed him acknowledged him with a nod. Occasionally, while Manny looked for a waitress to order a drink or checked his watch, he sneaked glances at the men in their Dockers or uniform slacks. He looked at the bulging muscles of the bikers, sweaty and covered in hair and tattoos, wondering at the firmness of so many years of alcohol packed into a dense loaf beneath their white T-shirts. He nudged the man next to him with his elbow and said man, I'd throw a couple kids up in her gut. The other guy laughed, shaking his head, and said man, that's some fucked-up shit, but she is fine, and they laughed some more and slapped hands. When Peaches came closer to them, Manny grabbed a five-dollar bill from his wallet, holding it out for Peaches, who took it and placed it between his lips. She pushed his drink out of the way and sat on the edge of the stage, rubbing her tits in his face, smashing them together between her fists to grab the bill from his mouth. She shoved her crotch in his face and rubbed it on his nose and she smelled like flowers and vanilla beans and better than any woman he had ever smelled. He smiled, yeah, I'm the man, the main man around here. He felt everyone's eyes on him—the jealousy, the sex—and he was content to think damn, that Peaches digs me. Then Peaches left.

Girl after girl came—Hope and Ambrosia and Rose and Deidra and Satin—each one testing the limits of the audience, pretending not to notice the urgency in the air but knowing that every man in the place would give a leg, would run a microwave at full power right next to his mother's pacemaker, would lick the pope's ass for even ten minutes alone with one of them. The music played on. The lights flashed. The smell grew stronger, almost unbearable for Manny, who was flinging bills onto the stage and yelling yeah, just give me a kiss, and the girls came up and smiled, sometimes sitting in front of him and rubbing themselves for a second, pretending that he, Manny Torres, was the reason they were there that night, as if the sole purpose for their existence was to give Manny a show and make sure he approved of them and their bodies and the way they did their hair and their clothes. Then they would move on to the next man waving money and give him the same treatment. But the time spent with each man grew shorter as men pressed their way to the stage, tripping over one another, slobbering, slurring out words of love, offering everything they were worth—their rank, their money, their very lives—to the women who moaned and made faces and slapped their asses, sending ripples of sex down their thighs, damn if they aint having orgasms right there on the stage, and licking their fingers.

Manny noticed Vinnie had finally moved away from the other men to order a drink. He waved at Vinnie and pointed to the seat open beside him. Vinnie walked over and extended his hand to Manny, who said I'm going to see if we can get one of these girls to give us a couch dance, unaware Vinnie had been considering whether or not to leave. He brushed the seat off and sat down beside Manny, thinking that's awfully nice of the captain, but I make plenty of money. I don't really need or want a lap dance from some slut in here. Why's he being so pushy? He beckoned to a waitress and asked her for two beers. Like a gentleman. No ass slapping. No crude jokes. Hey, thanks for the offer, Captain. You don't have to do this.

It's my pleasure, Vinnie. And call me Manny. Help me pick one of these ladies out. Manny scooted his chair a little closer to Vinnie, admiring the smell of his cologne, and they pointed at various dancers until they decided Hope was good enough. After waving her down, they got up and went to the back room, where dancers sat next to their clients or on their laps, sometimes kissing them on the neck or teasing them by rubbing their crotches on their legs or, if they were lucky, on their hands or faces, all the time not allowing the men to touch them back. The clients, desperate and bewildered, made proposals, invited the women back to houses they did not own, asked them on dates as if they were the first person to come up with the idea. The jukebox played Parliament, and Hope was taking off her clothes while Manny smiled at her until she turned her back to them and bent forward. While Hope danced in front of the two men, Manny sneaked glances at Vinnie, who looked over and gave him an awkward thumbs-up to show his appreciation. It was fifty well-spent dollars. For Manny, it felt good to share such a private moment with Vinnie, even though who knows what the guy thinks, at least he's happy he got a free show.

When the couch dance was over, the two men sat for a couple minutes making small talk. So, how about that chick, huh? She was sweet. He noticed Vinnie kept sitting up slightly, like he was going to leave but was having second thoughts, and each time a feeling of panic stabbed at Manny. Vinnie looked directly at him, then down at the floor, saying she kind of looks like my girl waiting at home for me, minus all those fuckin tattoos. Manny touched him lightly, as if it were an accident, or out of agreement. Yeah, well, that's better than most women these Air Force guys get. Mine's not so bad. Vinnie was oblivious, unaware Manny's hand lingered a second longer on his forearm or his knee than was acceptable. Manny felt this was the place where he should mention his wife, but he didn't want to. He felt an awkward sense of apprehension about admitting to being married. Not that he was ashamed. That wasn't it at all. He simply thought that if he mentioned his wife he wouldn't be able to talk to Vinnie the way he wanted to. His wife was beautiful, and everyone on the base knew her, but the last thing he wanted to do with Vinnie was compare notes on their two women.

Vinnie stood up and thanked Manny, and since there was no reason for them to stay in the couch room any longer, they parted ways, wishing each other a good night, saying I'll catch you around, and Manny said I'm going to take you up on that Vin, and then he staggered back into the main room of the Loveboat just in time to join in on the chorus of yo, ho, ho, and a bottle o' rum, while men swayed and crashed into each other, not feeling a thing, numb from the alcohol and happy with how much they had already accomplished, spewing up Jack Black and Coke or shots of tequila mixed with nachos, then wiping their mouths on their sleeves and downing the rest of their drinks with smiles and roars of contentment, each looking to the other for approval.

Amid the chaos of hundreds of drunken maniacs, Manny decided he'd try to convince Vinnie to stay a little longer, but he saw Vinnie was already going out the door, sucked into the night like a wisp of smoke. There was something about talking to Vinnie. The sound of his voice.

The way his Adam's apple bobbed when he laughed. The way he blushed and his eyes shifted, unable to meet those of the stripper when she sat on his lap.

Manny looked around, desperate to find someone he might be able to talk with over a drink. But the men around him were too drunk, or at least not in the mood for talking. So he looked up at Satin, a girl whose skin upheld her name and caused every man around her to clutch his ballsack for fear of exploding in his pants.

To Manny's surprise, Satin made eye contact with him and smiled. He wasn't even holding out money. She made her way toward him, switching her hips to the music, adjusting a bra that was so miniscule it could not even be made into a baby's sock, and rubbing her middle finger in the creases of fabric between her legs as she came closer. She winked at him while every man within spitting distance followed her movement, reached out to touch her, to sniff the flowery air trailing her, turning in her direction whether they wanted to or not, speechless, though if they had the time they could each come up with exactly the words she needed to hear to quit her job and move in with them, but she walked on faster toward Manny, and a universal awareness settled on every man that Satin had Manny in her sights, and they smirked in unison and said to one another goddam if she aint makin a beeline straight for Cap'm Torres, and snickered and then held their breath as they watched her make her way up to him and whisper in his ear, and he nodded and she grabbed him by the hand and led him out the back door and the bartender yelled, without conviction, time to get the fuck out, boys, while the gettin's good, and then he turned around and began wiping out glasses that he never used, only served plastic, but he liked to keep a pretty row of crystal on the rack above his head anyway because it made him feel like he was running a real five-star establishment, something that would one day make it into the Tucson Chamber of Commerce pamphlet for places that tourists must see, which is why he dressed every night like he worked at Caesar's Palace and not the Loveboat, that ungodly eyesore of a ship sitting in the middle of the desert like an absurd mirage, and to make his customers clear out he yelled some more slogans that he had read in the appendix to *The*

Bartender's Bible, which he studied each night over a glass of seltzer water after he got home and stripped down to his boxer-briefs and flexed a few times in the mirror while fantasizing about becoming the Southwest's most renowned bartender, the one that people came from miles around to see in action because his name, Chris Tall, was displayed on billboards all along Interstate 10 between Las Cruces and Riverside, but these patrons ignored him, more interested in Satin and the fact that she had nabbed some man and was making her way out with him in tow, and they all followed, silent now, as if the ensuing spectacle was something they could one day tell their grandsons about, and they shuffled in an orderly fashion as if they were out in the field on a drill in rows of two, no longer bumping each other or slobbering, but now intrigued because she had picked out the one man who was not known on the base as a philanderer—an anomaly in the service—and had decided to propose christknowswhat to the lucky bastard, but they all had to see with their own eyes how he would handle the situation, and when Manny walked past a few of them ribbed him good and said tear a chunk out of that ass, Cap'm, and winked or tilted their heads in a manner that promised the utmost confidentiality because what happens at the Boat stays at the Boat, and Manny flushed at the idea of so many men watching him at the same time, and he had to work some sleight-of-hand to tuck his hard-on beneath his starched waistband and adjust his walk in case of the small chance one of the men checked out his ass instead of Satin's, and he tightened his cheeks, pinching them together for a fraction of a second like a runway model, acutely aware that the men weren't cheering for *him* but for him to get a piece of Satin, which he supposed would work just the same, because if they were going to see him lay her, they would have to have a good long look at his cock too.

The next thing he knew he was standing behind a dumpster where homeless men slept on cold nights, sometimes forgetting to wake up before the garbage truck came to empty it in the morning. Then the dumpster was gone, pushed away by the throng of deprived men wanting to see him unleash a fury of fuck on the stripper who had probably picked him out of the crowd because he was the only one without a strand of drool as thick as linguine hanging from his lip. She had a point to prove. But all that was lost in the immense audience that began to chant TOR-RES TOR-RES TOR-RES and all Manny was aware of was their bodies, his and Satin's, surrounded by a panting brood of men who would not leave until someone had gotten their rocks off. They stabbed the air with their fists and yelled and hooted and laughed and chanted his name, yet he had no idea—what the hell do they want me to do? what does she want to do to me? and when Satin undid his belt and pants, a blast of chilly night air enveloped his body and he felt his nuts shrink up like a walnut shell, which was quickly taken care of by Satin, who dropped to her knees and began pawing at his sack, rooting until he came out of his shell and felt his balls drop like a bag of apples, which made him feel immensely better because I'll be damned if all these air-men are gonna see an officer with a weak pair.

He thought about Stella waiting for him in some new lingerie she had probably picked out from a Frederick's of Hollywood catalogue. He felt bile rising in his throat at the sight of this woman kneeling in front of him, the thought of what Satin had in store. They looked at each other. Her eyes sort of shrugged with lazy mischief, and she reached around and grabbed him by the ass, but suddenly he wanted nothing to do with her if it meant he had to get it up and slide it in her out there in the desert behind the Loveboat, next to a tower of empty kegs. He felt himself beginning to go limp, the very thought of it making him so self-conscious his dick shrank even further, to the point where he was certain it looked like little more than a piece of molted rattlesnake. But they didn't notice. They kept chanting and chanting and demanding that Torres do precisely to the woman what they'd had in store for her all night. Satin looked around as if she too were having second thoughts about the whole thing, realizing that to pick one of the bunch, especially a leader, might have been a mistake, until the crowd began pulling stacks of cash from their pockets and socks, and rings from their fingers, and chains from under their shirts.

The moment Satin saw greenbacks and jewels she shut out the faces in the crowd. They were all the same man to her, and she was ready to take requests and aware of the fact that whatever she ultimately decided to do would not only pay her rent for a couple months but would also have to include the nervous bastard she had pulled from the crowd of drunken airmen, what are the chances. All this to pay for my shitty studio and save for a ticket to Amsterdam, where I can make some real money for doing this shit. So close. Maybe this will be the last time I'll have to do this, if these cheapasses cough up enough money. She looked at the cash lying on the ground around her and tried to add it up. Mostly ones and fives.

The men chanted and someone fired up a joint and began passing it around and saying this shit's gonna be great. Manny realized he was tipsy now and beyond his better judgment, but that was all right because he noticed that not only had Satin taken off the rest of her skimpy nurse outfit while he was worrying about his appearance but several of the men were circled about them smoking cigarettes and laughing and calling out suck him off and let him put it in your ass, putting their hands down their own pants and staring at Satin touching herself slowly and smiling, while Manny watched as one, two, five, nine cocks flopped out of boxer shorts and between opened pants zippers and the men put their cigarettes to their lips and stroked themselves, laughing, shouting put two fingers in, yeah, that's it, and open wider bitch, and Satin complied because all she saw was the money lying in piles around her, and she put two more fingers inside, looked up at Manny, licked her lips, and moaned whatever you want, Cap'm. She ignored their yells and closed her eyes so she wouldn't cry because they had been right, all those kids she had grown up with. They were right when they said she was born be a porn star or something with a name like Satin Sheets. They made fun of her parents for not knowing any better. What kind of dumbass names their daughter Satin Sheets? Sassy. Call me Sassy. Oh, like Sassy Sheets is better. So, here I am. Satin. On my knees being what I was born to be.

By this point Manny was at full attention, watching the men who were pumping away while others sat atop the dumpster or on overturned kegs sipping their drinks and smoking cigarettes and laughing, all eyes on Satin as she pulled Manny toward her and ran her tongue over his kneecap and up his left thigh and finally licked his sack and grabbed his cock and kissed it and cuddled it against her cheek then buried it in her throat, and Manny jumped a little at her ferociousness but soon got used to it, pretending to close his eyes while she sucked on him and rubbed away at her cunt, moaning and grunting, but Manny was watching the men around him through squinted eyes and was overtaken with excitement and started shaking and heard the moans of the other men as Satin bent over in front of Manny and screamed fuck me, Cap'm, and he did just that while the men cheered and hollered and whooped and drank and smoked and pumped, the noise building into a frenzy of voices and grunts and yells that swirled above their heads and shook the sails of the Loveboat and flew above the city in a swarm of obscenities and primal moans crashing against the sides of houses and buildings and waking the people asleep within who thought it was a dream, and children hid their heads beneath their bedclothes and whimpered while wives shook their husbands and they turned on their clock radios or clicked their television remotes, but no mention was made of the event by the media so the wakened sleepers assured their wives and children that it was nothing unusual and tucked them back into bed and kissed them on their foreheads and shut off their televisions and their radios and all the lights in the house and went back to sleep while the spent men behind the Loveboat let out rushes of pent-up breath and zipped up their pants and stumbled into cars, onto motorcycles, and out onto the sidewalk, shaking their heads or whispering that fuckin maniac Torres.

⁓

Manny slid the key into the deadbolt and turned it slowly enough not to wake his kids or his wife. He was still trembling. He closed the door behind him and removed his shoes. A bath is exactly what I need right now. Even though it's past three in the morning and I have to get up for work in two-and-a-half hours, I need to sit in the tub and let my bones rest and my muscles relax. He stepped into the bathroom and shut the door. Since the master bedroom was at the very end of the hall and the kids' room was between it and the bathroom, Manny figured Stella would not wake to the sound of running water. But if she does, will she notice I'm still shaking? He looked in the mirror. What the hell was I thinking fucking that girl back there? Who knows where she's been? He grimaced at his reflection, then turned the bathtub faucet to the hottest setting and sat atop the toilet waiting on the tub to fill up, letting the steam fill the room and clear his pores and loosen his breathing. What have I done? What if Stella smells Satin on me? He didn't want to lose his wife over some cheap whore.

Manny inhaled the steam of the bathwater, remembering how powerful Stella made him feel as his wife, the same way he felt every time he went in front of a promotion committee and they awarded him a higher rank. Each time Manny came home with a new patch, Stella took great pride in removing his lower-ranking patches and stitching on the new one.

As he listened to the water pouring from the faucet, Manny glanced over at his younger son's potty chair, reminded of the time so many years ago when he'd wandered into the bathroom early one morning while his parents slept and lifted the lid of the toilet gently so it would not fall back down with a crash and wake his parents, and he tore off a piece of toilet paper—out of ritual instead of necessity—and placed it in the bowl of water and rubbed the sleep out of his eyes, wincing as the crust scraped the soft pad of skin in the corners where his eyelids met, and let loose a burst of urine that pained him with its initial blast because it had been testing the limits of his bladder as he slept. He did not hear his father enter the bathroom because he was lulled by the sound and the force of his pee crashing into the toilet bowl. When his father came up beside him and pulled a big brown monster from the front of his boxers, Manny almost cried out in horror. His father leaned over the bowl, placing his hand on the sink opposite him, and unleashed a roar of piss so loud it sounded as if the very heavens were crashing to the ground. Manny stared in disbelief. The tiny nub he held between his fingers suddenly baffled and embarrassed him.

Manny chuckled over that day in the bathroom with his father. He hadn't been able to look away. He'd even dreamed about it. The steam slowly began to clear and he removed his soiled clothes. The bath was full. The water was exactly how he liked it, almost unbearably hot. He eased himself into the large, claw-footed tub and let the water spill over him. The bathwater slowly broke down the film that covered him, the smell of Satin and sex and liquor.

Stella had not woken up, so he felt safe to ease the rest of his body into the water, taking a deep breath and sliding his head down the back of the tub to the bottom until only his knees were exposed to the air. Holding his breath until he could feel his lungs being pinched within his chest, he thought about the Loveboat. Even though he was ashamed, he wanted to do it again. It wasn't cheating on his wife or finally getting some stranger after years of being with the same woman. It was something else entirely. Something he couldn't quite put his finger on.

Little bubbles of air seeped out from his nostrils. Manny loved how it felt being underwater. It was the same way he had felt when Satin had him in her mouth and he saw all those men around him and it seemed like he was floating, finally relieving the terrible pressure that had been building within him for so many years, a pressure he had tried to press out so many different times, sleeping with several women before he married and even one or two in the year immediately following his wedding, though he had never enjoyed any of it. Not the way he enjoyed giving it to Satin behind the Loveboat.

Stella was unaware that Manny had been faking it in bed since before the birth of their first son, Justin. He felt bad because Stella seemed truly happy in their marriage. She scheduled family portraits at Olan Mills once a year. She's a good woman. She even referred to herself as Mrs. Torres when he introduced her to colleagues, not just Stella. If she finds out about Satin, it will break her heart. And the boys. If this story spreads around the base, I'm screwed. Kids hear and talk a lot. Justin will find out. He'll ask his mother. She'll come crying to me, and I'll have no explanation. She hadn't done anything to deserve a husband like him. He pinched his eyes together as hard as he could, trying to make himself cry. But the dialogue in his head was an act, and he knew it. He couldn't make himself truly care while he was lying in bathwater that smelled of sex.

He wished he could tell Stella that he'd had this weird feeling, like an itch, ever since he was a boy. One day he simply woke up and felt strange inside. A dull buzzing. As if he had sucked a gnat into his lungs and it was beating its tiny wings against the walls, trying to get out. At twelve he had scratched the itch for the first time when he and his friend Cory were walking home from school one day and Cory had asked him you ever punched your clown? Manny tried to pretend he knew what that meant while Cory motioned for him to follow him into a cluster of bushes and pulled a magazine from his backpack with pictures of women on their backs with their legs splayed, one man drilling into her and two more standing by her head while she held a dick in each fist, smiling at the camera. Manny's pants became very tight in the front. Cory flipped the pages and explained see, he's fucking her and she's sucking those other guys' dicks, and Manny knew he understood because his body was flushed in a way that it had never been before. He tried to shift his feet and adjust himself so he would feel more comfortable, but it didn't help. When Cory said do you feel it, Manny knew exactly what he was talking about and nodded and said yeah, so they're fucking, but paying more attention to the three, sometimes four or five dicks in each picture rather than the woman and the revolting crack between her legs that looked to him like the honey ham his mom bought from the deli for his school lunches, and when Cory asked do you want to feel something cool, Manny nodded and watched in awkward silence as Cory placed the magazine down on the ground and pulled down his pants and palmed his joint and then said spit on your hand like this, don't worry, I'm not a fag or anything, and he spat a glob onto his palm and rubbed it all over his joint and then wrapped his hand around it and started moving it back and forth and Manny watched in curious amazement, and Cory said damn, it feels good, you've got to try it, nodding toward Manny's crotch until Manny thought why not, since he was dying to get rid of the weird tingling in his pants, so he did the same thing Cory had done, spitting and stroking and looking from Cory to the magazine to his own dick, proud that he was actually slightly bigger than Cory but eventually only staring at Cory and his thrusting hand and his scrunched-up face and his head tilting back with his eyes closed and his thighs starting to shake and then he gaped in amazement as a few drops of clear liquid spurted from Cory's dick and left a strand hanging from the tip, swinging in the breeze and slowly stretching toward the ground, and Cory's face was flushed and he was panting a little and saying goddam, goddam, over and over, while Manny watched him and kept spitting on his hand until he felt a surge of energy shooting from the tingling head of his cock to all of his extremities, causing him to shake, and then with a burst it was over and Manny stood dizzy and breathless.

That was the first time Manny noticed the dull buzzing in his chest leaving and being replaced by a pressure that slowly began to build from that moment. But that time had been an accident. The first time he had consciously attempted to alleviate the pressure was at the age of fourteen when Hallie, a girl from school who had been giving him looks since he first started the seventh grade at Carson, walked through a dried-out wash with him one day smoking cigarettes as they headed toward their neighborhood and asked are you a virgin? When he said yes, she smiled and said I am too, but I don't want to be anymore, and since we're friends we should do it together. So they had met at his friend Jason's house three weekends later, while Jason's parents were away. Jason's older brother bought them a bottle of Kessler and they went to the den and drank until Jason finally got bored and went to bed and Manny and Hallie laid together on the couch and kissed and touched each other and she grabbed his hand and placed it beneath her skirt and between her legs where it was warm and soggy like mud after a flashflood. What came after had made him sick. It scared him the way she squirmed and moaned beneath him and got soggier. The sound of their bodies meeting was like a fat man chewing his food too loudly. And the smell was awful. He hadn't expected anything like it. With Cory it had been clean, out in the open. The tingling sensation shooting through his body happened again, but it wasn't right. So he thought it must be her, because the next day the burdensome pressure was still there, vaguely taunting him, begging him to appease it. He had no idea how to solve the problem, no idea until he had put himself on display in front of a crowd of drunken men outside a strip club.

Something else was bothering Manny too: his uncertainty about whether Vinnie had seen him behind the Boat. He remembered seeing Vinnie leave the club but wasn't sure if he'd had enough time to get to his car and drive away before Satin pulled him outside. Manny thought for a while, trying to envision the men and see if Vinnie's face was among those watching him, worrying Vinnie might become disgusted with him, or think he was a terrible man, what if he thinks I'm some sleazeball who'll screw anything that moves or that I'm a bad father and he never speaks to me again and that was my one chance, until he felt the pressure returning, somewhere beneath his heart but not quite in his stomach, as if he had an extra organ that was swelling, an organ that had developed while he was a teenager and kept growing and growing like a swollen piece of rice until it threatened to explode within his chest. He panicked, thinking something awful was about to happen to him right there in the tub. He threw his torso above the waterline, his chest heaving and burning.

In the solitude of the bathtub, he had forgotten all about Stella and suddenly he was overcome with guilt. He stood up and began scrubbing frantically at his skin with a soapy washrag. He scrubbed and rinsed desperately, splashing water over the sides of the tub and peering down at the layer of soap and dirt floating in the bath, ignoring the burns he was getting from the washrag. He pulled the plug and watched as the water level sank, leaving his feet and ankles covered in scum. He turned on the shower and rinsed the soap away and toweled off and tiptoed down the hallway to the bedroom where his wife was waiting. He edged beneath the covers, and she rolled over and put her arm around him and snuggled her head between his neck and shoulder, making sounds of contented sleep. Manny watched how peacefully she slept and wished more than anything that he could simply be at peace. His wife burrowed deeper, turning her head and smacking her lips, and Manny clenched his teeth to suppress a scream of anguish. He held his wife tight against him and wept.

Manny, get up. Stella was shaking him by the shoulder. She giggled at how difficult it was to wake her husband. Even though he could be a grump, she still enjoyed watching his eyes open every morning when she pulled the blinds and let in the Arizona sun. After a couple minutes, she put her hand on his rib cage and traced the gaps between his ribs with her fingers, tickling him.

How was last night, honey? You had fun, right?

Manny grimaced, thinking of something to say. Instead of speaking he turned to his wife and placed his hand behind her head. He drew her head toward his and kissed her. Then he lay back and closed his eyes.

Stella smiled, thinking how lucky she was to have found a man like

Manny. Genuine and caring. She knew plenty of women who were disappointed when Manny took himself off the market by proposing to her. In fact, when she went grocery shopping at the PX, she still got dirty looks from a few women who had thrown themselves at Manny when they were younger. He had been a real up-and-comer. Very few had moved up the ranks as fast as young Manny. It had something to do with the way he carried himself in public, Stella was sure. The way he walked, confident yet approachable, drew people to him. They simply assumed he was a man who should be respected, and in time, he had proven them right.

Respect was definitely something Stella held for her husband. And she liked making him happy. When he was in a good mood, her whole day seemed to go well. But he seemed tired today, so she quit tickling him to allow him a few extra minutes of sleep.

He gave her hair a little tug, and Stella squealed with surprise. Manny, what's gotten into you? She moved closer to him, pulling the blanket from between them so their bodies could touch. His skin was hot. His heart was racing. What's got you all worked up, baby? He said nothing, only pulled his wife closer and kissed her neck and rubbed his cheek against her breasts. Stella sighed and moved on top of him, whispering I love you, over and over like she did every time, and Manny kept his eyes closed and thought about the Loveboat, about the swirling blue lights inside and the stars outside above the dumpster; he heard the sails flapping and the men chanting his name and smelled the sweat and— oh god, Manny—smoke and a handful of dollar bills fluttered past his calf and came to rest on his foot—it's all yours, Manny—the stars swaying above his head until he felt Stella's nails digging into his shoulders, piercing the flesh, and then she collapsed on top of him—oh god, oh god, ohmyfuckinggod.

They lay in silence for a few minutes, waiting for their pulses to slow, breathing short breaths. Manny? You're amazing. She fell over onto her back. So are you, baby. He hated calling her pet names. Why don't you take a shower and I'll get the boys ready, Stella. He got out of bed and wiped himself with a towel lying on their dresser. Across the hall in the boys' room, Manny unplugged the GI Joe nightlight and picked his younger son out of his crib. He bent over and nudged Justin with his elbow, nodding toward the school clothes Stella had set out the night before. Keeping to their morning ritual, Justin groaned and Manny sang good morning to you, good morning to you, you look like a monkey and you smell like one too. His son laughed and sat up in bed. No, you look like a monkey, Daddy. Manny made a grunting noise and left the room.

He walked into the kitchen with his younger son, squeezing the boy's cheek before buckling him into his highchair and placing a frozen teething ring on the tray in front of him. He brought a carton of eggs out of the fridge and started whistling while he cracked them into a skillet. He heard Stella humming in the shower. The soapy-smelling steam drifted into the kitchen. Manny whistled and tapped his foot to the rhythm of an upbeat song, like one they might play in a club. Something easy to dance to. Something to set the mood.

Without realizing it Manny had stopped cracking eggs and stood with his hand suspended over the counter, clenched into a fist, an egg crushed inside. The yolk dripped between his fingers, hanging like strands of speckled mucus. The shower stopped running, snapping him out of his trance. He hurriedly finished breakfast and set it on the table as his wife and older son walked into the kitchen.

During breakfast Manny and Justin joked back and forth while Stella fed the baby. She was content, laughing at their jokes. Daddy, what do you call it when Scooby-Doo goes potty? Scooby-Doo-Doo. Hehehe. Well, what do you call Scooby-Doo's ghost then, Justin? Scooby-Boo. Stella shook her head. It was always the same terrible jokes. But every morning Justin and Manny acted as if it were the first time they'd heard them.

Gentlemen, I hate to interrupt your improv routine, but I need a favor. Manny tipped an invisible hat in her direction, winking at Justin. At your service, m'lady. He listened intently, like a true gentleman, as she told him about her hair appointment on post and wondered if he had time to drop the boys off this morning. Justin's little foot kept bumping against Manny's knee, trying to draw his attention to the butter knife clenched between his teeth and the egg he held over his eye like a pirate's patch.

After breakfast Manny buckled his sons in the backseat while the car warmed up. Stella waited until he was finished, then kissed him good-bye. She didn't see him flinch. See you tonight, baby.

When Stella was gone, Manny reversed out of the driveway and started singing Blow the Man Down, gently swerving the car back and forth. His sons loved it.

When they reached Justin's school, Manny pulled up beside the pole where the principal was hoisting the flag. Justin got out and saluted his father, then turned and walked inside. The principal saluted Manny too.

———

Inside the PX hair salon, three black women were cutting hair. The waiting list was already seven names deep and there were still appointments coming in, but it was like that every day, so the waiting wives of airmen and the few enlisted women sitting in a row didn't mind.

But girl, you shoulda heard this muthafucka go on bout Cap'm Torres. Talkin bout how he was drunk off his ass and some stripper come up to him.

You let your man go to the strip club?

Shit, I don't give a damn as long as he comes home to me and I gets mine.

Laughter. Hair fell to the floor and snipping scissors stopped and waved around, barely missing the heads beneath them. The waiting customers pretended not to be listening, reading their magazines.

Both a yall crazy, and you need to watch whatchou talkin bout up in here.

Shit. We got free speech, right? Aint that why our men out there flyin them damn planes and shootin at stuff? I aint come all the way from Atlanta to sit up in here and not say what's on my mind.

That's RIGHT girl. Spill it.

Yeah. So Torres is throwin money around, gettin titties in his face and drinkin beer while his woman at home watchin the kids and he runnin up in the Loveboat talkin bout I'm gonna get mine while all the other guys is there tryin to enjoy themselves and have a drink, maybe look at some titties. You know how Rodney is.

Shit, you know he a lyin bastard.

Whatchou know about that?

Girl, I just call em like I see em.

You both some silly bitches.

Who you callin bitch? So Rodney says Torres, the same guy who usually have a stick up his ass, is yellin and carryin on and gettin all cozy with the strippers.

And what's Rodney doin the whole time, coverin his eyes?

Girl, he was probably wishin he could afford to do the same thing, with his broke ass.

Everybody laughed again, putting down their magazines and watching the three women banter back and forth.

Why don't you both talk about somethin else?

Oh I got other stories, but lemme finish this one about Torres.

Yeah, now I'm all interested and you know yall are too, so quit trippin.

So, I guess the dudes figure Torres drunk so they just ignore him and watch the girls, and when it's last call, Torres ordered himself a couple shots and took em and went trollin for hoes.

Scandalous muthaFUCKA.

Yeah. And he went and found him this one name Satan or some shit and offered her money if she went in the back with him and gave him some head.

That's it?

Nah. Guess he took her ass to the back of the club and a buncha guys followed him out—

You mean Rodney went out there too?

Nah, he came home before the club closed, and his boys told him about what happened next.

Sure.

Girl, don't make me—she pointed her scissors at the woman in the stall next to her, then smiled. So Rodney says Torres went out back and whipped his shit out and was all wavin it in her face and tellin her bout how she had to do him right there in front of everybody.

Tell me that ho didn't do it.

You KNOW she did.

That's some NASTY shit.

Oh, it gets worse.

Then neither of you need to be talkin bout it up in here.

Damn, Kia, you gonna shut the hell up already? Let her ass talk. Keep goin, Sonya.

Girl, that bitch took off her clothes in fronta all them muthafuckas and start givin Torres head and all touchin her junk and lettin Torres put it in her ass—

Oh, HELL no. That's some sick shit.

And all of em just standin around and watchin and pullin money out and throwin it down on the ground.

She just goin at it?

Girl, lovin it like it gonna make her a movie star.

And Torres just had his thing hangin out in front of all them guys?

Wavin in the breeze like it was a flag and he all proud of his shit, like it's somethin.

Each woman sat with a gaping mouth, wondering if her man had been there, trying to remember what time he came home the night before.

I'll tell you both one thing.

Quit tellin us what we can and can't say.

No, it aint that. It just goes to show that all men are horny dogs and you better off not messin with em.

Shit, Kia, you think we don't know? But what can you do? I aint tryin to be no nun or some kinda lezzie.

Me neither. I'm STRICTLY dickly.

The salon filled with laughter and exclamations of agreement, and little conversations began between the women as they talked about how come men can't be faithful and sometimes think with their big head instead of their little one. And they laughed and talked and joked, Kia interrupting every now and then on principle, but the other two going on and on as if they were sitting at home with just the two of them and not in a salon filled with customers.

And shit if that son of a bitch, that sickass muthafucka with a wife and two babies at home, didn't put on a show for almost an hour doin God knows what—

Now don't you take the Lord's name in vain, Sonya.

Damn, Kia, you worse than my mom. I'm only tryin to let these females know what they men doin behind they backs and—

Stella walked in the door and the room fell silent except for the snipping of scissors and the rustling of magazines.

How are you ladies doing?

Oh fine, Stella. We just talkin bout the usual. You know, how men are dogs.

She smiled and took her seat and picked out the latest issue of *Us*. I wouldn't know about that.

Yeah. So this muthafucka try to run at me with a bump on his thang, talkin bout just kiss it girl, just put it in your mouth, and I say look at YOUR shit. What is that, a sore or somethin? You think you Herpules? Get that shit out my face.

More laughter, but everyone was watching Stella, wondering if she knew about what her husband had done the night before.

But at least there are some good men out there, like Stella's man, Cap'm Torres.

Yes, he's been very good to me. I consider myself blessed.

Girl, you better, cause a man like that don't come around too much and when he does, you got to snatch his ass up before one of these females here pounce on him.

Everyone nodded in agreement and gave Stella the sweetest smiles, telling her how lucky she was but not exactly meeting her eyes.

Weren't yall high school sweethearts?

No. We met in college. I still remember when he proposed on the day of his graduation, right outside the arena in front of both our families and the ten thousand other people who were there. It was the most embarrassing and romantic thing that has ever happened to me.

Damn. That's sweet, Stella.

Yeah, Torres is real.

Yes, he is. And he's a great father too. He takes the kids to Lakeside Park to play without me even asking. He even woke up with both boys when they were babies and fed them so I could sleep. But nobody's perfect, ladies. He's got his ass side just like the rest of them. There are days when he's terrible and I want to punch him. But for the most part, he's good.

Still, girl, you got yourself a real man.

Yeah, a good man.

Manny sat at his desk filing field tests on a handful of soldiers, taking phone calls, and preparing for a noon meeting, but he couldn't concentrate. He had come to work feeling great, returning salutes to the soldiers at the gate, happy to have gotten a few hours of restful sleep. When he checked in with his company for first formation he made more jokes than usual, subtly referencing his fling with Satin in case any of the men had been there.

Eventually the night before was virtually forgotten as he busied himself with work that he'd let fall behind over the week. And today was Friday, which meant the day would go by fast and everyone who didn't have to work over the weekend would be in a good mood, so it had the makings of a pleasant day. After he had been at work a few hours, he noticed that he kept rereading and reorganizing the same files. He laid his head down on his desk and tried to concentrate on his breathing. He sorted the files again. A to Z. They weren't even close to being in the right order. And that afternoon's meeting was when they were supposed to assign the officers to their training schedules. He placed the files on his desk and reclined in his seat. The itch in his chest grew into a tiny burn right beneath his heart and above his stomach. He placed his feet flat on the ground and sat up straight, hoping to give room to whatever was raging inside his torso. He shifted his feet and started tapping his pencil against his temple with no exact rhythm, shuffling papers and sipping his coffee, and he looked at the clock over and over and ignored his pager, which was beeping to remind him of the meeting in half an hour—I haven't even made a dent in the schedules—and got up from his desk and closed the door to his office and paced around the room and unbuttoned a few buttons on his shirt, looking at the clock again and realizing it hadn't budged. He held his nose so close to the face that it was almost touching the glass. But the second hand wasn't moving.

Wait. There. It moved.

His pager beeped nine, ten, eleven times, and he paced the room, going in circles around his desk and ignoring the beeper and suddenly he had his jacket on and was searching the pockets for his car keys and he'd taken the pager off his belt and thrown it in his desk drawer and slammed it shut, finally finding his keys as he walked out the door, past his secretary who tried to ask him if he would like to leave a message for anyone who might need to contact him, but he kept going through the narrow hallways of his building, ignoring the occasional soldier who stopped to salute him as he passed, increasing his speed, but that was not enough, and his heart beat faster while the pressure taunted him more than it ever had before and he tried to outrun it, slipping on loose gravel and catching his slacks on the cactus that lined the parking lot and stumbling, and by the time he reached his car his shirt was damp with sweat, but he didn't mind a bit because he felt a little better already now that he was out of his office. He started his car and drove toward the gate.

The rush that Manny felt the moment he passed onto Kolb relieved him long enough for him to breathe clearly and deeply as he headed toward the middle of Tucson. He had no destination. He simply needed to drive. He allowed himself to relax and look toward the boneyard where rows of dismantled planes were bleached white by the sun, purposely avoiding the direction of the Loveboat.

He tried to think of something to do. Anything that would take his mind off the tension. He could pick Justin up for lunch and take him to Chuck E. Cheese's for pizza. Justin loved the singing and the puppets. And the miniature ferris wheel. But the thought of screaming kids and flashing lights and the smell of grease made Manny nauseous. And even though he knew how excited Justin got when he surprised him at school for lunch—the way his tiny chest puffed out and his back straightened like a real soldier—Manny decided against the idea.

Of course, he could always surprise his wife. Reserve a table at a nice restaurant on Broadway and call her at home so she could meet him there. But seeing her right now wasn't a good idea. On Speedway he decided he wanted to get out of the sun and into a dark building, so he stopped at the first bar he saw and went inside to order some food. The bar was full of men, construction workers and plumbers and mechanics, all taking their lunch breaks. He made his way to a corner booth in the rear where he could be left alone. Just when he thought he would have to walk to the bar to place his order, a middle-aged woman dressed in cut-off shorts and a tank top approached him and pulled a notepad from her back pocket and asked what can I get for you. Jalapeño poppers. A cheese crisp. Oh, and a shot of Crown.

The shot went down real nice, melting the hardness in his stomach and clearing his throat somewhat. He ordered another one before she walked away. Then another one. And by the time his food arrived, Manny had finished off five shots and had a sixth sitting in front of him. For the first time since he left the base, whatever was constricting his insides had lightened its grip enough for him to move freely. He was thankful for that much. And for the additional shot he had after he finished eating his poppers. And for the cigarette he bummed off the waitress. He sat back and let the food mingle with the alcohol and the nicotine.

When he got up from the booth, he felt good, fuzzy and numb to the anxiety that had tormented him earlier. Most of the customers had gone back to work, so Manny relaxed as he walked toward the bathroom past the remaining men—two in a booth and a few singles sitting at the bar.

At the urinal, where Manny was relieving himself and reading the newspaper taped to the wall, another man stood beside him at another urinal. Manny rolled his eyes over as far as he could without moving his head and looked down at the guy, who had finished pissing a few seconds after Manny came into the bathroom but still stood there holding his dick. He stared over at Manny once in a while, not shaking it, not getting ready to put it away, just standing. The feeling Manny had relished the night before returned, and even though he too had finished pissing, he didn't move. The tingling in his groin made him want to close his eyes and stand there feeling it throughout his body, but instead he caught the man looking directly at his dick and was suddenly hit with a wave of disgust that overwhelmed him so much he forgot his excitement and he looked at the man and down at the man's hand, which had begun to move a little, waving his dick back and forth, and said what in the FUCK are you looking at, and the man smiled and looked down at Manny and said just you, and Manny felt rage begin to well up inside his throat, you're staring at my dick? you some kind of fuckin homo? you think I'm gay? and Manny noticed the longing in the man's eyes slowly change to an awareness, and he fumbled with his pants and his zipper and looked away and Manny, furious, was not going to let the fucker off that easy and he turned toward the man, is this what you're lookin at? you want to stare, go ahead and stare, you fuckin queer, cause it's the last one of these you're ever gonna see, and Manny could tell the man was trying hard not to look at him, that he was scared and worried but he looked anyway and immediately back up at Manny, and his eyes, even before they made their way back up to Manny's face, were full of the realization that he had just made a mistake, a big mistake, a mistake so huge that Manny snapped and watched himself—as if he were lying beneath a rushing body of water and everything was happening right above the surface—reach out toward the man, who did not move but stood with his arms hanging at his sides, and grabbed him by the neck and threw him against the wall, you just gonna stare at my dick like that? you must think I'm one of you, and the man tried to stammer out a response but Manny increased his grip around the stranger's neck, digging in with all his might while the man's face immediately reddened and his Adam's apple bucked beneath Manny's grasp, then the man's hands came up from his sides, as if he had just remembered that he even owned them, and he instinctively clutched at the clamp on his throat, trying to tear the hand from his neck or at least lodge his own fingers beneath it so he could get a sip of air, and Manny found that he suddenly did not care whether this faggot lived or died and he stood watching the man grow redder and redder and then he was beating the man's head against the tiled walls, not loud enough to draw attention out in the bar but certainly hard enough to draw blood from the back of the man's head as it hit the tile over and over again, and with each hit the man struggled less and the sound of his head hitting the tiles became less sharp, more muffled, and the man's hands fell to his sides again and his head slumped sideways, and Manny decided to stop before he killed the little fairy so he tossed the man aside. He washed his hands and checked his teeth and practiced a few smiles in the mirror to make sure he looked normal, then he closed the door behind him as he emerged from the men's room, wiping his hands on the thighs of his uniform slacks, ignoring the man's groans. He looked at no one as he left the bar, just waved a general wave in case someone was looking. The sunlight blinded Manny for a moment until his eyes grew accustomed to the brightness of the outdoors again.

His rage was gone. The man in the bathroom had drained it from him. But something was still there, growing more intense with the heat of the sun. He momentarily entertained the idea of going back into the bar and rousing the beaten man and letting him stare at his dick if he really wanted to. He'd tell him he was just kidding, you can look at it, want to pet it, maybe he'd even let the guy suck on it too. Instead he got back in his car. As he drove away, he thought maybe I should just run headlong into a semi or smash into a telephone pole and get it over with. He thought about his wife and his job—oh shit, what if that poor bastard saw my name, I'll be ruined—and he wanted to pull over and cry and tear the clothes from his body and claw into his chest and rip out the ever-growing mound of filth that had set up residence inside him.

He needed something. Silence. A place to clear his head. Maybe I can stop in that church up the road, what is it, Our Mother of Sorrows. It's Catholic, so it'll be cool and quiet inside. No, that won't work either. Something else. Dammit. His breaths were short. His hands and teeth clenched.

He parked in the lot of a flower shop and wept tears of rage and sorrow and frustration. He no longer felt like Captain Torres, the man in charge of hundreds of airmen. He was no longer sure of anything except that he must regain control of himself. He sat in the car trying to calm himself, wiping the tears from his face with his dirty shirtsleeve, rocking back and forth and thinking, thinking, thinking. It'll be okay.

When he had finally regained some composure, Manny decided flowers might be just what he needed. I'll buy my Stella some flowers and I'll water them for her. It was small, but it was something. Right after he bought the flowers, he would call the base and tell them he left because he was ill and they could brief him in the morning on everything he'd missed. Yes, then I can go home and give Stella the flowers and take the boys to the park. Or I could call the babysitter and take Stella out for dinner and a movie, something real nice so she'll be happy and we can go on playing house, the perfect family that makes all her friends jealous.

He went inside the flower shop and immediately felt better when the bells on the door chimed as it closed behind him. The smell was exactly what he needed, teeming with clean, pure life. He browsed through the flowers, trying to decide which ones were the brightest and the largest and would live the longest. A teenaged boy approached him and offered him assistance, and when Manny told him his requirements for the perfect bouquet, the boy dashed toward the coolers that lined the wall and motioned for Manny to come over.

These are the best flowers, he said, waving his hand over them. We only import them once a month but they last forever. He removed baskets filled with iris and cymbidium orchids and lilies and birds of paradise and plucked one from the bunch and handed it to Manny. The birds of paradise looked like a flock of cranes frozen in the moment of liftoff. He loved the way they seemed to be a cycle of life. How the stems morphed into crane bodies with wings shooting off of them. He told the boy to wrap them up. The boy took the flowers to an old man who sat behind the counter reading the newspaper. The old man smiled and punched the price of the flowers into an antique cash register with buttons like a typewriter. Manny paid with cash and, after he was given his change, went over to sit by the front window and wait for his flowers to be wrapped.

Across the street was Reid Park, Tucson's version of Central Park. Ponds, streams, golf. The zoo he had visited many times as a child, where he rode the same decades-old tortoise that both of his sons rode years later.

The boy returned from the rear of the store to wait with him while the old man wrapped his flowers. You know, there's a rose garden over there that's really nice. Manny turned to face the boy. Yeah. I've been to that park a few times.

Have you ever been to the garden?

I think once long ago, with an old girlfriend. No, it was with my family, and we had a bucket of Kentucky Fried Chicken with us and had a picnic in the middle of the garden. It was a little embarrassing. People walking by trying to enjoy the beauty of the garden and there we were gnawing on chicken bones.

The boy laughed. My name's Jaime. I just moved here, so the garden's pretty new to me. We didn't have anything that big where I used to live. So . . . you ever go there anymore?

Sometimes, but not to the garden.

I go there all the time. It's relaxing.

Really? All the time? He looked directly into Jaime's eyes and Jaime looked away.

Well . . . I go there a lot.

The old man came back to the front of the store with the flowers and thanked him for his purchase and Manny said it was no problem, his pleasure, and looked over at the boy, thanking him for his help and telling him he was going to head on over to the garden, maybe I'll see you. Jaime smiled and Manny left the store and decided not to call the base just yet, he wanted to go sit in the garden and see if Jaime would show up. There was something about him—how he had smiled and the way he spoke. He drove his car across the street and parked it, then walked over to the garden, feeling the anticipation of being able to talk to Jaime and maybe they could talk about flowers and life and anything to keep Manny's mind off the man lying beaten in the bathroom on Speedway and the dull throbbing in his chest and the itching at his temples. He walked through the rows of Sweet Dream roses and Magic Carpet roses and Freedom roses and Armada roses and Fellowship roses, stopping to smell each type and feel its petals, checking his watch from time to time and seeing if he could remember the names of the flowers without looking at the mounted placards in front of each row, and then he checked his watch and looked up at the sun, and still no Jaime, maybe he meant the pond, did he say the pond, and even though Manny knew Jaime had said the garden and not the pond he wanted to be sure, so he walked over to the pond where a few teenaged couples were dipping their feet and holding hands and geese lay sleeping beneath the shade of a giant oak tree, but Jaime was not there and Manny began to panic thinking shit, I'm an idiot and I probably missed him, walking, then running, back to the garden where a few old people meandered through the lanes of roses, but no boy. No Jaime. Manny's stomach tightened. He began to feel anxious and continued to check his watch every few seconds to see how much time had passed. He walked up and down the rows of flowers, passing the old people, overtaking them time after time, until he had fully memorized the names of each rose—the common names and the Latin names—and he walked faster and faster, creating ruts in the rows and getting dirty looks from folks who were out for a leisurely stroll, trying to enjoy the late afternoon when the sun began to cool. Manny stared in the direction of the flower shop and saw a figure coming toward him and his heart beat faster—it's him—and his anticipation grew and he forced himself to walk much more slowly, pretending to scrutinize each individual flower to see how they differed even within the same type, and the figure came nearer and nearer, Manny growing antsy and blatantly looking up now because he did not want the boy to think he was not there. Manny squinted and realized that it was not the boy, it was some scrawny old man walking through the grass—where is he?—his excitement wilting away, replaced by anxiety and anger. It was nearly five and most of the people were gone from the garden. Manny ran to his car and drove out of the park and over to the flower shop. It was locked. Manny was seething. He looked around for relief of any sort. It was too late to go back to work and he didn't want to see his wife yet, not like this.

A drink. That was what he needed. Not flowers. Not the boy. A good stiff drink. Rum or whiskey or gin, hell, I don't care. He left his car in the parking lot of the flower shop and walked north because he knew this part of town had a liquor store or grocery store every few blocks, so he walked and had barely passed three businesses when he reached the corner and saw Torchy's was open. He went inside and grabbed a bottle of Crown, his hands trembling as he retrieved the money from his wallet. The clerk wrapped the bottle in a paper bag and watched him leave, Manny shaking and fumbling with the lid of the bottle before he had even made it out of the store.

He took a long pull from the bottle. It burned his throat all the way down to his stomach where it settled but didn't bring complete relief. It was just enough for him to gather his thoughts. He decided to go back to the park just in case Jaime was there, so he walked to his car with the bottle tucked into his waistband, drove back to the garden, and sat on a picnic table, waiting. Manny lifted the bottle to his lips, letting it bubble two or three times, swallowing larger amounts as the afternoon turned to evening and the sun began to set. He knew Jaime wasn't going to come, but now he could laugh about it because he was just a kid anyway, why the hell would a kid want to meet someone almost twice his age? His laughter helped, but the tension was once again getting unbearable. The liquor was no cure, no help at all. Neither was sitting on a picnic table in the middle of a park at dusk when the cops would be coming soon to move everyone along. He got back into his car and drove away, bewildered, tired, and lonely.

What happened to me to make me feel like this? I mean, people like me. They like my family and are proud of all I've accomplished at such a young age. So why isn't it good enough? Manny brought the Crown to his lips, smelling the potent sting seeping out of the bottle, knowing he should just go home to his wife, go home and help give the boys their nighttime baths and tuck them into bed, then read Justin a chapter from *The Lion, the Witch, and the Wardrobe* and after that go into his room with his wife and pretend he just had a hard day at work and needed to stop off for a couple drinks. It would be easy. He could fix this. He could beat this. Except he couldn't figure out what *this* was. With his fingers he probed the bottom rim of his rib cage, trying to isolate the spot where maybe a tumor was growing. He pictured it—a gray smudge attached to his stomach, coiling its roots around his intestines, squeezing at the arteries around his heart like a closing fist. He felt its grip and thought I have to talk to somebody. I have to figure out some way to get back to normal, back to taking care of Stella and the boys and watering the lawn, pulling weeds from the cracks in the sidewalk. He needed someone to help him figure himself out. A good listener. Who can I call?

It suddenly seemed simple. He'd looked up Vinnie's number in the directory at work earlier. He could just call him and ask if they could meet somewhere for a drink. Surely Vinnie could help him make some sense of the flurry of sensations he felt pressing against his head and chest so badly it made him want to gouge his fingers into his temples and dig around until he found whatever was scratching the walls of his skull.

He pulled his car beside a payphone in a 7-Eleven parking lot and grabbed the receiver with a trembling hand. Twice he dropped his quarter on the ground and had to reach down to retrieve it. He finally managed to get the quarter in the slot and dial Vinnie.

The phone rang four times and he was about to hang up when Vinnie answered, sounding sleepy.

Hey, Vinnie. It's Manny. He was so glad he'd actually picked up. To hear him on the other end. The deep controlled voice, so sure of itself.

How'd you get my number?

Remember you said you were up for hanging out sometime? The first time they officially talked Manny had managed to get him to agree to a second meeting. He owes me.

I did? Yes, Yes. What night do you want to get together, Captain?

Tonight. I mean now. Can you meet me?

Sure. I mean, I guess I can. Is everything okay?

Fine, Vinnie. Fine. Everything's much better.

Um . . . the Tap Room? Is that okay, Captain?

Sounds good.

Okay, Captain, I'll be there in about a half hour.

In his excitement, he hung up the phone too fast to ask for directions, but then he remembered the Tap Room was on Pantano Road, where the wash ran beside Q Mart.

When he reached the Tap Room, he parked and got out to try to sober up in the brisk desert night air while he waited for Vinnie. He sat on the hood of his car, then eased his way back to lay his head on the cool windshield, enjoying the warmth of the hood beneath him and the wind cooling his skin.

It was during this period of waiting, while he listened to the clicks of his engine cooling down, that Manny began to wonder for the first time since his early years where the washes of Tucson led. Like all the other people in the city, Manny knew washes were dangerous during monsoon season. He didn't remember ever being told, just remembered that one day he was acutely aware of how dangerous the hardpan gutters that ran all over the city were. He'd seen plenty of news clips on TV where people were trapped in a wash during a flood, but the cameras never showed where the water went. Did the desert simply suck the water up as soon as it fell, or did it eventually drain into a secret underground river?

From the cockpit of an F-15 the washes looked like wrinkles in the desert's skin. But when they were this close, they looked like ancient sewers, a drainage system designed to carry away the filth of the city when the rains came and scoured Tucson's streets. Now that he thought about it, Manny realized it hadn't rained in some time. But when it did, he wanted to be there to see where the washes would end.

———

Stella put the babies to bed on her own. First she bathed the kids, taking care not to cry in front of Justin so he wouldn't be worried. Then she tucked him into bed and walked to the living room where she put the radio on Cloud 95 and sat down in a rocking chair with her baby. She held his head nuzzled between her breasts and hummed the songs playing on the radio. Cat Stevens. The Carpenters.

But she didn't pay any attention to the songs or the baby. It was Manny she thought about. His work had called at noon looking for him. Then they called back a couple hours later and they said he left and never came back for the meetings scheduled for that afternoon. This was not like anything he had ever done before. Her eyes were puffy from crying and her ear was sore from pressing the phone against it earlier when she called the base looking for her husband. By the time she had gotten through to someone who had any information about him, it was 8 p.m. All they could tell her was Manny had been seen leaving the west gate just before noon. No, they didn't know why. And now it was eleven and she was sitting in her living room wondering what was bothering Manny so much that he'd risk his job and his family to go AWOL. What if something was wrong with him psychologically? Maybe he was schizophrenic or hallucinating or something. But her biggest fear was the one she refused to acknowledge. That beneath his cover of perfection, he was actually disloyal. Maybe he was just too perfect. Too good to be true.

Manny, let it be anything except you leaving me for another woman. Please. We have such wonderful memories. A beautiful wedding at

Lake Havasu. Two handsome boys. IRAs. Nine years, for the love of God, and I'm not going to let one stupid little mistake come between us like this. But the later it became, the more she began to worry that maybe he hadn't left her. Maybe he was hurt somewhere. He wouldn't get involved in drugs or gambling, would he? No, he's on his way right now. Yes, that's my Manny. Something came up but he'll be back soon. He'll walk through the door any minute and he'll explain everything and then it will all be back to normal. I mean, he was fine this morning. He'll come home and explain everything and compliment my hair. We'll go to bed and wake up in the morning and life will go on. It always does, with Manny talking about his next promotion and where we'll send our sons to college and where we're going to build our retirement home. Stella hummed to the baby and listened to the swamp cooler whirring on the roof. The sliding glass doors shook a little as an F-15 flew overhead. He'll walk through the door and tell me he loves me and give me an explanation and I'll see all of this dumb worrying was for nothing.

———

So what's on your mind, Manny? Vinnie shook salt into his beer to keep the bubbles down. He looked up at Manny and smiled.

What's on my mind? he wanted to say. You're on my mind. He sipped his drink and said I'm a little tipsy Vinnie, but I just felt like talking, like getting to know you. Sometimes you see someone and they look like a person with things to say. You look like that to me. I see you around the base all the time and you know—shit, Manny thought, you're rambling. Making an ass of yourself. But Vinnie still looked interested, so Manny started over. Remember last night at the Loveboat?

The couch dance. Sure. Why?

Well, after you left—

Yeah, I heard.

Was that disgust that came across his face? Curiosity? Pity? Manny couldn't tell. The whole thing was going down wrong. It was all too awkward. He decided to take a different approach. His hand drifted across the table, stopping just short of Vinnie's. Look, Vinnie. Something's been happening to me. I have these mixed-up feelings. I need someone to listen.

I'm listening. He put his hand on top of Manny's, patted it, drew his own away again.

Manny stuttered, choked up. He couldn't think of what he had intended to say. On the hood of his car, he had worked it all out. And now, with the man he'd been thinking about so often in front of him, Manny was blowing it. Like a first date. He fumbled for words. Looking at Vinnie confused him. He was definitely still drunk.

Before he could check himself, Manny leaned across the booth. Vinnie sat back. Manny leaned in further, smelling his cologne. His face was so close Manny could see his pores, the place between his eyebrows where several fine stray hairs had grown in, the mole beneath his left eye. He needed to be closer though. He moved forward and tried to kiss Vinnie's lips, but Vinnie turned his head. Without thinking he tried again, but Vinnie leaned a little to the side and Manny's kiss landed on his neck. Then Vinnie lightly pushed Manny's head away.

I think you misunderstood me, Manny. And Vinnie was on his feet, pulling a ten out of his wallet, flattening it on the table. He patted Manny on the shoulder as if Manny were a little kid and walked out the door.

Stunned, Manny stared at the drink in front of him. He wasn't sure how that whole scene had just come about. Jesus, I just tried to kiss a fucking first sergeant, and now I'm sitting here with my drink and Vinnie's half-empty glass still sloshing in front of me. Then he looked down at his clothes. His pants were stained with dirt and sweat. The bars on his uniform hung like loose teeth. He looked like shit. Sloppy and unprofessional.

No wonder he'd just been rejected. He probably looked like some two-bit piece of rough-trade ass, coming at Vinnie like that. How embarrassing. Any decent person would've walked away at the sight of me. I just fucked up the whole thing and now I'm alone again. The sting of rejection crept up Manny's throat like acid. Where do I belong if I can't go home and Vinnie won't talk to me? First a kid stands me up and now him. He put on his jacket and walked out to his car, expecting to find a note from Vinnie telling him to try again later, he'd just done it wrong. But the windshield was empty. Only the moon reflecting off it. Manny felt tears again. In the passenger seat the bottle of Crown beckoned. He got in and lifted it from the seat. Just yesterday he'd been a completely different man. A captain in the Air Force, for christsakes. Look at you now, sitting in your car three sheets to the wind like a pansyass wino. He drank the Crown until it felt like the skin was burning off his throat. A fucking wino.

He needed to find a place where people were still drinking balls-to-the-wall at this hour. He drove south. Into a part of town he had rarely been to because there was never a reason to go. Everyone warned against going to the south side. It had the highest murder rate in the city, but he had never been there at night, alone and drunk, so he went, even though his vision was getting blurry and he had to close one eye to see better. This part of the city was swarming with nightlife. 6th Avenue bars and hotels and restaurants. But they were different from the ones he frequented. Their signs were missing letters, the sidewalks in front were littered with glass, the stench of beer and vomit and piss wafted by each time the wind blew.

He parked his car and stepped out. As he walked down the sidewalk, he heard glass crunching beneath his shoes and ignored the drunks passed out in doorways and curled up in the front yards of the most wretched homes he had ever seen in his life, bars on every window, the paint peeling to reveal paint peeling and more paint peeling beneath that, and taverns and boarded-up businesses everywhere—a huge pink adobe building that must have been a pharmacy many years before because Manny could just barely make out the sun-bleached remnants of the Rx painted on the wall—and lowriders cruised by playing music, the smell of marijuana seeping from their windows. How long Manny walked he had no idea. He could feel the burden in his chest and yet he could only keep walking, taking in the images of poverty and madness, smelling death and decay and a million unthinkable scents, hearing gunshots and sirens and wails and barking, seeing graffiti and the burned-out skeletons of cars and bums scavenging in the street for aluminum cans and looking for coins that had been accidentally dropped. What he saw terrified him in ways he had never been before, yet the place in his chest below his heart and above his stomach seemed to relish the wasted south side of the city. It throbbed and pulsed and grew within him, uncoiling itself like a snake.

He could see himself passed out in his vomit on the floor of an abandoned house with his finger hooked in the handle of a wine jug. He'd get rolled a few times, but eventually the cholos would figure out he was a waste of time and move on to someone else. The Tucson police, if they got bored, might drive him out to the desert and beat him with their nightsticks and flashlights and blackjacks and lead gloves. I'd deserve it, Manny thought. I've let my family down, probably lost my job, and made an ass of myself to a first sergeant. If he mentions it to my superiors, they'll have to fire me. Don't tell, Vinnie.

Manny stepped into the first bar he saw with English signs in the window and pushed past men who turned to look at him but made no path. He pounded the bar until the bartender came up and asked him what the fuck you want. Crown, a double straight up, make it two, and the bartender nodded and retrieved two Dixie cups from beneath the bar and filled them both to the top with Crown and told him you better hurry up if you don't want it to soak through the cup and then you've pissed away your money, and Manny did them one after the other and found a stool and sat down, resting his head on his arms until he felt someone put an arm around his shoulder and offer to buy him a shot, and he said sure and looked up and saw a man standing next to him in a leather vest with a threadbare T-shirt beneath, and when the man smiled it showed rotting teeth with wads of chew wedged between each one and the man said yeah, I aint seen you in here before, my name's Leonard. Manny told him his name and asked the bartender for another double shot of Crown and Leonard looked at the bartender and then at Manny and back to the bartender and nodded and the bartender poured Manny the drink and Leonard said you're a little pricey, huh, and Manny nodded, just keep the drinks coming, please, trying to blur everything out, but the Crown was not hitting him fast enough. The tattoos on Leonard's arms were too clear.

Leonard sat down next to him and took a slug of his beer. He watched Manny knock back the shot like Kool-Aid, hoping it would hit him soon so he would not have to spend all his cash on this guy who just kept putting them away, but Leonard did not mind too much because Manny was good-looking and Leonard rubbed Manny's thigh, slowly working nearer and nearer to the bulge beneath his slacks, and Manny looked down at the guy's hand and then just looked away. Leonard wanted to make sure Manny was going to keep allowing him to touch his leg before he bought any more drinks, but Manny completely ignored him. He didn't care if the guy wanted to rub him through his uniform slacks. He only knew that Leonard kept feeding him shots and he was thankful. Each time his head moved, the lights in the bar smeared, and he couldn't make out a single person's face but he didn't care at all, and another shot in a paper cup came to him and he drank it and teetered back and forth on his stool and fell backwards onto the floor and vomit burbled from his mouth—bile and liquor and his lunch—everywhere, his ribs contracting and heaving. Leonard picked him up and held him steady on the bar and ordered him another shot, hell, he just wasted six goddam shots at least. The voices and laughter in the bar became a throbbing swirling mass of grunts and moans dropping deeper in tone and speed with every shot Manny took until finally it was so low he thought his eardrums would burst and was sure that the sound had come alive and was burrowing its way into his head and Leonard wiped the vomit from Manny's chin and smiled and kissed him on the lips, yeah, I think you're almost ready, and Manny managed a nod, unable to discern what Leonard had said but willing to do anything to get out of the bar where the noise and the voices were probing him and threatening to drive him insane and then he was in the air and bumping up and down to the rhythm of Leonard carrying him to a nearby motel with rooms rented by the hour and a desk clerk who never looked his customers in the eyes or asked for identification, because he didn't want to actually see the human beings capable of what he found in the mornings when he unlocked the doors to be sure the rooms were empty—tomato-sized clots of blood lying at the bottom of the toilet, beds covered in piss and vomit stains, teenaged hookers passed out in the corner of the room with needles hanging from their arms—look, I don't give a fuck, just give me the cash and walk away—and Leonard paid for two hours because that was all the cash he had left and he carried Manny around to the back of the motel, room 289, and propped him against the wall while he opened the door and almost retched at the smell of sewage and off-brand Lysol and he didn't turn on the lights for fear of what he would see, instead he groped his way to the bed and threw Manny down on top of it and brushed aside godknowswhat, and then he pulled Manny's pants off and tossed them on the floor and told him just take it easy, which wasn't even necessary because Manny heard nothing, felt nothing, except the gray fist growing in his chest and breathing and sinking and sinking, then rising to the surface again, and it was daylight and the door was about to explode with the pounding of a fist that must have been the size of a pumpkin and a voice yelling YOU MOTHERFUCKER, I'M GONNA KILL YOU WHEN I GET THROUGH THIS DOOR, and Manny looked around and had no idea how he had gotten inside a room that smelled like the bowels of a dumpster and he ran to the bathroom because he felt sick, ignoring the voice, still drunk, his head throbbing and spinning, and he flipped on the light, dry heaved into the toilet, then ran gagging around the hotel room and grabbed his pants and pulled them over his legs, hopping up and down, terrified of what he might be stepping on, refusing to look down, and the pounding on the door got louder, I'M NOT GONNA CALL THE COPS, YOU COCK-SUCKING FUCKBAG, I'M GONNA PUT A BULLET THROUGH YOU IF YOU DON'T GET OUT HERE AND PAY ME FOR STAYIN ALL NIGHT, and Manny opened the door and said fuck you, you twisted fuck, and wiped the burning bile from his chin and ran out into the blinding daylight, stag-gering and sweating, thinking I need a drink, knowing he should go home, there's still time, wanting to be back in bed with Stella and his kids tickling him but sensing deep down the impossibility of that, and the impossibility of being able to look at Vinnie without feeling shame after last night, it was far too late, thinking Jesus, I need a drink, and he stumbled through the doors of a bar on some dingy street and the bar-tender asked him what the hell happened and Manny told him to pour him drinks and keep them coming, I don't care what it is, and the bar-tender poured shots of tequila and whiskey and rum and mixed it up over and over again, amused at the sheer volume of alcohol this crazy sonofabitch could drink, and he made Manny shots he had never made before, shots that were not even shots but bastard mixtures of the foulest liquors he could think of, but nothing would put Manny down, he even summoned the strength to get to the bathroom, and he splashed water on his face and used a towel on a spool to dry, but he would not look in the mirror because the thought of how he probably looked petrified him, and so he tried to scrape off a layer or two of whatever was on his clothes but he was unable to because he could not stand and he collapsed in the bathroom with his head lying on the rim of the urinal and woke in the alley behind some building and it was night and he had no idea what day it was or what had happened, only that he still could not breathe and the pressure was building and building like a tapeworm so long and thick it threatened to burst out both ends, and his wallet and keys were gone so he stopped a man in the alley and said I'll do anything for a bottle of wine or a drink of something and the man said okay and led him down to the wash that ran under 6th Avenue and into the corrugated steel tunnels that allowed water to pass beneath the bridge, and the man told Manny to get down on his knees, and he did, and in the darkness of the steel tunnel he felt the man rub his cock against his lips and Manny opened his mouth and let the man inside and the man grabbed Manny's head and pulled it toward him and Manny felt the fist in his chest begin to unclench the deeper the man plunged down his throat and he actually felt relief for the first time since the Loveboat all those years ago, or however long it had been, and his eyes suddenly shot open with a shocking revelation and it enraged and disgusted him so much that all along he had wanted this and he refused to believe it and while the man stood in front of him with his dick in Manny's mouth, Manny reached up and grabbed hold of the man's balls and crushed them between his fingers as hard as he could and the man immediately went limp in his mouth and dropped to his knees and Manny stood up and he brought his foot down on the back of the man's neck and pulled him up by the hair and scraped his face across the corrugated sides of the tunnels, grating his face off in chunks, over and over as the man screamed and kicked until he could scream no more but only gurgle and Manny finally stopped when the man was silent and looked through his pockets and found no money but did find a flask of whiskey and he drank the entire thing in two gulps and walked from beneath the bridge and into the wash and he followed it in a haze and Manny knew one thing, that he was sinking and breaking under an invisible ocean and he could not breathe and he walked through the wash as his breaths required more work and the pressure was so intense he fell to his knees and lay in the bottom of the wash paralyzed, not knowing where he was, if he was even in the same city or in the same state, and he could only inhale teaspoons of air at a time, mere teaspoons, and he closed his eyes as he felt rain begin to fall and the ground grumbled and in the distance Manny heard the sound of a flashflood breaking over the city . . .

EL CAMINO

THE SMOKE BILLOWING FROM BENEATH THE EL Camino's hood went unnoticed by the people driving past Food Giant. But even if they'd seen it, they wouldn't have stopped because the sight of a car overheating and catching fire on a summer afternoon was not uncommon. Everyone had seen plenty of burnt-out shells on the roadside, the metal carcasses deserted by their dismayed owners, or cops spraying a flaming car with a fire extinguisher. As common as cactus.

The driver pulling into the alley behind Torchy's to make his last delivery of the day wouldn't have stopped if someone paid him, because the flesh on his arms and face and chest was still scarred from two summers earlier when his car had overheated in a Circle K parking lot and he had lifted the hood and pulled off his shirt and wrapped it around his hand, then used it to grab the radiator cap and twist, thinking at the last second that maybe he should've let the car cool a bit, having forgotten his father's warning to always test the radiator hose first because he was rushing to get home to his new girlfriend, who liked to greet him at the door dressed in skimpy black lace lingerie and a set of handcuffs dangling from one wrist, which still pleased and baffled him—the way he'd scored this sweet güera—but remembering the danger of an overheating engine just as the threading on the radiator cap released from the lip of the opening and blew with such force that the bones in his right hand shattered when it hit the edge of the open hood, yet he didn't feel it and couldn't have screamed if he had because the white hot water that exploded from the radiator melted his skin on contact and temporarily blinded him, which was a good thing, he thought later, because he was glad he hadn't seen the looks people gave him when he had tried to scream but only stumbled backwards, skin sliding from his chest and arms, into the Big Block ice machine, which he collapsed next to on the sidewalk, convulsing and bleeding and gasping for breath. Three days later, when he awoke in the hospital, his first thought was to call his new girlfriend—just to tell her I'll be home soon and wait for me and then we can do that dom/sub thing you like so much, baby. But she never returned his calls. So even if he had seen the El Camino smoking in the Food Giant parking lot and the woman frantically ordering her kids out of the back, he wouldn't have stopped for every dirty dollar in Tucson.

Several of the Latin Kings were loitering in Torchy's parking lot, their systems blasting, admiring each other's lowriders, the murals painted on the hoods and the crushed-velvet interiors, waiting on the bitches to get out of school and come strut their shit like they did every day so the Kings could choose the lucky few who'd get to be their rucas for the night. No one heard the desperate cries of the helpless woman across the street. The music was too loud. And the new mural on Chuy's car was too impressive to look away from—a nude Aztec goddess with tears in her eyes and two dark-skinned men groveling at her feet.

But Peanut smelled smoke and looked over his shoulder in time to see a woman pulling her children from the bed of the El Camino, then jumping into the back and thrusting recently purchased bags of groceries into the arms of her three frightened children who ran, trembling, to the sidewalk where they watched as flames crept from beneath the hood of the car and their mother leapt from the back, her skirt billowing in the air. Peanut was happy he got a good look at the mommy's skyblue panties. He wished he had been closer when she had jumped because he could tell from across the street that she had a fineass body, even if her tits weren't *that* big, but her legs were nice and she had a real sweet curve to her ass and the panties were stuck in her crack just perfect when she jumped out of the back of the El Camino, her skirt pulled nice and high and hung there just long enough for Peanut to see her bottom half. The important half. He nudged Chuy and pointed toward the mommy. The moment Chuy turned to see what Peanut was pointing at, the front of the car erupted in flames and the woman jumped up and down screaming MY BABY'S IN THE FRONT MY BABY JESUS PLEASE FUCK-ING SHIT HELP MY GOD WHAT HELP I MY BABY PLEASE and Chuy shouted THE FUCK? and dropped his bottle of Mickey's and ran across the road, ignoring the cars speeding toward him, a taxi barely missing him as he reached the far side of the road with Peanut right behind him, Peanut having instinctively followed him, used to running from cops and niggers and bullets and not even thinking to stop running as he felt the bumper of a car graze his thigh, the pain failing to register because Chuy was just ahead so everything was fine. They always get away. Never get hurt.

Chuy reached the El Camino first and threw open the passenger door while the mommy screamed MY BABY'S IN THERE and held her children close. The door handle scalded Chuy's hand and he turned to Peanut, nursing his hand, and they looked at each other, silently debating whether or not they were actually going to help this lady's kid in the front seat. They had both seen enough cars overheat to know they only had a few more seconds before the whole thing blew up. Peanut told Chuy to wait, not feeling brave enough to go diving into the cab of a flaming car for a complete stranger, even if she is one fineass piece of work. But Chuy knew if he stopped to talk it over with Peanut it would be too late, so he dove into the front seat and winced as the leather interior boiled beneath his body. The buckles on the seat were too hot for him to bear, but he tried to undo the babyseat from the seatbelt anyway, using his thumb to stab frantically at the silver release button in the center of the melting seatbelt buckle and pulling on the opposite strap. It wouldn't give. Wouldn't unfuckingclasp. He tried again. Again. Three. Four. Five times. No luck. Then he tried to undo the latches on the babyseat, but, having never put a child into one of these damn things, he had no idea how to work the straps and get him out. He tried pulling on the baby but only managed to choke the kid on the chest straps and all he could think was I've got about two more seconds and then I'm gonna have to bail, sorry kid. He yanked on the babyseat, trying to rip it from the seatbelt, but it still would not budge. And that fuckin kid won't stop screaming. Chuy shoved his hand over the kid's mouth so he could think without all the racket and he kept pulling on the carseat and fumbling with the straps but no luck—how do people figure these things out?—the straps twisting every which way and only getting shorter and tighter and fuck it. It's just too late for you, kid. I'm sorry. He repositioned his hand so it covered the kid's mouth and nose to put it out of its misery and closed his eyes to wait for the car to explode and kill them both. At least you won't have to burn alive, little guy. I'll snuff you out and take the burn for you. How's that sound? Fair enough? He pressed harder, hoping to kill the baby before the car exploded—any second now—bracing his body, tensing every muscle for the pieces of metal that were going to come flying through the dashboard and puncture his body and maybe he'd get lucky and a cylinder would skewer his neck and take him out quickly. That was his only plan now. He knew that time was running out and the kid was still kicking, maybe I should punch the little guy in the chest. That'd crush his ribs and probably smash his heart, but that's better than cooking in here like a hotdog. He counted the seconds in his head, thinking bitterly of all the things he wanted to do that he'd never get to now. Now it's too late to go to NYC or Coney Island. Always wanted to see Vicente Fernandez in concert. Go to Vegas and bet on some roulette. Then he heard the first explosion and thought at least I died trying. He lifted his hand from the baby's face, his fingers stroking its soft cheeks. Then the baby slid away from him and Chuy lay down to die, at ease with his last act in life, happy he had tried to save the kid and at least spared him from burning death. He felt his body pulling away from the heat and was glad he couldn't feel the pain of burning alive—seemed the pain just shut off and here I thought this was one of the worst ways to die—but suddenly his forehead struck pavement and he was breathing water and choking and Peanut was yelling GET THE FUCK UP, MAN.

Chuy rose to his knees and looked around in confusion, wondering why he wasn't dead and the baby in its carseat was sitting safely on the sidewalk where the mommy was unfastening the straps, trying to remove her child and hug it and kiss it at the same time. And what the hell is Peanut doing with his 9mm out? Dumbass trying to get arrested? Then it all came together and Chuy knew the explosion had been

Peanut blowing the shit out of the seatbelt latch and that he'd saved both the baby and him, the crazy bastard, and the car hadn't yet blown up. Shit. It's going to right—

Peanut knew what Chuy was thinking, and he turned and knocked the mommy down on the sidewalk and threw his body on top of her baby. Chuy got to his feet just as the engine fire hit the gas line, erupting into a massive whoosh of flame, and tackled the three children who stood staring and screaming but fell silent as the heat of the flames overwhelmed them. And then the heat was gone.

Chuy and Peanut and the mommy and her kids and the people who had come out of Food Giant to see what was going on looked up to see the El Camino that had finished exploding and now sat billowing huge plastic-smelling clouds of black smoke and gushing flames. The worst of it was over. They all got to their feet and checked themselves for injuries. The only one hurt was Chuy, whose clothes had all but burned away and whose skin was red and black on his arms and face and parts of his back.

Everyone started clapping and whooping and smiling at the heroics of the two young men, and the mommy came over to Chuy and hugged him and kissed him and wept on his shoulder. The pain of his burns was too much for Chuy to bear so he pushed the mommy away, raising his arms so she could see he was hurt, and she turned to Peanut and started muttering thankyous and godblessyous and kissing his cheeks and mussing up his hair. Peanut let the woman hug him, feeling her tits heaving with relief against the front of his body. He wrapped his arms tightly around the mommy and then let his right hand drift down her back—either she doesn't notice or she likes it—feeling the bucking curve of her back as she sobbed in his arms. The rumply elastic border of her panties pushed at the fabric of her thin sundress. Peanut traced her pantyline gently, his eyes closed while he enjoyed the firmness of the mommy's ass and the way her body was so warm next to his. He wanted so badly to whisper into her ear for her to follow him back to his place so he could lay her down on his parents' bed while they were at work and let her show him her gratitude. He'd put on one of his dad's romantic Spanish records and feel her soft legs while lifting her sundress slowly and kissing her flesh as it revealed itself with each inch the sundress crept higher and higher until it was finally over her head and lying on the floor. Then he'd lick her legs and make his way up to her sky-blue panties and slip his tongue beneath the rim until he tasted her soft, smooth, wet lips, and she'd moan and scream out his name, and he'd climb on top of her while she continued to moan and writhe beneath him and scream and wail and WAIL and the wailing turned into the wailing of a firetruck, its horns and sirens growing louder as it neared, and Peanut opened his eyes, his hand still cupped on the mommy's glorious ass cheek, her children looking up at him, the two girls confused and the little boy with his fists balled at his sides. Peanut released the mommy, who continued to thank him and Chuy, and then turned back toward Torchy's, walking a jackleg walk with his hand in his pocket pressing his boner to his thigh so it would hopefully die down before he reached the other side of the street where the Kings stood drinking their beers and placing bets on who got fucked up worse by the El Camino.

REVIVAL

THE PREACHER IN THE WHEELCHAIR SHOUTED Jesus is here right now in this very place. Wherever two or three are gathered. Lift up your voices to God. Speak in tongues. Praise his name. Shandalaba-bababacondolo. Shandalababababacondolo. He waved his hands wildly above his head. The scene made David remember going to Sunday school with a friend back when he was a kid. Made him remember the teacher telling the story in the Bible where these people were sitting inside a church speaking in tongues and the Holyghost descended and flames were seen burning on top of the roof, but the building didn't catch fire. Just like the bush that was on fire and spoke to Moses but didn't burn either. He looked at the top of the Reid Park bandshell, half expecting to see pillars of flame dancing atop the roof, the Holyghost making itself known. No flames. But the roar of the crowd worshipping their Lord and King ricocheted off the back of the bandshell and echoed off the hill where the Jesus people sat. David laughed. Of course there were no goddam flames. The only flames were the faggot teenaged boys sneaking to the bathroom to suck each other off while their parents got their hearts right with God.

Roughly every two months the Door Christian Fellowship Church held revivals in the park, hoping to reach out to the impoverished and godless Latino communities that continued to grow in central and south Tucson. Before David's father died, he would complain every time the Door came around, always returning from the hot sunny afternoons at the orchard where he picked fruit all day and screaming about how those pinche Christians were back in the park again. They spit in the face of the Catholic Church and expect us to turn our backs on our culture. They say we worship false idols.

Because their father always got so worked up about the revivals in the park, each time the churchies came around, the Nuñez boys couldn't resist sneaking out of the house and walking to the park where they found a picnic table to sit on, passing joints back and forth and listening to the gringo in the wheelchair telling them how God loves Mexicans just like the rest of his people, he sees your pain and suffering here on earth and sent his son as a lamb to the slaughter to sacrifice himself so that you might be saved. Just like you come here to America to make a better life for your family back home. You toil in the fields. You are persecuted like the Christians were in the years following the death of our Lord. Look how much you have in common with us. Look to the Word. Look to the Lord and he will set you free—the words being translated into Spanish by a diminutive Mexican who kept wiping his forehead with a handkerchief and spraying spittle as he paced on the stage, gesturing wildly with his other hand, the veins in his forehead bulging from his attempts to keep up with the words of the preacher, who barely stopped to take a breath and allow the message to be translated so that the people who were slowly coming to see what all the ruckus in the park was about could understand what the hell the strange man in the wheelchair was saying.

The second time David and his brothers had sneaked out to the revival, they'd noticed the boys walking off to the restroom, and David said I've got to drain my gusano—hahaha—and walked to the dark restroom that smelled of stale beer and urine and the many years of beer shits and picnic shits and baby shits, whose stench was never fully allowed to dissipate but instead rotted in the restroom on hot summer afternoons and seeped into the walls. Inside the restroom he expected to hear the laughter of teenaged boys talking about the girls they'd like to screw and making farting sounds or probably pretending to piss in the urinals but really spraying their piss all over the floors and the rolls of toilet paper. He expected to see them writing FUCK YOU on the wall with a Magic Marker or crudely drawing naked women with little dot nipples or sketching gigantic cocks with absurd drops of spurting semen. Instead, he opened the door and saw only one boy standing by the urinals and thought maybe the others had snuck past the bathroom to have a cigarette in the bushes. Then he heard a muffled slurping and sneakers shuffling and saw a foot jutting from beneath one of the stalls and it took him only a moment to realize these little Jesus maricóns are sucking each other off while their parents are out there jumping up and down and beseeching Christ to prepare a place in heaven for them and for their little faggot sons kneeling on the filthy floors of the park shitters blowing their buddies, probably cupping their tiny ballsacks while they try to make sure they're sucking right—less teeth, goddammit, just pull your lips over them.

David slowly backed out of the bathroom, unnoticed by the kid at the urinal, and ran back to the picnic table where his three brothers sat, pointing and laughing at the Jesus freaks speaking in tongues—condolosai, shondolocobolosai—and raising their hands to the darkening sky. He explained what he had just seen in the bathroom, his brothers listening with disbelief. You mean those gringo dudes are all fags? Yeah, right over there, while their parents are praying, they're blowing each other and loving it. Let's go. And the Nuñez brothers walked quickly, trying not to draw attention to themselves, each one hoping the kids in the bathroom were still going at it so they could see for themselves, because they just couldn't believe they would really be doing it, here, in the middle of the park where anyone could bust them. Rogelio wondered what he was going to do—probably kick their fairy asses. He thought he wouldn't be able to stop laughing when they kicked in the stall door and found some kid sucking his friend's dick. Hey, guys, what if he's sucking more than one? Yeah, Chuy said, maybe he's double fisting and has a coupla peckers sitting on his forehead too. His brothers laughed. That'd be great. When they reached the bathroom, Rogelio raised his finger to his lips and slowly pushed the door open and held it while his brothers entered, and David tiptoed to one of the stalls and kicked the door in and it slammed into the back of the faggot on his knees with a cock buried in his throat, and Chuy and Rogelio dragged the kid out of the stall and held him while Felipe and David kicked him in the ribs and the nuts and Chuy clutched the kid's throat and said you like suckin dick, huh? you wanna take care of the four of us? and the Nuñez brothers laughed and whipped out their dicks, and Chuy said fuck it, piss on the fuckin queer, and his friends sneaked out of the bathroom and ran up the hill to their parents while the urine of the Nuñez brothers drenched the clothes and splashed the face and hair and sprayed into the mouth of the screaming kid pinned against the wall of the bathroom. When they had all run out of piss and shook the final drops onto the kid's forehead, Rogelio spat on him and said that's what we do to queers around here. You come around here again suckin dick, you better be prepared for a lot worse. Fuckin faggot. Pinche maricón.

And every few months after that, when the Door brought their revival around and their father came home screaming about the churchies and their bastard religion, the Nuñez brothers knew the time had come to go make fun of the Jesus freaks and kick some faggot ass.

But today David sat alone. He hadn't been to a revival in years. The last few times he and his brothers had gone, they had spread out through the crowd and pretended to place money into the KFC buckets the church sent around for collection and instead grabbed a fistful of cash, ignoring the glares of the freaks and walking to Torchy's to buy some forties and smokes. And after all these years, they were still using KFC buckets for collection. David saw the men walking with them, holding them in front of people who grudgingly pulled a crumpled dollar or two from their wallets, the rest of their money purposely left at home, just in case they felt the urge to pull out their pockets to prove they had no more money, or in case one of the fuckin wetbacks came along and tried to stick em up.

This time David didn't go to the bathroom to beat up the fairies. In fact, he hadn't laid a hand on anyone since that day behind Torchy's when he and his brothers and the rest of the Kings had beaten his baby brother Felipe to death. Instead he had quietly begun to distance himself from the Kings, disgusted with the rage that had overcome him and made him punch and kick so blindly he didn't know whom or what he'd been beating.

The wheelchair preacher rolled back and forth, telling the crowd of people that Jesus is here in this place right now and he wants to make his presence known. The KFC buckets were still going from hand to hand. God shall supply all your needs. Give to the Lord and the Lord will provide for you and your family. Remember the loaves of bread and the fish. Our God is an awesome God. Let's not forget the faith of the woman who used her very last cup of wheat during the time of famine to prepare a meal for the prophet Elijah. Her VERY LAST CUP. People dropping in singles and maybe some change. And how did our Lord reward her faith? That's right. He blessed her with an unending supply of wheat that lasted her and her son for the rest of the famine. That's the Lord we serve. What a mighty God we serve. The crowd clapped and sang as the buckets made their way toward the back, and the preacher said there's someone here right now who has just found out they have cancer. Someone who thinks it's all over. And I know you're tempted to hang it all up. Satan is whispering in your ear, saying see how your Jesus has forsaken you. Don't believe Lucifer, for he is the father of lies. The Mexican man paced the stage, wiping his forehead, loosely translating. A murmur went through the crowd and grew louder as the preacher described the person suffering—the spirit is telling me that you are here now, that you have given up on our everloving Savior, you have a wife, three kids, maybe four, and the Lord is pulling at your heart-strings right now. YOU FEEL IT. YOU KNOW WHO YOU ARE. The preacher paused. Everyone, including Davíd, looked to see if the man the preacher described was actually present when suddenly a woman yelled THANK YOU, JESUS and a man rose to his feet weeping, holding the hand of a little girl who looked up at her daddy, wondering why he was crying like that in front of all these people, having never seen her father cry, and he kissed his daughter and sat her on her mother's lap and contin-ued weeping as he stumbled over people sitting on the grass while try-ing to make his way toward the stage. People whispered to each other. Davíd smirked but couldn't help wondering whether or not he would witness a miracle tonight, here, in Reid Park, the place where so many sins had been committed that even if Jesus were real, it would be the last place he would make his presence known.

The man finally reached the stage and the crowd of people grew silent, shushing their children and looking expectantly toward the bandshell where the man stood with his back to them, his head bowed, his shoulders heaving with grief. Thank you, Jesus. Thank you, Jesus. Shandolokai. Shandolobobobosan. The preacher wheeled over to him and motioned for his translator to follow. Tonight the Lord will make Himself known. He will give a sign to all of you who disbelieve. He WILL heal this man and all of you who question the existence of God will know that He is real and that God loves His children.

The KFC buckets had reached the back of the crowd, and the ushers collected them and walked behind the bandshell. The preacher stopped speaking and rolled to the side of the stage, where someone handed him a package. He placed it on his lap and rolled back to where the broken man stood. As it says in the Word of the Lord, we will anoint this brother with oil and the laying on of hands, thank you, Jesus. We give thanks. He pulled a bottle of olive oil from the package on his lap and uncapped it, soaking the tip of his finger, and then beckoned for the afflicted man to bend toward him. The man bent over slowly. The preacher smeared the sign of the cross on the man's forehead and asked everyone to bow their heads and close their eyes. Reach your hands out toward our brother. Believe. Pray to Jesus—shandolobocosolo—for Him to cast the scourge from this man's body. Give him life, Lord. Cleanse his body and soul of evil. The crowd raised their hands toward the man and began to pray, and the preacher stretched out his hand and placed it on the man's chest and loudly cursed the devil. BE GONE, SATAN. FLEE THE BODY OF THIS MAN. HE BELONGS TO JESUS. HE IS A CHILD OF GOD. HE IS A VESSEL OF THE HOLYGHOST, AND YOU ARE AN INTRUDER IN THE SACRED TEMPLE OF THE LORD. SHANDOLOBOCOLOCOBOSAI. SHANDAL-ABABA—BE HEALED. He slammed his hand into the man's chest. BE HEALED. BE HEALED. Three ushers rushed onto the stage and stood behind the afflicted man, placing their hands on his back and praying in tongues. The preacher's forehead was peppered with sweat and the armpits of his silk shirt grew dark with perspiration. He rolled his chair back a foot or two and then rolled toward the man and slammed the palm of his hand into his chest—BE HEALED. OUT, FOUL DEMON. THY

NAME IS CANCER. THY NAME IS LEGION, AND THE LORD, WITH THE COVENANT OF HIS SON'S SACRIFICE, HAS ALREADY PAID THE RANSOM ON THIS MAN'S SOUL. OUT OUT OUT OUT OUT. BEGONE—the man began to shake, his hands flailing in the air above him—YOU HAVE NO PLACE HERE. YOU WERE CAST FROM HEAVEN IN THE GREAT BATTLE FOR THE THRONE, AND YOU ARE BEATEN. BE HEALED. BE HEALED. BE HEALED. SHANDABACONDOLOSAI. He rolled toward the man again and smashed his hand into his chest and the man fell backwards as if he had been crushed by a great wave, and the three ushers caught him from behind and gently lowered his convulsing body to the stage, and the crowd gasped and prayed, and the preacher rolled back and forth slowly, back and forth, thank you, Jesus, thank you, Jesus, thank you, Jesus, and the translator mumbled into the mic, while a woman came from the right of the bandshell carrying a floral sheet to cover the twitching and bucking man.

David let out a deep breath he had been holding throughout the healing ceremony. His heart beat heavily within his chest and he wondered if he had just witnessed a miracle. Un milagro. He'd heard of such things, but had always laughed them off. Yeah, like God's gonna heal some dude with a bum leg when the pope's barely able to sit up in his popemobile. Give me a fuckin break.

But now he wasn't sure. What he had seen had been so convincing. It was almost as if he had felt the spirit of the Lord come sweeping through the crowd and burrow into the man, flushing out the cancer, cleansing his body of all physical and spiritual impurities. While the congregation had been praying and reaching toward the stage, the hair on the back of his neck had risen for no reason. A shiver ran through his body, and he caught himself lifting his hands toward the man too. He wasn't sure why he had done it. Several women wept and people muttered in tongues, thanking God for showing Himself here tonight. Onstage someone started playing a keyboard and the volume slowly rose above the prayers of the preacher and the crowd of people giving thanks on the grassy hill in front of the bandshell. The keyboard player softly and respectfully pressed the keys, eking out sparse notes, then grew more bold and began playing a song that the people soon recognized, and the preacher began to sing Jesus, name above all names, beautiful Savior, glorious Lord—the crowd joined in—Emmanuel, God is with us, Christ our Redeemer, glorious Lord. Over and over. People who didn't know the words began to sing, caught up in the moment. Having just witnessed a miracle.

They sang song after song, each person praying in his or her own way, thanking God for salvation and watching the man who was now lying still beneath the sheet. After fifteen minutes the three ushers returned to the stage and lifted the man by his hands and feet and carried him from the stage. The preacher explained to the audience how they had just witnessed the blessing of the Lord, and now it's time to take up another collection, which makes these revivals possible and covers the expenses the city charges to rent out this bandshell—it's not free—and provides us with electricity and security. And we're expanding. We have outgrown—glory to God—our facility in the Southgate Shopping Center and we're building a new church on Irvington Road. But these things cost money. Find it in your heart to help the church and God will reward you. God is great. He is almighty and everlasting and He will not let his people suffer.

The KFC buckets reappeared. Parents dug deeper into their pockets. Children pulled change from their shoes that they'd been saving for after church to buy some saladitos or a Slurpee at 7-Eleven. David felt around in his pockets and found a five-dollar bill. He waited for a bucket to come to him, and when it did, he placed his bill inside. The buckets passed from person to person. The translator wiped his forehead and gulped from a glass of water. The preacher rocked back and forth in his wheelchair, lightly beating his hand on the chair's armrest to the rhythm of the music. He led the people in another song—our God is an awesome God—and then let the energy of the group dwindle, instructing the congregation to shake hands and welcome each other into the presence of the Lord. The people turned to one another, shaking hands and smiling, patting children on the head, each feeling a part of some greater work. The older believers wiped tears from their cheeks, pleased they had witnessed a miracle and convinced that the fruits of their labor were coming to pass before their eyes.

The preacher said tonight we're going to stray from the regular service. As you all know, this neighborhood has become afflicted with violence and hatred. Senseless drug addiction and lust and all things foul and detestable in the eyes of God. And lest the Lord decide to punish the people of Tucson by drowning them in flames like the sinners of Sodom and Gomorrah or those who turned their back on the Lord prior to the great flood, we should all take heed of the Word and repent. You, people of Tucson, lovers of sin and evil, must open your hearts to the message of the Lord. Davíd knew it was time to leave. He had had his moment and now this fucker was getting annoying. He stood, barely listening as the preacher explained they were going to show a movie geared toward the people of this community—it's called *The Cross and the Switchblade*—a movie about gangsters and how they found redemption despite being steeped in evil. Open your hearts and your minds to the word of the Lord. The lights on the bandshell dimmed. A projector placed high atop the hill started up and terrible seventies music blasted from speakers throughout the crowd. Everyone jumped with fright. Davíd turned to see what the hell was going on. After a few moments the sound was adjusted and the people settled back onto their blankets and chairs and discreetly opened cans of Coke and candy bars. Davíd was about to leave when he saw Eric Estrada dressed like a punkass Puerto Rican gangster somewhere in the Bronx or Brooklyn and decided he would stick around for the laughs. Eric Estrada. They couldn't be serious. In a Christian film? Didn't he play that sleazy Mexican motorcycle cop in *CHiPs*? The one whose dick was always getting him in trouble with the ladies? Maybe there'll be some tits or something. He sat back down on the grass and cringed at the horrible music, removing the flask from his back pocket.

The movie made him laugh more than anything. I mean seriously, what kind of gangs name themselves the Warlords and the Bishops? How scary was that supposed to be? They even met before they had battles to discuss the terms—chains, blades, and baseball bats. Oh yeah—and zips. Zip guns. How pafuckingthetic. Like they were going to play a game of soccer or have a bake sale. But there were some good asskicking scenes. There were also some slow parts because this white dude decided he was gonna save the gang members. Got them all to go to his church and be Christians. It was all such bullshit. David thought about running up to the stage and tearing the movie screen down and telling the people you have no fuckin idea what being in a gang is like. We don't sit around talking about fighting and getting together to plan wars. Man, the second some other cat from a gang tried to bring his ass anywhere near us, he'd have a fuckin knife in his throat. Look around, you sorry buncha fuckin churchy gringo muthafuckas. Right here, right where your kids are playing and sleeping and you're giving your money to Jesus, I have personally killed people. Yeah. And it wasn't no chains-blades-bats kinda shit. It was blades and guns. Real guns. Glocks. AK-47s. TEC-9s. You can spray em with bullets before they even get out of their cars. David wanted to jump up and put this movie to shame. And these Jesus freaks were looking at it and probably thinking how horrible, this street life. They'd go home afterwards and tuck their kids in bed and say their prayers and go to work in the morning and have a nice lunch at some restaurant and leave a good tip. He'd go home and fall asleep wondering who'd be dead when he woke up in the morning.

He thought about all the battles he'd been in. The last one before he began to pull away from the Kings had been right here in the park. Some of them had been sitting on the bandshell stage, smoking joints laced with angel dust, and a couple of them taking their rucas to the back of the stage where they could feel up on their titties and rub their pussies through their jeans until the weed kicked in and the girls didn't put up as much of a fight and pretty soon they were fingering their girls and pulling their pants down and eventually the sound of women moaning could be heard echoing through the bandshell and up the hill where Peanut came running down, shouting MAN, THEM NIGGER CRIPS ARE HERE, CMON WE HAVE TO WASTE THOSE FUCKIN MAYATES, and the Kings barely had time to tuck their pricks back in their pants and reach for their guns before they heard the bass booming and knew the cars were just on the other side of the row of bushes that ran between the road and the parking lot behind the bandshell. Then they heard the first shots. The girls crouching in the back of the bandshell, struggling to pull up their pants and button up their shirts, started screaming, and

David looked over and saw Cheeseburger take a shot to the chest and it exploded, splattering blood and shards of his ribcage, and pieces of his organs went flying and some of the guys standing by him wiped Cheeseburger's blood from their faces and stopped to watch as he slowly dropped his gun and fell to the ground. Then more shots. Then Peanut yelled THEY'RE GONNA KILL US ALL IF YOU DON'T SHOOT BACK, VATOS. SNAP THE FUCK OUT OF IT. They left Cheeseburger's body lying on the bandshell stage and scrambled down the front, crouching and running toward the bushes and firing in the direction of the bass, hearing the thunk thunk of bullets piercing metal and the cries of one or two guys who got hit. Tires squealed. The girls kept screaming. David broke through the bushes and ran toward the last car that was pulling away, emptying the clip of his 9mm into the back of the car. The car swerved wildly and crashed into a tree and more of the Kings caught up with David and shot their bullets into the car, screaming incoherently and firing firing firing, thunk thunk thunk. The rest of the Crips' cars had gotten away. They found the bodies of a few who had been hit by their bullets and thrown from their cars. David walked up to one of them and kicked him in the ribs, and the man groaned and blood seeped from his mouth and a hole in his shoulder. THIS ONE'S ALIVE. David stomped the man's head. Jumped up and down, landing on it with both feet over and over again until there was only a pile of blood and chunks of bone that felt like a squishy rotten apple. He heard more gunshots and looked behind him and saw eight Kings unloading their guns into the bodies of the other two niggers who'd been thrown from their cars.

Peanut finished last, and when he did they all heard the sounds of sirens in the distance and knew they had to run. RUN. THE POLI. They ran back the way they came, past the bandshell and Cheeseburger's destroyed body and over the hill toward 22nd Street, splitting up, knowing if they could just make it to the street then they had a million places they could hide and nobody, not even that pig Loudermilk, could find them.

On screen the niggers were running after the Puerto Ricans, hopping over fences and chasing them through the Bronx. Music played in the background. Maybe George Clinton. Eric Estrada ran the fastest and got away, but one or two of his boys were caught and beaten with chains and pieces of wood. The movie didn't show much. Bad special-effects blood that looked like watery Jell-O, not like the stuff that had come flying out of Cheeseburger's chest. That had looked like molé and was thick like syrup and never would have washed out of the shirt David ended up burning in the alley behind his house right after he stashed his gun inside the swamp cooler. He wanted to tell them the stuff in the movie isn't the way it looks in real life. He wanted to show them the scar on his back that he'd gotten when a Crip saw him riding the Sun-Tran bus one afternoon and walked up behind him and stuck a blade in his back. Before David realized he'd been stabbed, the nigger was already off the bus and running down an alley, down into a wash and out of sight. Fuck. That's all David had said. Fuck. He rang for the next stop, pulled the blade from between his shoulder and spine, stepped down from the bus, and passed out the moment his foot touched the ground. He woke up in a hospital the next day, his brothers sitting around him. His mother never came. They never told her. Her heart had long before collapsed over the loss of her husband and youngest son.

The movie kept going. Kept trying to tell the story of the street and failing miserably. Still, David kept watching, like there was something here he needed to see. Sitting on the grass, sipping his flask, he thought about all the people he'd killed or seen killed. Goddam lucky to not have been killed four or five times now. Maybe his was a life of miracles.

He watched the fags come sneaking back from the bathroom and ignored the urge to beat their asses. He didn't want that now. He was tired. He had the teardrop tattoos to prove he'd killed. Some were niggers. Some were wetbacks like him. Even his own brother. He remembered smashing his fist into his baby brother's face—the face their mother, every time Felipe walked through the door, said looked just like their father when he was that age, ay, que chulo—and he just kept going. When they had finally stopped beating Felipe and spat on his body and cursed his soul, they walked away and left him for the fuckin buzzards. Let the bitches stay there and cry over him. He's a bitch anyway. Not a fuckin Nuñez. But after many nightmares, David had finally gone back to Torchy's in the middle of the night, while his boys were passed out from drinking or dropping acid all day, and he'd sat next to the stain in the parking lot where his brother lost his life, and he wept uncontrollably. He lay on the ground where his brother had breathed his last breath and said I'm sorry. I'm sorry. I'm sorry. It wears me out, this guilt. It wears me out. And he felt the ground beneath him give and his body sank slightly and all of a sudden he was Felipe, watching as his oldest brother, Chuy, threw the first punch and feeling the unbearable pain from each punch and kick, and Davíd realized the last moments of Felipe's life had been utter terror and indescribable pain, yet there was the slightest bit of joy as Felipe's courage rose within his own chest and he realized that the youngest Nuñez was the biggest man in the family, the way he had faced his death knowing it was going to happen, and he wept more because it wouldn't stop, the hitting and kicking and swearing and stomping WOULD NOT STOP, and the faces were all a blur, all except for Davíd's, whose eyes possessed a rage and a hatred that nothing could quench. Nothing. And then it was over and Davíd lay on the stain of his brother's blood, gasping, his body sore from Felipe's death.

Sitting on the grass in Reid Park, the near-empty flask in his hand, Davíd decided he was ready. Something had to change tonight. He was ready when a strange man with long blond hair walked up to him and asked him if he had ever been saved.

Saved? What the fuck does that mean?

Have you accepted Jesus into your life and begged forgiveness for your transgressions?

Transgressions?

Like sins, wrongdoings. Things you know are bad but refuse to give up because the Devil has convinced you that you're right.

Davíd thought hard about the man's question. Was there really something out there that could save him? How could it be real when he knew those fags who sneaked into the restroom during the service were supposed to be Christians too? They sang and prayed right along with the rest of them. Davíd felt the man place a hand on his back and almost punched the fucker in the face, no man ever touches me like that. The guy was looking Davíd straight in the eyes and saying I can tell, brother, that you hurt inside. Christ can relieve that pain. He will ease the burden you feel each day. He will make it all okay. You have a place in heaven.

A place in heaven. Davíd thought about heaven. Would his father and brother be there? Or would they be in hell because they hadn't been Christians? Would there be naked chicks and more food than he could ever hope to eat? What the hell was there to do in heaven for the rest of eternity? he asked the man. Well, the Word of God says that in heaven there are many mansions. And we will worship God for all eternity. There will be no more sickness. No sadness. No death. All the aches of this world will be absent, and we will truly be able to enjoy the presence of the Lord.

How much fun could that be? Worshipping the Lord for all eternity? It didn't sound that appealing to Davíd. But the idea of no more pain sounded nice. No more fear and poverty and always having to look over my back to see if someone's going to shove a knife in it or blast me upside the head with a brick. That wouldn't be so bad. He was tired of living in fear. Tired of always having to be a fuckin macho who couldn't love or cry or do anything because he'd just be a bitch if he left the gang and tried to go to school or anything else that all the people in his neighborhood felt meant you were trying to be a gringo. Trying to be a gringo was one of the worst crimes you could possibly commit in his neighborhood. Be a busboy your whole life. Fix cars or pick fruit or be a drunk, but NEVER be a gringo.

So what do I have to do? The man said, come down to the altar with me and give your heart to Jesus. Ask Him to come into your body and cleanse your soul. Ask Him to save you and you will be born again. You will be given a fresh start on life. You will no longer be guilty of all the sins you've committed in your life. You will be free. You will be baptized with the Holy Spirit. The man gestured toward the bandshell. Will you come? Will you accept Jesus as your Lord and Savior?

Davíd said yes.

He couldn't believe he was doing it, but he figured why the hell not. Why not just try it and see? The worst thing that could happen is the churchies could all be full of shit and I'll be in the same place I'm in already, so fuck it. His brothers weren't there to make fun of him. The Kings weren't around because there were too many cops in the park when the Jesus freaks came around. Got to protect the gringos from the crazy beaners. In fact, Loudermilk was fewer than fifty yards away, standing over by the parking lot, leaning on his car and smirking at the churchies. Davíd said yes and the man took him by the hand, Davíd using all his willpower to keep from punking the sonofabitch in the mouth, and they walked through the crowd toward the bandshell, where the preacher was beckoning for sinners to come forward and give their lives to Christ.

David almost bailed out several times on the walk to the stage. He felt as if everyone was watching him, this hardcore vato, and wondering what the hell he was doing. I mean, I'm wearing a bandana and my zoot suit pants and an undershirt and it's obvious to these people that I'm in a gang. He looked over at Loudermilk, but the cop was looking at his fingernails and didn't notice Davíd coming forward to be born again. He was glad about that.

They reached the front of the stage, where several people were kneeling in prayer, and the man gestured for Davíd to kneel down. Davíd knelt. The man draped his arm around his shoulder and said you are about to make the best decision of your life. You will be a new man. Davíd nodded and felt a strange buzzing in his chest. Davíd, the man said, repeat after me. Okay. Lord Jesus. I know I'm a sinner. I know that you came to Earth two thousand years ago as a sacrifice for my sins. I ask you to accept my prayer. I beg you to come into my heart. Come in and wash away my sins. Jesus, I understand that you paid a debt you did not owe. That you gave your life for me so that I might be forgiven and have eternal life. I want to serve you. I want to be free. Please, Lord, take this burden from my shoulders. Accept me into your kingdom. Lead me into the Promised Land. Davíd said all these words and began to cry as he felt a great burden lift from his shoulders, the weight of his sins, the many people he'd hurt, the pain he'd brought upon his own house, and he wanted to call every girl he'd ever screwed and tell her I'm sorry, I know you're a human and more than a piece of ass and if you'll forgive me I'd like to make it up to you because I couldn't help having sex with you and never talking to you again unless you'd come hang out with the Kings so we could all have you anytime we wanted— don't you see? this is the way things have been around here for so long that it's completely out of my hands, and if it wasn't me fucking you and sending you home after maybe giving you a joint or something in return, then it would've been someone else, maybe someone who didn't believe in using condoms, someone who would've gotten you pregnant and wouldn't have had the money to pay for an abortion so he'd have to call up Smiley and have him do his operation, and then things would've been so much worse because you would have to choose between having your first kid at fifteen or risking Smiley's operation and maybe dying all because you fucked a King. Davíd wanted to call all the women he'd laid in life, the ones he'd bragged about to his brothers and the other vatos, and tell them sorry, sorry, sorry. But he could only remember a few of their names. He could barely recollect their individual features, since most of the time he bagged them in the dim bedrooms of various Kings, the girl usually so high she could hardly move when he climbed on her and pulled up her skirt or wrestled the skintight jeans down her legs.

Davíd began to sob and the man next to him patted him on the back and said it's okay brother—glory be to God—that's right, let it out. Davíd bowed his head and closed his eyes and was assaulted with images of all his wrongdoings. The robberies. The rapes. The beatings. Killing his very own brother. Oh God, please forgive me—and the grief he alone had caused his mother made him feel that he deserved nothing short of hell. He wept more. He wanted to find the families of the other boys he had killed or injured. To walk up to their front doors and knock and tear the shirt from his back and say here I am, the person who stole your child from you before he even had a chance to live, and maybe the father of his victim would kick him and beat his head against the porch floor and the brothers and sisters would come rushing from their rooms and join in, taking out all their anguish on the person who stole their brother from them, and the mom would come and beat him over the head with flour-covered hands until she tired and then she would run to her room and throw herself on her bed thanking God for the opportunity to avenge the loss of her baby, who had been so young and had so much to live for, so many years ahead of him to find a nice girl and a job and have some kids, happy deep down inside for finally being able to exorcise the anger and sadness that the punk lying beaten on the porch had brought on her household.

David wished he could replace everything he'd ever stolen, take back every punch he'd ever thrown and every curse he'd ever uttered. He knelt at the altar, before hundreds of people, and shed tears. The man next to him gave thanks to God for bringing another sheep into the fold, rubbed David's back and offered him his understanding. I used to be a gangbanger too. But I've been saved, just like you. And the Lord has forgiven us both. Yes. Yes, Lord. Sensing the intensity of David's remorse, the man decided to leave him alone to allow the Lord to purify the new convert's heart. He walked away, praising the Holiest of Holies, and David knelt back down to grieve more, to unburden all of his sins at the altar so he could leave the park with a fresh start on life. A new man. He bent forward and placed his head on the cement sidewalk that skirted the stage. The cement was slightly eroded and the uneven surface of pebbles poked into the soft flesh of his forehead. It hurt him a bit. But he pressed his forehead harder into the cement and as the pain became greater he cried even more, not for his suffering, but for that which he had brought on so many other people. The ache increased as he cried and pressed his head harder to the ground, moving it back and forth and wincing each time the rough surface broke through the skin. It hurt, but it was nothing compared to the families who'd lost their sons at his hands. He knew his pain didn't compare to the heartbreak he'd caused countless women who had lain beneath him, drugged eyes glazed and gazing at nothing while he thrust himself inside and ignored their whimpering and the click-whir of Peanut's Polaroid documenting another bitch to add to the Latin Kings' hall of fame.

David stopped grinding his head into the cement. He knelt quietly with his face to the ground, his blood trickling onto the sidewalk, and opened his arms to hug the earth. When he finally lifted his head, the lights on the bandshell were already raised and many of the believers had begun to pack their belongings and round up their children. He removed his bandana and wiped the dirt and drying blood from his forehead. The blond man who had witnessed to him returned, smiling, and welcomed

Davíd as a new believer into the flock, telling him where the church was located and when they held services. Davíd promised to attend.

He walked over to a trashbarrel a few feet from the bandshell and, making sure Loudermilk was watching, he wadded up his bandana and lit it with his lighter, holding it between his fingers until it burned too close to bear, and then he blew the flame off the scrap of cloth that remained and dropped it into the trash. He looked at Loudermilk, who was confused by Davíd's actions, and then he smiled at the cop, who instinctively went for his gun then stopped, hovered over the leather holster, ready to grab his weapon and fire it at Davíd if he made any sudden movements. But Davíd only smiled and shook his head, understanding that Loudermilk was simply playing his role in the game, the role of the man who had been commissioned by the city to protect its upright citizens. He smiled because he knew that Loudermilk didn't know he was out of the game. He had given up and he felt such relief he wanted to go home and hug his mother and tell her the exciting news of how he'd given his life to Christ—she'd be so proud. He wanted to sit on her lap while she rocked him in her rocking chair as she had done when he was young, rubbing his head and pressing it into the warm comfort of her chest while he would knead the rolls of fat on the sides of her torso. He wanted to run home and explain how he'd been thinking about maybe buying some paint and repainting the outside of the house for her. He knew it would please her to watch her son working on the house the way his father used to do after work or on weekends. Yes, that's what I'll do. Right after I find that preacher and thank him for bringing God's message to the park for all these years.

Searching the stage for the preacher amid the crowd of stagehands rolling up extension cords and packing equipment, Davíd finally spotted him in the corner. A young couple stood next to him, shook his hand, and walked away with their arms around each other and smiles on their faces. Davíd hopped up onto the stage and walked toward the preacher, extending his hand and telling him his name and being told mine's Pastor Warren, the pastor speaking much softer and more pensively than earlier, which surprised Davíd, who told Pastor Warren how he had just wanted to shake the hand of the man who's crazy enough to come here, to this fucked-up—sorry, messed-up—neighborhood, because it was just what I needed to hear and you never gave up, man, thanks for never giving up, squeezing the pastor's hand a little too vigorously, but the pastor allowing him to shake his hand, knowing how to play this game and realizing sometimes it means putting up with some poor gushing bastard who'd hit bottom because they might not be good for much money but it all adds up, and the pastor wanted the blathering idiot to just leave him alone so he could take the night's money, break off a piece for Carl, who'd agreed to do the cancer-daddy bit for a cut of the offering money, and after this pepperbelly finished gushing he could meet Carl for a drink on Miracle Mile and give him his cut and they'd toss back a few beers and talk about the fine women who had been at the park—they just keep getting better and better— and they might even plot out the next place they should take the revival, maybe Agua Prieta, or that Ciudad Juarez place where all those chicks are being killed, they'll eat the shit up cause they're probably scared to death, all of em, and on and on until Carl'd had his fill and headed home to his wife, shit, I'll have to remember to tell Carl, that hilarious sonofabitch, how he was killing me tonight with that whole convulsing thing, brilliant how those dumb brokeasses wanted so badly to think the whole thing's real, and he could barely contain his laughter at the thought of it and was relieved when the sorry prick shaking his hand finally let go and walked away, and he wheeled down the makeshift plywood ramp some suckup guy at the church had made for him, wheeled to the back of the bandshell where his car was parked, and he collapsed his wheelchair and placed it in the back, pulled himself up and into the driver's seat, and stretched his legs while he warmed up his car and thought about picking up some whore on the Mile—maybe Rainbow or Satin is working tonight—since his wife was out of town again.

When the car was warmed up, he slammed his foot on the gas and drove west to meet Carl.

KINDNESS

MUD SQUISHED BENEATH SAMMY'S FEET AS HE CROSSED the rain-soaked schoolyard of Buena High School, less than a mile from home. It was a cold night, especially for the desert, so he hunched his shoulders a little to shield his chest from the wind, slowing his pace to savor the moment and remember the eyes meeting and the wonderful conversation that had gone on and on between he and J—they had never wanted it to stop—until it was finally time for them both to go home. We have to go home. They had said goodbye and kissed one last time, braver than before, because they no longer had to stare into each other's faces and see the blush and shy embarrassment of first kisses. Neither of them had known how to kiss except for what they'd heard people talk about or seen in movies and practiced on their hands in the darkness of their own bedrooms, sometimes pecking and licking the mirror late at night while the rest of the town slept.

He was sure that if someone met him on the street, they'd see his toothy smile floating in the air long before they made out the rest of his features. Humming with the rhythm of his steps and walking like he had just conquered the world, Sammy didn't even give a shit because this was what it was all about—us against the world, and viva los amantes, and all the other sayings people made up for the feelings of love—and now he was halfway across the schoolyard, almost to the soccer field, thinking maybe tomorrow I'll get up and run or just watch the sun rise. Maybe we can meet up before school and walk together. Maybe I'll try to get another kiss, he mused, but not really caring if he did because it would be enough just to see J again and hear the voice that sent his heart flipping in his chest.

Five bodies suddenly appeared out of the drizzle. Look who's here. The bodies twitched and bumped, stomping in the mud like a herd of bulls. He looked around, knowing he knew them but unable to match faces to names in the confusion of his broken reverie. They came in closer. It's that damn wetback Sammy, someone said. Sammy's muscles tightened involuntarily, praying the confrontation would not get out of hand, trying to think of a way out but having a hard time because his adrenaline was on fire, in full gear. All pistons thrusting. He started shaking and someone said yeah, Sammy the Spic, Sammy the Faggot, hahaha, and his hands became slippery with sweat, Sammy the Spiggot, hahaha, that's a good one, and heads were nodding. The beaner faggot. They slapped each other's backs and drew closer and he could smell their breath, their shitass tobacco-eating breath, and one stepped close enough for his nose to touch Sammy's nose and his chest to touch Sammy's chest, which was heaving in terror, and he sneered in Sammy's face you're gonna die, you fuckin fag, you butt-pirate motherfucker, and Sammy kneed him in the nuts and brought his elbow down on the back of the guy's neck, thinking at least I'll take one of them down and show them who the fag is here, and then they all came at him, jumping from where they stood and looking to Sammy like they were floating in the air, giving him time to consider each one coming at him and to decide which one he would let hit him first so he would not feel the rest of what was coming.

He turned to his left and took a blow on the chin. Lightning flashed. Then they grabbed him from all sides and his legs buckled and he lay on the ground covering his face with his one free hand and looking at the fucker he had dropped, happy knowing at least I let one of them have it and he's lying on the ground right here next to me, and maybe I can get one or two kicks in on the guy, but after a couple of boots to the face he realized that's not gonna happen so he let his body relax and hoped it would be over soon, and the boys kicked and screamed and bit and growled and one of them broke away and grabbed a tow chain from the back of his idling truck, saying let me at that cocksucker, let me AT him, and the kicking and punching subsided for a moment only to be replaced by a clinking thud that wracked Sammy's body and sent fire shooting down to the marrow of his bones, and one of the boys saw that the chain was long enough for two of them to use so he picked up the other end, the end with the hook, and laid into Sammy good, over and over, tearing his clothes and leaving gouges in his ribcage and on his legs and the other boys looked around, hungry for more blood, wanting to hit him even harder with whatever they could find, scouring the ground in the murky moonlight, and one found a bottle and broke it over Sammy's head, and another found a loose slab of concrete from the corner of a nearby tetherball court and he threw it down on Sammy and timed the other two boys' hitting with the chain so he could pick the concrete up and throw it down again, and each time it made a small booming noise in Sammy's head until the bottle and concrete and chain had hit him so many times he could not figure out where his head or his hands were and he could barely breathe, only little wisps of air tainted by the exhaust of the truck idling nearby—its body shuddering like Sammy's—just enough air to remain conscious until he felt no more, except for the rain becoming more fierce, pouring down steadily, licking his wounds clean, and the boys, dripping with sweat and covered in blood, finally said fuck it, and one said let's roll, and the others nodded but they did not leave right away because they all felt good and pumped from showing this queer what they were made of, real man stuff, and they stood and grunted and caught their breath and finally ran back to the truck idling at the edge of the soccer field with its lights off, giving each other high fives—damn, that was fuckin sweet, yeah, fucked him up good, haha, damn straight— and the driver flicked on the headlights and adjusted his ball cap and reversed the truck until they could see what was left of Sammy through the shower of rain, admiring their work, eyes searching Sammy's twitching body—his pinky clawing at the earth, his soggy shoelaces—almost falling into a trance until one of the boys in the back shouted COME THE FUCK ON, WE GOTTA GET OUT OF HERE and they nodded to each other, fidgeting in their seats, and the driver pressed down hard on the gas and threw the engine into gear and drove over Sammy to put the finishing touches on the goddam faggot as they tore out of the schoolyard and drove home.

Interstate 10, a massive stretch of highway connecting Florida to California, is unwelcome in the desert. Like a crack in a mirror. Unsightly. For years the desert has tried to reject the asphalt tumor, where semis roar along every day and sometimes a careless driver flicks a cigarette butt out his window and it lands in the brush along the side of the road. Most of the fires last only a few minutes, devouring what little brush may be nearby before fizzing out and leaving nothing but the black skeletons of desert plants. Sometimes, the brushfire spreads and burns for weeks, roaring across the landscape, up into the mountains, burning down homes. The pavement is cracked from the desert's never-ending battle to shrug off its terrible burden. When the interstate first came to Arizona, the sun joined forces with the desert and has scoured the pavement with its harshest rays ever since, bleaching the asphalt until it starts to disintegrate. The summer floods patiently erode the highway each time they pass through, carrying along with them a few pebbles at a time.

Jaime used Interstate 10 as a guide—walking alongside it at a short distance—but found he was more comfortable among the various desert plants, away from the dangers of speeding vehicles. He kept his mind occupied by recalling the names of the yucca plants, the barrel, saguaro, prickly pear, and jumping cactus. He walked along the side of the road but didn't have his thumb out. He wasn't interested in a ride, even if one were offered. The driver might be an undercover border patrol officer assuming he was an illegal, since he carried no ID with him, and deport him to Mexico. He didn't want any trouble. All of his belongings were stuffed into a faded backpack. In his pocket he had seventeen dollars, all dollar bills except for four fifty-cent pieces he had received inside a ceramic Liberty Bell coin bank from his grandmother on his first birthday.

A semi drove past and sent a swarm of dust flying into Jaime's face, but he didn't bother covering his nose or eyes because he'd gotten used to breathing and seeing through dust the day before, on the first leg of his trip north from Sierra Vista, sneaking along the side of Highway 90, hiding behind brush and cactus whenever a car remotely resembling a police cruiser approached, even though he was sure his father probably hadn't noticed his faggot son was missing, and if he had, most likely wouldn't bother to put down his beer long enough to pick up the phone and report his disappearance. So instead of covering his face, Jaime blinked the biggest pieces of dirt out of his eyes and inventoried the backpack's contents in his mind for the fourth time that morning in an effort to break the monotony of his walk. He carried everything he'd thought necessary the morning before, when he'd hastily packed his bag after the door to their apartment slammed shut, signaling his father's departure for work. The backpack held three pairs of socks, three pairs of underwear, one pair of jeans, two undershirts, his favorite cassette, a half-empty canteen of water, and an old deck of cards. The cards were greasy and bent from the many nights he played solitaire, wondering what time his father would come home from the bar after a long day of janitorial work at Fort Huachuca army base. The deck was incomplete—missing an ace of spades and a three of hearts, which Jaime had replaced with two pieces of cardboard carefully colored in by a felt-tip marker to resemble the missing cards. He'd already eaten the fruit and beef jerky purchased the night before at a gas station in Huachuca City. Fifteen miles back, where he'd spent the night, Jaime left the empty sandwich bag he'd taken with him because he remembered his father telling him, when he was sending Jaime off on his first Boy Scout camping trip, that if he were ever stranded in the desert with no water he could dig a hole in the earth with his hand and cover it with an upside-down plastic bag and moisture would collect as it was pulled from the ground and into the sky to form clouds. The trick had not worked. He had placed the bag over the hole before he went to sleep, using stones to hold it in place, but when he woke there were only two or three drops in one corner of the dusty plastic.

Jaime walked past a road sign telling him he was still miles from Tucson. He did some quick calculations as he sidestepped a lizard carcass swarming with flies and estimated that he would probably arrive sometime around noon the next day. He walked at a steady pace, whistling songs that matched the rhythm of his footsteps and ignoring the heat of the sun. Mainly he was pleased that he still had seventeen dollars and plenty of energy to get to the city, so he was optimistic about things working out after all, something he had not been so sure of when he left his house the morning before, after putting everything in order for his father so he could make his own meals and find his own clothes and not have to clean for at least a week or two—all the work that Jaime used to do. He smiled and forced himself to think of all that lay ahead—the possibilities for work, and living in a big city where no one would notice, much less care about, a gay kid—instead of dwelling on his father and his classmates, who certainly weren't thinking of him right now.

He watched the tumbleweed and a dust devil far off in the distance, ignoring the reasons he was walking. He ignored the time his father came home and found him sitting in the bathroom with a pair of women's stockings pulled up to the knees and slapped him across the face with his left hand, knocking him unconscious. Jaime came to moments later to find his father standing above him with his belt in his hand saying I ain't raising no fairy, beating him on his bare legs and shouting IF YOU'RE GONNA ACT LIKE A BITCH, I'M GONNA TREAT YOU LIKE A BITCH. This was easy for Jaime to forget when he looked at the mountains lining the distance and focused on wondering why they looked blue when they were actually brown up close.

When he sat down for lunch among a cluster of boulders and ate a few prickly pear fruits, he had no problem keeping his mind off bad memories. After he removed the needles and peeled the skin off the jelly-like fruit beneath, he lay back and enjoyed its sweet, watery juice and didn't think about the night his father stumbled upon a Hallmark card from the only other outwardly gay boy at school. The card said how he was thankful for the time they'd spent together the weekend Jaime's dad was out of town and how nice it was to lie next to him in bed and feel his warm body and smell his hair and wake up beside him in the morning and how he missed him even though it had only been a few days. And it thanked him for being the most thoughtful person he knew.

His father read the card and immediately grabbed Jaime and held him down while he pulled off his belt and whipped his son with the brass buckle that had Jesus with outstretched arms engraved on the front. With each lash his father hit him harder, and Jaime smelled the whoosh of leather swinging toward his head and heard his dad yelling MY ONLY SON, A FAGGOT and WHAT WILL HAPPEN TO THE FAMILY NAME? and another lash and he heard, a goddam QUEER, and another lash, which left a distinct ringing in his ears as the buckle connected, a pinche maricón, a goddam puta, a disgrace to the family. None of this crossed Jaime's mind when he stood up from his lunch and began walking toward Tucson again, happy that he'd be there tomorrow, excited about finding work and people like him.

What Jaime did remember was the day he'd realized Sammy knew he was gay, when he caught him peeking during PE class as they dressed in their gym shorts. Every PE class after that one, as an act of kindness and flirtatiousness—a little testing of the waters—one or the other spread his legs a little too wide when tying his shoes, or bent over a little too far when reaching down to pull on his red shorts, allowing the other to have a quick look. Jaime looked forward to taking showers, but he also worried he'd get caught staring at another classmate and immediately be called a faggot and get knocked around or thrown up against a locker. Or worse.

He remembered how weird it was that no one thought the school's three toughest kids were gay when they danced around the shower with their dicks flopping, chanting yeah, yeah, check out my daddy longleg, bitch, which made the other boys do everything imaginable not only to avert their attention but also to cover up their own dicks, which didn't flop around but instead had shriveled up like uncooked biscuits. Jaime and Sammy showered at opposite ends of the room. Better not to be noticed, even though the longlegs offered a diversion with their taunting of the other boys, who in return went behind the gym after their showers and smoked cigarettes while concocting elaborate schemes to kill them fuckin pricks. Except they didn't have the courage to approach even one of them, so they contented themselves with talk of killing them and, as long as they all agreed those longleg boys were fuckin assholes, they were happy enough.

Jaime and Sammy ignored the talk of the other boys, standing far from the group and shyly making small talk. Eventually they decided they should get together sometime and do something, kicking rocks and saying yeah, that would be nice, maybe some night after school you could come over before my dad gets home. And Sammy did. He came over one afternoon when school got out and walked in and the smell of freshly baked cookies—how Jaime had managed that in the time between the final bell and Sammy coming over was something Sammy would always marvel at fondly—led him to the kitchen where Jaime had coffee steaming in a pot on the stove, and they sat down and talked for two hours about music and school and their favorite actors, until Jaime looked up and realized how late it was and said sorry, but I have to get dinner ready for my father, with enough conviction in his voice for Sammy to understand the importance of Jaime's task. Jaime walked him to the door and they brushed hands as they reached for the knob at the same time. After he watched Sammy walk through the gate, Jaime went back to the kitchen, humming, and seasoned chicken breasts with lemon pepper and put water on to boil for the rice and turned on the oven to heat some rolls.

Their afternoons became a routine. So, in addition to his daily chores, Jaime had to clean up that evidence before his father returned. He took advantage of his father's smoking habit by lighting a cigarette and walking around with it to mask the smell of cookies and gourmet coffee. He had so much to do that once he didn't notice his father had returned and stood in the entrance of the kitchen watching his son sing songs, using a ladle for a microphone, while his oven-mitted hands flailed about, gesturing like an exaggerated vaudeville performer. His father snuck up behind him, grabbed him by the hair, and dragged him through the house until he found something out of place that he could punish Jaime for neglecting—an unchanged toilet paper roll or a sock wadded up under his bed. This memory would have bothered Jaime, except it helped him remember his times with Sammy.

The day dragged on, and Jaime noticed creatures like the horny toad and wondered if they were miniature descendants of the stegosaurus. Even though he knew he was foolishly crossing the desert on a very hot day, he felt comfortable and was even amazed when he realized that seven hours had passed since he'd last taken a drink of water and he wasn't even thirsty, which reminded him of cartoons he had seen growing up where people were trapped in the desert with no water, dragging themselves over sand dunes and leaving trails behind them in search of an oasis. He looked around to see if such a thing existed, but saw nothing except for cactus and mountains and a roadrunner. He thought about finding a place to sleep. By the time nightfall came, that place ended up being between two boulders with his navy blue flannel shirt serving as a blanket and his backpack beneath his head.

As Jaime slept, he dreamed he was the kid again who had hidden in the laundry room taping ninety-nine pennies inside an envelope accompanied by an ad from a music club—twelve cassettes for ninety-nine cents. He wept with the sadness he'd felt three years later when he was suddenly and inexplicably reminded that he'd sent away for the cassettes all those years before and had never received them. He'd forgotten what he had ordered. But it didn't matter now because he was lying down beneath his coat in the desert, sleeping comfortably.

When he woke up, he made his way back to the interstate, so close to the city now he was passing billboards for Old Tucson and Breakers and the Lazy 8 Motel, and the billboards got hazier and hazier as the day got hotter and signs of life in the desert began to show. For the first time since he ran away two days earlier, Jaime felt exhausted and knew he needed to get out of the sun and get a real meal, so he stopped at the first roadside diner he found and walked inside, where the air was thick with the smell of grease. The sign inside told him to sit wherever he pleased, and he did, in the far corner, where he wasn't visible to anyone unless they made a trip to the salad bar. The muggy mom-and-pop establishment had been built in the early 1900s, a newspaper article pinned to the wall informed him, by a Mexican gold smuggler named Francisco Arroyo, who, according to legend, had buried gold in the restaurant's walls and foundation. Several years after his death, people came from all over the Southwest to pry the boards from the walls in the middle of the night, searching feverishly for a glint of precious metal while the new proprietors slept upstairs. Eventually a sheriff was deputized whose sole purpose was to watch over the building at night and keep would-be looters away, and he remained there until he retired in 1976, but by then most thieves had stopped believing in the myth of Arroyo's gold, so no other men were sent to protect the restaurant.

Jaime was fascinated by the history of the building and wondered if it was true, even asking his waitress whether or not Arroyo's gold had ever been found. She told him no one had mentioned it in a long time, but she knew for a fact that once or twice a year they would have to call the coroner in from Tucson to salvage the remains of a person who had gotten trapped under the building while searching for treasure. And she told him, when she brought his eggs and bacon, that every now and then the owners had the building repainted and the painters sometimes quit the job before it was completed because they were deeply disturbed by the teeth and fingernails they had to extract from the walls of the building before they could put on the first coat of paint. Sometimes, she said, in the middle of the night they heard clawing and scraping in the walls, but they didn't bother getting up to look because they knew no one would be there. She left the check overturned in front of Jaime and walked away.

When Jaime finished his meal, he paid his check and counted his remaining money—thirteen dollars and fifty cents—and as he walked out the door, the newspaper rack taunted him with images of what he'd left behind in Sierra Vista. He looked around to be sure no one was watching, then quickly grabbed a newspaper and left. Startled by Sammy's picture on the front page, Jaime couldn't resist glancing at the story, recollecting the events that made him leave home in the first place. He feared for his life. But more importantly, he wanted revenge.

He wanted to make his father pay for coming home later than usual, almost too drunk to speak but coherent enough to tell Jaime that a couple of fellas from Buena nailed themselves a fag, got him real good, beat him with a chain till he couldn't move and one of em even ran him over, and then his father went to the bathroom and passed out on the toilet. Jaime sat in silence until he was sure his father wasn't coming out of the bathroom and then quietly picked up the phone and dialed Sammy's number but it only rang and rang—thirty-six rings—and then he hung up and knew. That was when he decided he had to leave, because if they knew about Sammy then they had to know about him. He wasn't safe, and it was just him, alone, against everyone who knew his secret.

The paper said the police had labeled it an unfortunate accident.

Jaime, finally piecing the whole story together from what his father had said and from what he read in the newspaper, hardly noticed that he'd reached his destination a little ahead of schedule. He collapsed in the back of a Sun-Tran bus and fell asleep, trusting in the fortune of the bus's route to lead him somewhere safe. The bus took him downtown to the depot, where he awoke, amazed at the amount of homeless people milling about, asking for change. He'd heard that Tucson was overrun with homeless vets, but he'd never expected to actually see so many. Despite their weathered skin and sun-bleached clothes, he felt a kinship with them. They too were lost, wandering from place to place with nowhere to sleep, little food to eat. God, Jaime thought, I can't believe it's come down to this—me and these men sharing the same streets together. The bustle of downtown traffic and all the vets made Jaime anxious, so he hopped another bus at the depot, tossing the driver his transfer, and headed east, nodding off to the rhythm of the bus's motor. It was almost noon when the driver finally brought the bus to a halt in front of Reid Park and walked to the back and shook him awake and asked you ever getting off, kid? while motioning to the door. I've got to take my lunch. Jaime grunted and left the bus and squinted his eyes in the fierce light of the sun until he could focus on something. The desire to get out of the sun and into someplace cool led him from the bus stop to a flower shop across the street from the park. Unsure whether or not the shop, Floreria Gutierrez, was open, he pulled on the door anyway and was relieved when it swung open and blew a gust of cool air in his face.

—————

Rudolfo Gutierrez awoke to the smell of burning feet. It was a common occurrence dating back almost forty years to a time when his wife and son were still living. He had been having the same nightmare and waking to this godforsaken smell all these years, though there were occasional nights when he dreamed nothing at all.

Unfortunately, the nightmare was the most vivid memory he had of his son, and it often caused him to wake with tears in his eyes and a feeling of solitude so intense he almost welcomed the scent of burning flesh, because at least it was something. But he knew he was alone in his home—his wife and son both long dead—and he listened to the whoosh-click of his oxygen tank, trying to exorcise the image of his son walking out of the house one day when it was one hundred and twenty degrees outside, while his wife, Gloria, balanced the checkbook for their plumbing business and Rudolfo wrote up bids for commercial contracts.

Back when his little Alberto was still a toddler, three days after asphalt had been introduced to their neighborhood in Tucson, his son walked barefoot through the front yard, past the lonely palm tree they had planted the year Alberto was born, and out onto the freshly lain asphalt of their cul-de-sac, bubbling under the burning sun, where, as soon as he stepped onto it, his feet planted themselves firmly in the black, lumpy, licorice-smelling goop, and the boy stood, unable to move or breathe or cry out, until finally, in a burst of immense pain, he released a scream so terrible and tortured it sent every mother and father within two miles to the window, their parental instincts forcing them to drop everything—cooking meals, reading to their children, sewing Halloween costumes, watching television, making love, relieving themselves in restrooms—and each parent looked outside, holding their breath, expecting the worst, praying it was not their child whose awful scream reached into the depths of their hearts, even though some of them had thrown their only child from their laps, or ran past their children watching television or working on puzzles, seeing their kids were safe but unable to think anything except maybe there was a kid they had momentarily forgotten who was now outside, wailing so horribly that panic sent them to their doors, thrusting their heads out hurriedly, looking around, under cars, up in trees, in neighbors' yards, until eventually they were satisfied it was not their child, so they wiped the sweat from their foreheads and went inside and hugged their children, crossing themselves and thanking the good Lord it was not their child who had experienced such overwhelming pain. Then they returned to their meals or their televisions or their newspapers or their waiting beds to finish what they had started.

Everyone was finally calm except the Gutierrezes, who ran to their door, stumbling over toys and slipping on receipts and invoices and cancelled checks strewn on the floor. They stood at the door searching for their son, clutching their chests until they finally saw him, pobre Alberto, standing in the street, stuck in the boiling asphalt, and the smell was so unbearable, so putrid, they could hardly approach him without gagging, were it not for the simple fact that it was *their* son's flesh burning.

Alberto stood motionless, his flesh an unearthly purple, looking more like a bruise than a little boy. Rudolfo's gut response was to run up and tear him from the asphalt, so he reached down to grab him but was stopped by his wife, who had wisely considered the ramifications of such an action, telling him to hold Alberto, my God, just hold onto him, please, I'll be right back. She ran inside the house, leaving her husband to stare at his son, who could not breathe, whose face was contorted with so much agony that Rudolfo could bearly stand to look at his child's eyes pleading, failing to understand the pain and the burning and why his dad could not make it stop, just make it stop, Daddy, and Rudolfo could bear it no longer and looked away, and he raised his head toward heaven, fuck, fuck, what do I do? my son, my son, then he closed his eyes and put his fingers over them and pressed down hard while Alberto reached out and grabbed his father's pant leg and wailed again and finally Gloria returned with a metal spatula and began digging their little boy's feet out of the asphalt, furiously digging, digging through black mush and gravel until she had freed one tiny foot and then the other and had her baby cradled in her arms, running back to the house with him and leaving her husband in the street with his fingers pressing into his eyes and his son's wailing echoing through the cul-de-sac.

And the smell.

The smell would never leave, even when Rudolfo called an ambulance while his wife soaked her son's feet in a tub of cold water and wept and stroked his head and prayed to la virgen y todos los santos to heal her son, please. The smell lingered in Rudolfo's nose while he waited in front of his home for the ambulance to appear, chain-smoking and pacing and damning the asphalt and his own foolishness for forgetting they had only just pressed a fresh sheet into place three days earlier and the heat was so strong the swamp cooler did nothing but push hot air around inside so of course the asphalt was still sticky and treacherous. The smell was still clinging to Rudolfo's nose even after they returned from the hospital where Alberto had been admitted for third-degree burns and severe shock, staying for three days to recover with bandaged feet and doctor's orders for him to not walk for at least one month, maybe better to wait six or seven weeks. And be sure to change the dressing every two hours, even when he sleeps. Which was fine with Gloria, who spent the next two months lying in bed with her son and kissing him all over, especially on his delicate bandaged feet, and cooing in his ears while praying to the Virgin Mother to please deliver me from the pain of motherhood and save my child from the despair of the cruel, cruel world.

Rudolfo knew she could never forgive herself for her negligence. At least that's what he believed when she died of cancer two years later—she who had never smoked and who forced her husband to go outside and not smoke around her or the baby—and he found it unsettling that she had passed away in the same hospital where her son had lain in agony, the vicious circle of despair growing wider. He knew the cancer was not from ill health, because he had heard her sobbing every night in her sleep and could practically feel the guilt that stood thick in the air of their home. That was what killed her, he was sure. The cancer of guilt.

But his curse was the smell. He, too, would pay the price for not noticing Alberto walking out the front door, for forgetting that technology and municipal taxes had finally brought asphalt to the desert. For not noticing until it was too late that his son was stuck in the middle of the cul-de-sac, cooking beneath the desert sun.

He smelled his son's burning flesh, a grotesque mixture of bacon and mayonnaise, every moment thereafter. He smelled it when he dropped his son off at school every morning. He smelled it when he read him bedtime stories and kissed him goodnight. He smelled it when he attended Alberto's school plays. During holiday masses. At parent-teacher conferences. He smelled it when he helped him knot his bowtie before the senior prom. When Alberto's orders arrived, Rudolfo smelled burning feet as he drove him to the army recruitment center to board the bus for basic training so he could be turned into a soldier and deployed to Vietnam. He even smelled it two years and four months later when his son came home from the war in a crude pinewood coffin, after being burnt alive by miscalculation on the part of an unseasoned bomber dispatched on a napalming mission. Standing over his son's open grave, he imagined his poor Alberto, not even twenty-one years old, screaming and burning and abandoned all alone in the wilds of some foreign country, betrayed yet again, looking for his father's pant leg to grasp, Alberto turning purple and black, his flesh melting off in greasy clumps, crying out while the flames devoured his body. And Rudolfo Gutierrez wept furiously behind his sunglasses as the men in military uniforms fired their guns into the sky three times and presented him with the Stars and Stripes, once draped over his son's coffin, now folded into a neat triangle with three warm, spent rifle shells from the twenty-one-gun salute tucked inside. Even then, when they laid him in the ground, the smell never went away. It only got stronger.

Even though he tried to smoke and smoke—chain-smoking filter-less cigarettes, inhaling deeply and holding the smoke trapped in his lungs until he was about to collapse—in an attempt to kill off his olfactory nerves and coat his lungs with so much filth that one smell was indiscernible from the next, it did no good. Now, because of complications from emphysema, he was on oxygen, each gust from his tank issuing a new surge of fresh air tainted with burnt feet. Every breath was like this. All day long. Every single day.

And so he had grown old and suffered the same nightmare, a ghoulish adaptation of that day's events back when everything in Rudolfo's life had suddenly and inexplicably altered its course. Back before he'd developed the nervous twitch beneath his left eye that sometimes became so violent it nearly drove him to insanity. Back before he began rubbing Vicks under his nostrils so he could alter the smell, if even a little, and perhaps dream of something else.

But now Rudolfo lay in bed, succumbing to the smell's inevitability and adjusting himself to the reality of his solitude as the nightmare began to mercifully fade from his mind and was replaced with the warm light of sunrise. And, like every other morning, he sat up in bed and plucked the oxygen tubes from his nostrils. Then he reached over to the nightstand and tapped a cigarette from his pack of Benson & Hedges. He lit it, taking care to avoid the oxygen tubing with his flame, and lay back on his pillow, relishing the burning in his throat, the sandpapery smoke scratching its way deep inside him, and for the briefest moment, diminishing the smell of burned feet.

When his cigarette was finished, he lit another off the dying ember of the first, then sat up and began the laborious process of getting out of bed and trudging to the restroom. The getting up and moving in the morning was the hardest part of each day. Just lifting himself up from the bed and then putting one foot in front of the other. It was so hard. But he did it because what else could he do? Lie in bed and rot?

When he finally made it out into the hall, Rudolfo stopped occasionally to rest against the wall and take a lengthy pull from his cigarette. Then, after blowing out the smoke and pausing for a brief coughing fit, he took a sip of oxygen from the tubing and gathered his strength for a few more steps.

Eventually, he made it to the restroom, and he carefully lowered himself onto the rim of the bathtub and cranked the faucet handle as far as it would go, basking in the steam and praying this time it might scour the smell from his body. And maybe today would be the day the bath would relax him enough and his eye would stop twitching and throbbing each time he thought of his burning son and his guilt-stricken wife. Rudolfo pressed down on the bag beneath his eye with all his might, ashamed that he had neither the strength nor the courage to gouge the offensive thing from its socket. He wished he could rid himself of his curse. But there was little he could do. This much he knew. How to bring back a dead wife and son? How to forgive himself for having failed both as a husband and father? It had been his job, he knew, to protect his family. It was he who should have died in battle, not his son. It was he who should have died from cancer, not his Gloria. Yet, inexplicably, after nearly forty years of serious smoking—what his doctor called chronic smoking—it was Rudolfo Gutierrez and not his wife or his son who continued to breathe. Even now, sitting on the edge of his bathtub and watching the water rise, he was the one alive to feel the steam lending its moisture to his tired skin and penetrating his blackened lungs. And he simply could not reconcile this harsh fact with how he believed things should be. For this, he could never forgive himself. To Rudolfo, each day he was alive was an inexcusable crime against his wife and son. Against nature and its order.

Of course, when he was finally in the water, soaking in a hot bath of Epsom salts, Rudolfo considered, as he often did, pulling the oxygen tubing from his nostrils and lowering himself completely beneath the water. But he was scared even that wouldn't work. His bathtub was neither long enough nor deep enough, and he knew how foolish he would feel when he inevitably burst through the water's surface gasping for breath. After all, what kind of person could actually stay beneath the water and allow his lungs to give in, allowing himself to die when mere inches above his head was the lifesaving desert air, despite its being tainted with the smell of burning feet? Certainly not me, he thought. I'm not that strong of a man. Still, it was something to think about as he lay in the tub, preparing for another day of trying to keep his small business afloat.

In a meager attempt to cope with his overwhelming sense of guilt and his inability to forgive his failures as a father, five years after his son's death, Rudolfo Gutierrez decided to sell his plumbing business. Besides, he had tired of laying the clay pipes that carried the city sewage. He had tired of waking to the smell only to spend the remainder of each day working in the none-too-pleasant occupation of human waste. The stink of shit was an affront to his already traumatized sense of smell. And he felt humiliated to be bending over all the time, as if in supplication, yet getting no sense of relief out of the act. There had been a time when he installed expensive bathroom fixtures in the glorious new homes climbing up the foothills, and there had been a time when his many lucrative contracts had even included plumbing the food courts of Tucson's malls. But when the recession hit, those contracts had dried up, and it was back to the sewers and unclogging toilets and replacing the aging water lines in Tucson's oldest homes and snaking out industrial-sized drains in the filthy backrooms of the bars on Miracle Mile. Always digging, piping, snaking, burrowing, plunging. It was simply too much.

So, he made up his mind to move to a different part of the city, far away from Siglo Place, that accursed cul-de-sac. Within six months of his decision, Rudolfo had laid off his employees, canceled his contracts, and opened a flower shop, with the hopes that working around the pleasant smell of flowers might make breathing more bearable.

Yes, opening the shop had been a good decision, Rudolfo believed. It made sense even now, as he rose from the steaming bathwater and pulled on his heavy terrycloth robe, to at least take some control of his life all those years ago. No, the flowers didn't completely mask the smell of burning flesh, but they did take a little bit of the edge off.

As he dressed and groomed himself for work, Rudolfo truly hoped today was one of those days. He decided it might even be a good idea to have a Christmas in July sale to do away with some of the products that weren't moving quickly enough for his liking. I'll get to work and draw up a nicely lettered sign and post it in the window. He visualized the layout and the size of the lettering as he pulled on his socks and underwear. He remembered the bright yellow roll of paper in the back of the store above the cleaning supplies. It would work perfectly.

Once he was finally dressed and had tightened his bolo tie around his collar, Rudolfo left through his front door, locked the two deadbolts, bent down to retrieve the *Arizona Daily Star*, and began the fifteen-minute walk to work, pulling his portable oxygen tank behind him. The front page said temperatures were expected to be in the 120s. Of course, Rudolfo knew this was something that certainly happened out here, but it was infrequent enough that when it did, it was newsworthy. To his annoyance, next came the usual gamut of articles about checking on the elderly, upkeep of swamp coolers, maintenance of refrigerators, proper levels of hydration, and so on. He hated how they condescended to readers, as though the people living out here in the desert did not know to drink water when it got extra hot out.

He stopped at Torchy's for a cup of fresh coffee, and Torchy said the same thing he said every morning, yep, good ol' Rudy G. A well-oiled machine, a man so punctual I set my clock by his movements. Haha. If Rudolfo Gutierrez aint in my shop buying his brew at exactly three minutes to eight, the birds'd fall from their telephone wires, cars'd screech to a halt, the sun'd freeze in the sky, not sure if it was actually on schedule. What Torchy didn't know was how hard it was getting for Rudolfo Gutierrez to pull himself out of the bathwater every morning. Still, he thanked Torchy, as was their custom, tapped the face of his watch, and walked out the door with a minute to spare before it was time to open up shop.

It only took him half an hour to make up a Christmas in July sign, advertising 50% off select items. An hour later, he had dusted and marked and organized all the baskets and teddy bears and vases he was having trouble moving. Then he sat on his stool behind the counter to read the paper while waiting on customers to arrive. The bright colors at Floreria Gutierrez made him smile each morning. The iris and cymbidium orchids and lilies and birds of paradise were like his children. Each time he arranged bouquets for weddings, anniversaries, proms, valentines, or even for funerals, he realized he preferred dealing with things that grew out of the ground, things that bloomed and blossomed and colored. Every day he sat by the front window and gazed at the old three-by-five of his wife that he kept folded in his wallet. The photo was faded, its corners disintegrated by years of being pulled from the wallet and pushed by sweaty fingers back behind old receipts and business cards. Beneath a web of creases his beautiful wife sat in her wedding dress, perched on a wrought-iron bench in front of the San Xavier Mission. He did this every morning until the sun warmed the flowers and brought life into the shop.

The string of gold bells hanging from the handle of the door chimed. A teenaged boy walked in and Rudolfo said let me know if I can be of service. The boy wandered slowly through the store smelling each type of flower in stock, closing his eyes and breathing in every one as if he had never smelled a flower in his life. He went to the cooler and picked out a half-price carnation that had only a day or two left to live, feeling obligated to make a purchase. What do you think? he asked Rudolfo, who nodded and asked him for thirty-five cents, reducing the already lowered price because the boy obviously needed the money.

The boy walked back to the cooler and opened the glass doors, letting the cool air blow over him and smoothing as many wrinkles out of his shirt as he could, and then, apparently satisfied, he gathered up his backpack and walked toward the exit. Rudolfo, who watched from behind the business section of the newspaper, lowered his paper and asked do you like flowers? and the boy said sure, it's nice to see them in the desert. Rudolfo agreed and said there's a rose garden in the park across the street that's great for wandering through on lazy afternoons like this one. The boy thanked him, then he left, again jingling the bells on the door as he closed it behind him. Rudolfo gathered up his box of deliveries and walked out of the store. He flipped over the will return at two o'clock sign and locked the door behind him.

Hungry once more, and with his money dwindling fast, Jaime decided on lunch at a taqueria. He ordered huevos con chorizo in a tortilla and after he paid, he left the store with his food wrapped tightly in tinfoil. He could feel the warmth of the food in his front pocket heating his leg, his body reacting to the touch, as if his leg could taste it through the foil and denim. He crossed six lanes of traffic and went into the park, searching for the rose garden.

He wanted to relax for a moment and then try to find a relatively safe place to sleep for the night. But when he saw the pond in the middle of the park, with families and couples loitering in paddleboats, he was overcome with the desire to lie beneath a tree with his feet in the water. He surveyed the outline of the pond, looking for an area with the fewest amount of people, and found a spot where it trickled slowly over rocks leading down gently sloping steps. There, two boys walked through the stream, sneaking along its edges where they suddenly plunged their hands into the water to overturn a slimy rock and emerge with a crayfish. It was peaceful enough for Jaime to eat his meal and finally relax. When he finished, he crushed the tinfoil into a small wad and removed his shoes and socks and placed his bag beneath his head so he could doze off for a few minutes.

What woke him two hours later was the thumping of bass from the lowriders cruising through the park. He sat up and rubbed his eyes while he let his feet dry in a patch of sunlight. He admired the lowriders skulking by, and in the distance he saw Rudolfo Gutierrez coming toward him, wheeling his oxygen tank down a hill. He hurriedly put his socks and shoes back on.

When Rudolfo finally reached him, he looked at Jaime's dusty clothes and started to turn around to give the boy some privacy, saying I figured you'd be here somewhere, since you didn't look like you had anything else to do. I had a little extra lunch and came to see if you wanted any. In spite of his lack of money and work and a home, Jaime acted disinterested. He shrugged and mumbled thanks, leaving the food untouched. But after the old man nodded and walked away, leaving behind half a sandwich and a bag of chips, Jaime devoured the food.

He was having an inner celebration for getting to Tucson intact. The problem is, he thought, I only have eleven dollars and I can't get a hotel room for that. And even if I could, I wouldn't have anything left for eating or otherwise living. So, while he watched people slowly meander over the hills of the park toward their warm homes, Jaime tried to think of a place to stay. He'd felt safer in the desert than he ever had in his life, as if some outside force were protecting him. But now, in the bowels of the city, he was a stationary target. The sun began to go down in the west and the park emptied out and he realized he had absolutely nowhere to go. He got up and walked toward the sound of traffic. When he reached the edge of the park, he sat on a boulder by the entrance and passed the time watching cars and motorcycles cruise past. Eventually, he crossed the street, past the closed flower shop and Torchy's, and turned left at the corner.

Behind the liquor store, he saw a mattress and wandered over to it to see if maybe it was in good enough condition to sleep on. It wasn't. But at least there would be no cold desert floor that night. He pulled the mattress behind him and continued wandering up the alley until he came to a McDonald's. There were two large brown dumpsters behind the restaurant, covered with graffiti. Between the two dumpsters, which stunk of a thousand half-eaten hamburgers, Jaime dropped the mattress and then climbed into one of the dumpsters and rummaged around until he found cardboard boxes to use as sheets. He broke the boxes into flat panels and arranged them on his mattress and then climbed back into the dumpster and removed a few bags of trash. He tore them open, using the plastic to cover the cardboard.

He lay down and immediately fell asleep and dreamed he was running through the desert, his pants getting caught on cactus needles. He felt the needles implanting themselves into his jeans, their tips scraping away at his flesh as he ran from the headlights of a monster truck with a bunch of guys screaming HEY FAGGOT, WE FINALLY FOUND YOU, YOU ASSLICKING QUEER, and the cactus kept cutting at his feet as he ran farther and farther, his lungs threatening to cave in, his pants wearing down as the needles slowly tore at the seams and disconnected the fibers, but the truck was always bearing down on him, and the voices kept yelling FAGGOT and SHITDICKED COCKSUCKER.

Jaime thrashed around in his sleep. He kicked the plastic and it coiled around his ankles while he dreamed his legs were trapped in a sea of rolling tumbleweed and he could feel the breath from the truck's engine pulsing on the back of his neck while the guys whooped and yelled and gunned the motor and laughed as he ran, trying not to trip on whatever it was that was catching his legs, afraid to look down, only able to look back over his shoulder and in front of him, his vision blurring as the dust blew into his eyes and scratched their surfaces and lodged in the corners and he had to find a place to hide, a wash to jump into where the truck wouldn't be able to follow him or something, but all he saw was flat land ahead and he wanted to weep but was too afraid, fearing he would get run over by the truck but knowing they were only toying with him, waiting for him to collapse or trip or simply run out of steam so they could stop the truck and get out and beat him to death with bricks or bats or whatever they were banging on the roof of the truck as it nipped at his ankles. And while Jaime slept, he kicked the cardboard panels off the mattress and tossed and turned and felt the moisture of the mattress beneath him. In his dream his legs were still caught up in something, and he fell and the truck came to a stop and one of the boys threw something from the bed of the truck and it rolled toward him. Sammy's head, staring him in the face.

When Jaime woke, his heart was racing and his eyes were bloodshot. Shaking with rage, he balled up his fist and punched himself in the face because he didn't want to cry from missing Sammy, he wanted to cry out of anger. He had never felt like this before. He had never wished harm on a single soul, not even his father after he beat him with his Jesus belt. Not even his father had provoked what Jaime now felt toward those boys from Buena High School who had taken the life of the only person he'd ever loved. The only person he'd ever been able to sit down with for hours and talk about anything. The only thing that mattered now, the only thing that allowed Jaime to open his eyes after that terrible dream, was his desire for revenge against the fuckers who killed Sammy. He had to make a plan. Once he got settled, he had to. He would figure out a way to get back to Sierra Vista and pick them off one by one. It wouldn't be that hard. He had plenty of time. They were only juniors in high school, and so they'd be in school another year, maybe more. Stupid assholes. If it weren't for metal shop, they'd be lost. Yes, he would get settled here somehow in this lonesome, crowded city, and then he would get back at each one of them. He would get them when they least suspected it, as if they really even expected a faggot to come after them and try to avenge the death of his fairy boyfriend. Yeah, to them he was just a donut puncher. But he would get them. He would surprise them.

The fuckers.

Jaime sat up and realized that the plastic he'd placed over the cardboard panels was wound tightly around his ankles. When he looked behind him in the mild blue light of the Arizona sunrise, he saw the figure of a girl kneeling next to the dumpster smoking a cigarette. She made no move to injure him, merely looked and puffed her cigarette.

My name's Lavinia, she told him, gesturing toward Jaime with her cigarette. He took it from her, trying to act cool. Nice to meet you. He looked at the plastic around his ankles. Guess I got a little carried away in my sleep. He tried to laugh it off. She nodded, as if to say hey, you don't have to talk about anything you don't want to. Jaime unwrapped the plastic from around his feet. So, how long have you been sitting here?

Well, long enough to have a couple of cigarettes and watch you kicking and squirming in your sleep. This is the first time I've ever seen you around here.

Oh, so you come here all the time?

Well, every day on the way to school I come here because—where'd you get that mattress, anyway? She scratched delicately at her head, trying not to disturb any of her slim braids.

I found it down the alley, behind some liquor store.

Lavinía flinched. Behind Torchy's? That mattress has stories attached to it. If you had any idea, you wouldn't be sleeping on it. Trust me. She shook her head. It's kind of a neighborhood artifact.

Jaime grimaced. I don't need to know. But it was better than sleeping on the ground.

That's probably true. I won't tell you how it gets used, besides, you can probably guess.

The thought had never crossed Jaime's mind until now that maybe there was a good reason why the mattress was sitting untouched behind a liquor store. Right now it only smelled of rain.

You know, someone died behind that store once. A boy that I used to have a crush on. His name was Felipe. You kind of look like him, actually. Same features. She stared at him for a few moments. Yeah, you both have this look, like you think too much. It's kinda creepy how much you remind me of him. A softness to you. He had the same thing. Made me sick what they did to him.

How'd he die?

Well, his brothers killed him. His brothers and their gang. That's why I was so surprised to find you here. Usually if someone comes around they don't know, they make him pay. Don't worry. If they find you here with me, everything will be fine. Anyway, I have to go to school soon. Maybe you should go over to the park or something until I get out of school, then I can meet you back here if you want.

Jaime stood up and gathered his things to walk back to the park. He wanted to check out the zoo or something today anyway, and maybe look for a place to work, something that might pay him under the table since he didn't have any ID.

Lavinía stood and waved goodbye. So, maybe I'll see you after school?

Sure. Jaime thought he probably wouldn't see her, but when he was alone, he began to think maybe he should see her again. After all, she had mentioned the neighborhood gang. If she knew these guys, then maybe he could get to know a couple of them too, and maybe he could hit one of them up for a gun one day. It was an option.

It had been less than a day he had been in Tucson, and already things were starting to fall into place. Driven by his mission, and knowing that it might even be attainable, Jaime hid the mattress behind the dumpster and walked back up the alley toward the main road. Before he began his job search, Jaime had one thing more he wanted to do.

He needed to find a church. He needed to show God that he had forsaken the world, and people were starting to take notice. Sure, he thought, I could pray to You, but that wouldn't bring Sammy back. And I could pray the rosary and put ashes on my forehead and crawl on my knees through the desert to some shrine where la Virgencita had appeared in the desert, but that's a bunch of shit. Why would I want to pray to the saints who've been dead forever? I'm sure Sammy prayed while he was beaten to death, and what good did it do him? I'll make You notice, Jaime thought, shifting his backpack to his right shoulder.

As he walked he kicked stones into the street and ground his teeth until finally he stood before a Catholic church. He opened the door and stood in the back of the sanctuary, allowing his eyes to adjust to the dimness. Except for an old woman praying silently in the back row, the church was empty. Jaime didn't bother crossing, dipping his fingers in holy water, or kneeling. Instead he made his way over to the shrine for the Virgin Mary surrounded by hundreds of burning candles. He looked around to be sure no one was watching and then turned back to the statue, pretending to light a candle. He reached toward a candle and let his hand move past it and on toward the statue of Mary in her powder blue and white gown. Jaime traced its folds and felt Mary's face, her soft features tickling his fingertips, a mother whose eyes spoke undying love and devotion. He let his fingers fall around Mary's throat and squeezed as tight as he could. Her unchanging features—her absolute belief in the holiness of her son and the goodness of the world—made Jaime want to smash her into a thousand pieces. He lifted the statue, placing it beneath the waistband of his jeans, and covered it with his shirt.

Then he waited. He braced himself for the lightning that was sure to strike him down. He waited for the church floor to open up and devour him and hurl him into the pit of hell. Any minute a priest would come forward and start flicking holy water at him and then it would be all over. Mary avenged. God's wrath satisfied.

But nothing happened. No one noticed. Not even the old woman praying at the back of the sanctuary. Staring at the life-sized crucifix hanging behind the altar, Jaime flipped his middle finger at it and mouthed fuck you. He turned around and left, slumping over a little bit so no one would notice Mary in his pants.

The traffic was heavy enough that no one paid attention to the slouching figure of Jaime as he left Our Mother of Sorrows and walked toward the park.

Jaime salvaged a few empty Coke cans from a trashbarrel and filled them with dirt. Using some twine he found tied around the base of a tree, he bound the dirt-filled cans to the feet of Mary and raised her above his head. He threw her as hard as he could into the pond where ducks split trails into the calm face of the water, bobbing for breadcrumbs. She hit the water and didn't sink right away. Jaime was terrified. He thought maybe he was witnessing an act of God. What else could explain a floating statue?

But Mary finally sank and Jaime knew there was no turning back. He was committed. He had defied God and now he answered to no one except the voice inside him telling him you're letting those fuckers get away clean. You're letting them take away the only thing that ever mattered to you and you're the one running. It should be THEM running. They should be the ones hiding from headlights behind cactus on the side of the highway. Jaime agreed with his inner voice, but he knew he would have his revenge in plenty of time. He walked to Floreria Gutierrez and asked the old man if he needed any help today watching the store, and Rudolfo thanked him and said yes, it would be nice for a change to be able to leave the store open for business while I make deliveries.

The old man trusted Jaime. He couldn't explain it. Instead of doubting Jaime and his honesty, he decided to prove to himself that there were still good people left on the earth. He didn't lock the register. He didn't turn on the camera he'd installed all those years ago to deter robbers, something he had done religiously for the first three years until he figured out that no one thinks to rob a flower shop. He gave Jaime brief instructions on how to take orders for arrangements, showed him how to ring up merchandise, then left for his afternoon deliveries. He knew this kid was special. This boy comes to me completely helpless, and I can give him some direction. He thought, I'm going to offer my place to him in exchange for his help at the store. Do a good deed, try to make a difference for once.

Jaime stood by the door, waiting for the delivery van to leave the parking lot. Once the van turned north, Jaime went behind the counter and sat in front of the register. I could just clean out this drawer, he thought, when he opened it and saw the cash inside. He shut it and sat for a moment, taking in the store's details. The smell of so many different types of flowers was relaxing. Jaime wanted to take a nap, even though he'd only been awake for a few hours. Instead he poked around behind the counter, digging through paperwork and orders and stacks of receipts. Jaime kept searching beneath the counter, looking for scrap paper or a notepad. He couldn't find any. All there was were old orders written in Señor Gutierrez's meticulous hand-writing and boxes full of unused order forms. Using one of the forms and a pen, he started scribbling frantic notes. Sierra Vista. Sammy. The Buena students. He listed the names of all the potential killers. He jotted down plots for revenge—sneak into the school with a gun and make his way to the gym and hold the students hostage until the murderers confess and then force them into the showers and shoot them up against the wall, firing-squad style; or he could go door-to-door, pretending to sell magazine subscriptions, until he found the houses where they lived, then he could ask to speak to the kid who lived there and when he came to the door, he'd shoot the bastard right there in the doorway, his mother crying out from the living room and Jaime laughing as he pumped bullet after bullet into Sammy's killer. He flipped back and forth between order forms stained with harried ink. So caught up was he in his project, he ignored the phones and failed to hear Lavinía walk through the front door, standing in front of him with a look of confusion as she watched Jaime's reckless scrawling. She couldn't get his attention until she reached across the counter and grabbed his hand. Then he looked up.

Lavinía tilted her head to the side, saying what are you doing here? Did he give you a job? She looked around the shop. Not a bad gig.

Jaime shook his head and stacked the order forms into a neat pile, then slid them beneath the counter. Just watching the place for Señor Gutierrez. He's off doing deliveries or something. Not sure whether or not I have a job, but I think the guy could use a little help around here, so I'm going to hit him up and see if he'll let me wash the windows or something.

Lavinía nodded, looking around at the tables and coolers overflowing with flowers. Look, today at school I was thinking about what we could tell the Kings if you run into them. First I was going to introduce you as an old friend. But they might not buy that.

True.

Anyway, I thought we'd just wait a little longer. You know, no reason to make things more complicated than they have to be. I just figured you would eventually want to get out from behind those dumpsters. You can't stay there forever. You're too nice to be sleeping in an alley like some kinda bum.

They both laughed. Jaime shook his head and told her that mattress is probably the closest I'm going to get to sex around here anyway.

Eww. I'm probably one of the only girls here who hasn't slept on it— and no, Jaime, I'm not going to let you talk me into joining you behind McDonald's. That's, like, super trashy.

This was the first opportunity for Jaime to test the waters in this neighborhood. He wondered what Lavinía would think if he told her he was gay. He could pretend to be sad because she would never sleep with him, or he could take the plunge and let his secret out. He braced himself and said, Lavinía, don't get me wrong. I think you're cute. Truly. But if you slept next to me on that mattress, the only action you'd be getting would have to be from someone who wandered past. I'm not interested.

Not interested. In this? She smirked and turned around, poking her butt toward him and shaking it slowly in her tight jeans. She licked her finger and made a sizzling sound when she touched it to her thigh. Everybody wants a piece of this, baby. She giggled. I didn't mean to tease you.

Seriously. It's fine. I'm not interested in girls. Women. I . . . how can I say this?

So, you're gay? Like a *real* gay? Seriously, if I got naked, you wouldn't want to touch me? She leaned over the counter toward him. He didn't move. He didn't look down her shirt like every other guy she'd met. He held her gaze. Maybe he was telling the truth.

Yes. I'm a real gay. I don't like girls.

Lavinía leaned lower, her breasts almost touching the counter. She looked into Jaime's eyes and pulled her shirt down, dramatically, painfully slow. Jaime looked completely unimpressed.

That, said Lavinía, was one of the most amazing things I've ever seen. Guys practically break their necks to look at me. Sometimes I forget and I bend to pick something up. Next thing you know, people whistle or walk up behind me and grab my ass. I've even caught my teachers looking down my shirts, or up my skirt. It gets old, actually. I hate it.

I understand. Well, not that people look at me and want to have sex with me, but you know what I mean.

Yeah. She took a step back and looked at Jaime again, examining his features. His clothing. Looking for some sort of telltale sign that he was indeed gay. She squinted her eyes. Peered hard at his face. You really *are* gay. That's too much.

Yep. A real gay. Queer as a three-dollar bill, as my dad always said. Anyway, just thought you should know. I won't be one of the guys chasing you. But please keep it to yourself.

Well, I like you. You're pretty cool for a guy. Different, you know? Not like the ones around here. They're too macho. Always strutting and showing off. My two friends Rosa and Rosa love it though. They walk around here all the time and flirt with the guys. They're kind of slutty, but they're my friends, you know? I think both of them have even been on that mattress of yours.

That's nasty. Jaime pretended to throw up. They both laughed.

But if I *had* to pick one guy around here, it would probably be Ricardo. He was Felipe's best friend. Felipe was the one, though. He was so romantic. You could just see it in his eyes. Smart. Sexy. He had everything you could ask for in a man.

Jaime frowned. So why don't you ask him out?

Lavinía looked away, toward the window and the traffic outside. He's dead. Remember? He's the one I told you about the other day. Brothers killed him. I don't like talking about it. She walked to the front door, then turned back to Jaime. Anyway, your secret's safe with me. But whatever happens, we can't let the guys around here find out. It'll make your life hell. She waved and walked outside.

My life's already hell, Jaime thought.

As the days passed, Jaime fell into a routine. Each morning he shared a cigarette with Lavinía, who stopped by the dumpsters on her way to school, then he went to work for Rudolfo Gutierrez, arranging flowers, taking orders, stocking shipments. Lavinía stopped by after school to share another cigarette and they stepped behind the store to smoke while she filled Jaime in on all the latest gossip. In the evenings Señor Gutierrez invited him for dinner and then the two would talk late into the night about flowers and horticulture. Señor Gutierrez always offered Jaime a place to sleep, and for the first few days Jaime didn't accept, content to sleep between the McDonald's dumpsters on the mattress. Since the restaurant closed at ten, everyone usually cleared out by eleven and the alley was dead. And even when people did walk by, they couldn't see him unless they knew he was there. The fence on either side of the dumpsters saw to that. So he declined Señor Gutierrez's offer.

One of the main reasons Jaime hadn't stayed at Señor Gutierrez's was because he looked forward to his morning cigarette with Lavinía. He had always liked the smell of smoke. It was pungent, but something beneath it hinted at sweetness and mystery. He'd never smoked, though, before Lavinía. The pain of his first drag from her cigarette was almost unbearable. His lungs had heaved in rejection of the smoke. But Jaime had been patient and soon enough he was thoroughly enjoying each hit off of the daily cigarettes she brought for him. She taught him how to blow smoke rings and how to inhale through his nose. She taught him tricks with her lighter—how to throw a ball of butane fire, how to open bottles.

He told her about the offer Señor Gutierrez made to him—a place to stay and meals, plus a small weekly sum of a hundred dollars cash.

She suggested Jaime take him up on his offer. I mean, you haven't found anywhere else offering work *and* food, have you? He shook his head. You know, Gutierrez is quiet, keeps to himself. I've heard my mom talk about how lonely he is. I think you could both use the company. You don't expect to stay here on this mattress forever, do you?

He shook his head again, considering her point. She's right. I am alone. I'm just as lonely as the old man. He'd gotten comfortable around the harmless Señor Gutierrez. But there was something else. Something in the way the old man's fingers sometimes probed at the soft flesh sagging below his left eye. Whenever he did this, his eyes would widen, as if he were witnessing some horrifying scene.

That's it, Jaime thought. He's got some dark secret too. Something he's running from. What's he scared of?

Jaime had been so involved with his plan for revenge that he'd failed to notice the man with whom he spent most of his days was harboring deep pain too. Maybe it wasn't such a bad idea to take him up on his offer. He decided to accept.

—

Who the fuck is this guy? Peanut glared at Jaime with obvious distrust. Jaime shifted his stance a little, trying not to look too stiff. He hoped he didn't look too soft, but he also didn't want to appear confrontational. Maybe this wasn't a good idea.

I told you already. This is Gutierrez's nephew up from Sierra Vista. He's gonna be staying around here for a while, and I thought you guys might like to meet.

Who you down with? What's your set?

Set? What do you mean?

Your clica. Your homies. Your fuckin posse, man. You in a gang or what?

No. That's not really my thing. Besides, there aren't really any gangs in Sierra Vista.

Listen homes, there are gangs everywhere. You got that? Here, we ride with the Kings. Latin Kings, por vida. Just so you know.

I've heard. I can respect that.

Peanut looked over at Lavinía and gave her a hard stare. He waited a few moments, letting the tension linger in the air, savoring the look on

Jaime's face. That's cool, man. You're cool. Long as you're not with some other clique we got no problems with you, homes.

Lavinía breathed deeply and squeezed Jaime's hand. Then she looked at the Kings sitting on the couches and chairs. The room was thick with pot smoke and the electronic music of Nintendo. Ricardo and Gordo were playing some sort of ninja fighting game.

Anyway, guys, I just wanted to bring him by to meet you, so that way if you see him around, you'll know who he is.

Jaime resisted the urge to blurt out I'M GAY TOO. LET'S JUST GET IT OVER WITH. Instead he looked around and said this is a pretty nice setup you've got here, trying to appear comfortable.

Peanut invited them to stay a few, have a couple tokes with us, cocking his head toward the loveseat a few feet away. They sat down and Peanut passed Jaime a joint, just to make sure he wasn't a cop or anything. Jaime took a hit, coughed, took another, then passed it to Lavinía. She took a tiny hit and passed it back to Peanut. Then she started telling him about some shit that went down at school between Rosa and that bitch Suzy and the joint kept being passed, seeming to Jaime like it went on forever. It never got any smaller. And he wondered how high he was going to get and whether or not he'd say something stupid and couldn't really tell how long he'd been sitting there, zoning out, listening to the Nintendo, watching as they rolled another joint, and he realized he hadn't ever really been high before, uncertain what to expect, and he started giggling a little, man, this shit's pretty good, feeling cotton in his brain, and Lavinía grabbed his arm and shot him a look that said get it under control, which was all she needed to do. He snapped out of it and found his way out of the fog.

Lavinía told Peanut they had to go and pulled Jaime to his feet before he got too high and maybe let something slip that made him seem gay. Jaime started to follow her out but suddenly stopped and faced Peanut. An awkward silence fell over the room. The Nintendo made the only sound. Lavinía pulled lightly on Jaime's shirtsleeve. Look, Jaime finally asked Peanut. Can we talk out back or something?

The other guys in the room looked at Jaime, a little more critical than before, now that he was trying to get himself alone with one of their own.

After all, since the only thing they had to go on that this kid was all right was Lavinía's word, it struck them as wrong that Jaime would just walk through the door and then demand an audience with a King.

Jaime considered retracting his question. He hadn't realized it would be such a strange request. But it was now or never. It wasn't like he was just going to walk into their place uninvited someday and ask to speak with Peanut again. No, it was best to try to get it out of the way, since Lavinía was here with him and he getting a pass. So he rephrased the question. Look, I'm not trying to interrupt or anything. I just wanted to ask a quick favor. But if you don't have the time, it's cool.

Peanut gestured with his head toward the back of the room, where a doorway led outside to the carport. He rose from his seat and Jaime followed, trying to ignore the disapproving glances from the others in the room.

Standing outside, Peanut lit a cigarette and turned to Jaime. He peered at Jaime through the cloud of smoke that surrounded his head, waiting until he'd finished half the cigarette before he spoke. So what do you want? You trying to get in with us or something, cause it's not that simple, man. You can't just appear from nowhere, smoke a little weed, and think we're gonna let you in, no questions asked. This is some orga-nized shit we got going on here, with connections in most of the big cities in the southwest and even up in Chi-town. If that's your question, you can forget about it.

That's not what I was going to ask. Jaime stood his ground, his gaze meeting Peanut's. What I was going to ask might be out of place, so don't take offense.

Peanut raised his eyebrows, blew the ash off the cherry of his ciga-rette, and nodded for Jaime to proceed.

It's like this, man, what I left behind in Sierra Vista was some seri-ous shit. Jaime tried to match the way these machos talked. I can't get too deep into the story, so let's just say that some dudes back in Vista took out my boy. Me and this guy were like this—he crossed his index and middle finger together—we knew each other for years. Hell, we grew up together. Same schools. Same church. Our moms were tight. The whole thing. Anyway, these guys, well, I guess you could say they're a gang, sort of. But not like you guys here, with the organization and network. This was just a pack of dudes who were out fuckin around one night and decided to off somebody for the fuck of it. Just for the fuck of it. Not over turf, not over bitches or drugs. They just trapped my boy one night and took his ass out. The simple answer is that I want revenge. I need it. I'm sure you've had that happen around here. Someone takes out one of your own and you have to retaliate, right?

Peanut didn't say a word. He smoked and blew on his cigarette. His eyes remained locked to Jaime's, weighing the truth of his claim. Maybe this guy is just tryin to blow smoke up my ass, tryin to seem all tough and shit when he's really just testing out how we take care of our own. He might even be from a gang, though his threads are kind of weird. Nothing like the dudes wear around here.

Murmurings from inside the house distracted Jaime, hurrying him to get to the point before he lost Peanut's attention for good.

I'll just be up front with you. I need to get my hands on a weapon. A gun. A blade. Anything. It's just that I can't keep sittin here and let-tin those assholes get away with takin out my boy like that. I don't know anybody here. Only Lavinía, and we just met through Gutierrez. I'm workin now, helpin out at his shop and shit. So I can come up with the money. I just need to get back at these guys. These fuckin faggots. It stung him to say those words. But he knew he'd made the right decision when Peanut's eyes squinted. Jaime held his gaze, then moved a step closer. So, can you help me or not?

I'll see what I can do. Just watch your ass around here. Flipping his cigarette into the driveway, Peanut turned his back on Jaime and retreated to the house, slamming the screen door in Jaime's face.

Dinners at Rudolfo Gutierrez's house went something like this: Jaime set the table for two while Rudolfo whistled over the stove in the kitchen. When the food was finally set out and they both took their seats, Rudolfo asked little probing questions. After three months of dinners together, he'd managed to find out Jaime's reasons for appear-ing in the shop one afternoon with a backpack full of his belongings. Jaime had eyes that reminded Rudolfo of a one-way mirror. Rudolfo was certain something hid on the other side, just beyond reach, pictures or shadows or something to explain the premature wrinkles around the boy's eyes.

By telling Jaime little bits and pieces of his own past, Rudolfo managed to extract parts of Jaime's story, and what he heard was enough to make him want to grab the boy and hold him close to his chest. To rub his hair and rock him in his lap, telling him the world is indeed a harsh place, but you must not let it get the best of you. You must learn to forgive yourself. And you must learn, especially, to forgive those who have harmed you.

He never touched the boy, but he did try to teach him forgiveness. He told Jaime how he had learned to forgive himself for losing his son and his wife, which was a lie. But each time he tried to help lift some of the burden from Jaime's shoulders, Jaime cut him off. He simply stopped listening and hunched over closer to his plate, shoving the food into his mouth. This always made Rudolfo feel as if he'd failed miserably, and he wondered if he could help the boy at all. Maybe Jaime was beyond help. He feared what the boy would do, because on the night Jaime revealed his friend's murder, his eyes clouded over. His entire face turned red, the veins on his forehead crisscrossing and bulging. He clenched his jaw together and kept mumbling, those fuckers, those fuckers, they'll pay, and Rudolfo Gutierrez shook his head. No amount of coaxing or explaining was going to change the mind of this young man, who was harboring enough hatred in him to keep him fighting day after day.

Rudolfo eventually let the subject drop and tried to lighten the mood by telling jokes he remembered from his school days. Or he would tell Jaime funny stories about the people in the neighborhood. Such as the time he told about the little Nuñez boy who, one morning years ago on his paper route, had fallen over into a row of cactus and had to stay home from school while his brothers and mother picked each individual needle out of his flesh. Jaime liked that one. Rudolfo laughed heartily when he told these stories, but after the dishes were cleared and cleaned, he shuffled off to his bedroom where he threw himself onto his bed, buried his face in his pillow, and wept until he fell into a fitful and bitter sleep.

This was how the dinners always went, so it was no surprise when Jaime revealed one night that he had finally worked out a way to avenge Sammy's death. Rudolfo listened in horror as Jaime described his plan to get a ride back to Sierra Vista, where he would corner the murderers one at a time and subject them to the worst tortures he could imagine. He might superglue their mouths shut, then watch as they suffocated themselves with panicked breathing when he glued one of their nostrils shut and left a hole in the other one the size of a pinhead. It's enough to breathe if they're calm, but they'll be too freaked. They'll drown themselves.

Rudolfo tried to talk the boy into scrapping his plans, but knew deep down he still wanted to walk into the army recruitment center downtown and line the recruiters up and shoot them one by one for convincing his son the army was not only a great way to build a future but also a completely safe venture. They had promised Alberto no harm would come to him. All he had to do was enlist and serve four years, and then Uncle Sam would cut him a check. Alberto's eyes had lit up, overwhelmed by the glory of being able to serve his country. When they slid the papers across the desk for him to sign, Alberto had barely been able to hold the pen to the page he shook so much.

If he could go back to that day at the office, Rudolfo Gutierrez would grab the papers up when they slid them under his son's nose and tear them to shreds and shove them down the throats of those animals. How could he really tell Jaime to forgive the sick kids who had beaten his friend to death with their bare fists and chains and rocks? If given the chance, Rudolfo knew he would not hesitate to grab each recruiter by the throat and fling him down on the floor and put his knee to the bastard's neck and flog his head good until the man promised to never take another son from his mother and send him out, scared and ignorant, into a wild jungle halfway across the world to be burned alive by napalm and sent home a twisted and unrecognizable corpse with his weapon welded to his hand and his dogtags melted into his chest.

So he listened to Jaime's plan and knew there was nothing he could say to change the boy's mind. Instead, he merely picked up Jaime's plate and told him to get some sleep, tomorrow is going to be a busy day. But

Jaime didn't get up and go to bed, instead he stared at the spot where his plate had been moments before and clenched his jaw and his fists, his whole body trembling.

More than anything, Rudolfo wanted to persuade him to reconsider. He worried the boy might get hurt. And he couldn't help wondering what all this rage might do to the kid. *What if he tries to do something to me? I'm too weak to defend myself. I don't own any weapons.* But he went to bed anyway, resolving to lock his door at nights from now on. Just in case. Just in case Jaime flipped out one night and turned into a monster.

But in the morning, the boy was a different person.

After his bath Rudolfo left the bathroom and wandered out to the dining room, where Jaime had a plate of chorizo and a warm stack of tortillas steaming on the table for him.

Jaime sat down, looking refreshed, as if he had no worries other than how to help Rudolfo meet the recent demand for wild orchids at the shop. Jaime was full of smiles, cracking jokes and ribbing Rudolfo about being old and living alone. *How in the name of sweet baby Jesus did you ever get by before I got here?*

Rudolfo offered to take Jaime to see a bullfight in Agua Prieta, to drink his first beer in the blistering heat while watching the splendor of the matadors. He told Jaime *if you just come, if you just get out of here for a while, then maybe you will see things differently.* Jaime grunted and said *where would you stash your oxygen, viejo? What if the bull ran up in the stands and punctured your tank, then where would you be?* And they shared a good laugh while they cleared the dishes and readied themselves for opening the shop.

If he caught Jaime spending more time in a certain portion of the store, he said *why don't you see if you can do something with those flowers? Make some sort of arrangement to put in the window.* Sometimes the boy listened, and sometimes he ignored him and went right on examining the flowers, as if memorizing every detail.

Though Rudolfo knew he had little time left, he decided only to wait. Wait, even if it gets to be too much, wait and let the boy have his pain. And his revenge.

Jaime flipped the switchblade open and pressed it closed. Señor Gutierrez slept in the next room, snoring and coughing at intervals through the night. For Jaime, the sound was a bitter one. Here was a man who had a good heart, and had been punished for trying to take care of his family. This wouldn't have bothered Jaime, except that he had seen the way Señor Gutierrez's loss tormented him. He had woken up to the old man's moans and screams on several occasions, frequently enough to know that Señor Gutierrez often relived burying his son and his wife side by side in Holy Hope Cemetery.

Why is it, he thought, that there are so many horrible parents out there, like my father, who never get their children taken from them? Is there really some sort of reverse justice in the universe that allows the good people to suffer?

Jaime flipped the switchblade open again and made slashes at the air. He was in good with the Kings now, and he enjoyed hanging out with Güero and Peanut and the Nuñez brothers. They treated him with respect. Almost as if he had already proven his street credibility. But he didn't have the teardrop tattoo on his face, nor did he have the crown tattoo. No, to them, Jaime had the look of a disturbed genius. A powerful glare set into a pleasant face. He looked kind and dangerous at the same time.

Not that they considered him violent. In fact, Güero and the Nuñez brothers were equally surprised when Jaime asked them if they could get him a switchblade or a gun.

A switchblade? they asked. The fuck you want a switchblade for? Someone's givin you trouble?

Nah, just for protection, you know. In case. Oddly, the guys all felt uncomfortable giving Jaime a weapon. Like they were being asked to teach their mothers how to kill a man. It just seemed wrong. But when Peanut told them why he really wanted a weapon, they understood and gave him a switchblade and taught him how to use it, and he practiced every night, pulling it out of his back pocket and pressing the button while stabbing at an imaginary target. He practiced grabbing someone from behind and slitting his throat so fast the victim wouldn't have time to react. He mastered several swift, fluid movements so that when the opportunity for revenge arose, he would be able to take out an enemy regardless of the circumstances.

$$\smile$$

When Jaime didn't return home for dinner at his usual time, Rudolfo Gutierrez knew he had finally decided to go through with his plan. The boy can only take so much, he thought. In fact, he had watched the inner struggle take place before his eyes when each night Jaime fought the urge to lash out with all the anger built up inside him. Every morning the boy woke with a fresh outlook on life, as if he could stave off his demons all day long, but as soon as it got dark, they had free reign to taunt him and remind him of his failure to pay back Sammy's killers. Each day it seemed as if a new person took over Jaime's body. Dark circles formed beneath his eyes and the bright, twinkling happiness permeating Jaime's entire face gradually gave way to a somber, clouded, slumping cluster of features. Each morning Jaime'd have breakfast ready, and by the time Rudolfo finished his meal and put on his windbreaker, the boy would be halfway out the front door, joking and laughing the entire walk to the flower shop about how he couldn't believe he had slept on that nasty mattress behind McDonald's. It always made Rudolfo think maybe the boy will pull out of it yet. He was so convinced with his self-deception that when Jaime didn't come home for dinner, he really thought maybe he's down at the park, hanging out by the pond, but he knew he was wrong because no matter what the boy was doing, he always made it home to set the table for whatever meal Rudolfo had cooked.

Sitting in front of a steaming plate of albóndigas, poking at the meatballs with his fork, Rudolfo waited for Jaime to come bursting through the door full of apologies for his tardiness. He made elaborate excuses for the boy, thinking of all the possible alibis, places a teenaged boy could go, inventing friends' houses he could be staying at, until the sun slowly faded out in the west and a thick layer of grease formed on the surface of his uneaten dinner, and Rudolfo remained seated, ignoring the long shadows coming through the picture window and over his shoulder. The knot of worry in his stomach grew into a ball of paranoia. The boy's actually going to go through with it. He was scared and proud of Jaime at the same time—like he had been training the kid for the big game and now he would get to watch with pride as the kid scored a winning touchdown.

But this was no game. He knew it. It's no game when you want something as bad as that kid does. I guess all I can do is sit here and wait.

———

Each time Jaime's nerves threatened to get the best of him, all he had to do was flip his switchblade open, rub the sharp metal edge with his thumb, and press the blade back into the handle. He had done this several hundred times by the time they turned onto Charleston Road, heading for the San Pedro River, the streets of Tucson almost two hours behind them. Meanwhile, Güero and his friends ignored Jaime's nervousness, bobbing their heads to the radio instead.

Surely one of them will be there, thought Jaime. When they had driven down the main drag in Sierra Vista, the road had been relatively quiet. Of course, that doesn't mean they're not out at the river. They're always at the river banging some girl or smoking weed. At least, that's what they boasted about each day in gym class when they spoke loud enough for everyone in the locker room to hear, trying to make the others jealous. Not that anyone cared. But there were only so many places for people to go in this town, and if they had the urge for some ass or some drugs, they took it out to the river because no one ever drove by during the night, since the only thing out in that direction was Tombstone, and who cares about old dead cowboys?

Jaime flipped the blade out again and told Güero to pull over. Ditch the car for now, he said. We'll come back for it.

They left the car hidden behind a cluster of paloverde trees, not particularly worried because Jaime assured them no one ever drove down this road. Maybe two cars a night. They walked in silence, following Jaime as he led the way through the grasping limbs of trees. With each step closer to the river, Güero and his friends felt the adrenaline beginning to pump through their veins. It was a familiar feeling for all of them, the main ingredient for survival on the streets. Always be prepared.

Jaime, on the other hand, was practically bouncing with energy. He was so close, just a few hundred feet from facing the guys who killed

Sammy. The quiet atmosphere of the desert made the whole scenario seem unreal. But this *is* real, Jaime reminded himself. He wanted to see the fear in the eyes of his victims and relish the moment. He'd imagined this scenario hundreds of times, dreamed about it even more, and yet he had no idea how it was going to play out. Would he actually kill one of them? Might they actually kill him?

But those questions only lasted for a moment, quickly replaced by the reassurance he had received from Güero when the two of them sat in Güero's garage and Jaime explained his plan—the route from Tucson to Sierra Vista, the other two Kings they might take with them, whose car they should use, what they should do if they were outnumbered. Jaime had considered all of it, each possible obstacle weighed, even the possibility of getting caught. For him, it was worth every risk. He'd rather be sitting in a jail cell somewhere sleeping peacefully than walking the streets knowing he had let Sammy's killers back him down. And luckily Güero had agreed.

Güero had picked the two people closest to him, Chuy and Peanut, who went on missions without asking questions. They knew if Güero was willing to risk it, then it was something that had to be done.

And now they stood at the bank of the parched San Pedro River. Looking down, Jaime could see that it was dried up except for a thin ribbon of water perhaps six inches across. He squatted on the edge, holding on to the trunk of a tree so he could lean over and gauge the distance of the jump. The riverbed was littered with shattered beer bottles and torn condoms and the occasional shred of material caught on a cactus or some brush. Jumping down into the river, Jaime motioned for the others to follow him to the cover of the bridge. They waited for a moment, letting their eyes adjust to the shadows.

There it is guys, Jaime pointed. That's one of their trucks. Güero and his friends looked and made out a vague outline of a truck idling in the darkness.

You sure you ready for this? Güero asked, remembering the terror he had felt the first time he went into battle, at the age of fourteen. He had ridden in the backseat of the Caprice Classic, slouching down with three other Kings as they drove onto South 6th Avenue to rough up the black kids who were trying to come into the neighborhood and steal their women. It had been a long and terrifying drive across the city while the wind whipped through the car and Güero trembled, fearing bullets slicing through the side of the car at any moment. When they pulled into the parking lot of the shopping center, time became a blur of bodies jumping out of the back and running toward a group of cars where a bunch of black guys stood around passing joints and drinking forties. Güero was a little slower than the rest, running a few feet behind Cheeseburger and his brother when they leaped into the air, slicing at whatever came into contact with their knives. They took the black guys by surprise, and there were more Kings running to back them up, but in those first moments, when Güero felt his blade sink into the soft flesh of a crouching black kid's neck, he felt a rush of relief. He knew it would be okay. Knew these niggers would be the ones who would pay tonight, not them. And when it was all over, when all the black guys were lying in puddles of blood or crumpled on the roofs of their cars or rolling around in agony clutching whatever parts of their bodies they wanted most to protect from the beatdown, Güero knew this was what it was all about. Protecting our vatos and our ladies. It was the reason they were crouched beside the San Pedro River a few miles from Sierra Vista, peeking through the shadows of the bridge at the outline of a truck that held Jaime's enemies. The boys who had taken out Sammy.

So Güero wanted to make sure Jaime was ready, because once they stepped onto the other bank of the San Pedro, it would be too late to stop, and it would be us or them.

Jaime thought for a moment, flicking the blade in and out, feeling the sweat run down his back. Yeah, it's them. It's them who aren't ready. And he stood up slowly, straightening his back, and took his first step toward the other side of the river.

Jaime tuned in to his surroundings. He felt each pebble scrape beneath his foot, heard coyotes howling somewhere in the mountains, watched the moon cast shadows in front of him. He flipped the blade of his knife out over and over, holding it at his side, shuffling along the riverbed toward the waiting truck. They reached the other side and scrambled over the edge of the bank, clutching at roots and rocks and whatever else could help them get over the top of the river.

The smell of truck exhaust lingered close to the ground where Jaime pulled his body over the side of the riverbank. The others followed, scrambling up the riverbed, then standing to brush themselves off. The truck was only a few feet off. Luckily, it faced away from them, so they crept over to the back of it on their hands and knees. Güero whispered a three-count and they all ran toward the cab, racing to get to the truck before the passengers inside noticed they were being attacked. Güero reached the passenger door first and ripped it open, pulling on a young man wearing a baseball cap. The kid yelped in fear, half choking on the seatbelt caught around his neck. Is this one, Güero shouted, and Jaime, not entirely sure yet, said yes, that's one of the fuckers, and he watched as Güero beat the bastard over the head while he pulled him loose from the seatbelt and threw him to the ground. Chuy and Peanut were yelling and cursing, trying to get the driver's door open. The driver threw it into gear and peeled out of the gravel parking lot, the passenger door swinging wildly as the truck turned onto the road.

FUCK, YOU LET ONE OF THEM GET AWAY screamed Güero. Jaime didn't care. He didn't want to waste time so he grabbed the boy squirming beneath Güero's knee and dragged him to his feet. Yeah, you are one of them, aren't you? You took Sammy and beat the shit out of him behind Buena, and the boy shook his head, tears dropping onto the front of his shirt. Who . . . no, I didn't do anything . . . I'm sorry, stammering to save his life, but only making things worse because Jaime was running on nothing but nerves. Güero punched the terrified guy in the breadbasket and said you fucked with the wrong vato, homie. I heard you don't like us wetback, river-hopping Mexicans. The boy shook his head hard enough for his neck to pop. Jaime said let's get him away from here before his friend comes back. It took all four of them to drag the boy down into the river, his terror giving him a surge of strength.

They dragged him through the riverbed and walked east to a saguaro standing amid a cluster of yucca and ocotillo plants. Strap his ass to this thing, Güero told the other Kings, ignoring the cries of their victim.

Güero punched him in the Adam's apple so he couldn't speak, left him gasping for air and unable to cry out as the needles of the cactus pierced his clothing, the barb on each needle burrowing beneath his skin and taking hold of muscles and tendons as his captors pressed him harder into the cactus. They tied rope around his wrists and pulled his hands behind him, around the trunk of the saguaro in a way that seemed impossible, felt impossible, too, when his arms popped from their sockets.

Look at me, Jaime said, pressing the guy's head into the cactus, the needles breaking off inside his scalp. I said look at me, you fuckin piece of shit. But the boy couldn't focus on Jaime. His body twitched, trying to fight against the sting of the needles.

Jaime pulled out the switchblade. He and his victim watched mesmerized as it quivered for a moment in Jaime's grasp and then, pulling his arm along with it, dove at the midsection of the young man lashed to the saguaro cactus, his back bleeding from countless needle punctures. The knife struck again and again. It slid through the flesh of Jaime's victim, a boy who had, only moments before, been planning out his future with his friend in between drags on a joint. Got accepted to U of A, you know, the land of milk and honeys. Girls everywhere—from California to Florida—ripe for the taking. Sunshine sweeties. Girls with real tits and trimmed bush and everything we ever dreamed about. Bitches outnumber the guys three to one. Slapping hands, passing the joint. Not thinking of Sammy's death. That was old shit now. No one had asked any questions. They never mentioned it. His thoughts were on all the women in the world and all the fucking and the booze and the romps through the desert, and mountains, and swimming naked in Sabino Canyon. He thought about everything except the possibility of someone actually coming back to avenge the death of that mousy little queer, Sammy. He paid no attention to the cactus surrounding him, never thinking that in a few moments he'd be tied to one of them, its needles tearing into him, plucking at every tissue of his body, his back an infinite cluster of pain, burning and pricking, but worse, burrowing still farther into his body, taking root, sucking out his moisture, his life. But that was only half of it. He watched Jaime flip the blade but could not comprehend the click of the switch and the metal, a menacing silver smile, grinning at him and charging toward his stomach. And when it finally and effortlessly pierced his stomach, sliding through skin and muscle, the boy realized he no longer felt the pain in his back. And then the knife was gone, and the pain in his back returned. Then the knife returned, confusing the boy, whose body was a swirling mass of nerves screaming at his brain, his mind unable to process the pain, growing sluggish, watching Jaime who stood in front of him screaming, slobbering, stabbing. He wanted to lay his head back and look away. To close his eyes and die, but he could only watch the knife come at him again and again. Could only wonder how long it was going to last. Wanted to pray, but knew there was no point.

The knife was alive with fury. Jaime didn't want it to stop, but was still surprised by how it kept going. Jumping at the body in front of him. Hungry for blood, searching it out like one of those sticks for finding water buried in the ground. His arm was sore from stabbing over and over, from hammering away at the boy's stomach like a punching bag. The kid was actually deflating before his eyes. He's fucking watching the whole thing. Just watching it. He isn't crying or anything. Like he knew I was coming. Like he'd been waiting for me the whole time. Jaime watched the knife continue to punch holes in the shirt and come away with blood on it. He kept stabbing while he looked around at the other guys. They don't want me to stop either. They can't make me stop and they know it. They can't stop the blade because it needs to be fed. He looked to them and then back to the knife. So many holes. So much blood, it was hard to imagine what was holding his victim's entrails in his torso. Jaime's hand was covered in blood. His sleeve was saturated from the elbow down, clinging to his arm.

A thousand holes later, Jaime looked up from his hand and saw Sammy's killer in front of him. Their eyes met and the knife stopped, buried in the stomach of the killer tied to his green prickly cross. Jaime felt the kid's ragged breathing against his knuckles. He leaned forward, the knife cold in his fist, and laid his head on the shoulder of the dying teenager, then vomited down his back with so much ferocity he felt some of it splash off the cactus and splatter his face. He closed his eyes and saw Sammy smiling and hugging himself as he walked down Jaime's driveway in the middle of the night, and then he retraced his journey to Tucson, cactus and brush and tumbleweed and dust devils and cars and highways slicing through the dusty skin of the desert, and up to the home of Señor Gutierrez and into the shadowy dining room where the old man sat in silence, staring at the wall, blinking tears out of his eyes and stirring his cold and pasty plate of albóndigas, waiting for Jaime to walk through the door and apologize for being late, to tell him he'd been held up over at a friend's house or gotten lost in some unfamiliar part of the city so he could pat Jaime's hand and say everything's fine, everything's fine.

Everything is fine, thought Jaime. Finally. I finally got one of them, and now the others will know I'm coming. They'll look over their shoulders now, worried for their lives. The warm, bloody stomach in front of him finally stopped moving, and Jaime opened his eyes and backed away from the slumping lifeless body, unaware he had been grasping the knife the entire time his body was pressed against his enemy, until he let go of the handle and looked at his hand, then to the three men standing around him. He turned and walked back to the car.

The lights were off in Señor Gutierrez's house when Güero dropped Jaime off in front. Jaime stood and watched the car drive away, then turned and walked through the yard and up to the door, where he paused and looked at his hands. They were shaking. But he wasn't scared like he thought he would be. Instead, he felt like he had grown a foot taller in the two hours it took them to drive back to Tucson. He was proud he had finally done it. Made a plan and stuck with it, that's what I did. But there was something else present now. Not quite disappointment or defeat. It felt like being rescued from drowning in the ocean only to be pulled to the shore and deserted with your lungs still full of water.

It wasn't shame. He knew he should be ashamed, but did not care. This was his own brand of justice, an old-fashioned type that used to rule these lands. It was desert justice. So, no, he wasn't ashamed.

However, the burden of vengeance he had been carrying had not lifted. He wanted a second opinion. He needed to tell Señor Gutierrez.

He turned the doorknob carefully, not wanting to disturb the old man, whom he figured would be asleep this late at night, probably thrashing around in his bed. But he was sitting at the dinner table, his hands on either side of his plate. A pot of albóndigas sat in the middle of the table, and there was an empty plate where Jaime should have been. Rudolfo did not turn to look at him, did not even seem to notice Jaime was late. He acted like he had only just sat down to dinner a few seconds before Jaime had come into the house.

I did it, Jaime said. He blurted out the news as if he was simply stating the time. He sat across from Rudolfo, looked at the old man, and listened to his oxygen tank clicking. Me and some of the guys went down and paid a visit to Sierra Vista. Jaime was getting excited.

Rudolfo did not speak. He only listened and, with every word, felt a flaming sphere wedge itself in the back of his throat. His eye started throbbing again.

Now they know I'm not playing. When they find that prick in the river they won't get a decent night's sleep again. They'll only come out in the daytime.

The eye was really going now. And Jaime was jabbering, playing with his spoon, twirling it between his fingers. Yeah, they'll look over their shoulders constantly. Oh, when they're together, they'll pretend it doesn't bother them. Like his death was an accident. A fluke. But they'll wonder who's next and that's perfect. Sammy's laughing his ass off. I just know it.

Rudolfo pushed his chair back, grabbing at his eye, this goddam twitching is too much. The entire time Jaime was telling him how the night had gone—how they had taken the fuckers by surprise and managed to take one of them out, as if the boy they had just murdered was an unwanted kitten they dumped somewhere on the outskirts of town—the pulsing beneath his eye had grown worse. He was certain Jaime could see it, but the kid was still too fired up because he rambled on and on about how sweet it was to see the look on that fucker's face when he realized—when he finally *knew*—he was going to die.

He didn't plead, Jaime said, he only closed his eyes and let the knife come to him.

The kid's done something I never had the nerve to do. He's finally done it. Got back at those sonsabitches—

You should've seen this guy, roped to a cactus, and he *knew* he'd
fucked up—

Rudolfo's eye pulsed along with the inflections in Jaime's speech,
getting faster, more excited, beating inside his eye socket like a kick
drum. It was worse than maddening, it was terrifying. This is it, Rudolfo
thought. If I don't put a stop to this once and for all—

—saw he was outnumbered and probably shit his pants—

—he can't see it. How can he not see?—

—Güero and his boys fucked him up a bit before I could—

Rudolfo pushed his chair back from the table. He stumbled to the
bathroom in the middle of Jaime talking. Then Jaime was yelling.

BLOOD ALL OVER—WE GOT HIM.

Jaime waved his blood-soaked sleeve around like a victory banner.
Rudolfo slammed the bathroom door behind him. His eye slowed. Stay
calm. Cold water on the face will take care of it. Use a washcloth.

Jaime stood at the bathroom door knocking and asking, hesitantly,
Señor Gutierrez, are you okay? Inside, Rudolfo was desperate, haunted
by so many things now he had to confide in someone or he knew he'd
go crazy, so he asked Jaime to clear dinner and set the table for tea.

When he emerged from the bathroom, Rudolfo told Jaime to have
a seat. Dinner doesn't matter right now, only listen. Jaime looked at him
with concern but kept silent. Rudolfo asked him look at my eye, do you
see anything funny? and Jaime peered closely and said yeah, I see a pulse
but isn't that normal? which bothered Rudolfo because he prayed, oh he
prayed he was only imagining it. Jaime was worried, unsure of what was
the big deal about the old man's eye. Rudolfo told Jaime about losing his
wife and son and how it haunted him and the smell and how he had lied
to Jaime all along. He wanted revenge too.

He fidgeted with his cup of tea, turning it around by the handle and
picking it up to play with the ring it left on the table, anything to keep
his eyes from meeting Jaime's. The more he thought about it, the worse
it became. He fingered the bag beneath his left eye, pinching it softly,
then grabbing it and probing it until he felt a pea-sized lump and his
eyes grew wide in terror. The more he played with the lump, the more
it grew, until it felt the size of a walnut. Unable to bear it anymore, he

ran back into the bathroom, slamming the door and flipping on the light switch. He brought his eye up to the mirror and examined it closely and knew that whatever it was in his eye, he was sick of it. So he started rubbing it hard, faster and faster, and poking at it. He felt the pulse building as if his heart lay not in his chest but beneath his left eye, and he fumbled around in his medicine cabinet looking for anything he could use to relieve the discomfort. His eyes rested on a pair of tweezers and he grabbed them and began pinching the lump and moving it around beneath his skin, and though he was repulsed he was certainly more annoyed, so he pressed the sharp-pointed tips of the tweezers hard against his flesh until they pierced the surface. He opened them, widening the gap that streamed blood down his cheek—his pent-up tears and guilt and loneliness all in one. Rudolfo pulled at the mass, muscles ripping and veins disconnecting, yet through all the pain he felt cleansed and relieved as he stared into the hole beneath his eye and the pink and purple tissue between his tweezers and brought it to his nose and smelled it and even touched it to the tip of his tongue in an effort to determine its origin, but when it touched his tongue he thought his heart would burst from the pain, and he cried out. A thunderous river of red poured from the wound in his face, cascading against the rim of the gouge beneath his eye, a clumpy fluid seeping between his lips, the tinny sap of blood creeping into his mouth as it rushed past, down his chin, streaming along the creases in his face, which seemed as if they had undergone years of construction for this moment when Señor Rudolfo Gutierrez opened his dam and let the wrinkles carry the swell of liquid along the arroyos of his face, each line chiseled into place by the years he carried like a pack mule, cowering a bit more each day in the shadow of his torment, waiting for the opportunity to finally be allowed to lay down his load, his throbbing and twitching anguish pinched between the arms of the tweezers and soon half his face was painted with blood, and he banged his head against the mirror and wept and moaned and held the mass of flesh he had torn from beneath his eye—it had finally stopped twitching, it had finally stopped—and then he laughed and laughed and laughed, even when Jaime kicked in the door and stood staring at him, his face full of disgust and horror and his skin becoming pale as he drew near to Rudolfo to lift him onto the toilet seat while the old man laughed and laughed and laughed and held out his hand and showed the boy the source of his torture and then terror returned to his face when he took a deep breath so he could continue his laughing and he smelled his son's burning feet again, the feet again, AGAIN, as the twitching returned worse than ever.

Rudolfo slumped over and fell into Jaime's arms. Jaime reached into the tub with one arm and rinsed a washcloth with warm water. He tried to stop the bleeding beneath Rudolfo's eye, but realized he needed more than a washcloth to wipe up the mess. He grabbed the first thing he could find—an old sock lying in the corner—and rolled it up into a tight ball and forced the sock into the cave on the left side of Señor Gutierrez's face, tying a towel around it as fast as he could.

He dragged the old man to his room and placed him on the bed, then climbed on top of him until he quit flailing. Señor Gutierrez's body trembled and convulsed and then he lay silent. Unconscious.

After he had tied Señor Gutierrez to the bed with spare sheets, Jaime scoured the house for every flower he could find—orchids and xenias and red anthurium and protea. He arranged them carefully throughout the room—on the bed, the nightstand, the floor. He even held some in his arms while he sat at the foot of the bed and watched the man stricken with terror and insanity, weak from the years of grief and anguish. The house was silent except the whoosh-click of Señor Gutierrez's oxygen tank pumping beside his bed. Whoosh-click—I wonder—whoosh-click—if—whoosh-click. He reached toward the old man's face, feeling for the tube beneath the bloody towel and tracing it up to Señor Gutierrez's nose. He pinched the tube lightly and listened—pfft-click—but no breath—pfft-click. He let go and Señor Gutierrez struggled to breathe, but didn't put up much of a fight. Jaime waited a minute, thinking about Gutierrez and how kind he'd been to him.

Me. A complete stranger on the run. I needed a place to hide and lick my wounds, and this man—with wounds of his own—opened his home to me. His excitement from before was completely forgotten in light of Señor Gutierrez's pathetic, collapsed body.

Jaime reached for the tube again, knowing the man in front of him was still smelling his son's feet, and he pinched and held it a little longer and—pfft-click pfft-click pfft-click—he let go and, for a long time, watched the old man struggling for breath. He gathered all the flowers in the whole room, pulling them from their pots and vases and baskets, and laid them on Rudolfo's chest and face. He searched beneath the flowers and the bloody towel for the oxygen hose and—pfft-click pfft-click pfft-click—did not let go—pfft-click pfft-click pfffffffffffffft-click click click. Click. Click. Click. Finally the old man's breathing stopped, and Jaime hoped more than anything in the world that the last smell Señor Rudolfo Gutierrez smelled was the flowers.

PEANUT

 PEANUT SMELLED HIS FATHER'S WORKBOOT WHEN IT landed by his nose. But he ignored it. It was a smell he was used to because every morning his father did the same thing. He stepped between his children sleeping in a row, tastefully separated by two-foot intervals, on the living room floor of their one-bedroom house.

His father never turned on the lights in the morning. He didn't need to. He knew the spots where each of his children slept and had memorized their patterns of sleep—Yolanda on her side; Gordo on his back, legs splayed; Carlos on his stomach; and Peanut in the fetal position. And each morning Peanut awoke the same way—the smell of his father's leather workboots, the coffee machine clicking on and gurgling Folgers. The one-bedroom house filled with the smell of coffee and the sound of his father brushing his teeth—hawking up spit to the beat of some childhood rhythm that perhaps his mother had taught him. Brush, brush, hawk, brush, gargle. Repeat. Then the sound of the shower and his father blowing his nose under the running water. Never used toilet paper. He constantly lamented the cost of toilet paper and the vast amount that the women of the house consumed on a daily basis. He was the only man Peanut knew who actually used handkerchiefs to blow his nose. Every time he saw his father pull out his handkerchief and blow snot into it, then fold it over and stick it back into his pocket, Peanut thought, who does that anymore? That's some serious Huck Finn shit.

And the last thing Peanut heard each morning before his father left the house for work, while the sky was still black outside, was the clink of the spoon in the coffee mug, and his father hawking up more spit as he closed the door behind him and made his way to the old Ford truck, where he sat and pumped the gas for five minutes, sipping his coffee, until he was sure plenty of gas had worked its way into the carburetor, and then he turned the engine over and drove off.

But today Peanut smelled his father's boot and the smell didn't leave. His father stood above him with his legs spread and breathed deeply. Then he spoke, knowing each of his children was awake, waiting for the coffee, the shower, the rituals of morning.

He spoke softly at first, in the low tone lovers use after they turn out the lights for the night. Kids. Get up. Get up. Your father's not going to work today, so we're going to have a family outing. All four of his children moaned, longing for the ritual, not wanting to wake up and acknowledge his comment, but knowing they had to because he so rarely asked anything of them. And you don't question Dad. Besides, there was something different in his voice today. Something pathetic. Beaten.

Peanut didn't want to get up. But he was the oldest—one year out of high school. And he knew he had to be the first to make a move because somewhere along the line an order had been established. Oldest to youngest. Peanut does something, and the others follow suit. It was the same with everything. Peanut showered first in the morning. Then Gordo. Next Carlos. Last Yolanda. And at dinner. And when their mother dragged them to mass at Our Mother of Sorrows.

Their father stood above his oldest child, legs apart, voice directed toward his head. He enjoyed that his children had consented to this order without being shown. As if given divine instruction in the womb, they had come into the world and known their places. They helped each other. Looked after one another while their parents were at work— Freddie at the music store, Isabella at Circle K. He was proud of them.

Peanut sat up on the floor. Then Gordo, Carlos, Yolanda.

When all his children were sitting up, Freddie said today we're going to the park as a family. You guys stick together. And you're each to take a trashbag and fill it with cans. There're so many cans. Always going to waste, or some drunk gets his hands on them to buy another night of denial. And that's the problem, children—Peanut rolled his eyes, thinking great, another fuckin sermon. His dad went on, that's how the white man keeps beating us. He takes our land and gives us liquor in return. And so many of us fall for it. We take the drink and say thank you, white man, and then pass out. When we wake up, he's piled us all into a corner and told us to stay there together, living on top of each other like roaches, until they need us for harvest season or to watch their livestock while they vacation in the Virgin Islands. We have to do our part to stop this. No matter how small our role. One less drink and maybe the drunk will wake up one day and see he has nothing. See his home gone and a mall standing in its place.

Peanut glared up at his father, saw he wasn't looking, and flipped him off—so did Gordo, Carlos, and Yolanda—thinking fuck you, Dad. Just because you have no one who'll listen to you but your kids. You sad man. He was tired of always hearing his father bitch about the gringos. Like it was only their fault. Like tequila didn't exist before them. Like we weren't smoking weed before they came. He didn't feel like showering just to walk all day in the sunnyass park, so he got up and put on yesterday's clothes.

When Peanut and his siblings finished getting dressed, they gathered in the front yard, where their parents sat on lawn chairs, sharing a cup of coffee. The family sat in silence, watching the sun come up over the mountains. After Freddie and his wife finished their coffee, he placed the mug down on the hard dirt, and they walked in a group toward Reid Park. Peanut walked just ahead of his family with his head lowered, hoping none of the Kings were up this early to see him with his family. Oh, they wouldn't dare say anything to his face, but he knew they'd talk all kinds of shit behind his back.

Peanut knew once they reached the park, he could have his bag filled within a matter of minutes because he knew exactly where to find a shitpile of cans. Behind the bandshell where he and his boys sometimes drank and where all the drunks passed out each night in a mound of empty beer cans, clutching their brown-bagged beers to their chests. Let the rest of em dig around in trashcans like a bunch of bums, Peanut thought. I'll go right to the stash and be done with it. He barely gave any thought to why they were searching for cans. He'd heard enough of his father's goddam sermons by now.

They stopped by the rose garden, and Freddie picked up a can of Crystal Light and poured the brown liquid on the ground, crushed the can with his boot, and tossed it in his trashbag. And that's how it's done, children. Empty it, smash it, throw it in your bag. You can even tie your bag into your belt loop like this—he demonstrated—then your hands are free for searching. And whoever finds the most cans gets a prize.

This excited Carlos and Yolanda, who talked rapidly with each other about what the prize might be, comparing search techniques, inventing strategies for finding the most cans in the smallest area. They didn't notice that their mother had yet to speak a word. Or the frown on her face. And while they had been sleeping, they hadn't heard Freddie whispering to his wife in bed, telling her that he had finally been canned. The Creasys, who had come to Tucson all the way from Marietta, Ohio, nine months earlier to buy the music store where he'd been teaching guitar and violin for the past twenty-three years, had told him they were willing to accept his resignation. The pinche gringos are still moving west and pushing us on top of each other, he'd whispered to his wife. Twenty-three years and they dump me like a stock boy. And I asked them how am I going to feed my family now, like someone will really hire a Mexican to come into their house and teach their pretty white kids to play the violin or flamenco guitar. They'll bring the kids into a shop because it's safe there. Where in Christ am I supposed to go now? But the bastards only shrugged and pretended they were making budget cuts when they're really just trying to bring in a higher-class clientele. Let the hispanos—that's what they call us—go to the YMCA or join the orchestra at school if they want to learn violin. It's the new money they're after, Isabella. The gringos who finally figured out they can get land cheap here. They're the ones. Scooping up forty or fifty acres a pop to build what they think is a ranch. Some Spanish tile, cactus, a couple horses, and a lame cow, and you're a regular caballero.

I know, Freddie. I know. You've worked so hard.

I loved those kids. When they scrunch up their faces and try to figure out chords on the guitar. Or notes on the violin. Remember a handful of them even got a mariachi band together to play every Sunday at the Southgate Shopping Center?

I know, Freddie. I've seen them. Back when we lived down there and I went shopping at Fry's.

Freddie sighed and threw off the covers, too sad to speak. So he had walked out to the living room and stood over the head of his oldest son and came up with an idea. There's all kinds of ways to make a little money until I find work. He only hoped this scheme might at least feed his family for a few days while he hunted for a job.

Standing next to his wife beneath a palm tree, Freddie watched the enthusiasm of his two youngest children scrabbling for cans and thought I'm pathetic. This isn't happening. I've got my children collecting cans, gathering their next meal, and they don't even know it. He avoided his older sons' eyes. He grabbed his wife's hand and told Peanut to watch after the young ones, your mom and I will be looking over by the zoo, and he and his wife walked, shoulders subtly slumped, away from their children.

Peanut took them over by the bandshell and pointed to the trashcans by the bathrooms. There's your goldmine, guys. Really? Yep. Guarantee you'll have your bags full before you're halfway through with those cans. He watched his brothers and sister race to the cans, smiling when he saw that they were letting Yoli win on purpose. He walked behind the bandshell and saw a drunk lying on his side with vomit dried in his beard. Look at that fucker. Maybe Dad's right. This guy's worthless. He walked up to the drunk and rifled through his pockets and found a dollar crumpled inside an empty softpack of Basics—yeah, good trick dumbass—and then he kicked him in the ribs as hard as he could just for being such a fuckin fuck, and the drunk grunted and rolled over onto his back but didn't wake up, so Peanut started filling his bag with cans, not bothering to empty any—they're sucked bone dry before they hit the ground—and too lazy to crush them, thinking maybe I should kick that bastard in the head again, maybe smash in his face or—

Why'd you kick him, Peanut? Yolanda stood just behind him.

I didn't kick him.

But I saw you.

You didn't see anything. I was picking up cans. He grabbed his sister's hand and led her back to where his brothers had dumped the trashbarrels over and were picking through the spilled trash. Look, guys, just kick the trash out of the way and pick up the cans. Jesus. You're gonna kill yourselves. Get AIDS like some homo. Yolanda let go of her brother and walked over to a trashbarrel and tried to push it over, but the metal barrel was too heavy for her. Here, Yoli. Peanut kicked it over. There you go. Just don't touch the trash.

For the next hour, they kicked trashbarrels and grabbed cans, racing against each other. Peanut was on Yolanda's team, so they finished first, then sat on a nearby picnic table to watch their brothers and invent prizes. Peanut didn't really care about the prize at all, but he was amused by how excited Yoli was over the whole thing, so he played along with her. Yeah, Yoli, maybe they'll take us to Disneyland finally and you can go on the teacups.

You really think so?

Sure, I mean, why not? We love Disney as much as the next family. And everyone gets to go to Disneyland. Yolanda trembled, trying to actually come to terms with the possibility of going and getting her picture taken with Minnie or in front of Cinderella's castle. She smiled and grabbed Peanut's hand and asked him do you really think they'll take us, because I have to pick out my nicest outfit, maybe the one I wore for Easter this year, the sundress with the matching gloves and the hat with the daisies. What do you think? Would that be a good one? Peanut just nodded and decided to let her live in her little dream a bit longer. She was so happy. He didn't have the heart to tell her that Disneyland would never happen because not only was it too far away, but just look around you, Yoli, for fuck's sake, we have nothing. But you're still too young to know that. Too young to realize that your beautiful Easter outfit has been the beautiful Easter outfit of at least four other girls before you—and those are just the ones I know about. And all of them had gone on to become neighborhood whores. She grabbed his hand and smiled up into his eyes and loved him. He didn't have to wonder what her eyes meant. The way she looked at him like he was one of her favorite cartoon characters or something made it obvious.

For the first time, he realized that this baby girl sitting next to him, holding his hand and loving him, was going to grow up one day. Soon she'd stop asking for My Little Ponies and Care Bears. There would be no more Dr. Seuss books. Instead she'd start hiding makeup in her purse and putting it on in the bathroom at Mansfield Junior High with the rest of the girls who spent more time fixing their hair than they did in class. In fact, most of Peanut's friends never bothered trying to peek into the girl's bathroom whenever a girl entered or left because the sticky cloud of hairspray that escaped each time was practically intolerable. Yoli's next step from there would be to become one of the neighborhood bitches.

He looked away from Yoli. He loosed his grip on her hand and felt disgust burrowing into his stomach. But it was natural. Fuck, it was more than natural. It's the God-given right of the Kings to have any bitch in the neighborhood that we want. That's why they come to us in droves, practically begging us to pull trains on them. Shit, last time Lucy came, she brought two friends over to Güero's and they put on a sweet girl-on-girl show, pulling off each other's bras and panties with their teeth, real slow, looking out the corners of their eyes at the guys sitting around them, leaning in to see if the chicks were really into it or if they were putting them on with the whole lesbo thing—since every bitch knows that all guys have lesbian fantasies—but they weren't putting on, they were kissing and moaning and sliding their fingers into each other's snatches and then licking them and smiling and writhing around in a pile on the floor while the Kings watched and passed joints around and decided which bitch they wanted to shove a cock up in. After Lucy and her two friends made each other come, they each turned around and grabbed the Kings nearest them and opened their zippers and pulled out their cocks and started jacking them off, and the Kings smiled and leaned back to enjoy the sluts rubbing their knobs until Peanut couldn't stand it anymore, so he went up to the tiny little thing with the beautiful tits that had come with Lucy, and he got on his knees behind her and pulled out his dick and slapped it up against her sweaty back a few times and then he stuck it in her and fucked up a storm while the other Kings finally decided Peanut had the right idea and stood up and filled the various holes made available to them by the three slutty cunts in the middle of the room. And none of them were surprised because this is what being a King is all about. You kick a lot of fuckin ass and you get even more pussy. Sure, you might get killed, but this is your family and you look out for each other and the neighborhood and get pussy on the off nights and life is good like that. But one day Yoli would be full-grown too, and she'd either be one of the rucas that fucked all the Kings or join a gang and get herself killed or knocked up, and fuck that.

Maybe there's a way to warn her. He could write her a letter and leave it for her to find but not open until she was thirteen. Of course, she'd definitely open it long before that. He could threaten to kill anyone who touched her, but that wouldn't work. There's no way to be around her every minute, and someone somewhere would get his hands on her, and then she'd just be a slut like every other puta in this goddam neighborhood. He tried to stop himself but couldn't help looking down at his sister and imagining her writhing beneath some kid on the mattress behind Torchy's, or in the tunnels under Park Mall, or in someone's living room smoking weed and letting the bastard feel her up because that's what she's supposed to do. Peanut had to get up and walk to the bathroom to sneak a cigarette where Yoli couldn't see him. He never let her see him do anything wrong.

In the bathroom he thought maybe he could cry, but there's no point in that pansyass shit. He took a long pull off his cigarette and felt the soothing smoke burn down his throat and into his lungs, where he held it and thought about never letting it out so it could swirl around inside him and then his lungs would stop working and they'd find him in the bathroom dead on the toilet with a chest full of smoke. He blew the smoke out. He took another pull. The burn was nice and it calmed him enough to let him think his new problem over. There was a solution and he was going to find it. There was a way to save Yoli.

When he finished his cigarette, he went back out to the table where his brothers and sister sat waiting on their parents, talking about what the prize might be and who would be declared the winner. He stayed a few feet away until the wind had aired the smoke out of his clothing. The breeze blew through the trees and ruffled Peanut's shirt, and he watched it lift Yoli's thick, beautiful hair and wrap it around the back of her head. He didn't want to think about her growing up any longer, so he told them follow me to the playground because Mom and Dad will know to find us there. With his brothers trailing behind him, Peanut grabbed Yoli's trashbag full of cans and dragged it behind him while she ran ahead to the rocket slide, her favorite. The cans clattered and the liquid inside them sloshed around.

When Freddie and his wife finally appeared over the hill behind the playground, Yoli ran toward them screaming I'M GONNA WIN THE PRIZE. Peanut could tell by the looks on their faces that they had forgotten about that little detail. His father wrapped his daughter in his arms and lifted her up to his chest, nodding yes, someone will win today, and winking at his wife, who forced a smile. Peanut pretended not to notice and grabbed his and Yoli's trashbags, ignoring the cloud of beer stench mixed with Coke and Sprite and the smell of park trashbarrels. He turned and began walking back toward their home, trying to push the thought of Yoli from his mind. No, she'll always be good. She'll always have us to protect her. He said this to himself, knowing it was a load of shit, because there wasn't a single girl like that in the neighborhood—at least not that he'd ever met.

He stopped at the corner, waiting for the light to change and his family to catch up with him. By the time they did, the light had gone through three cycles of walk and don't walk, and he was irritated by how slowly they walked. The light changed to walk again and six lanes of Saturday traffic came to a stop. Peanut and his family stepped into the crosswalk, and he listened to his baby sister singing the Strawberry Shortcake song, ignoring the clatter of cans scraping against the asphalt as he dragged the bags behind him. Suddenly the bags became much lighter and Peanut heard the cans explode out of the bottoms and he stopped and looked toward his family, who watched in horror as the cans spilled all over the street, rolling down the sloping road toward the cars idling at the stoplight with a crash and slamming into tires and bumpers and burying Peanut in cans up to his shins. Lifting the empty bags up, Peanut looked down at the saggy bottoms, wordless. The stench was unbearable. In the middle of the intersection, Peanut tried to react, finally throwing down the bags and running out into the street while his family stayed on the median and turned around to watch him kick cans toward the side of the road, using his foot like a rake and trying to ignore the embarrassment pushing against his cheeks. He didn't look in the cars stopped at the stoplight, afraid of seeing someone he knew. If someone sees me, I'm gonna fuckin snap, cause here I am in the middle of 22nd kicking cans like an idiot with my brokeass family standing on the median and holding their trashbags like a buncha pathetic Mexicans. We look like goddam bums. Jesus. The light changed to green. Car horns blasted at Peanut and drivers leaned out of their windows and yelled for him to GET THE HELL OUT OF THE ROAD, YOU GODDAM ASSBAG, and Peanut flipped them off and tripped over the cans trying to make his way to the median where his family stood looking at him and at the angry drivers and at their own shoes, and he thought if I only had a gun with me I'd pump every one of these pricks full of lead.

When he finally made it to the median his mom put her arm on his shoulder and whispered I'm sorry. Peanut shrugged it off. His dad patted him on the back and asked if he was okay. You're not too shook up are you? Peanut didn't answer. Instead, he stood with his back to them and waited for the light to flash walk so he could just go home and get the hell away from those goddam cans crumpling beneath the cars driving by, still honking at him and screaming obscenities, the cans bouncing off of cars and beating up against the legs of Peanut and his family. Each one that hit him pierced like a cactus needle and made him wish he could jump in front of an oncoming car and feel his body break and scrape against the street as the car pulled him along and ground aluminum shards and asphalt into his body until he was an unrecognizable mass rolling into the gutter. The bottoms of his pants were soaked with the beer and soda that sprayed out of the cans each time a car smashed one.

Finally the light blinked walk and Peanut crossed the street, leaving his family behind him. Yolanda called for him to slow down, but he didn't. He couldn't be seen with them. We're all miserable enough. And I know one of the fuckin Kings will catch wind of the whole thing and I'll be the laughingstock of 24th Street. When he reached his street, he turned the corner and ran the rest of the way home.

Fifteen minutes later, he sat in the bathroom catching his breath, and waited to hear his family walk through the door, wishing he had a room of his own to lock himself in. But the front door didn't open. He waited to hear the unlatching of the handle and the creaking of the hinges, but eventually too much time had passed without a sound and he grew curious and walked out of the house, only to find his family tearing open their trashbags and throwing the cans all over the driveway. The sound made him cringe and he wanted to scream WHAT THE FUCK DO YOU THINK YOU'RE DOING? Do you want to bring every neighbor out of their house so they can stare at us and laugh and point their fingers at how pathetic we've become? Collecting cans like a family of immigrants. He opened his mouth to yell but was shocked to see his dad's truck back up in the driveway and roll over the cans, spraying sticky liquid everywhere, and his family laughing. Laughing? Yes, they laughed and jumped around while his dad put the truck into drive and then into reverse and then back into drive, smashing the cans flat on the concrete until the driveway was covered with an aluminum mosaic.

Peanut was speechless. His brothers were running through the cans, kicking them up into the air and sliding on them and falling over, laughing. Yoli grabbed handfuls of the cans and threw them up like metal snowflakes, giggling when they clattered to the ground. And the whole time, his mother sat in the passenger seat of the truck cab with her hand over her mouth, attempting to smother her laughter because she knew she should say something stern about how dirty the children were getting and what a mess this whole thing was going to be.

Peanut thought fuck it, and he ran to the driveway and said Dad, you missed a couple, and kicked the cans into the path of the truck. The sound that had been driving him mad a few moments earlier had now become funny, and he laughed along with the rest of his family, knowing there was nothing he could do about how goddam broke they were. He was old enough to know that his father would never make them go collecting cans unless something bad had happened and they really needed money. He went to the garage and grabbed three shovels and handed them to his brothers and told them to help him shovel the flattened cans back into the trashbags.

While the three brothers filled the bags with crushed cans and tied the full bags and tossed them into the bed of the Ford, their father shut off the engine and got out, walking around the front of the truck to open the door for his wife. Isabella put her hand out for her husband to help her into the yard because she was afraid of slipping on the liquid that was trickling down the driveway toward the street. All that filthy sticky junk sticking to the bottoms of her shoes.

As Peanut finished shoveling the last of the cans into his trashbag, a large brown roach appeared from a small hole in the ground—a hole a tenth the roach's size—and fluttered its wings before scurrying toward the liquid covering the driveway. Peanut had to choke back vomit when hundreds more roaches suddenly began streaming from the hole, each one fluttering its translucent brown wings before dashing into the stream of soda and beer. Yoli saw the roaches and screamed and Freddie let go of his wife and rushed toward the truck, grabbing Yoli and waving the boys out of the way. He fired up the truck and drove back and forth over the driveway. The roaches crackled beneath the tires and their puss-filled bodies discharged all over the cement. Peanut felt bile burning its way up toward his mouth, eating at the lining of his esophagus and threatening to burst from between his lips. He covered his mouth with his hands and forced it back, looking up from the roaches being ground into the cement, and saw his little sister pressing her face against the window of the passenger door, her mouth wide in a scream, and then her eyes suddenly grew wider and she turned away from the window and disappeared onto the floorboard of the truck. Peanut slowly let his eyes drift down to the driveway. The roaches weren't dying. Even though the driveway was covered with their puss, and the sound of their backs snapping filled the air, they continued to race around the driveway, licking at the slime of their own bodies mixed with the leftovers from the cans. Thousands more streamed out into the sunlight and the sludge until Freddie parked his truck atop the hole and yelled for Peanut to get the hose and spray the fuckers out into the street. Peanut ran to the side of the house and ordered Gordo to turn the hose on. Water came out of the hose and Peanut placed his thumb over the nozzle and formed a powerful spray that blew the roaches and the slime and the one or two cans they had missed out into the street where the sun would bake the mixture into a paste.

Freddie shouted THERE MUST BE MILLIONS OF THE BASTARDS LIVING BENEATH THE GROUND RIGHT UNDER OUR HOUSE. JESUS. Peanut threw the bags of cans into the bed of the truck and ran to the shed to get the gas his father kept in a milk jug for cleaning his hands. The gas slopped inside the jug and Peanut removed the cap and told his dad to back up the truck. Back it up and give me some room so I can kill these fuckers—nauseated by the thought of ten million roaches burrowing beneath the house and bursting through the floor like a geyser, overrunning the house and eating the flesh off his baby sister as she slept on the floor of their living room. When his dad had backed the truck down the driveway, Peanut poured the gas into the hole, watching as the roaches retreated and the gas bubbled from the jug and spread over the driveway, mingling with the muck. He grabbed a lighter and his pack of cigarettes from his front pants pocket and lit one, then flicked it toward the hole. The fumes erupted into flames, and Peanut's family watched as the roaches scrambled out of the hole and onto the driveway with their backs on fire and their legs melting beneath them even as they tried to run from the heat. Eventually they stopped running and the crackling of burning roaches filled in the silence left by Peanut and his family.

Shaken, Peanut's mother told the boys to pile into the truck, and Yoli, stay in the front with me and Daddy. The boys hopped into the truckbed, careful to avoid the bags of filthy metal. They drove to Safeway, ignoring the cans still scattered all over 22nd. Since it was Saturday and Safeway was crowded, Isabella told them to wait in the truck. She grabbed a shopping cart and pushed it alongside the truck so Peanut could hoist the bags over and into the cart. He was happy to be rid of the damn things. When his parents disappeared into the store, he ordered his brothers to watch Yoli, I'll be right back. Slipping between the rows of cars, Peanut lit a cigarette and his thoughts returned to saving his sister. He tried to think of any girls in the neighborhood who hadn't become used-up whores by the time they reached eighteen, but the only ones he could bring to mind were the nasty skanks from school who wouldn't lose their virginity until they went off to college and got broken in by someone too pathetic to care about her looks. And even these girls were sad. They knew that the only thing that mattered was whether or not they were fuck material. If you aren't fuckable, you might as well stop wasting air.

But he knew his sister was going to be pretty, unless some terrible accident occurred. Of course, there was nothing he could do about that, so he tried to think of loopholes in the system. Surely there was a really hot chick at his school that no one had gotten his hands on. There must be. The last time he could remember fantasizing about a chick and not actually managing to bag her was back in the sixth grade, before he'd railed anyone. But as soon as he started running with the Kings, as soon as he'd gotten his crown tattoo, there had been so many women he never had to chase any. They came to him. Maybe he could tempt one of the lesser Kings into doing something to his sister one day and then kill the poor bastard and make an example of him. Except killing another King would mean he'd have to die too. Goddam, he thought, this is way harder than I thought it would be.

He walked back to the truck and hopped into the back just as his parents emerged from the store with a bag of food. Yoli jumped up and down in the front seat and waved at her parents crossing the parking lot toward the truck. When they reached it, Yoli shouted WHO GETS THE PRIZE, MOMMY? HUH? WHO GETS THE PRIZE? Her brothers knew she would get it. She was the youngest. Besides, they knew from the look on their mother's face and the bag of food she carried that the can collecting had been no game. So they sat down in the back of the truck and waited for their father to start it and drive away, hoping they wouldn't get caught at a stoplight and have to stare awkwardly at the people in the cars behind them. Isabella fished a tiny package of saladitos out of the paper grocery sack on her lap and handed them to her daughter. Do I get a lemon too, Mommy? Isabella shook her head no. Her husband pumped the gas pedal, put the truck into gear, and headed back home.

—

Peanut woke to the smell of his father's workboot, but the actual shoe wasn't there. It must've been part of a dream. Or just habit. He looked up at the clock and saw it was past one thirty in the morning, then he sat up and looked over at Yoli sleeping peacefully on her side next to Gordo. He knew he was onto something earlier, when he decided he would simply have to get her out of this place. Maybe to another city or something. That's it. She wants to go to Disneyland, so I'll just take her away to where Disneyland is, somewhere over in California. I know I'll be able to find it. Just drive west and ask around. He knew it was a great idea, even if it was kind of complicated. So he quietly stood up and tiptoed to the hall closet, where they kept most of the kids' clothes. He opened the door slowly, inch by inch, to avoid making the door creak and waking his parents. The clothes hung on hangers and were separated into neatly folded piles on the floor. First he found himself a pair of Dickies and a hooded sweatshirt, and then he rifled through Yoli's pile, taking care not to disturb Gordo's or Carlos's. When he had found a nice warm outfit for his sister, he put his clothes on and sneaked through the kitchen and out the back door of the house, happy for once that, unlike so many other families in the area, his family couldn't afford a wrought-iron screen door, because it surely would've creaked badly and woken the whole damn house.

Outside, Peanut walked to his father's truck and opened the door, throwing Yoli's clothes onto the seat next to him. He pumped the gas and placed the keys in the ignition. Realizing he would definitely get caught if he fired up the truck in the driveway, Peanut forced the gear shift on the steering wheel down into neutral, letting the truck roll quietly down the driveway and into the street. The truck continued to roll once it reached the street and Peanut wrestled the steering wheel—no fuckin power steering, of course—and turned the truck onto the road, its momentum allowing it to roll a few houses down the block before it stopped rolling, and Peanut was able to safely start the truck without having to worry about waking anyone. The truck started right up, and Peanut put it in park, with the lights off, allowing it to idle while he went to get his sister.

He crept back into the house through the back and wrapped Yoli's blanket tight around her, shushing her when she woke and opened her mouth to ask him what he was doing. Shhhhh. Just be quiet for a minute. I've got a surprise for you outside, and Yoli's eyes opened wide with excitement, but she only nodded to show her approval and to assure her brother that she wouldn't make a sound. He held her tight to his chest and stood up, looking at his brothers and wondering when he'd see them again, if ever. It made him want to bundle up his whole family and place them in the back of the idling truck and sneak them off to someplace where Dad wouldn't lose his job, and Mom wouldn't have to work as a cashier when she'd probably rather be at home cooking or planting a garden or something. Maybe she'd rather be in the PTA or volunteer as a class mom at Yoli's school. He wanted to bundle them all up and tell them, here, leave the driving to me, you just relax back there and soon we'll be out of this desert and we'll all be happy and find a house with four bedrooms and a staircase and a basement, and a swimming pool—that way we don't have to pay fifty cents each to go swimming in the piss-filled pool at Jacob's Park. We'll have our own and we can invite our friends and Yoli won't ever have to grow up to be somebody's bitch. She'll go to dances and fall in love and marry someone nice who hasn't dealt drugs his whole life or killed people. But Peanut knew this was impossible. He had only planned for him and Yoli, and so he turned his back on his sleeping brothers, holding Yoli against his chest, and crept from the house one last time.

He held his finger over Yoli's lips until they were safely inside the truck, which was still cold because the heater was broken. She hopped up and down on the front seat and laughed and asked him where they were going. What's the prize? I'll tell you in a minute, Yoli. Put these clothes on while I drive. She let the blanket fall from her shoulders and stepped into the pants and pulled on the sweater he had picked out for her. Then she settled into the seat and giggled when Peanut reached over her to fasten the seatbelt across her chest.

Yoli. We're going to Disneyland. Remember what I promised you? That you'd get to go? Well, if you're good and you don't tell anyone, I'll take you there and we'll have so much fun. She looked at him with amazement. It was hard for her to understand how they were going to Disneyland, but she didn't want to question her brother because she had wanted to go for so long it didn't matter how she got there. She started singing a song from *Sleeping Beauty* and Peanut hummed along, driving the truck slowly away from the house and out onto Country Club Road, then he pulled the truck into Torchy's parking lot and dimmed the lights.

Okay, wait here for just a minute, and I'll be right back. You want some chips or something like that?

Doritos.

Okay. Peanut reached over and locked the passenger door. After he opened his door, he locked it too and told Yoli not to open the doors for anyone but him. No one. I don't care if it's the cops, or Mom, or a friend. You just lay down on the seat and wait for me to get back. It'll only be a minute. Okay? She lay down on the seat and pulled the blanket up to her chin. That's right, Yoli. Just like that. Lay there and sing your songs. He started a song from *Snow White* for her, and she quietly sang along with him, singing so softly in her high little voice that he could barely hear it after he had shut the door, checked the locks, and pulled the hood from his sweatshirt over his head.

The neon lights outside Torchy's were flickering, many of them burned out already, and the few remaining had maybe a couple days of life left. Peanut turned the corner of the building, out of Yoli's view, and lit a cigarette, then took several deep drags while he considered his next step. He'd always had a fondness for Torchy's. The owner, a guy they assumed was named Torchy, though none of them really knew, didn't mind the kids loitering outside his liquor store. Probably because their parents were his primary customers, and so he didn't want bad relations with the rest of the community. But either way, he'd been nothing but kind to Peanut and his friends and the rest of the neighborhood kids, so Peanut felt badly about what he was about to do. He fingered the barrel of the pistol in his front pocket. The rim was cold but the handle fit his hand perfectly. It was the only gun he'd ever owned, the one he'd gotten from Chuy the day after he was initiated into the Kings. While he'd been lying on the living room floor of his house, a cold washcloth on his forehead and Neosporin smeared on all the cuts and bruises they'd given him, Chuy knocked on the front door and ordered Peanut out of the house. Peanut had thought he was in for another asskicking, but instead Chuy reached behind his back, pulled out the 9mm, and handed it to Peanut. This, he said, is a gift from us. Don't lose it. And he walked away immediately, not allowing Peanut to reject the gift. It wasn't a matter of whether or not Peanut wanted it. The Kings wanted him to have it, so he had to accept.

Peanut stood outside Torchy's, hoping his plan would work and everything would fall into place so his baby sister would be able to live her life somewhere better. All we need is a few hundred to get us started, which Torchy's would probably have because it was the first of the month, so everyone rushed right over after cashing their checks to buy tequila and beer, or maybe some whiskey, and definitely cigarettes. Torchy's *had* to be brimming with money.

He snuffed his cigarette out on the sole of his shoe, blew out the last of the smoke, and peeked around the corner of the building to make sure Yoli was still safe in the truck. The exhaust pipe was vibrating, sputtering out little clouds of thin smoke while the engine rumbled beneath the truck's hood. He couldn't see Yoli, which meant she was fine.

Fuck it, let's go. Peanut turned back toward the front door of Torchy's and pulled it open. The bright rows of neon lining the ceiling flickered and made him squint. He walked to the back of the store where they kept the forties—Mickey's and Colt 45 and St. Ides—and pretended to look for a specific brand. Really, Peanut was counting to thirty in his head, ignoring the cashier asking can I help you find anything? Young man, can I help you? Peanut shook his head, lowered his chin to his chest to hide his face in case there were cameras he hadn't noticed, and walked swiftly toward the counter.

He stopped and lifted the gun out of his pocket. It's not too late to give up, he thought. The guy hasn't even seen the gun yet and I haven't asked for any money so I could just pretend I can't find what I'm looking for, go outside, and tell Yoli that we'll have to postpone the trip. But he knew if he didn't do it now, if he gave up so easily, he would fail his baby sister. Yoli, sitting out in the truck cab all excited at the thought of finally going to a place none of the other kids in the neighborhood had ever been. Yoli, who deserved better than this place with these sad fucked-up people who always hurt each other because they're too afraid to hurt the people they really hate. No. He would not fail Yoli.

He pulled the 9mm the rest of the way out and felt the handle settle in his palm, the grip familiar and calming, and he raised the gun and placed it between the clerk's eyes, cocked the trigger back, and flicked his eyes toward the register. Open it. Open it, asshole, and give me the money. All of it, in the bag, and don't forget the safe on the floor behind you too. Don't give me that shit about how you can't open it because this 9mm between your eyes says you can, says you better if you want to see the sun rise, old man. The clerk stared at Peanut, not even glancing at the gun between his eyes that was cold and made goose bumps stand up on the back of his neck, but instead looking deep into Peanut to try and see what was making this boy rob him when all he had ever done was act nice toward Peanut and his friends, never called the cops or shooed them off with a pushbroom, and up until now it had been fine—sure, a little graffiti behind the store every now and then, but he honestly liked most of it—yes, until now it had been fine, but he knew it was inevitable, was a bit surprised, actually, that no one had robbed his store just yet but he'd still planned for this moment, and while he looked into Peanut's eyes and tried to warn him with his own eyes, to say just turn around and leave and we'll pretend this never happened, since I know you're just desperate and doing something stupid, like you have something to prove to the other guys you hang out with, but I can't—*won't*—let you get away with it so put the gun down—I won't even hold it against you that you put it up to my forehead—and turn around and walk out the door and go home and get some sleep and don't ever come back, it's that simple, trying to get this message across to Peanut so he wouldn't have to do what he was doing at that moment, his right hand slowly, slowly going toward the cash drawer while the other reached beneath the counter for the cold steel barrel, ah, there it is, and wincing as he wrapped his finger around the trigger of the shotgun and aimed in the general direction of his attacker—that ought to be about level with his arm—then he asked Peanut once, please don't, just walk away, just go out the door, boy, and Peanut shouted BOY? I'LL SHOW YOU A BOY and the clerk knew this was his only chance to get out of this alive, he'd heard how these gangbangers killed for sport, so he closed his eyes and squeezed and felt the shotgun buck in his hands, heard the buckshot spray through the counter and opened his eyes in time to see Peanut looking down in surprise at the counter as it burst into splinters and the lead pellets buried themselves in his chest and face and the arm holding the gun, and Peanut cried out as he felt the molten lead ripping through his torso like a thousand metal spears being thrust all at once, Jesus it hurts, and he stumbled backwards, dropping his 9mm, tripping over warm cases of Milwaukee's Best, then landing on his back and lying still and wondering if Yoli was okay in the front seat and hoping she would never open the door for anyone, but grow old in the truck and maybe one day figure out how to drive it so she could finish what he had started.

FLASHFLOOD

THIS IS THE PART WHERE I'M SUPPOSED TO BASH OUT my window and crawl onto the roof, Rebecca thought, when the cab of her car had been underwater for more than two minutes. Her car shook and turned and flipped beneath the water, knocking up against the walls of the arroyo, scraping small boulders and crashing into turns while the flood-water swept it from the city into the bowels of the wilderness. Yes, this is the part we've seen a thousand times on the news. I kick out the win-dow with the heel of my foot and don't worry about cutting myself as I climb onto the roof—because it's better to get a few cuts than to drown—and up on top of the car, where I hang on until some Good Samaritan throws me a rope or a police helicopter shines its spotlight on me and lowers down a man with a safety harness to lift me away.

But Rebecca did not bother to kick her way to safety. She did not try to roll the window down. She did not try to undo her seatbelt. She sat completely still and let her lungs fill with water, feeling purified as it splashed against the back of her throat and down her windpipe until it boiled inside her lungs and they threatened to—aren't they supposed to burst?—collapse. She could feel each water molecule seep into the lin-ing, burrowing, tickling almost, and was a bit disappointed because this was supposed to be the most painful way to die—waiting on the rem-nants of oxygen left in her blood to dissipate and then for her brain to get all mushy and foggy and slowly wink out, and she was supposed to be in complete terror while her hair floated around her head in a sea-weed dance—she'd be dead but still able to see. But the oxygen wasn't dying out, even though she knew she hadn't taken a breath in at least three minutes because the dashboard clock was still blinking.

It was during these minutes that Rebecca saw the last bubble of air float by her head from the backseat and lodge itself between the windshield and the dashboard. She leaned forward to pick it loose. She felt it wedged in the corner of the windshield directly below the Grease Monkey sticker from her last oil change. She remembered the grand opening of the Grease Monkey on Pantano Road and how there was a man in a blown-up vinyl monkey suit who sputtered around on the street corner with a plastic monkey wrench and a pair of overalls, beckoning the drivers to stop, and kids peeked over the ledges of backseat windows or from the rears of station wagons and smiled and waved at the monkey. She lifted the bubble tenderly between her fingers and brought it to her face with the intention of biting into it and sucking out the few air particles it might contain, but instead of placing it in her mouth she raised it up to her ear and pinched it until it burst and a scream escaped and shot into her ear, down the canal like burning wax, reminding her of something that mattered before the flood and the car filling with water and the turning and twisting.

Less than two years into her marriage, Rebecca took up crying as a hobby. Ever since her husband, Rogelio Nuñez, had withdrawn her from Pima County Community College, Rebecca often found herself weeping at her kitchen window, her forehead resting against the glass. She wanted to write a series of essays on crying. How sometimes scrunching your eyes really tight while the tears poured down your face would keep your eyes from getting red. That was the trick for not getting caught. So people wouldn't stop and ask you what's wrong all the time. But there was also something nice about crying. A deep pleasure in being able to release the emotions inside her in a tangible form, the salty liquid drops she could wipe onto her sleeve, leaving a darkness that would lighten after a few minutes. The taste was the dry salty feeling of hopeless disappointment, like the time Rogelio came home to find her studying at the dining room table. He ripped her books from her hands and threw them on the floor, saying you think you can just go around behind my back reading when there's things that need to be done around here? But she did not cry then. She couldn't give him that luxury. Instead, she got up and took the meatloaf from the oven and set it in front of her husband with pursed lips, making sure to hold back her tears and act like it was nothing when it really felt like he'd thrown her to the ground and stomped on her throat, and he screamed MEATLOAF AGAIN? the fuck do you *do* with our money? and they ate their dinner in silence while her husband's chewing, the squishy chomping and sucking, tested the strength of her resolve, mocking her even when she carried her dirty dish to the sink and thrust her hands beneath the water like she was searching for the washcloth but really she was clasping, smashing her hands and fingers together as hard as she could and wondering if there were a butcher knife beneath the water would she finally use it on her ungrateful and worthless husband, but then her rage and discontent waned and she felt guilty for questioning him, he was doing the best he could, they only pay Mexican mechanics so much, they're too easy to come by, and she released her hands and found the washcloth, not watching her husband or letting him see her as she scrubbed food from her plate and it fell into the sink and mixed with the white soap bubbles until they turned orange. When he got up and left his dirty plate at the table, ignoring Rebecca, she knew he had gone to the bathroom to wash his face and sit on the toilet until he'd read the newspaper from cover to cover. This she used to love about him—the way he'd sit on the toilet every evening, relating the news stories to her that interested him while she brushed her hair or washed off the day's mascara. But he hadn't read to her for a while, and now it just annoyed her, his sitting in there, hiding behind the paper. And she knew there was no use in bringing up any of her worries now, because she had lost her window of opportunity. If he was in a better mood she could try to explain to him that she wasn't being selfish. She simply didn't want to be another broke mojado family. Didn't want to give her neighbors a reason to laugh at them and say to each other, see, they're all the same, living off our dollar and taking our goddam jobs. And while she waited to hear the toilet flush, Rebecca thought maybe if he would let me work too— a paper route, a cashier at Thrifty's, anything—that would be enough.

Instead, I'm wearing a hole in our kitchen window where I lean my forehead every afternoon and watch the birds and the rain and the kids and try to name the cactus—ocotillo, saguaro, prickly pear, jumping, barrel, aloe—while I wait on you to come home mad because you hate your job. Have you seen the groove where my forehead rests? Or are you too busy going into the kitchen and searching for the grilled government-cheese sandwiches that we both hate so much? I'd like to buy tamales from the old woman who lives down the road, the one who knocks on our door on Tuesdays and Fridays carrying a steaming pan covered with a handwoven towel, but I have to turn her away like I'm not interested, like she's a Jehovah's Witness, when she knows, can see it in my eyes, that I want nothing more than to taste the warm, squishy masa and pork on my tongue. And what do we do when the ice cream man comes down the block and our baby comes running inside and I have to say no, we can't afford it, when I want to say yes, buy a Bulletpop or some Lemonheads or a Flintstones push-up or one of those ice cream feet on a stick with a gumball for the big toe? Do I close the door so I can't see him running down the street after the van, hoping for a handout he'll never get?

But it was hopeless. Rogelio had already gone to bed. She couldn't talk to him for the rest of the night. The only thing remaining then was for her to lean against her kitchen windowsill in their apartment, her elbows on the ledge and her forehead pressed against the pane of glass, and teach imaginary math lessons to the birds or the cactus or the paloverde trees—wishing they were real children—so they could better themselves, so that not a single one of them would ever have to lean against the windowsill crying, or stand in line at the mission for government cheese and peanut butter and powdered milk, wondering what could have been in their lives, because tomorrow Rebecca would be here again, resting her forehead against the window, crying and wishing.

But what she could not understand, what had eluded her since the first date she had ever gone on with Rogelio, was how he could slap her sometimes and other times weep in front of her. How sometimes he needed her and she meant everything to him. Like the night at Mama Inez's Cocinera when he had cried while telling her how he'd witnessed the beating of his brother behind a liquor store in his old neighborhood and how his mother, hearing of her son's death, never left her rocking chair again, not even to eat or sleep or bathe, and he and his two remaining brothers brought her badly cooked food and blankets and washed her off with sponges, turning their heads out of respect, and clothed her in freshly cleaned robes of mourning. Sometimes when it rained, Rebecca gazed out her kitchen window and wondered where did the man go who used to write me poems, even though they were often stolen or, at best, badly written? Do you remember going to the Tanque Verde Swap Meet, even though we knew we couldn't buy anything, and looking at all the booths and pointing and laughing, wondering who would buy Chinese stars or get a tattoo in front of all those people? Or the time we went out to Gate's Pass up in the Tucson Mountains and were amazed at how far we could see, and you held me tight because I didn't want to go up there where the cops found dead bodies all the time tossed over the side of the cliff like dirty diapers or empty coffee cups. Rogelio could change so quickly it wouldn't have even surprised Rebecca if he came to her one night to make love and, in the middle of that beautiful act, pointed out each flaw in her body and personality, yelling YOU DISGUSTING WOMAN, LOOK AT THIS FAT BOILING OUT FROM YOUR STOMACH AND YOUR TITS SAGGING LIKE A PAIR OF LEAKY BALLOONS AND YOU'RE ONLY TWENTY-TWO while he still made love to her, his face buried in her neck, his hands pulling her hair so hard that she wondered if her scalp would tear. Rebecca wished she could return to the moment when he'd asked her to marry him, right after he'd praised her attempts at getting an education and promised her with every part of his body that *he* was the one who would be blessed if she accepted his offer. If she could only go back, she would turn him down. She would tell him please leave me alone to go about my business. She would give him back the ring he'd saved an entire year to buy, fling it at his feet in a dramatic fashion, like something they did in the movies, so it would be all symbolic.

She longed for the times when Rogelio came home after work with a smile on his face and scooped her into his arms, twirling her around, and thanked her for being his wife. How he used to sing her to sleep with boleros and tell her of his plan to save up enough money for them to drive down to Zacatecas on their anniversary and make love under the magical Mexican stars. Even though they'd always been poor, there had been a time when he would do side jobs at restaurants in exchange for free meals for the two of them. He even helped with some minor plumbing at Breakers, the new water park, and got free passes, and they pumped five dollars of gas into their car and drove to the water park one Saturday and slid down the slides together and flirted in the wave pool like a couple of teenagers and made plans to bring their child when he was big enough so they could teach him how to swim.

But that was the past. Pregnant with their first child, she spent every afternoon, while a pot of pinto beans boiled on the stove, sewing little unisex baby outfits and poring over magazines and ripping out decorations they could never afford for a nursery they had no extra room for. She thought maybe she could make more baby outfits from her old dresses and clothes she picked up from the free store and sell them at a consignment shop. After she cleaned the house and hung the laundry on the line to dry, she spent her afternoons sewing bloomers and jumpers and onesies and capri pants and sailor outfits and Easter dresses and first communion dresses. She even found a little shop called Guadalupe's Second-Go-Round that agreed to place a few of her items on the shelf for two weeks, and for the first time in years she was excited to wake up each day because there was always the chance that when she called Lupe at the shop she would give her news of her items flying off the shelf. It made Rebecca happy to think that a child some-where would be wearing an outfit with a tag in the collar that said Lovingly crafted by: Rebecca Nuñez. Her name handstitched in cursive with her finest pink silk thread. Would they wonder who she was? Would they ask their mothers when they were old enough to read, who is Rebecca Nuñez? is she my aunt, or my grandma? and their mothers would say oh she's a lady who got her start making baby outfits down the road, but we never imagined she'd get so famous that now she has a factory down in Agua Prieta, where the best seamstresses sew each item by hand, under Rebecca's watchful eye, before shipping them around the globe.

But weeks later, after Lupe told her quit calling, I'll call you, she still had not sold a single article of clothing. And even after she convinced Lupe to reduce the price by half and keep the items in the shop another week, she still had not managed to sell any clothes. More than anything she wanted to tell her husband about her disappointment, share with him the sting she felt each time she hung up the phone with Lupe's words repeating over and over, no we have not sold anything yet, *we'll* call *you*. She wished she were wrong, but experience told her otherwise. If she told Rogelio how she had failed at her small-time business, he would only tell her she should have been spending that time cleaning or shopping or learning to cook better food or getting the apartment ready for the baby.

He'd say what makes you think you can do better than me? I've worked my hands down to nubs, slaved away for Ruth down at the shop, and how far has it gotten me? And I'm a *man*. And what could she say to that? She couldn't sneak behind his back and make things better. She'd already tried, and Lupe wanted no part of it. He was right. She had failed. So she had given up on that endeavor and returned to tearing photos and advertisements out of *Good Housekeeping* and *Parenting* and *Better Homes & Gardens* and wishing some fortune would befall her. But she refused to fail as a parent. Sometimes she was so desperate about succeeding she wanted to grab her husband by the collar and scream DO YOU WANT OUR CHILD TO GO TO SCHOOL AND STAND IN THE FREE LUNCH LINE THAT TELLS OTHER KIDS, LOOK AT ME, I'M POOR AND MY PARENTS ARE WORTHLESS AND I HAVE TO WEAR THE SAME SHOES EVERY DAY AND PROBABLY THE SAME DIRTY UNDERWEAR BECAUSE MY DAD CAN'T PAY THE BILLS AND MY MOM DOES NOTHING BUT CRY AT THE WINDOWSILL EACH AFTERNOON WHILE I'M AT SCHOOL AND DAD'S AT WORK? Rogelio, will we have succeeded as parents then?

Should I tell our baby, let's call him Junior—cause if he's a boy, don't we have to name him after you?—that he will spend the majority of his years fighting and playing tough because that's what all the boys do, the ones I sometimes see walking home from school. They find the smallest one and push him and steal his lunch and call him a pussy and his father a cocksucker and his mother a puta until he runs home crying to her.

Sometimes she considered playing the lottery, which kept her mind occupied for a while when she drove to the grocery store or to visit her old friends from high school. She found herself stopping behind cars and gazing at their license plates and adding the numbers together and dividing them by the number of digits on the plate or trying to break them down into prime numbers or multiples of three or five with the intention of playing them in the state lottery. She tried to store these numbers away in her mind, but they melted together in the heat of the desert, and she inevitably forgot them and realized it was fruitless to play anyway because the only ones who ever win the lottery are the old retirees who were already rich or else they wouldn't be able to afford living in Green Valley or the foothills. Yes, they win the lottery and forget to cash in the ticket because they're too busy celebrating their good fortune at the clubhouse of their golf resort or in the smoky dim rooms of the Elk's Lodge over sushi or filet mignon. Or maybe they would lose the slip of paper beneath all the stock certificates wedged under a Jamaica magnet on their refrigerator. Every so often some young person might win too. Someone who could actually use the money. Of course even they didn't appreciate it. Didn't need it the same way she did, to pay bills and send her kids to the U of A. They'd get to use the money to party and get girls or travel the world. But she'd never win. Not Rebecca Nuñez, who was a month away from bearing her first child, feeling like Mary of the Immaculate Conception because she sometimes forgot she even had a husband, pushed him out of her mind. Though sometimes she wished he'd massage her head and brush her hair and listen to her. Rogelio, she'd whisper, I'm drowning, like I'm trapped in a fishbowl with no food and I'm a goldfish and there's a piranha chasing me, laughing and biting, and I can't get away from it cause my fins are torn and my tail won't move and my gills are cemented shut with tears and I suffocate with the effort and I'm helpless and for what?

The day Junior was born, Rebecca's girlfriend Vivica drove her to Tucson Medical Center because Rogelio was working downtown at the auto shop where he was swamped and wouldn't be able to get home in time to take Rebecca to the hospital. It had rained all afternoon and the city looked dismal from the window of Rebecca's maternity room, gray and solemn, although she normally loved a good rain shower, loved to run outside and twirl around and smell the freshly washed air. It rained all that day and the next because it was monsoon season finally. But, to Rebecca, something seemed different about it, like it was a rain of mourning instead of rebirth. Her husband had arrived before Junior was born, and the day after she had delivered a healthy nine-pound baby, Rogelio was sleeping on the couch a few feet from her bed. He had been there for the birth but he hadn't watched. He'd stood by her head while Rebecca tried to figure out whether he was disgusted or bored. Will he be able to touch me again after watching me stretch and gush blood from the only place on my body that was sacred, now that another man has passed through me, even if it was his own son? These fuckin pachucos. They can have as many women as they want, but god forbid I sleep with another man—I might as well have fucked the whole world. She lay in bed and watched her husband wake up and rub his eyes and look around in confusion. He could just as well have woken up in a jail in Mexico from the look on his face. He realized where he was when he spotted Rebecca in bed, and he walked over to her.

We named him Junior, Rogelio smiled and rubbed his wife's hair. He's Rogelio Eduardo Nuñez the Second and he looks just like me. So, what do you think? Do you feel better? Did the drugs help the pain? He looked like he actually wanted to know, not the usual way he looked when he asked a question and didn't expect, didn't want, an answer. Most questions were usually accusations or threats. Things like, just what *do* you do while I'm slaving away downtown? So Rebecca was surprised the kind Rogelio was resurfacing and, although she didn't trust him, she answered anyway.

Yes, they helped a lot, but I had the worst dreams. She struggled to remember visions that would not come or could not be explained. She had been at the Rodeo Day parade, next to the statue of Pancho Villa where she'd first met Rogelio, and he drove up in a car, even though the road was closed for the parade, and beckoned toward the backseat, come over and help me unload these pigs, and then the back door flew open and pigs came pouring out of it like popcorn overflowing from a pan, some covered in mud and others with beautiful long hair, and the whole time Rebecca was trying to explain to him how she didn't want to help with the pigs, how she was having fun sitting next to the statue of Pancho Villa and watching the marching band members step in the shit from the horses that had come before them in the parade because everyone knew the musicians had been specifically instructed not to step out of line, even if it meant stepping in shit, but she could not explain it to him because her mouth was muffled and filled with cotton and the pigs came running at her squealing and squealing like babies, like her baby when it burst from between her legs and took its first breath, and then the pigs had the face of her baby—all of them—and they circled her and beat their snouts against her legs and she ran out into the street while Rogelio laughed and everywhere she stepped was shit and it splattered all over her pants and splashed up onto her arms and face and she was covered in shit, running and crying and the parade was gone and the band was gone and the pigs were gone and she was left there alone, covered in shit with grass and oats and hay in it, and the only thing that was left was the statue of Pancho Villa looking down at her from his horse reared back on its hind legs, and beneath the horse's front legs, right where they were going to land if the horse ever came back down with all of his eleven hundred pounds, was her baby.

Rogelio asked her what kind of dreams, Rebecca? But she could not articulate them. She could not begin to tell him because he would only laugh and he would not understand why it had been so terrifying to her.

Do you remember the statue of Pancho Villa?

You mean where we sit when we watch the Rodeo Day parade?

Yeah, that's the spot. Well, I just had some weird dream about the statue and you and pigs. But, I don't remember any of it now. It's all washed away.

And it was. Sort of. But the feeling lingered with her for the rest of the day, and so when it didn't stop raining by the time Rogelio went home, she wondered if the dreams would return or if she could stay awake until he came to pick her and Junior up in the morning.

When she first came home, Rogelio treated her with kindness. He woke up and changed the baby's diapers in the middle of the night. No complaints. Just got up and did it. He started singing boleros to his son and whispering excitedly in his ear how he was going to take him to see his first bullfight down in Nogales when he was old enough to appreciate it. Sometimes, when he saw Rebecca was listening, he winked at her and announced, when Junior's tall enough to see over the counter of a cantina I'll buy him his first beer. And he promised to teach his son to play baseball and work on cars. If the weather was nice after work, he pushed his son in the stroller, pointing out passing cars. That's the new Celica. Pretty sharp, even for a rice-burner. The new Mustang though, that's where it's at. And his son gurgled and squealed with delight and Rogelio straightened his back and waved at passing cars when the people inside smiled and pointed at him for being such a good father.

But when their financial situation didn't change and the newness of the baby had worn off, he became frustrated again. He started hiding money from Rebecca and spending it on beer, coming home drunk and trying to kiss his wife but missing her mouth and struggling to pull down her panties while she groaned in her sleep, tomorrow, Rogelio, wait until morning, but he kept trying, climbing on top of her and pulling his cock out and pushing it into her but it kept flopping out, limp, and she tried to help him, kissed him back, played with his joint, but it didn't help, and after a few more minutes he gave up and rolled over, cursing his wife and his beer-soaked dick, and passed out while Rebecca tried to block out his snoring and fall back to sleep before the baby woke up to feed. She lay in bed waiting for sleep and imagined the conversation she wanted to have with him. But they never had the conversation.

Then one evening the radio said flashfloods were coming. Rebecca said it over and over. Flashfloods. Don't drive near washes or on roads prone to flooding. Cover your swamp cooler with a tarp unless you want water dripping into your house. She knew the rules. If you have a leak in the roof, you set out the pots and pans, Tupperware bowls, whatever. You can sit under the drip with your mouth open and taste the rain mixed with your house. You call the kids in from playing and tell them it will only be a few minutes and then they can go back out into the street and play soccer or steal the neighbors' mail or sneak cigarettes in the alley. You close windows and shut doors, bring in pets, run and hide and watch as nature reminds you how insignificant you really are.

So when the radio said flashfloods were coming, she decided to make her husband take notice. She whispered flashfloods, and plucked Junior out of his crib, put him in her favorite outfit, the one with red and blue dinosaurs—T-rexes and triceratops—which reminded her of the boys in elementary school who found horny toads and pushed them up into girls' faces, because she'd always thought that horny toads proved dinosaurs weren't extinct, they'd only gotten smaller. It was the outfit he wore for his two-month pictures. She never bought any of the portraits, instead she scraped together the three-dollar sitting fee at Sears and when the notice came in the mail saying your child's portraits are waiting for you in the Sears photo lab! she went to the store and looked at her son in all the different poses and smiled and handed them back to the woman at the counter, shaking her head so the woman knew she wouldn't be buying any of them, and she walked out cursing her poverty with Junior in her arms slobbering down the back of her left shoulder.

When she finished dressing him, she put on the dress she had worked on during the final month of her pregnancy in anticipation of being skinny again. She loved the spaghetti straps and the low-cut back. How it showed just enough skin but was still classy. She had earned the money for every scrap of its fabric, a task that had taken the better part of her pregnancy. A dollar here, a dollar there. She had handmade little Easter purses in the shapes of rabbits' heads or stuffed miniature skeleton dolls for Día de Los Muertos or little Mexican flag pillows for Cinco de Mayo and sold them door-to-door in her neighborhood while the husbands were at work and the women who stayed home cleaning and cooking and feeding their children were susceptible to her sales pitch. She knew how to get them to buy, if they could truly spare the money. She had even traded two Easter purses for tamales with the old woman down the road and set the table with pride that night—a votive candle; two matching plates; full glasses of whole milk, Rogelio's favorite—and when her husband came in from work and sat down, he scooped up the tamales and beans without even asking where they'd come from. Rebecca was sure the dress made her look like a queen, or at least a princess, and she turned around several times in front of the bathroom mirror before pinning her hair up like she had seen girls do for their proms, leaving a few strands on the sides.

Tonight Rogelio had to work late and wouldn't be home until around eleven. She thought about writing him a note, explaining how she needed to drive out in the rain, to see the desert momentarily become an ocean. She wondered if he'd even worry. She wanted to tell him how she felt when she went grocery shopping, to ask him do you have any idea the evil eyes shooting at me in the grocery store when I take my food stamps or my WIC vouchers and buy milk, bread, ground beef—not the fancy reduced-fat ground chuck—and people, you can see what they're thinking, that worthless woman milking the system and buying steaks and Coke and candy with our hard-earned tax dollars. And they don't even know what it's like to come home and turn on the lights and find roaches in our cereal and to pick them out of the box, wondering if they've lain eggs—what do they say? for every roach you see, there are ten thousand scurrying around in the walls—and to have to eat the food and serve it to you and Junior and wonder if the eggs will make the baby sick or if they'll hatch in your stomach and you'll wake up with night sweats, your body infested with insects chewing their way out?

She picked up her purse and her son. Junior, we're going to break the rules. We're going to drive during a flashflood and be brave. She buckled him into his seat in the back of the car, taking care not to wrinkle his outfit with the tight straps. He didn't wake up, but instead nuzzled his face into the receiving blanket Vivica brought to the hospital on the day he was born. She took care to keep her dress from wrinkling beneath her, stretching it out before she sat down on it, buckling her seatbelt and placing the strap behind her back. She was pulling out of the driveway when the first drops of rain began to fall. She passed through her neighborhood, her home for the last four years, and noticed her neighbors looking from their windows, watching for the downpour.

The roads were mostly empty, and the few cars that remained began to pull to the shoulder of the road or beneath the canopies of gas stations for safety. But Rebecca drove on, undeterred by the rain that now fell so hard the windshield wipers had no effect, and she sang to Junior the songs her mother had sung to her during storms, Si Tú Te Vas, Dos Gardenias, wondering if he would wake and notice the rain hammering on the roof of the car, happy that he was quiet but sad that he was not awake to notice how clean the desert smells when it rains, which was one of her favorite smells.

Now he's going to see, she said to her son in her bravest voice, minutes after bringing her car to a stop in the Santa Cruz River, the arroyo that runs crookedly along the west side of Tucson, longer than the whole city and deep enough to remind Rebecca of the huge ditches they used for mass graves in old war footage on TV, an invisible river as dry as the rest of the landscape, with only the ghosts of fish swimming past and specters of ancient tribes washing their animal-skin clothing in the river that no longer existed, that wound into the desert past the city, past the lighted buildings of the downtown and the missions, fleeing the businesses and the roads creeping closer every year, a moat between the mountains and civilization, whose smoke-coughing cars and asphalt streets branded and gridded and crisscrossed the once pure land, and knowing the flood water was coming—she wanted to get out of the car and place her car to the ground to gauge the approaching swell—she was determined to let nature decide her fate, trusting in the decision, watching the city lights in her rearview mirror and thinking how pathetic that she had lived her whole life in Tucson and only known the smallest portion of it and had never seen where Geronimo lived or where Dillinger was arrested or the ranches Mexican bandits looted at night for supplies, because she had been too caught up in her own life, brushing hair, learning how to do makeup, wishing she could meet Prince, and sneaking behind Q Mart for kisses with boys, which she had never mentioned so no one would think she was a slut or a chingada and beat her for trying to steal their boyfriends, and even now she felt like a fallen woman, especially now, sitting in her idling car gazing at the walls of the arroyo lined like the rings of a bathtub, rising above her like the walls of an ancient city, the vessel that carried the flood water, which was the gift for the rain dancers who collapsed with exhaustion when the first drops fell while their fellow tribesmen rushed to collect as much of it as possible in clay containers before the thirsty desert drank it up, and Rebecca thought she had fallen asleep at her windowsill and dreamed the flashflood, of course, so convinced it was a dream that she wanted to wake her son sleeping in the backseat and say to him, come with me out into the wash and we'll walk and pick the buried hairs of our ancestors from the dry walls of this river, and Rebecca wanted to pick up the arrowheads of fallen warriors while she pointed out the stars to Junior, but she let him sleep, allowed him to dream while her hands trembled and her breath went cold, and she wondered if the other people who had drowned in this very arroyo, or other arroyos—Santa Rita, Rillito River—had done so by accident, or had they purposely gone there so they could fling themselves, their women, and their children, into the water, sacrifices to the desert spirits, carried away to wherever the river deposited its spoils, the place where the bones of lost children and tired parents sank into the earth and scraped against one another until they were ground to a fine powder like the blush a much younger Rebecca used to brush onto her cheeks as she sat in her room waiting on boys to come pick her up and take her out for a meal or to the zoo, the same color she brushed onto her cheeks minutes before she buckled her son into the backseat and kissed him on his forehead and then went back into the house to put Rogelio's dinner in the oven so it would be warm when he got home, except that he would probably not find his dinner without her help, without her carrying it to him and setting it on the table in front of him the same way she had set her heart before him a few years earlier and he had stabbed it with his fork, slicing into it and chewing tiny pieces covered in gravy, consuming it slowly until she could no longer feel anything but shame and sadness, even though she'd had a son, which was supposed to be life's most beautiful gift, yet she was ashamed to be his mother and ashamed to give him the name of a man who was capable of looking through her as if she were no different from the windowpane she rested her head on every afternoon, the same man who hadn't held his own son in two months and had once come home so drunk he stumbled to the dresser and pulled open the top drawer and pissed all over her stockings and her panties, despite her attempts to stop him by shouting and shaking his arm, and he never did apologize but instead ignored the stench of piss that filled the entire house for two weeks and lingered in Rebecca's nose for three more, and although she scrubbed her undergarments repeatedly the fumes were impossible to remove, so she wore them to bed thinking maybe the smell would remind her husband of that night, because it was a night she would never forget, the first time she realized that she could hate the man she had taken vows to love, and since she had learned to hate him, she took advantage of the energy it gave her, shrieking at the walls while he was away and damning them to the same fate as her own—I HOPE RATS BURROW INTO YOU AND CHEW OUT YOUR HEART THE SAME WAY MY HUSBAND DOES TO ME AND TERMITES SLOWLY EAT YOUR FOUNDATIONS AND TURN THEM TO DUST WHILE YOU SLEEP—and she pulled out her hair and tore the sleeves from her shirts and the pockets from her pants and then sewed them back together while she sat naked in her sewing chair, seething with fury, hurling curses, words she had never dared to utter before, a la madre chingada and everything damnable she could dredge up from the recesses of her soul, a soul so utterly crushed by decayed love she wished she had never been given a soul and that she had never met her husband, dios mío, why didn't you just stay in your neighborhood with your cholos and your vatos and your rucas, the women you fucked without even looking at their faces so you wouldn't have to speak to them if you ever saw them on the streets afterwards with hickeys on their necks and babies in their bellies, vile women scratching at their asses and digging in their crotches riddled with warts and crawling with lice, you could have made a better life for yourself dealing weed or angel dust to your friends so you could roll around the south side in your lowrider and your chain-linked steering wheel instead of dragging me into your twisted world where I'm an afterthought and your baby might as well be a hamster for all the attention you show him, and the rain fell harder and the rushing water finally came, seeping under the doors of the car, rising to her ankles, and she fought her reflexes, forcing her feet to stay on the floor—this is the part where I'm supposed to bash out the windows and pull us out to safety—but she did not bother to kick out the window, did not try to roll the window down or undo her seatbelt, instead she sat completely still, feeling the cold muddy water bathing her feet like one of Jesus' disciples, and she thought of her last supper, the leftover menudo with the tripe still floating in the middle, solidified grease clinging to it even after she had reheated the soup on the stove and split it between herself and her son, spooning it into his mouth while her own bowl grew cold, and the water lapped at her calves and rose faster and higher until it was in her lap, tickling her and freezing her and taunting her until she lost control of her bladder and felt the warmth of her urine spreading between her legs, and her son stirred in the backseat because the water had begun to soak through his shoes and socks, and she could hear the frightened tremble in his voice crying out for her in confusion, and he kept crying while she sang him bedtime songs and all the soothing melodies she could call to mind, which became more difficult as her car lifted off the ground and was carried away by the rushing water, and the lights of the city circled around her and became blurry above the surface of the water, but she sang on even while she wondered why the car was underwater but not yet full, clenching her teeth when her son's crying suddenly ceased as the water rose above his head and crept up toward her neck, but refusing to turn and look at him because this wasn't what was supposed to happen, her chest heaving with the terror inside her, and when the water reached her chin she let out her breath and bowed her head, feeling the splashing in her ears, letting her lungs fill with water, relieved when the car became full and she was left with her thoughts, now he's going to see how hopeless our situation really is, and momentarily confused by the purple dinosaur sock floating slowly past the steering wheel.

ICE CREAM

CARMELLA SANTIAGO BEGGED HER HUSBAND NOT TO pull the trigger. But when he did, she fell in love with him all over again.

The mob outside the courthouse, the very next day, had fallen in love with her husband too. They had all watched him, on live television, walk straight up to the man being escorted into the courtroom by six sheriff's deputies. The accused shuffled down the hall, his shackles confining his footsteps to an awkward trot. He wore a bulletproof vest and held his head low with his hands cuffed together—as if in prayer—attempting to hide his face but really only obscuring his chin. Cameras flashed, reporters shoved microphones in front of him, but he only pushed onward while the deputies shooed the cameras and microphones away as if they were a swarm of flying ants. And there, in the chaos of newsmen and law enforcement officers, Alejandro Santiago came into the frame of the television, walking up to the accused and pulling out his gun, raising it slowly, deliberately, and the deputies didn't even react—who would think of pulling a gun in a courthouse?—and the accused looked up just as the deputies began to process the scene in front of them and Alejandro clenched his teeth and pulled the trigger and the back of the accused's head exploded all over the deputies and the fuzzy microphones and the reporters and the cameras and Alejandro let the gun drop from his hands and held out his wrists and by then the deputies finally grasped what had just occurred so they wrestled Alejandro to the ground and cuffed him and took him into custody amid the screams of women and the stampede of frenzied people toward the exit.

Carmella had watched the entire event live on Channel 4 and was moved to tears. She stroked his face when it appeared on the TV screen, feeling the cottony static build up and imagining that it was her husband's cheek. That he had forgotten to shave that morning in his haste to leave for the courthouse. She had begged him not to go, told him to leave it in the hands of the law, Alí, please, they will make him pay, that's what they do, but she knew she had no power to stop him. She hadn't really wanted to stop him anyway.

The TV showed the footage of her husband for three days straight. Nonstop. On every newscast. Footage from every angle. One cameraman from Channel 9 had unwittingly captured Alejandro's approach—they liked to freeze the picture, zoom in, draw a white circle around her husband—and you saw him pretending to be talking on the payphone, nodding his head and glancing nonchalantly over his shoulder at the approaching deputies and the accused, and he simply turned around and the phone slid from where he held it pinned between his shoulder and his ear, and before the receiver had time to smash against the wall, the gun was already appearing from out of his waistband as he took large confident strides toward his enemy. That was one of their favorite angles. It puts a face on what might otherwise be considered a cold-hearted killer, they liked to say. Carmella chuckled whenever she heard that phrase. Her husband, cold? Anything but.

Carmella's favorite angle was the one captured by Channel 18. It showed the look on her husband's face right before he pulled the trigger and covered the camera lens with blood. They liked to freeze that angle too. Right before the gun goes off. It was the frame they had used for the front page of all the newspapers. Alejandro's steeled jaw, his furrowed brow, and his eyes. His eyes made the photo. Those eyes that spoke his soul in a way she had loved immediately the first time she'd met him through a mutual friend over coffee in a night that ended with him stroking her cheek and brushing her forearm without her noticing because it had been perfect and his hands felt as if they had been there on her skin all along. And in the photo, her husband's face taking up the top half of the *Arizona Daily Star*'s front page, on the rim of her husband's eye, Carmella saw a tear lingering, ready to drop, the bottom of it heavy and filled with just enough liquid that gravity would inevitably coax it over the edge of the lid. It clung to his eyelashes. Carmella thought if I had the technology, I'd blow up the picture until it was just the tear so I could see the reflection of that bastard right before my Alejandro blew his filthy brains out of his godless head.

She liked to look at the picture of her husband's eyes—so determined, so unselfish. She could see what so many others had failed to see—that her husband had killed the man out of love, not out of hate.

Carmella had taped every newscast she could manage and she watched the tapes endlessly—Alejandro walks up to the man and BLAM. He puts out his wrists. It's like a ballet. Alejandro, so graceful. He holds the gun out like a rose being offered to a lover. He lifts it tenderly and when it bucks in his hand, he releases it, and it drops to the floor like a dying bird. One fluid movement. Arms go up, he shoots, gun drops, and his hands are there, empty, like he had never had anything in them in the first place.

The part they stopped showing on the news was the accused. The way his head exploded yet his body continued to walk forward—she had counted—one, two, three more steps before it collapsed, finally accepting the idea that its head was missing. As if it wanted to go forward with the trial anyway to prove its innocence.

The story became national news. A man in Tucson is accused of the rape and murder of a seven-year-old girl. The public is outraged. The morning of the alleged killer's arraignment, the victim's father, certain that the State of Arizona will not be able to impose real justice, takes the law into his own hands and murders the accused. It's the oldest tale in the Southwest. Cowboy justice. *USA Today* loved the idea. Victim's Father Corrals Accused. Standoff in the Southwest. New Sheriff Comes to Town. And on, and on.

The mob outside the courthouse had fallen in love with Carmella's husband too. They demanded that he go free. They stood outside holding signs and chanting that his actions weren't punishable. That he should be rewarded. The mob had appeared almost immediately upon seeing the live telecast of the murder. The mayor of Tucson had ordered riot police to set up a perimeter to contain the enraged crowd.

Carmella felt an immense pride in her husband as she watched the crowd grow in front of the courthouse. People had come from as far as Maine and Florida. They liked to tell the TV crews this sort of thing wouldn't be an issue in OUR state. New York would just let Alejandro Santiago walk free. Florida would name a park after him. Oklahoma had already set aside an honorary stretch of highway for just this sort of event. Carmella liked the sound of the Honorary Alejandro Santiago Freeway. It flowed nicely from the tongue. She said it over and over again. The Honorary Alejandro Santiago Freeway. It made her happy.

The kidnapping of Samantha Santiago was not at all uncommon for Tucson. Children were abducted on a weekly basis and were never heard from again. Their faces were in constant rotation on milk cartons and post office walls. Not a month went by without some unfortunate parents coming home to find their child missing, only to call the police and get the brush-off because their missing persons division was swamped. It was the circumstances surrounding Samantha's kidnapping that had made her case so high profile.

Twelve days before Carmella watched her husband live on TV shoot the accused man, Samantha, after spending the clear Saturday morning watching cartoons, had disappeared on the way to a friend's house. All they'd found, after three days of relentless searching, was a melted ice cream cone lying beneath Samantha's favorite Care Bear, Grumpy Bear, that she had taken with her. All the parents in the neighborhood had been notified of her disappearance, and someone called the Santiagos three days after she had disappeared to tell them of the ice cream cone and the stuffed doll lying in the street in front of their house, which was only two streets away.

The police chalked it up as another missing child to add to the ever-growing list of missing children in the greater Tucson area, and they sent a patrol to give the Santiagos the usual speech concerning children whose disappearance had lasted more than two days. So, three days later, with no leads and no clues other than the doll and the ice cream, two officers arrived at the Santiagos's house in the early evening, parked their cruiser in front of the house where the neighbors, who were gaping out their windows, shook their heads in grief for the mother and father, and knocked on the front door. Alejandro and his wife answered the door, hesitating when they saw two police officers who so obviously had no good news, then inviting them in for coffee so they could talk in private.

Both officers were rookies, which is why they'd been sent to do the taxing job of telling Alejandro and his wife that the odds, Mr. and Mrs. Santiago, that your daughter has been taken out of state—and of course there are exceptions—are pretty good. Perhaps she's even been taken down to Mexico where children are often smuggled only to resurface many years later fluent in Spanish, having forgotten all their English and bearing an entirely new identity. That's the worst-case scenario. There's also a small chance that the person who abducted her may be contacting you about a ransom. If that's the case—the officer cleared his throat, looked at his partner, who nodded for him to continue—please contact us and we'll try our best to work something out with the criminal.

The officers didn't tell the parents what is most common, that their daughter was either dead or maybe had even been smuggled down into the belly of Mexico where she'd be sold into slavery or prostitution. Most likely in Mexico City. But there was no point in telling them that.

On the fourth day following Samantha's disappearance, the Tucson Police Department received an anonymous phone call from a family living on A Mountain. Their son had come home late at night from visiting his girlfriend down in the city when he had almost run head-on into an ice cream truck speeding down a secluded mountain road without its headlights on. He hadn't been able to read the license plate number and waited a few days to tell his parents about the event because he worried he'd get into trouble for staying out too late. When he finally told his parents, they decided to call the police because nothing good could come from any vehicle driving on A Mountain at night with its lights off. Besides, ice cream men never came up there. It was mostly retirees who lived on the mountain.

And so, five days following the disappearance of their daughter, while the Santiagos lay in bed, pale and unable to do anything but pray for her safe return, the police sent a search team up to A Mountain to check out the tip. The search team, consisting of four police officers, stumbled upon the body of Samantha Santiago at 1:36 p.m., in the blazing 115-degree summer heat. The sight of the little girl's body caused two of the officers to faint immediately, their minds rejecting the picture of the dead girl bound by five lengths of bungee cord, and the other two officers, who had thirty-two years combined experience on the force and who'd found countless bodies in the desert over the years, grabbed on to each other for support and wept and vomited for almost half an hour until they could only dry heave and spit up blood and their tear ducts were incapable of producing another drop.

The image of the little girl's ravaged body burned itself permanently into their memories. When they'd recovered enough to speak, the search committee radioed dispatch and told them to send homicide and the coroner, and then the members of the team sat in a circle to wait for the arrival of the others and took turns praying for the girl's soul so that it might rest peacefully and forget the violent death it had endured.

The coroner arrived shortly after the call came in and couldn't bear to look, forced to turn away as he snapped pictures from every possible angle, hoping he had gotten close enough to document the ragged hole in her abdomen where her entrails had been eaten away by vultures or coyotes or other desert creatures—or so he hoped. He told the officers to cut the bungee cords and bag them for evidence, then rope off the scene and place the girl facedown in a bodybag so he could photograph the gouges that riddled her arms and neck and back and legs. The coroner grieved silently as he snapped the pictures, then zipped the bag and carefully lifted it into the hearse and drove slowly down the mountain toward the Tucson Medical Center, where he and his assistants would perform a full autopsy on the remains.

It wasn't until the next day that the Santiagos were notified that a body had been found up on A Mountain that fit the age and general description of their missing daughter. Alejandro trembled as he put down the phone and turned to face his wife in bed to tell her the news.

They think they might have found Samantha's body. Carmella shook her head and turned away. Morena, we have to go see. She pulled a pillow over her head to shut out her husband's words. We have to go. We must know. Carmella. Mi corazón. Come with me. Don't make me go alone. Alejandro placed his arms around her shoulders and scrunched his eyes closed and relaxed every muscle in his body to absorb the heaving of his hysterically sobbing wife. He held her while she wept and told her not to worry. It probably isn't her, but we have to go check. After many hours her weeping subsided, turned to shudders, then finally dwindled to the occasional twitch.

During the entire drive down to the Tucson Medical Center, Carmella stared out the window and forced Alejandro to slow the car each time she saw a girl with black hair on the street. Slow down, Alejandro. What if it's her? Could you forgive yourself if our baby is just lost and we drove right past her to go look at some dead girl in a morgue? COULD YOU? Well, I couldn't. No. And I'll never forgive you if you don't at least slow enough to LOOK at a girl who just might be ours. She has to be SOMEWHERE. Carmella said all of this with her face to the window while Alejandro shook his head and bit the inside of his cheek to keep from bursting into tears. He slowed for his wife when she asked, not even bothering to look at the girl in question because it was bad enough that one of them was keeping their hopes up. He slowed each time she demanded it and clenched the steering wheel in tight fists, waiting to hear the sigh of resignation when his wife had verified that yet another girl with black hair was not their Samantha.

Less than a mile from the medical center, Alejandro was steeling himself to view the body of a dead girl who might be his daughter. But how do you prepare for such things, he wondered. How does a parent ready himself to look upon the corpse of his child and wrap his mind around the idea that the child lying lifeless in front of him was just yesterday playing in the backyard with her friends? How do I, if it's really her, look at our daughter for the last time? And how do we go home and clean out her room and destroy all the cards she ever made us? What do we do with all her clothes and her stuffed animals and her Disney posters? Do we really have to pretend she never existed to get used to the idea that she won't be coming home again and asking for an after-school snack?

He tried to imagine all the possible questions that would rise to the surface of his mind, tried to guess how it might be if his little girl was truly gone forever, when his wife screamed and began pounding on her window and kicking her legs trying to get the car door open, suddenly remembering the lock and bursting through the passenger door before Alejandro could stop the car. She tumbled out into the street and was back on her feet and running toward the public library screaming IT'S HER, IT'S OUR SAMANTHA, before Alejandro slammed the car into park in the middle of the road and switched on the hazards and ran after her with all the hope and desperation he could muster to pin on this last little girl. Carmella screamed after the child, yelling for her to stop, PLEASE STOP, BABY, and the girl turned and saw the woman running frantically toward her, and she dropped the books she was carrying and bolted toward the library entrance, running between parked cars, barely able to breathe when she tripped over her untied shoelaces and fell to the ground, skinning her knee on the parking lot asphalt. She immediately began to cry, terrified of the woman coming after her and in pain from the gravel buried in her knee, yelling MOMMY, HELP, MOMMY. Carmella heard the girl's cries and found her sitting on the ground holding her injured knee up to her chest, and she collapsed beside the girl and hugged her and told her it's alright, Samantha, Mommy's here. We found you. Mommy and Daddy did. You can come home now. You can come back to your house, baby. She held the little girl close to her and rubbed her head and kissed her knee and was muttering words of love and encouragement when Alejandro reached the two of them and stopped running. He stood panting for breath, unable to believe their good fortune at having found their little girl. He wept and laughed as he stepped forward to hug them. He reached out to touch his daughter's head, to feel her beautiful cornsilk hair once again, but stopped mid-stride when an electric shock shot through his back and into his kidney, paralyzing him, and as he fell to his knees he saw a woman charge past him and shove a stungun into his wife's neck and his wife's body went limp and lay still in the library parking lot, her lips covered in blood from the little girl's scraped knee that she had been kissing.

The woman stepped over his wife and, with the rage of a mother's protective instincts in her eyes, she spit on Carmella's face and said this is MY girl, you witch. Bruja. Whore. You're so lucky my husband isn't here or he would've crushed both of your child-snatching skulls.

Carmella's leg twitched, but she lay still, curled into a ball with tears streaming down her cheeks onto the asphalt where they sizzled and dried up immediately.

Alejandro rose to his knees and reached out toward the woman and whispered Samantha, please come back, Samantha. The woman turned around and pushed her daughter behind her, protecting the girl from the two crazed predators. She is NOT Samantha. Her name is Erica and she's MY daughter. The mother reached back into her purse for her stungun and held it out in Alejandro's direction and pushed the button. The stungun hissed and popped in the woman's hand. She took a step toward Alejandro and then, in a voice so sweet it almost broke his heart, the child grabbed her mother's arm and said don't, Mommy. Please don't. And the exhausted mother relented, allowing her daughter to lead her away.

Alejandro gathered his wife's limp body off the ground and carried her back to the car waiting in the middle of the road with its flashers blinking, a line of traffic behind it honking at the abandoned vehicle.

———

In the morgue the Santiagos waited with thirteen other couples. Some were certain their child wasn't lying dead in the other room and had only come because there was nothing else to do while awaiting the call from the police telling them their child had been found and could be picked up at the downtown precinct. Others had given up on seeing their child alive again but hoped that she was still alive somewhere. Maybe lost in a mall or asleep under a bush scared and waiting to be found. Still others were aware that their child was most likely dead. They had accepted this fate and only needed proof. A body. A finger bone. A tooth. A strand of hair. Anything they could place in a pine box and bury so they could get on with their lives and just maybe the nightmares would finally go away.

The Santiagos were among the first group. Parents who had yet to give up hope. They were both certain Samantha was still alive somewhere and weren't expecting the morgue visit to help anything. Nobody looked at one another. The air in the room was thick with despair and no one wanted to look at a couple exiting the examination room and see the relief of two parents who had just seen the corpse, trying to contain their happiness because it hadn't been their child lying dead on the table, but ashamed to show any joy in front of the other people whose child might be lying mutilated beneath the sterile and impersonal lights of the morgue.

Six couples entered and left. The Santiagos still waited. Alejandro didn't have to look up to know the child in the other room didn't belong to any of the people who had gone so far. He could sense the relief pouring from them as they walked back through the waiting room and out the door. Besides, the coroner would quit calling off names if the body had been identified. And he hadn't stopped calling.

Finally, the Santiagos were called. Carmella, unable to bear the strain—even if it wasn't Samantha—buried her face in her husband's neck as they entered the examination room. The coroner's assistant led them to the farthest table in the room, past more than a dozen covered bodies, to a table with a bright lamp shining down on it. The assistant asked them to hang on a second, and the coroner entered the room and walked to the head of the table, tucking his clipboard beneath his right arm. He avoided looking directly at the Santiagos, letting his eyes dart about the room— floor to ceiling, left to right—as Alejandro stood by his wife at the foot of the shiny metal table. The tips of two tiny feet stuck out from beneath the gray plastic sheet. Hanging from the big toe of the child's right foot was an identification tag. The coroner spoke, warning Alejandro and Carmella of the severity of injuries to the child's body, attempting to tactfully explain the cause of death without going into any details that might potentially drive the parents to madness. But Alejandro ignored the words and lightly shrugged his wife's head off his shoulder. She turned away from the table. Alejandro looked at the tiny foot. The way the pinky toe curved under and the toenail seemed to slide down the side was exactly like Samantha's. The coroner kept speaking, preparing the parents for the viewing, but his words went unheard. Alejandro raised the tag where it hung from the child's body and read the words scribbled on it. No name or age. Sex: F. Height: 47 inches. Weight: 35 pounds. Alejandro was relieved. He turned to his wife and placed his hand on her shoulder and told her Carmella, it's not her. It's not Samantha.

She turned to face her husband. How do you know? Did you see her face? Alejandro shook his head. But look here at this tag. It says this girl's thirty-five pounds. Samantha is more like forty-eight pounds, right? Right? Carmella hugged her husband, overcome with relief.

The coroner shook his head and spoke again. Mr. and Mrs. Santiago, this girl weighs thirty-five pounds *now*. But she weighed more when she was alive. That's what I've been trying to tell you. All you need to do is come up here and look at her face. That's all I'm asking. Just look at her face.

Alejandro didn't move. Carmella squeezed her husband's arm tighter. The coroner spoke again. Please. Just once. Look and look away.

Alejandro grabbed his wife's hand and led her to the table. The coroner pulled the sheet down to the girl's shoulders and asked is this your girl? Take your time. When you're sure, let me know.

But he didn't need to hear an answer. He'd seen the look so many times. The look of denial when a relative sees the face of death clouding the once-recognizable features of a loved one. The way they blink their eyes and bring their hands up to their mouths to hold back the cry of recognition that wants to leap out and make itself heard. The way they look a second time, their brains denying the truth while their eyes seek to confirm it. It's an awful look, and the Santiagos had it all over them. The coroner put down his clipboard. Is this your daughter, Mr. and Mrs. Santiago?

Carmella shook her head and said no, no. No. It's someone else's baby. Our girl is brown, not purple, and she smiles. She has little smile wrinkles in the corners of her mouth and a dimple high in her left cheek, so this cannot be Samantha.

She bucked and then collapsed into her husband's arms because as she spoke those words her brain and eyes finally connected with one another and verified the undeniable fact that it was indeed *their* baby on the table whose purple and sun-dried face was practically unrecognizable. Alejandro knew it from the first glance and was glad his wife didn't seem to be aware, but when she collapsed in his arms he knew that she knew and he wanted only to leave the death-infested basement of the medical center, but he could only seem to stand there, still, holding his wife until the intercom paged a doctor to come to trauma two stat, and then he broke from his trance and pulled his wife to him to lead her out of the morgue before the reality of Samantha's death registered in her mind and she snapped.

Carmella pushed her husband's arms away and turned back toward the table, smoothing her hair, then her blouse, then her wrinkled skirt. She took a deep breath and said let me see her. The coroner raised his hand to object. His assistant, having seen this look on Carmella's face on a hundred parents, reached instinctively for the plastic sheet to re-cover the body. Mrs. Santiago, it's best that—

She stormed toward the coroner and grabbed his collar and yelled IF YOU DON'T SHOW ME MY BABY'S BODY I'LL CHEW THROUGH YOUR ARMS—YOUR GODDAM NECK IF I HAVE TO—BECAUSE I WANT TO SEE HER AND I *WILL* SEE HER.

There were only two reasons Alejandro didn't try to stop his wife. The first was that he knew she would never forgive him if he tried to deny her wish to uncover the body. The second was that he needed to see, too, so he could know whether she had simply wandered off and gotten lost and died a naïve child's death in the middle of the desert or if she had been taken from them and misused, which is what his gut knew had happened.

The coroner said no and wouldn't release the sheet. He dropped his clipboard and grabbed the gray plastic with both hands and begged Carmella to listen, to please use some reason. Listen. You DO NOT want to see this body. If it's your daughter's face, that's enough. We'll mail you a report concerning the cause of death when we complete the full autopsy, then we'll release the body to you as soon as possible for you to grieve over.

Carmella only replied in a seething whisper, if you do not remove this sheet so I can see my daughter, my husband and I will kill you here and now. She turned to Alejandro for his support. He didn't deny his wife's threat, which was all the support the coroner needed to see.

He let go of the sheet and stepped back from the table. She's yours. Then he knelt to retrieve his fallen clipboard. He continued to kneel as the Santiagos uncovered their daughter's body, bracing himself for the rage that was sure to burst from the two parents of this unfortunate child.

But the rage never came.

The morgue fell silent.

The coroner held his breath.

Samantha's mother and father looked at their daughter in shock. It wasn't disbelief. They both knew it was Samantha on the table. She had the same knobby knees. The same muscles and well-fed legs of a child who had spent most of her free time outdoors, playing soccer in the street, riding her bike up and down the park trails. But it was the delicate fingers grabbing at nothing, reaching out for her mommy in her final moments of life, that wracked Carmella with sadness.

Neither Alejandro nor Carmella realized it, but when they saw the gaping and waxy hole where their daughter's poochy belly used to be, they both emitted a slight howl—like a distant pack of coyotes—that grew steadily louder until the room where they stood began to expand slowly, the floor dipping slightly beneath the weight of the Santiagos's anguish and rage and confusion.

The other tables in the morgue began to slide toward the center of the room as the howls of Alejandro and Carmella became so unbearable that the coroner had to throw up his hands to cover his ears and the couples still in the waiting area grabbed their belongings and ran to the parking lot, well aware that the proper parents had been found and terrified to see the reckless grief that would result from the mother and father whose child had been found, bound and murdered, in the middle of the heartless desert.

Samantha's parents wailed together. They howled as they scanned their daughter's empty body. Her torso looked as if it had been gouged and scraped out by an enormous ice cream scoop. Her eyes held a sadness so intense and so forlorn that even the coroner, unable to avert his gaze from them, began to weep, adding to the flood of tears.

Unlike her husband and the coroner, who both seemed unable to move, the way they stood there with their eyes locked on Samantha's body, Carmella collapsed beside her daughter, the bottom of her skirt floating in the river of tears flowing past her legs, and rested her head on her daughter's, feeling for the last time the cheeks she had wiped clean on so many occasions with a dab of spit on her thumb, the two loose teeth her daughter had been looking forward to losing so she could put them beneath her pillow with a note for the tooth fairy. She felt the little eyebrows that she had been planning to one day teach Samantha to pluck and the hair she'd never get to style for yearbook pictures.

All of her daughter's features Carmella committed to memory by touch while her heart split. But it wasn't until she felt Samantha's fingers grasping her own in death that Carmella, with her forehead resting on the cold surgical metal of the examination table, stopped weeping and looked up at her husband. She asked only one question.

What are you going to do?

And she didn't speak another word to her husband until, a week and one day later when she sat crosslegged on the living room floor in front of the TV, hugging Samantha's favorite Care Bear to her chest, and whispered to the screen, please don't pull the trigger, Alejandro.

Then he did.

⸻

Octavio Flores became a father at the age of eighteen. He and his then-girlfriend, Claudia Sanchez, decided to name their daughter Lavinía after Octavio's great aunt, who'd died the year the couple had met. Octavio, a ladies man with the charm of a poet and a voice that made women warm below the waist, had no intention of marrying the pregnant girl because he had three other, more promising prospects at the time, as well as an established pattern of bedding at least two strange women each month and keeping in contact with them by leaving behind small notes that he slipped into their purses or under their pillows after long afternoons of sex.

He could afford to date many women because he smuggled marijuana across the border every Tuesday night, passing through Nogales, Mexico, and into Arizona, then driving the back roads into Sierra Vista, where he broke up the shipment in the storage shed behind his parents' house, bundled it into pounds, and distributed it among a few of his closest friends, who sold it in smaller towns like Bisbee, Benson, and the south side of Tucson.

His dreams of remaining a bachelor changed one day when he was captured by the border patrol just east of Sahuarita with two hundred pounds of marijuana in his trunk. Had the officer not been a rookie,

Octavio could've easily bribed the man into taking a portion and letting him go. Instead Octavio found himself, a week from turning eighteen, in a holding cell at the Cochise County Jail, awaiting arraignment on charges of possession with intent to distribute and the smuggling of illegal narcotics over international borders. But the arraignment never happened.

His pregnant girlfriend, Claudia, after hearing of Octavio's arrest, broke down in front of her father and begged for his intervention, knowing he had many connections with the highest officials in Sierra Vista and Cochise County. After hearing his daughter's confession of pregnancy out of wedlock and the situation her boyfriend had gotten himself into, Esteban Sanchez placed a few phone calls to ensure the charges against Octavio never became official. And so Octavio, two days later, was surprised to find himself face-to-face with the Cochise County superior court judge, trying to understand why he was talking privately with the man in his chamber instead of being formally brought up on charges in the middle of a courtroom. The judge gave him an ultimatum, telling Octavio, who was shaking imperceptibly, that he had two options. He could face several serious felony charges for international drug trafficking that would cost him a minimum of twenty years in prison, or he could marry the daughter of Esteban Sanchez, a retired army colonel who commanded the respect of some of the most important people in southeast Arizona and had the best interests of both his daughter and his unborn grandchild in mind.

The choice was simple. And so, in the summer of 1972, Octavio and Claudia were married in a quiet ceremony at St. Martin's Catholic Church.

In an effort to avoid the rule of Claudia's father, Octavio convinced his wife that his employment options in Sierra Vista were severely limited. She agreed and, less than two months after their marriage, they moved their fledgling family to Tucson, where Octavio immediately secured a job as a used car salesman at a small lot on the corner of Speedway and Kolb.

Although he'd planned to get a fresh start in Tucson, Octavio continued his philandering during his lunch breaks or on the way home from work, resentful of the debt owed to Claudia's father and hopeful his new wife would eventually tire of his infidelity and return to Sierra Vista to live under her father's roof. Much to his dismay, Claudia seemed to grow fonder of Octavio the longer their false relationship wore on. The later he returned home from work, the more extravagant Claudia's meals and their presentations became.

He even tried to offend his unwanted wife by coming home with the stench of sex in his clothes and purposefully refusing to wash up because he wanted his wife to smell and taste the proof of his disloyalty and leave him in a fit of rage.

Each night on his way home, he visualized what he longed to occur. He would come home and take his seat at the perfectly set dining room table, silverware glinting in the light of a dozen candles, trying to determine which fork to use for what and which plate matched which food and what the shit he could possibly need two spoons for. He ate and ignored Claudia's questions about his day at work and how many cars he'd sold down at Betancourt's Used Car Sales, telling her not to worry, sales were going just fine. Then he finished his meal, wiped his mouth, and told Claudia to put the baby in her crib and meet him in bed. She left the candles burning, bundled up their daughter in a nice wool blanket, and carried her to the nursery. When she came into the bedroom Octavio was already beneath the covers, the bedside light extinguished, scratching his balls and sniffing his fingers and wincing at the smell of stale sex, certain his wife would gag as soon as she lifted the sheet to lie beside him, or at least when he forced her head down between his legs and made her suck him off.

But it never worked out that way. Instead of vomiting or complaining about the smell of another woman, Claudia, who had mixed and sampled so many herbs and spices as she prepared their elaborate dinners that her palate had become distorted, mistook the smell and taste of other women, when it mixed with the bouquet of her culinary experiments, for the unabashed arousal of her husband, so she devoured him all the more.

Octavio was frustrated, but he began to accept Claudia for what she was—a fine mother, a wonderful cook, and an untamed lover—and he slowly resigned himself to the unwritten pact he'd made with her father.

He decided to make the best of his unfortunate circumstances, so he began cheating on his wife less and less and actually stayed at work late selling cars instead of bedding old lovers or hunting down a new piece of tail at the bars on Speedway.

Eventually he realized he'd molded his wife into a lover any man would be more than pleased to have, so he quit talking to other women altogether and devoted himself to becoming a good husband and father. He focused more closely on his sales technique, using a mixture of sarcasm—often poking fun at the stereotype of the used car salesman—and an air of nonchalance that made buyers feel as if they were trying to sell themselves to him as good customers. Once Octavio refined his technique, his sales doubled in the next six months, then tripled, allowing him not only to provide for his family but also to put away healthy sums of money so he and his wife could eventually buy a house and maybe one day he could go into business for himself.

On his daughter Lavinía's seventh birthday, Octavio bought her a brand-new bike and locked it to the front porch railing of the house, whose mortgage he'd secured two days earlier—a fact he hid from his wife until he returned home from work with a birthday card for Lavinía, telling her and her mother to get in the car, we're going for a drive. He drove north toward central Tucson, eventually turning east on 25th Street and stopping in front of their new home.

When he pulled the car into the driveway and pointed out Lavinía's gift chained to the porch, his daughter let out a squeal of delight and raced from the car to examine her new bike with its beautiful flower-print wicker basket attached to the handlebars, its pink frame and pristine white tires, begging her father to please unlock it, please, so I can ride it down the street and try it out. Octavio's chest swelled with pride at having pleased his daughter so well, and he could barely contain his joy while trying to insert the key into the padlock to release Lavinía's present.

After he removed the bike and helped Lavinía climb onto the seat, he gave her a gentle push to start her down the driveway, then stood watching, with his arm around Claudia's waist, smiling as his little girl rolled into the street, a little wobbly at first but quickly righting herself and laughing as she pedaled to the opposite sidewalk and rode down to the corner of the block.

He and his wife watched Lavinía ride her bike up and down the sidewalk for a couple minutes, then he turned to Claudia and said there's one more surprise. This house. She looked at her husband in disbelief and asked how much is the rent? There is no rent. It's ours. Our first home to call our own. You can put a garden in the backyard if you want and, come back here—leading her to the back of the house. I was thinking I'd put a swingset for Lavinía and her new friends back there in the corner, next to the mulberry tree. Claudia squealed and threw her arms around his neck, overjoyed with Octavio's thoughtfulness and the way he'd come around from a drug dealer to a man, a real man, who not only succeeded at his career, but also had become an enviable husband and father. She laughed until she was on the verge of tears, telling Octavio I love you, I love you, until her throat was sore. Octavio waved off the words, explaining that he was only doing what he was supposed to do—providing for his wonderful wife and their gorgeous princess Lavinía.

While Claudia was thanking her husband and hugging him and kissing him all over his face, Lavinía returned to the house, excited to tell her parents about a girl named Rosa she'd met down the street and her awesome outfit with butterflies on her jeans that matched the butterflies on her pink and purple shirt—Lavinía's two favorite colors. At first she thought her parents had abandoned her and a pang of terror pierced her chest. Then, thank god, she heard her mother's laughter coming from behind the house and she ran to the backyard to find her parents. The smile on Lavinía's face when she came bursting through the gate running toward Octavio almost made his knees buckle. It was so pure and innocent and full of beauty and life, and at that exact moment his mind fast-forwarded fifteen years to see the respectable woman his daughter was going to become. All of a sudden he decided he must guard her at all costs. He devised a set of strict rules in his mind that would keep his only daughter from ever being mistreated by the boys who would inevitably try. He'd kill them first. At that moment he saw the awkward flaws of adolescence beginning to surface in his child—the crooked teeth they'd fix when all her grown-up teeth came in, the way her face would grow strange as it stretched out to form the face of an angel—and he vowed to protect her to the death.

And at the precise moment Lavinía hugged herself to her father's legs, Octavio fell deeply in love with his daughter. Not in the way a parent often falls in love with his child at the moment of birth, after seeing his own flesh and blood emerge from between the legs of the mother. No. This was deeper. He felt it in his chest. It was her delicate hands with dimples above the knuckles that he wanted to kiss in place of his own wife's hands. Her hair that looked so fresh and full of life. He fell in love with her smoothness and the way she naively flipped her hair over her shoulders after her mother finished curling it. How she stepped into her panties after a bath, as if they'd been handwoven out of the finest Chinese silks just for her, contoured to every curve of her body. These were the things he fell in love with in the backyard of their new house on 25th Street.

From that day on, Octavio became obsessed with Lavinía. He went to work forty-five minutes late so he could drive her to school, just in case someone tried to mess with her. His wife laughed at him when he told her his reasons for wanting to drive her to school, but she didn't know, as he did, that young boys were capable of the same passion and cruelty as adults. He remembered—but didn't tell Claudia—how he'd been madly in love with a girl in grade school named Heather, and often fantasized about bringing her home and tying her up so he could caress her hair and face, pull off her shirt and smell her beautiful white and freckly skin. And yet, despite his passion and distorted sense of love, the day her mother came to school to inform the teacher of her daughter's absence due to diarrhea, she whispered a little too loudly, and he realized she wasn't an infallible creature but was as flawed and human as himself, and he wanted to take her long red hair and cut it off and use it to choke the life out of her. It made him sick to know that Heather, the epitome of perfection, could fall ill to the same common and disgusting sickness that infected boys like himself. He wanted to strangle her for being normal. For being human, goddammit, because he had elevated her to a pedestal reserved for perfection. And she had failed him.

Octavio never told his wife these things, but he had good reason for going in late to work—to protect his daughter. So each morning he made sure she was well fed and, on the way to school, he allowed her to apply the slightest bit of lipstick and he pulled out a trial-sized stick of deodorant and told her to put it on because it made him happy to have the best-smelling girl—her armpits already developing a very slight stench to them.

This became the ritual every morning, and each day when he pulled up to the entrance of Robinson Elementary he hugged and kissed her goodbye, his arms lingering around her small body just a second longer every time. But after a year of this—now Lavinía was eight and in third grade—he slowly became aware of his obsession and began to back off his daughter a little, disgusted with his secret desire.

He reminded himself that he was simply in love with his daughter the way a father should be. But deep inside he knew it was sick and he slowly began to despise himself for wishing he could take his daughter home and lay her down in his bed in place of his wife.

Over the next few years, Octavio watched his daughter grow into a teenager. Her features were changing into those of a young woman. The fingers growing longer. The pudgy baby face becoming slimmer. The slight, graceful curves of womanhood appeared, and the elegant gestures to match. He longed for the lost innocence of his Lavinía's childhood. The eager way she used to throw herself on her father had begun to dissolve as she grew older, and by the time she reached the eighth grade at Mansfield Junior High, his little girl rarely spoke to him. On the few occasions when she turned to her father for help or conversation, it was distant and sterile and it tore his heart in two.

Octavio knew Lavinía's actions were typical of a girl her age, but he couldn't help feeling betrayed. She used to need him so much. Used to come crying to him in the middle of the night when she'd had a bad dream. But no more.

Octavio developed a number of techniques to deal with his daughter's maturation. He began to seek out other young girls to be around, in the hopes that one might notice him and smile and bring that feeling of innocence and pure love back that he'd been missing for so long.

At work he was always relieved whenever a customer brought a little girl along. He kept a jar full of lollipops on his desk for these occasions and even if he was busy with a customer, when he heard the squeal of a girl, he'd excuse himself and run to the child, pulling a lollipop out of his pocket and offering it to her with a warm smile, patting her head and maybe complimenting her eyes, dying to lean in close and smell her skin and kiss her just once, to feel her tiny soft lips pucker and return his kiss. But he always stopped short of grabbing up the young girl and, instead, began the self-deprecating sales pitch he'd refined to the point of being able to do it without thinking, pointing out the makes and models his years of experience had proven women with children preferred while concentrating his thoughts on imagining what the child's skin might feel like and wanting to run his fingers in between each of her ribs, to press down on the springy muscles that attached them together, to kiss every part of her tiny body while he sang her to sleep so he could pull her close and feel her heart beating and her chest rising and falling while she lay dreaming in his arms.

It didn't take long, after his own daughter had grown foreign and distant, for a feeling of emptiness to engulf his body, a vacancy in his heart that temporarily filled with joy each time a young girl came into Betancourt's Used Car Sales, but emptied again when he sealed the deal and the mother or father buckled their child into the backseat and drove away. It made his chest hurt every time.

And even these, his chance meetings with children at the dealership, began to leave him unsatisfied, merely whetting his appetite for the companionship of children, or at least the constant presence of a youthful and pure girl. He knew they all grew up eventually and became tainted by the hands of men, and it made him nauseous. Everywhere he looked girls were growing into women and spending every waking moment trying to capture the attention of men. But when they're still young they laugh and it isn't fake. They aren't trying to impress a boy who only sees them as a new piece of ass. He knew. He'd been there.

The more he looked around and became disappointed in his own daughter and the other boy-crazy girls, the more bitter and sad he became. Each day the vacancy in his chest grew greater, and it required the vision of youthful girls to temporarily fill itself and once again be happy so Octavio could go on with his daily routine. If a day went by without coming into contact with a girl, Octavio's life reflected it, from his sales to the way he greeted his wife when he came home at night. Certain he would go crazy if he couldn't find a solution, Octavio began taking his lunch breaks away from the dealership. There were several elementary schools and parks nearby and he decided the best thing to do was to park a short distance away during recess, so he wouldn't be noticeable, but still would be close enough to see the playing children clearly. He kept a detailed record of the schools he visited, so as not to become repetitive and draw attention to himself. He varied his methods as much as his creativity would permit, pulling his car up outside of schoolyards during lunch and putting on a hardhat he'd bought at Goodwill so it would look like he were a construction worker on his break. The type of man who often eats in his car. Each day he sat, wearing his hardhat and eating his lunch with no concern for what he consumed because his eyes watched the girls being chased by boys, their scraped knees and calf-length socks exciting him. He silently thanked the boys whenever they caught up with a girl and flipped up her skirt.

Other days he parked beside a playground in one of the nearby parks and gazed in fascination at the girls whose mothers pushed them on the swingset, the wind blowing through their pigtails and fanning their hair out. And every now and then, if he was lucky, a gust of wind sent the skirt of a swinging girl flying up around her waist and Octavio would stop chewing and stare, his mouth full of mushy food that he didn't taste, the image frozen in place for a few glorious seconds until the swing reached the end of its arc and the girl rushed backwards, laughing as her skirt fell around her legs again.

His routine eventually grew stale. It wasn't enough for him to merely watch the girls from a distance. He wanted to hear the laughter and smell the dust kicked up into the crisp desert air. It made the pain in his chest grow even greater, to be so close and not be able to touch them. So, seventeen weeks after he first began his lunch break visits, Octavio pulled up to the playground at Reid Park and stepped out of his car with his lunch pail in one hand and a fistful of lollipops in the other. He was nervous and afraid someone might recognize him from one of the other days he'd sat in his car eating—even though he'd only been to this particular park seven times over the last seventeen weeks—and they'd call the cops on him for stalking kids. But he knew his fears were foolish and the chances of him being recognized were very slim, so he strode confidently and calmly to a picnic table in the middle of the playground and opened his lunch pail, taking out the ham and cheese sandwich Claudia had packed for him.

As he ate he realized he hadn't thought about his wife in some time. Claudia. She was nice enough. In fact, she'd turned out pretty well—had mastered the craft of cooking, kept a pristine house, always made sure the laundry was done and Lavinía was where she needed to be. But she bored him. Terribly. There was something missing that he couldn't quite place. All he knew was that he never grew excited about returning home anymore, now that Lavinía was growing into a woman. And even when his wife was freshly bathed and treated him like a prince—removing his loafers, massaging his feet, serving up a plate of steaming food on a nicely set table, making entertaining conversation—he wasn't satisfied. He spent the whole time wishing Lavinía were eating with them instead of out at a friend's and that she was young again so he could watch her flip her hair out of her eyes or push food around on her plate or giggle with a mouthful of food. Now, whenever she did eat at home, she barely made eye contact with either of them. She spent the entire meal scowling and picking at her food and looking at her nails until everyone finished eating and she was finally excused from the table. After that she disappeared into her room for the rest of the night to talk on the phone or dream about boys.

There was nothing at home that made him happy anymore. Sure, their house was beautiful, and Claudia had done fine things with it, spending his earnings wisely on redecorating and remodeling, but it no longer brought him any joy. Not the way it used to when Lavinía met him at the door and jumped into his arms.

He wasn't sure why happiness eluded him when, by all rights, he should be thankful that the woman he'd accidentally gotten pregnant turned out to be so perfect. And Lavinía, well, she had changed his life.

All he knew was being at the playground right now, so boldly and in broad daylight, was giving him a sense of wholeness that filled the place in his heart left vacant by his growing daughter.

He'd placed a couple lollipops beside his lunch pail when he first sat down, and as he sat eating his ham and cheese he watched the children at play with their mothers or babysitters. Their shrieks and laughter delighted and excited him so much it became difficult to finish his meal because he could only think I'm so close. So close and maybe I can think of a way to approach the girls without being too obvious.

He sat thinking, tuning out all of his surroundings and focusing on a girl in overalls who was sitting alone atop a concrete tunnel just a few feet away, playing with a lizard whose tail had fallen off. She raised the writhing lizard to her lips and kissed it, saying I'm sorry, poor lizard, your tail all gone, and Octavio's heart swelled with love for the girl he longed to talk with, to sit her on his lap and play with her hair while she told him about the lizard and how it was probably so sad to have lost its tail and maybe was lost and looking for its mommy, and he'd ask her about her mommy and her favorite flavor of ice cream—I'll bet it's neapolitan, but you probably call it napoleon, hehehe.

Before he realized it, he was standing beside her with a lollipop in his outstretched hand, smiling a reassuring smile that made the girl feel comfortable enough to take it, not really paying attention to him as he reached down to tie her shoes while she slowly unwrapped the candy, placing the wrapper between her teeth and biting it open. He let his hand brush the dirt-stained skin of her ankle, feeling a great sense of relief and happiness at the softness of her skin, smiling at the tiny hairs that covered her legs and shone blond and wispy in the afternoon sun. He wanted to feel each individual hair, to pull lightly on each one and scrub the dirt off her legs in a bathtub full of nice warm water. Just as he was about to propose a bath to the little girl, a police cruiser pulled up to the playground and an officer leaned his head out the window and honked, waving Octavio over. As Octavio approached the car, his heart beating wildly in his chest, he tried desperately to appear calm. Excuses raced through his mind, reasons for being in a playground in the middle of the day when he had no child with him. But the reasons were all so lame, so transparent and foolish, he began to imagine the officer slamming him up against the car and cuffing him, roughing him up good for the worried parents who saw the arrest of a potential molester going down in the middle of the day, parents who would want to be sure that the sick fucker not only was taken off the streets, but that he was also beaten for being such a despicable creature.

He reached the police cruiser and looked at his reflection in the cop's silver-tinted shades. The officer looked at him with a smirk on his face and asked what he was doing with that little girl over there.

Little girl? Oh, that's just Sarah, one of my kid's friends.

So where's your kid?

He ran off with some of his other friends. They're probably by the pond catching crawdads.

Officer Loudermilk removed his shades and looked deep into Octavio's eyes. Octavio tried to will his hands to stop shaking, shoving them deep into his pockets as if he were looking for something.

You got some ID? Loudermilk asked. You got a license or something on you?

Octavio reached around to his back pocket, pulled his wallet out, and handed it to the cop. It's in there.

Take it out.

Octavio opened the wallet, flipped the plastic picture holder over, and pulled his driver's license out, praying that the cop hadn't noticed his trembling fingers. Here you go, sir.

Just hang tight for a second. I'm just gonna run your name and make sure there aren't any warrants out for you. You're clean, right?

Yeah, I'm clean. Then he remembered his deal with the judge in Sierra Vista and wondered if that was going to show up on his record. He waited, listening nervously to the cruiser's engine as it idled and the radio inside the car crackled and sputtered out police codes to the various crimes happening in other parts of the city, hoping that a call would come through for a real emergency so Loudermilk would have to speed off and forget the whole thing. But none came. Loudermilk called in Octavio's name and license number and sat back, waiting on the information to check out, looking at Octavio from behind his mirrored sunglasses to see if there was anything about the guy that would justify taking him in. But Octavio just stood beside the car with his hands in his pockets, looking off into the heart of the park and avoiding the playground.

The radio crackled at Loudermilk and he picked up the CB and held it to his ear, nodding his head and then pressing the button and saying ten-four, just making sure everything's kosher with this guy. He handed the license back to Octavio, told him he'd checked out okay, then said you better go find your kid because there's a lot of weirdos around this park and it's really not safe to let him run off like that.

Octavio nodded and assured the cop he was going to find his kid immediately. He walked back to the picnic table, making sure to do it calmly because the cruiser still sat idling behind him, and he packed his lunch back into the pail, waved goodbye to the little girl with his lollipop in her mouth, and walked toward the pond, pretending to search for his nonexistent child with a sense of great urgency, even calling out Junior loud enough for the cop to hear him.

When he'd made it over a hill and out of Loudermilk's sight, he stopped to catch his breath. It had been too close. Not that he'd done anything wrong, he'd only been innocently tying some kid's shoes. Shit, it wasn't like any of the parents there had noticed or freaked out. But he realized how close he had come to getting in big trouble. The cop was definitely suspicious. He'd practically looked like he thought I was raping the girl right there in public, on top of the concrete tunnel while the other parents watched in horror. He wiped the sweat from his brow, looked down at his perspiring armpits, and sat down to calm himself before he went back to work. It would only raise more questions if he showed up looking like he'd just finished jogging in his shirt and tie. Shit, he thought, I should've given the cop one of my business cards. Offered him a real nice deal on a used car. That would've been so brave there'd be no way he'd think I was up to something. But what's past is past. Scared the shit out of me anyway, he muttered as he started up his car, so paranoid he resolved never to return to the park again.

For four weeks Octavio kept that promise. Instead of taking his lunch outside the fences of schoolyards, sitting in his car, pretending to listen to the radio while he watched little girls playing, or unpacking his lunch at a picnic table in a park with a handful of lollipops by his side, he spent the next few weeks eating in the food court of Park Mall. It was almost as good as parks or schoolyards, though it fell a little bit short. There were plenty of children, but most of them were being rushed from one store to another by their mothers shopping for clearance items or bargain clothes while their husbands were at work. The mall was a different place in the daytime. It had the air of a library or church. Women shushing their children if they spoke too loudly. Merchants standing calmly behind their counters or stocking their shelves, visibly relaxed because all the teenagers who stole from them after school were nowhere to be seen. But despite the abundance of children, Octavio preferred the playground to the mall because the kids were truly happy there, running and playing together and laughing and not having to worry about being too loud.

Eventually Octavio forgot about the terror he'd felt the day Loudermilk questioned his presence at the park, and so he began visiting schools again, but only once or twice a week to keep from drawing any unwanted attention. He made a conscious effort to stay away from Reid Park.

The once- or twice-a-week visits soon grew into everyday visits, and once again Octavio found himself walking up to one of the many tables surrounding the playground, where he unpacked his lunch and pretended to revel in the peacefulness of the quiet afternoon, watching the girls playing from behind a pair of shades he'd recently purchased. They weren't excessively tinted. That would draw too much attention. Instead, they had a nice brown hue to them that allowed for people to see his eyes if they came close enough, but from afar, they ensured that no one would notice what he was looking at while he sat eating his lunch and concocting ways to get girls to accept his gift of a nice lollipop.

A few weeks of this went by and then Octavio found himself talking to a child who came up to him and asked for a stick of gum. He smiled and apologized for not having gum but told her I do have a lollipop. Do you want orange, lemon, or grape? and the girl's eyes lit up and she said I dunno, I like all three, and he laughed and said me too, and rifled through his pile of lollipops and found a yellow one and an orange one and a purple one and handed all three to the girl, who thanked him and then turned and ran toward the playground, flaunting her treats to the other kids playing in the sandbox and on the swings and they all shouted gimme, gimme and where'd you get them? and the girl pointed back at Octavio, but he was already packing up the remainder of his lunch and walking back to the car because he was afraid of drawing too much attention.

In his spare time, he tried to come up with a way to be around children all day long and have the trust of their parents. Each night when he came home from work, he began to plant the seed of this new idea in his dinner conversations with his wife, but Claudia largely ignored the hints, worrying more about the recent changes in Lavinía's attitude. She told Octavio about how she'd seen Lavinía's best friends, Helena and the two Rosas, hanging around with those gangbangers outside Torchy's. Octavio, not wanting to think about his daughter hanging around the very crowd he'd tried to protect her from, repeatedly tried to change the subject to his dream of going into business for himself, but Claudia kept cutting him off with a sharp look. You used to care so much about Lavinía. What happened? I remember when you used to rush home to be with us right after work, and you'd take her out back while you built her a treehouse and a swingset, always asking her opinion—do you want a trapdoor, or how about a swing that seats four?— and treating her like she was the only thing in the world that mattered. And now look at you. You act like you don't care if our baby falls off the face of the earth. I'm telling you, something's WRONG with her. I saw a hickey on one of the two Rosas the other day—the short one—and she didn't even try to hide it.

Octavio only shook his head in disgust, not bothering to interrupt.

Say SOMETHING, Octavio. This is our girl I'm talking about. She's only fifteen. When did you stop caring?

Octavio had stopped caring the first day his wife came home with a training bra for their daughter. That day he'd gone to the bathroom and knelt beside the toilet, resting his head on the cold plastic seat with an overwhelming feeling of nausea, unable to deal with the concrete proof his little girl was making the first transition to womanhood. A *training* bra? What else might she be training for while her he was away at work? He could only imagine the worst. Could only picture his daughter lying in bed with some boy, or worse, losing her virginity in a public bathroom in some mall while he and his wife thought she was spending the night with Helena or one of the Rosas.

He continued to avoid the subject each night, only speaking enough to assure his wife that there was little they could do. They could only hope their daughter was out there making the right choices, because ultimately, Claudia, there is nothing we can do to stop her. She will have sex when she feels like it. She will try drugs or steal or maybe even be a saint and make wonderful grades, but right now there is little we can do. We can only hope and pray that we've raised her to use her head.

While his wife knew he was right, these answers were not the ones she was looking for. She wanted to hear him say everything would be all right. Tell me, she wished, our Lavinía is just as sweet and innocent as we raised her to be. Tell me our girl is growing into a smart and fair woman who will be the envy of everyone around her. She knew that probably wasn't true. And she was mad at her husband for vocalizing her worst fears. After all, Claudia spent more time around the neighborhood than her husband. Over the years since they'd first moved in, she'd watched the neighborhood change. She could barely take naps anymore during the day because it was a constant battle trying to think over the sounds of cholos working on their car stereos, the bass shaking her windows and the cat running and jumping up in bed next to her, trying to burrow beneath her pillow to escape the awful sound of rap beating at the walls of their house. She worried that someone would break in while her husband was away and hold her down at gun or knifepoint—all those punks carry knives and guns—and rape her while the neighbors looked the other way. Nothing like that ever happened, but she constantly fretted about it. She thought about it so much that one evening, when she sat across from Octavio at dinner and listened to his rambling on about starting a small business she decided that she'd play his little game, offering to support him if he promised to move the family to a better neighborhood as soon as they had saved up enough money. You know, for the good of the family. Maybe it's just what Lavinía needs. Just a better environment. I mean, what would we do if she came home pregnant or something? And Octavio pretended to care, pretended he was genuinely concerned with Lavinía's growing independence and foolish choice of friends. He convinced his wife that he was looking out for the best interests of the family. Yeah, we'll get out of here and everything will be fine.

And so, while Octavio sat at a picnic table on his lunch break handing out candies and lightly touching the girls who ran up to him when word spread that someone had candy, he thought hard about the type of job that would allow him to be around kids constantly without seeming obvious. His own child had failed him. And he had loved her so much. He'd had many dreams about living the rest of his life with her frozen at seven, the age when he first fell deeply in love with her and her innocent voice and her childish breath and her laughter. So many nights he'd sneaked into her room and knelt beside her while she slept, kissing her face and pressing his cheek against her flesh, smelling her soft child skin and imagining what it would feel like to undress her and then himself and climb into bed next to her, feeling her cool skin against his own, wanting to touch and taste every part of her body and imagining she'd wake up and welcome him into her bed, snuggling up to him and wrapping her legs around his waist, and he felt a throbbing in his pants and realized that his thoughts were horrible and disgusting and yet he still liked them and relished them and he would leave his daughter's room immediately and crawl into bed with his wife, who lay waiting for him, legs open, because he always came to bed in the mood to make love to her roughly, just the way she liked it. But those days were over. All he could see now was a girl growing into a woman. A girl who was only concerned with looking good for the boys in the neighborhood and at school. But those boys only wanted one thing and he tried to tell her they don't love you. They only want to get into your pants and they'll say anything to do just that. Once you give them that part of you, they'll get bored and move on and they'll break your heart. But the bigger tragedy is that you set yourself up for that by looking and acting like a whore.

The cheerful music of an ice cream truck rang out across the park and mixed with the cries of children who ran from the playground in a pack, yelling for their mothers to come and bring money quick, it's the ice cream man, it's the ice cream man, tripping in the playground sand, skinning knees and bruising legs and arms, which they ignored because the music flowing from the ice cream truck's loudspeaker rang out like a beacon, drawing the children toward it as the truck pulled to a stop, the driver turning the speaker down to hear the children hollering their orders over one another at the side window covered in stickers of Nestlé Crunch ice cream bars and Bulletpops and Lemonheads and Dreamsicles. The driver smiled and hushed the children, organizing them into two rows and taking their orders. The mothers came behind, pulling bills and change from their pockets and purses while the ice cream man tried to keep track of who had what, handing out frozen treats with one hand and collecting money with the other.

Octavio was in awe of all the children crowded around the truck—so many kids, look at all those beautiful girls—and the driver smiled and continued to take orders, nodding to the mothers, who were happy their children got a nice cold treat on such a hot summer day, and more children appeared, unable to resist the music that called from the farthest reaches of the park. It was brilliant. Perfect. He only had to watch for a few moments to realize that this was exactly the business he'd been searching for. A little tune played at the right volume, a white van with ice cream stickers—the prices written in Magic Marker—and the kids will flock to me like the sick flocked to Jesus.

When he finished his lunch and drove back to work, he knew he was going to be an ice cream man.

He returned to work full of joy and managed to sell two cars after lunch, and when his boss came and congratulated him on the impressive number of sales Octavio had been making lately, he nodded and accepted the compliment, relishing the immense happiness of being such a success in every endeavor he chose and confident when he told his boss that he was going to need a few days off to work out some things with my family—you know that personal stuff that comes when you have a wife with PMS at home and a daughter all synced up with her, my home's a madhouse and maybe it'd help my family and me out if we could go on vacation for a few days, like down to Nogales or maybe up to Phoenix to catch a game, plus that'd free up some sales for my fellow salesmen, who seem to be suffering a drought anyway. Wink, wink. A pat on the back and Octavio loosened his tie and walked quickly to his car, started it up, and drove home.

Now where the hell, he wondered as he sat in rush hour traffic, does a man find a van with a window cut out like that? With the little counter for leaning on my elbows so I don't tower so high above the little ones. There are probably hundreds of ice cream wholesalers. Finally, no more tirekickers coming in and wasting my time and getting my hopes up when I could be out selling ice cream in the gorgeous Arizona sun. The car days were over.

And that is what he told his wife over dinner that night. She rolled her eyes and asked him if he was serious, you really think you can make enough money nickel-and-diming kids all day to get us out of here? He put down his fork and removed his tie, rested both hands flat on the table, and calmly said have I ever left us wanting? Have we ever been hungry? Look around—he picked up his fork and waved it at the walls—you've been able to do all this. Think how much better it will be, how much easier, selling a product to people who chase after me instead of the other way around. I won't have to kiss ass anymore. They'll be kissing mine.

His wife shook her head and finished her meal in silence. When she stood to remove the dishes she mumbled at least your daughter can be proud of what her father has accomplished, you ass, and she walked into the kitchen and threw the dishes into the sink.

Octavio awoke the next morning before the alarm went off. He sang in the shower and hummed while he shaved. After he rinsed his face and applied lotion, he grinned into the mirror, trying to conjure up his best ice cream man face and said what'll it be? What can I get you, sweetie? At your service. Please come again. Be careful crossing the street. Tell the other kids. All the useful slogans for making children feel special. To give them that extra touch. He'd be their favorite ice cream man. The best ice cream man ever. Probably even see a profit after the first month or two, and by year's end he'd have to buy more trucks and hire a couple people and eventually he'd own a fleet. An ice cream empire.

A week and four days later, he pulled up in the driveway in a customized Ford Econoline van painted powder pink, with an automatic stop sign like the schoolbuses have and shiny new stickers encircling the windows on both sides. He parked in the driveway and blared a cheery, unmistakable ice cream song that drew stares from the neighbors.

Sitting on the floor of the living room folding laundry, Claudia knew Octavio wanted her to come running out and throw herself on him, to publicly show her pride and support, but she couldn't do it. Not because of the embarrassing pink van, and not because she wanted the business to fail. She didn't. She only worried her husband had made a hasty and foolish decision, and she wanted to make a point to him one last time before it was too late. So instead of rushing out the door, she lifted the clothes she'd been folding, tossed them into the laundry basket, and walked out the back door to the clothesline, where she slowly and deliberately pinned each dry piece back onto the line.

After stubbornly playing the same song three times and shooing away the children who had gathered, telling them I open for business in a couple days, you'll know, Octavio finally shut the van off, locked down the side panels, and went inside. It didn't matter what Claudia thought anyway, or if Lavinia and her friends called him a freak behind his back. He hadn't felt happiness this great before. It could only get better.

And it did.

The first day he took the van out, he'd hardly backed out of the driveway before he had his first customer. Then another. Then six more. By the time he made it to the end of the block, he knew he'd made the right decision. The kids were happy. He could tell they loved him and felt so grown up when they handed him their money, warm and damp from their sweaty hands. His heart swelled when they looked up at him, and each time a little girl's fingers brushed his hand when she handed him money and took the Popsicle, his entire body tingled.

Over time the ice cream song burrowed into his head. Much to the annoyance of his wife, he hummed it while he slept. He whistled it when he shaved each morning. He memorized each note, every nuance, the subtle inflections in the chiming melody. The way it echoed back at him from the houses and mingled with the children's voices as he drove down the street made him wonder how he'd ever liked any other song. This was his song.

He couldn't remember ever feeling happier getting ready for work. It'd always been a chore to wake up exactly when he'd set his alarm—which is why he'd set his clock eighteen minutes ahead, two snoozes. But now he woke early and mentally plotted his route while his wife slept beside him. Okay, first down Country Club to Fort Lowell, then hop on Campbell and make a huge circle back toward home, snaking up and down the streets, lingering in the parks. He did this as he watched the sun come up and counted the minutes on the alarm clock, the minutes going slower and slower each day as he waited, his heartbeat galloping and his palms sweaty. He watched the clock. He watched the sky shift colors and grow brighter, and he waited. And when the alarm finally went off, he let it buzz for a couple moments—so Claudia would know he just woke up—and he opened his closet and took a deep breath of his five starched uniforms hanging in the middle. The uniforms were one of the best parts. All part of the business, he'd said to his wife when he came home with five suits as white as God's beard and two bolo ties—one with a large onyx stone in the middle and one with smooth turquoise. It's all about presentation, he told himself in the mirror as he dressed. Can't have an unkempt ice cream man. That'd make the parents worry. Plus, the kids have to trust you. That keeps em coming back.

And sure enough, the kids came back. Time and again. No matter how often Octavio visited a neighborhood in his shiny new ice cream truck, the crowds of children grew larger and larger. Even the ones whose parents had no money to spare ran up to the truck with their friends because Octavio had planned in advance for those children who couldn't afford his treats. He brought along penny Bazooka Joe gum so they'd remember him and his kindness, because one day they'd have some money and his van would be the first place they'd want to spend it. It's all about business.

But really it was all about making each and every child who saw his van come running. He fed off their excitement. He knew they needed him as much as he needed them. The boys and the girls. Although he didn't really care for the boys, he understood it would be half his clientele, and at their age they were still innocent too. So he could forgive them. At this age neither boys nor girls were involved in the cycle of flirting and fucking. No, not these kids. They were the picture of innocence, Octavio decided. These were his children. The replacements for the one he'd so quickly lost. The one who'd grown up so fast and was at this very moment probably in a movie theater somewhere getting fingered beneath a denim jacket spread across her lap by a classmate who'd invited her to study after school. Getting the old stinky pinky, as he and his friends had called it.

But these children weren't like that yet. They loved him and trusted him and even came into the van when he invited them—it's so hot out there, just come in and pick out your treats, kids—and he left the door wide open so all the parents would know he wasn't up to anything. He waved out the side window to the moms and said hi and gave the boys and girls a piece of gum for each parent, tell em it's from the ice cream man. Oh, he loved calling himself that. It fit him. Lovable. Humorous. A perfect sense of hygiene. A model adult the children could look up to and aspire to be like one day.

He let them calculate their own change—no, Carly, if that's thirty-five cents total and you gave me fifty then what would the change be, sweetie?—so they learned even while they played, which their parents had to appreciate. He played thumb war with the boys and handslap games with the girls. Bo-bo-skee-wot-en-tot-en, eh-eh-boom-boom-boom-boom-boom. He learned the handslap games fast. He memorized all the words circulating in the different neighborhoods of central Tucson—Miss Suzy had a baby, his name was Tiny Tim, she put him in the bathtub, to see if he could swim—and he shared them with the kids in his own neighborhood. And vice versa. He complimented the girls on their sundresses and asked them where'd you get that nasty scrape on your knee, honey? that's awful, make sure your mommy kisses it and makes it all better.

Some kids even knocked on Octavio's door after he'd already parked the truck in his driveway and sat eating dinner with his wife. It drove Claudia mad, but Octavio was overjoyed the first time it happened. He jumped up from the table, his forgotten napkin sliding to the floor, and asked the kids inside and took them to the back room where he stored his stock. Such a wonderful business that children even wanted to buy off you after-hours. He'd struck gold.

But Claudia grew irritated about her husband's new obsession. She scolded him frequently, trying to get him to pack up this business of his. How secure could an ice cream business really be? she asked, and he told her to look, goddammit, Claudia, look the hell around. You see the kids beating down our door for ice cream? You know I only have to back the van out of the driveway and I'm loaded down with customers until I pull back in when the sun goes down. And even *then* they come knocking. Even then they can't get enough, and you're worried about business? You think this is stupid? Well, it's not. And if you ever want to move someplace nicer—remember that part?—then I have to keep going. Besides, I like this job.

And that worried her too. But she didn't say anything about how he spent time with all the other children in the city except his own. She didn't tell him how she worried about Lavinía, who came home a little later each day from her friends' houses, who ignored direct orders from her mother to be home before dark unless you call and check in. You're still a child. Yes, I know, you're a teenager and you know everything, but I still worry about you and you're still living under our roof. As long as you're living here you obey me, young lady, or I'll tell your father and there'll be hell to pay. But it was an idle threat. And she knew her daughter knew and that's why she didn't tell Octavio any of these things, because he'd just shrug them off and go outside after dinner to restock the van for the next day. That was all Octavio cared about anymore.

He never even took a day off.

Seven days a week he drove around the city. On the weekdays he did the parks during school hours, then made the rounds of residential streets until the sun went down or the stock ran out. Saturdays and Sundays he drove to the parks that had pools. He drove to special events. The PGA and LPGA tours when they came to Reid Park, the after-church crowd, the parking lot of the swap meet. Ice cream consumed him, and he'd never been happier.

Less than six months into his new career, on a clear and warm Saturday morning, Octavio drove his ice cream van into a neighborhood he'd only been to a few times. It was a rundown neighborhood by the veteran's hospital, two blocks off of South 6th Avenue. He slowed his van and turned on the music and a lone girl came running toward him, waving a dollar in one hand and a Care Bear in the other. He gasped and slammed on the breaks when the girl was close enough to make out her features. She looked exactly like Lavinía when she was seven years old, and when she reached the side window of the van and asked can I please have a chocolate chip ice cream sandwich, mister ice cream man, sir? his heart felt as if it would burst. Everything about her was identical. Her hair. Her fingers. The way she twitched her lips and chewed on the bottom one while talking to an adult. He told her she didn't have to call him sir, Lavinía, you can call me Daddy.

Her face scrunched up in confusion, uncertain whether or not she'd heard him correctly, but when she finally loosened her features and asked again in her tiny voice please, ice cream man, can I have a chocolate chip sandwich? he fell in love with the sound. She brushed a hair out of her mouth. Tiny pinheads of sweat appeared on her hairline from running in the unforgiving sun to catch up with Octavio's van. He reached out and wiped the sweat from her forehead and told her to come out of the heat and into the van, and she came, excited to see the inside of every child's favorite vehicle. The air inside was cool as she stepped into the cab and climbed over the passenger seat. He led her to the cooler in the rear and when he opened the lid and pointed to the neat rows of frozen treats, her eyes grew wide, seeing so much ice cream in one place.

Pick out whatever you want. Her hand stretched toward the sandwiches, then drifted over to the Super Friends ice pops, then to the Flintstones push-ups, and finally came back to rest on the chocolate chip ice cream sandwiches. She plucked one from the pile and handed him her crumpled dollar bill, but he only shook his head and invited her to join him for the day. Come be my helper and you can have all the ice cream you want. She shook her head the same way Lavinía did when she was little, but her eyes drifted back to the cooler and all the ice cream inside and she was visibly torn—to go back outside into the blazing heat with one treat and no money, only to go home and help Mommy with her chores and picking up the dog poopie, or to spend the day helping the ice cream man sell treats, which would be awesome because all her friends would be sooooooo jealous when she went to school on Monday and talked about riding in an ice cream truck while the rest of them were playing Barbies or helping their mothers babysit their younger brothers and sisters. Octavio reached out and wrapped his hand gently around the little girl's wrist and said don't worry, your mom will be so proud when she finds out you were a big girl and helped me out all day. I'll let you run the music and take the money and hand out the ice cream. You can even sit on my lap and help drive if you want.

His speech closed the deal. The girl nodded and said I just have to ask my mommy. Octavio felt a surge of adrenaline. No, no. I already asked her this morning, and she said as long as you're home by lunch, you can come. We'll just be around the neighborhood so she can find us if she needs you. Her mom had said those same words not ten minutes earlier. Be home by lunch, and call me when you get to Hannah's house so I know where you are. It was close enough, so she giggled and said okay.

Octavio went back to the driver's seat and looked around. Not a person in sight. He checked the mirrors. A half a block behind him some boys were running toward the van and waving their hands. He ignored them and shifted into drive, turned onto Veteran's Boulevard, and sped south, easing the volume down on the speaker and telling the girl Lavinía, honey, come up here and buckle in so you don't get hurt. She climbed into the seat but couldn't get the seatbelt buckled, it was too clunky, so he slowed the van and helped her.

They drove out of the neighborhood. He knew just the place to take her. She'd love the 4th Avenue Street Fair. It was like a circus, and he told her she'd love watching all the people and their colorful clothes. The clowns walking on stilts. The jugglers and the street musicians. The magicians and the crafts for sale. With every description he gave, the little girl grew more and more restless with anticipation.

When they reached the fair, he slowed down and pulled to the side of the road. Okay, come here, Lavinía—my name's Samantha—let me show you how to work the music, and the lights, and the stop sign. He pulled the lever that activated the sign and the lights. He showed her the knob that started the music. Samantha cranked it and squealed with delight when the cheerful ice cream song blasted from the speaker atop the van. Octavio took the white paper hat off his head and gave it to the girl. There you go, Lavinía—my name's Samantha—this makes you my official helper. A real live ice cream girl. Her back straightened with the seriousness of the title, and she gave the knob a little extra turn to make the pretty music just a little bit louder.

They cruised up and down the side streets of the fair, and every few yards Octavio brought the van to a stop and Samantha pulled the lever to activate the stop sign and then they walked hand in hand—Octavio crouching to avoid hitting his head, and the girl copying his actions—to the side window and took orders. He grabbed the ice cream from the cooler, placed it in her hand, and whispered the price in her ear, savoring the sound of her voice when she repeated the price back to the hippie chicks with their ratty hair.

After each sale he told her you're doing a good job, relishing the happiness on her face.

Lunchtime passed.

She mentioned it once or twice, but he distracted her each time by offering her ice cream, walking her back to the cooler and telling her try something new this time. Think about it. How many times in your life will you ever get to do this again?

After lunchtime her belly began churning grossly, trying to warn her to not eat any more ice cream or you might get sick, but she couldn't help herself, she had to reach into the cooler and pull out a Nestlé Crunch ice cream bar, and Octavio patted her head and said that's it, that's a good girl, then he sat her on his lap as he had each time she chose a new treat, which didn't seem to bother her as long as she had ice cream to eat, so he pulled her close and helped tear open the wrapper on her Nestlé bar, and while she ate he made up stories of being a brave ice cream man who helped children who got picked on in school, or rescued animals hit by cars or mistreated by the neighborhood boys, and when the ice cream got warm enough and started dripping down her Popsicle stick, he laughed and said let me get that for you, grabbing the Nestlé bar from her and bringing her hand up to his mouth so he could lick the sticky and cold sugary milk from between her fingers and from the back of her hand and her wrist where the ice cream had crept, and she tasted so sweet, so much sweeter and softer than the melting ice cream, he could hardly stand letting the girl up from his lap, where she felt so good, as if his lap and her body were a perfect match and should stay together forever, but it was broad daylight still and someone could come to the window any minute, so he handed Samantha's bar back to her and waved her to her seat, biting the inside of his cheeks hard enough to forget the longing in his lap, his molars grinding deep gashes into the soft, gummy flesh.

After a minute of waiting, he stood and walked, crouched over, back to the driver's seat. He turned the engine over and Samantha turned on the music and bounced up and down as it streamed from the speakers. He was astonished at the way each and every time she started the music she carried on like it was the best thing that had ever happened to her in her short life.

Of course it was. Samantha could barely contain her happiness over the ice cream man inviting her to spend the day with him, almost weeping with joy at her good luck—this was exactly what she might have wished for if one of the many times she had rubbed an empty Coke or beer bottle a genie had actually appeared and granted her a wish—at getting unlimited ice cream and also making her friends jealous because she got to be inside an ice cream truck. Plus, the ice cream man loved her. It was obvious because he liked to fix her hair, and he kept her clean, and all the same stuff her mommy did—sitting on their laps and all that. And everything was so perfect it didn't bother her that he kept forgetting her name.

Instead she ate and ate and ate until her tummy got sore and she didn't feel good at all anymore and the sun was starting to go down and that meant it's past lunchtime and I'm going to get in trouble, and she felt so yucky and sad and scared she didn't notice that Octavio had slowly turned down the music and she slumped down in her seat and held her belly and it hurt like someone had kicked her and it was too full of sweets and felt like it was going to explode, she just knew it, and it grumbled and growled and churned and she opened up her mouth to

complain to the ice cream man about the pain and instead of her voice
coming out she heard a splashy sound and her sides and stomach hurt
and heaved and she couldn't breathe because she couldn't close her
mouth against the push of the sweet chunks flying out of her and
scratching her throat, it burned so bad, and then it stopped for a second
and just when she started to catch her breath her mouth flew open again
and she tried throwing her hand over her mouth but the stuff shot out
between her fingers and she felt the warm splash of it in her lap and
burning her arms and legs, and when it stopped again she sat gasping
for breath and reached out to the ice cream man, hoping he wasn't mad
at her and that he would help her, can I just go back to my mommy,
please can you take me back please? and he held her hand and said yes,
we can go right now, and she tried to say thank you but her mouth filled
with warm chunky sweetness and she opened her lips and let the mixture ooze from between her lips and down the front of her shirt and she
just wanted to cry and wanted it to stop and wanted her mommy but the
ice cream man pulled the van over and undid her seatbelt and carried her
trembling body to the back of his van and said first we have to get you
cleaned up and out of these clothes or your mommy will get really mad,
and she knew that he was right but that he was also wrong because out
of the van's back window she saw that it was dark and she mistook the
city lights for stars and knew that if it was late enough to see the stars
then she was already in big, big trouble, young lady.

Octavio laughed about it later, but when the little girl first started
vomiting all over the van, his only thought had been how the hell he
could get her cleaned up before he took her home. He was genuinely
horrified when he saw the bright bile of melted ice cream covering the
front of her outfit, and he worried how to explain the puke-stained
clothes to her mother. It wasn't until he had her in the back of the van,
parked atop A Mountain, that he realized he couldn't take her back
home even if he wanted to. He was in too deep. Several days later, when
the cops were beating down his door in the middle of the night, he supposed the decision had already been made—though he hadn't realized
it—when he drove away from Veteran's Boulevard with someone else's
kid. But when he first drove to the top of A Mountain with a sick child

in the passenger seat, he'd only planned on showing her the view of Tucson at night, then maybe taking her to dinner before going home and tucking her into bed.

He didn't think about what he was saying when he carried her to the back of the van, only said what came naturally, that yes, he'd take her back to her mommy—no, I won't, I CAN'T—and then placed her fragile body on the floor of his van and knelt over her. We have to get you cleaned up. The girl tried to nod, but she was afraid to move her head and get sick again. I'm just going to take off your clothes and rinse them out. She let him pull her sticky shirt over her head, and she was happy he kept his hand between her head and the floor of the van the whole time because his hand was so much softer than the floor. Your shorts are sticky too, honey. He pulled her shorts down her legs and over her socks and shoes. You're covered in it. Let me rinse you off. He uncapped a gallon jug of water he kept for emergencies such as overheating and told her to stand up for a minute. She tried, but it was so hard. She had to lean on him and wrap her arms around his neck. Sweetie, you'll get us both wet. You don't want wet shoes, right? She shook her head. The shoes came off. Then the socks. And you want dry panties, too? She nodded and stepped out of them when he pulled them down to her ankles. Now stand up. She couldn't. She wanted to lie down so bad. He poured the water down her front and rubbed his hands over her skin to get the stickiness off. I'm gonna take off my shirt because you're getting me all wet too. His shirt came off. His pants came off. She didn't notice his nakedness. He sat on the floor of the van and the cold surprised him for a moment. He didn't care.

He pulled Samantha over to him and sat her down on his lap, relishing the feeling of her wet body naked against his, and he poured the water over both of them and worked his hands softly over the girl's body, through her hair, down her legs, while she laid against his chest and wished for home. She was too sick to feel his hands touching her in a bad way because the water made her feel better, and she didn't mind him kissing her forehead and holding her close because she was too worried about her belly and how yucky it felt until he touched her *there* and her eyes shot open and she let out a scream and then felt his hand clasping over her mouth and it tasted like the battery she licked once that shocked her and made her run crying to her mommy.

—

Governor Babbit scratched at a pimple on the back of his scalp, parting a small section of hair with his middle finger and thumb, trying to scrape the head off with his fingernail. If I could just get my hand on that bastard for starting this whole thing, he thought. He glared across the black walnut conference table at the members of the emergency cabinet he'd summoned when the news of the Tucson murders reached his mansion.

That little cunt has opened up Pandora's box down there. Anyone have a brilliant proposal about how to handle this?

The cabinet members fidgeted in their leather chairs and tried to think of possible solutions to the disastrous scene developing at the Pima County Courthouse. Surveillance photos were strewn across the table. The helicopter shots showed thousands of people crowded into the courthouse plaza, pressing toward the dome, holding signs and shaking their fists. The front pages of the *Arizona Daily Star* and the *Tucson Citizen* had close-ups of snarling faces, weeping mothers, bewildered children.

LOOK at those goddam pictures and tell me how I'm supposed to disperse a crowd of pissed-off parents, all law-abiding voters, rallying around a man who blatantly murdered someone in OUR courthouse. This, in case you don't know why the fuck I brought you here, is what we call a no-win situation. Should I order riot police out to beat down a swarm of soccer moms and PTA members? These are our constituents. Any ideas?

Erect barricades?

Erect barricades where? *Around* the crowd? They're already there, camped out and practically storming the doors. News cameras are out there filming mothers and children, playing to the emotions of anyone who watches the damn TV. Fathers are foaming at the mouth, and you want me to ask them to please move back and let us bring order to a trial that will take months, or, god forbid, YEARS?

The governor swiveled around in his seat and faced the picture window overlooking his browning lawn. The Beat the Peak campaign to conserve water was making his yard unsightly, but it was his campaign so it'd be foolish not to abide by the same rules. Besides, throw the Tempe hippies a stupid bone like saving water and that freed up a little pressure to do some behind-the-scenes scheming.

Governor Babbit? The governor swiveled back around and nodded to the lieutenant governor. Why don't we just send in some National Guardsmen and have them barricade the courthouse doors and keep traffic flowing downtown while we hash out what to do with this Santiago guy? It's not the soccer moms and Boy Scout dads that we have to worry about. We have to maintain commerce or all hell'll break loose.

And the guy? What do we do with the dad? the governor asked.

He already knew there was no point in asking. The last year and a half had Arizonans enamored with Babbit and his policies. He cut the amount of money doled out to drunk Indians. He'd made several appearances at public schools with Nancy Reagan to promote her futile Just Say No campaign. There was no way he wouldn't get another term, unless he actually allowed the state to bring Alejandro Santiago up on first-degree murder charges. There's the right thing to do, and there's the *right* thing to do.

In almost any other state where kidnapping wasn't such a large problem, he could simply leave the guy to rot, citing loopholes in the law and smoothtalking the pushy liberal journalists until the next big story came and Santiago was buried in a landfill of paperwork and legal problems that ensured his trial would be long and unresolved until years after Babbit moved on to greater things. The Senate. The White House. But his state was plagued with missing children and mysterious bones found protruding from the desert hardpan. Then he had the Mexican problem. And the developing gang problem. Those he could deal with. Missing, sexually assaulted, murdered, and brutalized children was a touchier issue. Of course something of this magnitude had to happen on *his* watch.

He swiveled back around and ordered the cabinet members to leave him alone for a while, just give me a few minutes to figure out an angle. Call up the TPD and make sure they have every officer there until we send reinforcements. And NO outbursts. This mob is just waiting for the chance to riot, and we're gonna be directly in the line of fire.

The cabinet members rushed out of the room with the lieutenant governor leaving last, closing the door slowly while peeking at the back of the governor's head, relieved that this wasn't his problem—a real bitchofa nightmare.

The mob pulsed with anger, chanting and demanding that Santiago go free for doing what any parent would have—should have—done. They took turns screaming into the news cameras. The heat was incredible, reflecting off the courthouse dome and adding to the growing uneasiness. Children splashed around in the fountain to escape the heat, and the out-of-town journalists looked on with envy, annoyed that their jobs required them to wear ties, pantsuits, polyester. If the story unfolding in Tucson wasn't so wonderfully scripted, most of them would have packed up their gear after filming the mob from various angles. But it was impossible to leave. The Santiago murder had all the makings of Pulitzer journalism. The fact that he shot his daughter's murderer point-blank in the face—and on live television—had sparked the interest of the entire country. And his reasons for doing it? It couldn't get much better. Of course some of the reporters tried to incite the crowd—holding up that year's school pictures of the murdered girl while asking questions. Did you know her? Do you have kids? What would you have done if your daughter was found raped and mangled in the desert? And the cameramen zoomed in close when a father clenched his jaw or narrowed his eyes. Up close action. The people at home will eat it up. And they did.

They came to the courthouse in ones and twos. Carloads of people with out-of-state plates cruised around Congress and Church and Granada, trying to find parking, eventually pulling onto the lawn next to the statue of Pancho Villa and swarming over the Allande Footbridge where police were stationed to block them. But they walked right past them, knowing they wouldn't be stopped because any one of them would have done the same thing. You can't possibly beat a parent for defending his child, even if she is already dead. It's the principle, someone said to one of the officers assigned to block the bridge. It's the principle and you know it, and the cop, even though he knew better, let the people pass, because he was too ashamed to stop these parents, united in grief and anger, from completing their pilgrimage.

The courthouse plaza was bursting with people. They stood on benches to get a better view. Some climbed the trees, hiding from the sun and trying to get a glimpse of anything happening inside. One sighting of Alejandro Santiago walking in shackles would make the discomfort of waiting in a tree for two days worth all the inconvenience. So they waited. They shared stories of child abduction in their own states, praising Alejandro for skirting justice and blasting the head off that sick sonofabitch. Full of joy that he stood up to the law and took care of business instead of cowering in his home, taking all of his sick days at work, coming before a jury and reliving the painful experience of losing his child over and over and over again while her murderer maintained his innocence and sat smugly listening to his actions being recounted. To hell with that, they said to each other. We will not back down just because we're supposed to. We're not SUPPOSED to lie there and let the scum of the earth snatch everything from us that we work so hard for. They yelled in agreement and waited for some word from inside the courthouse. Waited to see Alejandro. Waited for anything.

What they got, in the early afternoon, three days after Alejandro Santiago had committed Arizona's most famous murder, was his nervous wife appearing at the courthouse entrance. A podium had been wheeled out two-and-a-half hours before, and the crowd had pressed in, waiting to see who was coming out to give them some news. The reporters had gone to work immediately, setting up their microphones on the podium, turning the mics just right so each TV station's logo could be seen clearly by viewers at home.

Carmella Santiago, flanked by police officers in riot gear, walked to the podium and squinted her eyes in the sunlight, surveying the mob that had grown quiet in anticipation. She tried to smile, to show the people that she was so happy they were here. But she couldn't do it. There were so many kids in the crowd, holding their parents' hands. Looking up to their mothers and fathers. Looking at her. She walked around the podium and sat on the ground, cross-legged, and beckoned a young girl to join her. Ven aquí, mija.

The child didn't want to go, but her mother pushed the back of her head lightly and said go. Just go on. She needs you right now. The little girl walked over to Carmella and sat down on her lap and Carmella held the girl's head between her hands and looked into her eyes, felt the individual folds of her braids, smelled her scalp, then broke into tears and hugged the child's head to her chest. Everyone was silent. While the news cameras were trained on the podium, waiting for Carmella to stand up and address the crowd, one cameraman, who left a camera recording on the ground between his feet, captured the scene between Carmella and the little girl. Every other person present—parents, children, police, politicians, reporters, cameramen—watched in silence as Carmella held the girl and traced her ears and her tiny lips and her knobby knees.

Even the little girl was transfixed, looking up at the sad woman who touched her like a mommy. Like someone who knew children and knew how to admire by touch, without offending. She was proud that this woman noticed things like her new cross earrings, her big brown eyes, her braids that she liked to squeeze during school. She didn't even mind that the front of her dress was soaked with this woman's tears, because somehow she understood that this mommy isn't a mommy anymore and that's why she's sad. Her baby is gone, and so my mommy is sharing me.

The one camera capturing the moment was on a live feed to WGN, and soon the scene was being aired nationally, much to the dismay of the governor, who was eating lunch at a small diner in Phoenix when he noticed that all conversations had ceased, replaced by sniffling and coughing and an uncomfortable silence as, one by one, the customers looked up at the TV in the corner of the room and watched as a child comforted a woman sitting on the ground in what appeared to be an outdoor market or something—who's that woman?—and then it suddenly clicked, and a gasp went up from everyone when at the same moment they understood who was on television, her name flashed across the bottom of the screen, and the governor knew he was screwed, absolutely fucked. He ran out of the diner and into his limo waiting outside and yelled at the driver GET ME HOME NOW, RUN PEOPLE OVER IF YOU HAVE TO, and he dialed the lieutenant governor and told him get the chopper ready because we're flying down to Tucson as soon as I get there. For the rest of the drive back to the mansion, he bit down on his tongue and scraped at the pimple on his head and prayed that the crowd would stay calm until he arrived. He stared out the tinted windows at the city of Phoenix, watching the cars and the people milling about and wondering how he was going to stifle the overheated and heartbroken swarm of people down in Tucson. And every time he closed his eyes, he saw Carmella and the little girl holding each other and a surge of panic overcame him.

The courthouse plaza was overcast with dread. After Carmella finished holding the young girl and calmed down a bit, she returned to the podium and the crowd released a collective sigh. The microphones crackled to life, and she leaned in and began to speak.

I'm so glad you all showed up to support my husband, Alejandro Santiago. I'm not sure what to say exactly, but the mayor thought I should explain to everyone why you should go home so there won't be any trouble. But, the way I see it, there already *is* trouble, don't you think? The people roared in unmovable agreement, proving their inherent understanding of exactly what the trouble was.

Carmella continued, urged on by the shouts and bellows from the parents who wanted her to speak. Since the day we went to the site of our daughter's murder, I've been unable to look at the desert—which is impossible in this city—without seeing her face. Don't you think that's what the trouble might be? I'll never get to make another Halloween costume for her. This year she wanted to be a toothbrush. She thought that'd be funny. When she first told me about it, she smiled her wonderful smile. Yes, I think that's what the trouble might be, Mister Mayor.

The crowd shouted in agreement, a wave that tore through the trees of the courthouse lawn, through the streets of downtown Tucson, cascading against buildings and causing businessmen in their offices to cringe. It was more than anger. It was the sound of pure animal rage barely held at bay by the last remnants of human reason.

But the shouts held a different meaning to a young newlywed named Rudy who was on his way to the courthouse, barely able to contain his excitement at the good fortune of having such a large, hungry crowd of people gathered in one place, standing in a huge cluster—as he had seen them on TV—sweating and on the verge of being overcome with what he had misinterpreted as heat exhaustion. Especially those who'd traveled from other parts of the country, whose climate was a bit more forgiving, whose children huddled at their parents' feet, seeking the shelter of bodily shade while the parents tried to suppress a pent-up fury so close to boiling over that the people in the crowd had stopped shouting in any recognizable language. They had even stopped looking at each other for fear of what they might see in the eyes of the person standing next to them. They could all feel the tension in the air, a mighty weight of rage and injustice bearing down on them like a massive storm cloud, a weight so heavy that even seasoned TPD officers given orders to maintain calm outside the courthouse found themselves wishing they could strip off their helmets and vests because it was stifling, this feeling in the air that made them shift from one foot to the other and practically demanded that they maintain radio silence.

Yes, this crowd was perfect. A captive market, thought Rudy the newlywed, who knew the reason the mob was gathered at the courthouse, who knew the tragedy of Alejandro Santiago's imprisonment but did not know the man Alejandro Santiago murdered had been an ice cream man, this detail only briefly mentioned when the story first broke—as Rudy and his wife were returning from their honeymoon and were distracted by the romance of their new life—but quickly forgotten as the growing tension at the courthouse between the parents and the law became more and more palpable. So Rudy drove onward.

The roar of the mob that had been music to Rudy the newlywed's ears finally subsided, and the air pulsed with the overwhelming silence of anticipation for more words from the mother whose daughter's life had been so wrongfully stripped from her and yet so poetically avenged, just one word, a directive, a cry of pain, a call to arms, anything, and the people would have immediately been behind this woman who held undeniable power in the words she had not yet spoken.

Even the governor, listening to the speech on the radio as his helicopter sped toward downtown Tucson, found himself holding his breath and silently praying she would have the prudence not to utter any word that might incite the crowd, praying that she could stave off the dormant wrath of the mob in front of her just long enough for him to get there and free this Alejandro Santiago. To free the same man whose actions had single-handedly turned the country upside-down and transformed downtown Tucson into a wasp's nest of parents ready to strike at anything they deemed a threat to their young. The same young who were beginning to feel uncomfortable with the deep silence and lack of movement in a mob of people who had, up until this point, been frantic with action. The same young who heard far off in the distance the first strains of music coming from Rudy the newlywed's Good Humor truck, which was crawling through the blocked traffic, navigating sidewalks, and squeezing around parked cars and makeshift lean-tos that forced him, on occasion, to drive over the lawns of municipal buildings.

He drove his van over curbs and past deserted roadblocks and fruitless detour signs, pushing onward toward his goal of delivering his frozen confections to a swarm of famished and heat-stricken people who would undoubtedly welcome him. Yes, they would make him enough money that he'd be able to retire early and move down to Sahuarita with his wife and the three kids they were planning to have. These images of his early retirement brought waves of happiness to Rudy the newlywed because he'd invested every last penny he and his wife owned to stock his van with as much frozen cargo as it could bear. He even added two additional freezers in the back and one more in the front, where only two days earlier a passenger seat had been. The night before he had painstakingly washed every inch of the van's surface, repainting over some of the faded price stickers with his wife's fingernail polish, cleaning the radio antenna and the cracks around the headlights with a toothbrush, washing and polishing the exterior until it sparkled like an ice sculpture, then vacuuming the interior. He stood in the dining room for his wife, who took her husband's measurements and made adjustments to the uniform for the thirteen pounds he'd gained in the short time they had been married, letting out the waist of his polyester slacks a half inch on each side, then sewing in tiny pie-shaped pieces of elastic so that the pants would fit perfectly, allowing a little give for the slight swelling in his stomach after a meal and the subsequent shrinking once his food had been properly digested. After she had made a couple more slight alterations to his uniform, she carried his work clothes with the tenderness of a midwife to the bathtub and delicately handwashed each item—the white cap that resembled a short order cook's, but looked much more professional on her husband, like he was the pilot of a luxury jet; the slightly thinning oxford button-down shirt that she starched heavily each night and then hung on a plastic hanger in the kitchen doorway, where the breeze that swept beneath the back door always managed to have his shirt dried and crisp and smelling like the purified desert air after a rainstorm by the time the sun came up; the red bowtie that gave her husband's uniform an approachable touch; the newly repaired pants; and the red argyle socks that matched his bowtie and offset some of the blinding whiteness of the spotless uniform that gleamed as brightly as the Good Humor van. When her husband stepped into it that morning and leaned out the driver's door while he warmed the motor, he took off his hat and waved it above his head as if leaving for a great voyage, a search for treasure in the desert from which he would return wealthy. The image of Rudy waving so happily from the door of his ice cream truck engraved itself onto his wife's mind as she turned to begin tidying the house, where, at random intervals throughout the morning of her husband's journey downtown, the sepia-toned image of her Rudy distorted and shifted in her mind until what she saw was a faded portrait of them both waving goodbye to their friends and family as they boarded an ocean liner on a three-week cruise to reap the rewards of hard work, smart investment, and frugal spending.

Rudy the newlywed was imagining a similar picture as he drove closer and closer to his goal, failing to notice the shocked and offended looks from pedestrians, who couldn't believe someone could be so insensitive as to drive an ice cream truck through the the city so soon, and Rudy drove on, nearly to the courthouse where the now-quiet mob was awaiting a word from Mrs. Santiago, who'd fallen silent upon realizing the volatile nature of the horde of people in front of her, and she wanted so badly to speak, to shout out vengeful phrases for all the parents who had ever lost a child and for all those who would lose children in the future, but suddenly, in the moment that the crowd ceased its yelling and the children began to hear the first far-off notes from Rudy's van, Carmella Santiago had a moment of clarity and finally noticed the cluster of microphones on the podium before her, and she counted them silently and realized that there were forty-three of them, which was forty-two too many, and she looked up and into the unblinking eyes of the cameras staring back at her, expecting, demanding that she make something happen, and the scope of the tragedy drove itself into her chest and she silently swore to herself never to utter another word, that she would wait until her husband was released, no matter how many years that might take, and the silence grew deeper and the grounds of the Pima County Courthouse became a vacuum into which no noise entered except for the strains of Rudy's ice cream truck, still only heard by the hungry and overheated children who clutched at their parents' legs and began tugging at the hems of mother's skirt or father's belt, looking at one another and verifying that the universal sound for ice cream was indeed a reality and not some sort of twisted hallucination put on by the adults who were acting so strangely today, and Rudy continued to maneuver around the many obstacles that stood between him and the thousands of people he and his wife had watched on television that morning, knowing these people had so hastily appeared in the city of Tucson that there was little chance they had thought to bring snacks to cool their children, most of them probably hadn't even thought to bring hats, which was why he also had a small rack of Good Humor sun visors he intended to sell in addition to the ice cream, the ice cream that would offer these people a moment's reprieve from the oppressive heat—yes, ice cream makes people happy—and as the sight of the courthouse's mosaic dome appeared amid the various downtown buildings, it took every drop of his resolve not to break the unspoken ice cream man's code against speeding, even though he knew there were no children to accidentally run over because they were all with their parents, he had seen them being clutched by their parents on the news while the reporters asked questions and speculated about the outcome of the tragic events that had unfolded in this once peaceful desert town, which had therefore tainted yet another profession in which parents entrusted their children to men who only abused that trust, as had also happened in the backrooms of churches or during the naptime at a daycare or after a victory at a Little League game when the coach took the boys back to his house for pizza or during choir practice for the Tucson Boys Chorus, and yet here was another group of people who had to serve penance for the actions of one of its brothers— having just returned from their Mexican honeymoon when they schemed together about the great opportunity presented by the growing throng of protesters downtown, the likes of which hadn't been seen in Tucson ever and was such a grand opportunity that both Rudy and his wife knew it would be foolish to ignore this chance, it would be ludicrous to pass up the opportunity to take the money they had received at their wedding and use it to stock the van to capacity and dive headfirst into the good fortune that had befallen them, and blinded by a shared dream, they focused on the screen filled with people, and they noticed the hotdog stand that always stood across from the courthouse fountain was providing the people with some food, and a VW minibus sold grilled cheese sandwiches and steaming plates of watery spaghetti, but nobody was seen holding a Bulletpop or a push-up or a Fla-Vor-Ice, and so they agreed while lying in bed two nights after Alejandro Santiago blew the head off of his daughter's murderer that it was an untapped opening created for them—it's a great tragedy, yes, but people still need to eat, even sad people—and they went to the bank together to withdraw every last cent to purchase hundreds of pounds of ice cream, which Rudy carried with him now as he neared the fringe of the gathering and saw that his goal was so close, less than two blocks away, so he adjusted his hat and turned the music up slightly and relaxed his neck muscles by rolling his head and then drove the final block and a half at a slow pace while the faces of children peered from between and behind their parents' legs and Rudy searched for a good spot to set up shop, within view and easy walking distance of each one of these potential customers, and the music from his speakers brought happiness to his heart as it did each time he heard it because of the fond memories he associated with the tinkling cheerfulness of ice cream music and smells, the same smells that drifted into the crowd of protestors, tickling their noses, tempting their senses, the smell of cream and fruit and summertime and laughter wafting through the crowd and finally settling in the nostrils of Carmella Santiago, whose position afforded her a view to the farthest reaches of the crowd, which was where her eyes darted, searching, glaring, trying to locate the source of that cursed smell that had assaulted her before she had time to identify and acknowledge such a commonplace and delightful smell, and the cameras recorded the shifting of her eyes back and forth and the way they widened as the music of Rudy's truck drew closer and became louder and mocked the silence that enveloped the plaza, and the people who stood watching Carmella, their hearts breaking with hers as they understood the blasphemy of those sounds and smells disrupting the sentiments of the group, but they didn't react, they continued to watch as Carmella searched for Rudy's truck, and the very moment she spotted the shiny white van, the source of the jingly music and lovely smells, the dreadfulness of her poor daughter's fate came crashing down on her anew, and she watched in horror as her child's murderer was free while her husband was imprisoned, unaware that at that moment reality had slipped completely from her grasp and she broke her vow of silence less than three minutes after she resolved in her mind to never speak again when she whispered the words *it's him,* and the microphones in front of her carried the sound over the airwaves of the entire country to the ears of millions of listeners, *it's him,* words barely conceived and released before they were transmitted and translated into other languages as they crossed the borders of this country into others, *it's him,* she said, and the governor threw down his headphones and knew he'd failed to reach his destination on time, down there on the courthouse lawn where the crowd turned to face Rudy's Good Humor van, and in the front seat the unwitting man who thought for the briefest of moments that he had hit paydirt realized at the last second, when it was too late to run, that the mob rushing toward him had no intention of buying anything, that the people didn't have the look he was used to seeing—the unadulterated longing of children who craved something cold and sweet, the look of only minor annoyance the parents often gave him for showing up at a time that was financially inconvenient—but instead what Rudy saw was the fury of unbridled revenge in their eyes and he searched desperately for an escape, but there was nowhere to go unless he wanted to run over the crowd, leaving dead bodies in his wake. He frantically tried to locate a cop to flag down, but there were none to be seen. There was no help. He was trapped. So Rudy the newlywed threw his truck into park and crouched down on the floorboard, thinking what a shame and baffled at what he might have done to provoke the mob as his truck began to shake, picturing his wife waiting for him back home and saddened that she'd spent all that time on his uniform when it wasn't even going to make it through one day.

The scene from above was too much for the governor to bear, so he motioned for the pilot to turn around and muttered fuck these madmen. Maybe we should pray for plague.

RAINBOW

WHEN RAINBOW CAME UPON A DEAD BODY LYING IN HER path, she did what people often do—provided the body doesn't belong to a relative or friend. She stopped, held her breath, and bent down to rifle through the dead man's pockets.

She didn't do this out of cruelty. Rainbow was not a cruel woman. Sure, she'd seen a vast amount of cruelty in her time walking the blocks of Tucson's squalid hotels and strip clubs named Miracle Mile—the thefts, the beatings, the "doctor" who performed fifty-dollar abortions in the back of his van, even an occasional hearse parked tastefully behind a hotel to collect the body of one of her fellow streetwalkers—yet after almost six years of full-time hooking, she was practically the same woman she had been going into the business. A little older. A little less pleasing to the eyes. Slightly more bitter. More self-protective. But not cruel.

She knew this much about herself, and it helped her reconcile her line of work with the way the public frequently spoke of it. Cruelty and desperation were two completely different demons, after all.

So it wasn't cruelty that made Rainbow rifle through the pockets of the dead man lying in her path. She was just barely old enough to drink legally, and still wishing some kindhearted man might save her. Hoping he might look beyond her past and take her away and give her a nice home where she could raise two or three kids, maybe plant a garden and put up a clothesline. She'd dress the kids real nice for school every morning, teach them to brush their teeth, maybe even take them to church on Sundays if her husband wanted them raised as good Catholics.

In the corpse's pockets Rainbow found three dollars, a pack of E-Z-Wider rolling papers, and an expired Sun-Tran bus transfer. She kept the three dollars.

After staring silently at the body for what she felt was the appropriate amount of time, having long ago given up on prayer but unable to break herself of certain habits, Rainbow crossed herself, stepped over it, and ducked into the entrance to one of the three concrete drainage tunnels that ran beneath Park Mall and emptied into the Alamo wash. The body would be gone soon enough, carried away by desert animals or the next flashflood, whichever found the body first.

Despite the danger of going down into the cement labyrinth alone, and she knew how dangerous this was, Rainbow still made it a point to visit the tunnels every few months, because she often grew nostalgic for the days when she lived there beneath the city with a homeless Vietnam vet named Brightstar. At fifteen, when her mother abandoned her shortly after Rainbow's grandfather passed away, it was Brightstar who'd first protected her and taken her to his concrete hideout running under the length of the sprawling mall parking lot, a claustrophobic hallway that provided protection from the sun, the police, and the gangs prowling the neighborhoods in central Tucson.

When Marísol Delgado lost her virginity to her grandfather at the age of thirteen, she didn't make a sound. She was too surprised it didn't hurt like the girls at school said it would. Instead, she actually felt a deep sense of relief, as if she'd finally scratched an unreachable itch. The sensation of her grandfather lying on top of her, breathing heavily in her ear and whispering I love you more than you'll ever know, Marísol, my little pomegranate, was the same feeling she got when she received more valentines in her basket at school than the other girls—which had, admittedly, only occurred once, in the second grade—or when she came home waving her straight-A report card and her mother wrapped her in a big hug and told her how proud she was of her smart baby girl for doing so well in those hard big-girl classes.

After the first time her grandfather had lain with her, after he finished and kissed her goodnight, Marísol lay awake trying to remember how to French-braid hair. How you're supposed to grab a new strand as you go along, incorporating more and more hair with each pass. Luckily her fingers were long and nimble, so it wasn't hard for her to manipulate the bulky clumps of hair that built up somewhere around the middle of the braid, becoming almost unmanageable. Her mother, after years of promising to teach her to French-braid, had finally shown her the previous weekend, and now Marísol was excited to practice on her dolls and one day move on to braiding her friends' hair. It would be fun.

Right before she fell asleep, she had the idea of changing her name because there were like fourteen other Marísols in school and she hated being the same as everyone else. She wanted to be different. When she woke the next morning it was raining outside, and as she sat on the porch waiting on her mother to pick her up after her night shift at work, she decided her new name would be Rainbow. Not Rainbow Delgado. Just Rainbow. It was the perfect fit.

When her mother pulled up in front of her grandfather's house and honked, Rainbow ran to the car full of energy and excited to reveal her new name. She tried to get her mother's attention, to tell her mom how she was a brand-new girl, not like everyone else, but her mother was too exhausted and preoccupied to be bothered. So Rainbow kept her new name to herself until she got to school, where she announced the change through a series of notes that circulated the classroom as they studied for the CAT test.

Rainbow preferred her grandfather's house to her own, despite her home's cleanliness—and it truly was immaculate, she actually *had* eaten off the floor a few times, just because it was clean enough to do so and because she'd even heard other people say your floor's clean enough to eat off of, back when she was younger and her mom still had friends to invite over. Her home gave her an eerie feeling when she returned from school each day to find all the blinds closed, the swamp cooler running full blast, and her mother passed out on the couch, a forgotten cigarette dangling from between her fingers, the whole ash still intact and curiously defying gravity while her mother snored and sputtered in a deep drunken sleep. Her house was *too* clean. Everything was in order. Perfectly aligned. All at right angles. As if her mother thought that keeping a perfectly clean house would make up for her other shortcomings. As if her mother were trying to make up for the fact that she'd somehow lost her husband—Rainbow never did find out how or why.

Each day, when Rainbow—and now everyone but her mother acknowledged her new identity—walked home from school, pulled the house key from where it dangled on a piece of yarn beneath her shirt, and unlocked the deadbolt as stealthily as possible, she cringed at the quiet and darkness, fumbled with her backpack, and placed it as silently as she could on the floor inside the front hallway closet where her mom had a box labeled MARISOL'S BACKPACK that sat between neatly arranged rows of shoes and flip-flops and Rainbow's galoshes that she sometimes got to wear during monsoon season.

To pass the time between her arrival home and when her mother miraculously rose for work without the aid of an alarm clock, Rainbow tiptoed to her bedroom and pulled from beneath her mattress a manila envelope she'd hidden away seven years earlier and carried with her from house to house each time she and her mother were either evicted or had to find a new home because of yet another ASSHOLE landlord who can't cut a single mom a fuckin break. Rainbow called the envelope her wedding plans envelope. It contained pictures of wedding dresses and gardens and swans and beautiful smiling women she had painstakingly cut from the pages of her school library's and mother's magazines over the years. Each afternoon she spent her alone time carefully arranging clippings of everything from the cakes to the minister, and then she gently put on her dress, which she had taped together from pictures of beautiful lace and the remnants of white and pink tissue paper salvaged from the gift bags she received from her mother each birthday and Christmas. And there, in the privacy of her room, while her mother slept off the morning's alcohol, Rainbow unfolded a years-old piece of notebook paper containing the wedding vows she'd hastily copied down during her aunt's wedding in LA—the only time she'd ever been out of Tucson—and she whispered the words while dabbing imaginary tears of joy from her eyes as she stood at the foot of her bed, her makeshift altar adorned with glossy magazine cutouts of extravagant springtime wedding bouquets.

The one thing she never included in her wedding was a groom. Throughout her childhood her mother had raised her to be a princess—good manners, perfect posture, impeccable hygiene—but every time she asked about her prince, her mother huffed there's no such thing, and stormed out of the room. So Rainbow never bothered to include a groom, since she wasn't entirely sure what would make a good one anyway.

With each day that passed Rainbow felt her mother growing more distant, and she longed for the time when her mother didn't work nights and the mornings when Rainbow used to dress up in her plastic tiara and her feather boa, sneaking into her mother's room while she slept and slipping on her mom's high heels like a grown-up princess. In the days before her mother took the night-shift job, Rainbow always woke her up and presented herself, and her mother smiled and cooed what a beautiful girl. You'll grow up to be a fine woman. Yep, I'll be beating the boys off you. After their morning ritual her mother got out of bed, patted her daughter on the head, and said let's go to the kitchen so I can show you how to be a real princess. Her mother taught her how to poach eggs and make omelets and toast the bread just right. And for snacks she gave her celery with peanut butter, so she could watch her princess figure.

When her mother took the job as a janitor at Davis-Monthan Air Force Base, all that had changed. No more breakfasts together. No more dress-up. For years now, she saw less of her mother and more of her grandfather.

Rainbow never told her mother how she lost her virginity to her grandfather. And she never mentioned that it had become a routine. To her, it seemed perfectly natural. So natural, in fact, that Rainbow often felt something was missing during the hours she spent locked in her bedroom after school, waiting until it was time for her mother to go to work again. When her mother finally woke and called for her, she hastily stashed her wedding plans envelope and packed a bag with her overnight clothes, a book, and her next day's school outfit, then she went straight to the car to wait for her mother to come grumpily staggering out of the house with a freshly lit cigarette and wearing her janitor's uniform. It made Rainbow sad to look over at her mom driving, then at the ID badge with her mom smiling so happily in the little picture. She often compared the smiling face in the badge to the scowling face of her mother, and inevitably looked away from both. During the entire silent ride to her grandfather's house, Rainbow stared out the window as her mother drove to the neighborhood where her grandfather had lived since he and his now-deceased wife had first married and raised their two daughters.

She and her grandfather quickly grew close through her visits. He read her stories and patiently explained the rules of golf while they watched tournaments on TV. He took her to the Randolph Park golf course, told her sometimes the PGA and LPGA tours come through here and said look, right over there I saw Jack Nicklaus shoot an eagle during the Chrysler Classic. It was incredible. Then he promised to take her to Golf & Stuff and teach her how to putt.

Sometimes they shopped for groceries together at Food Giant, and she laughed when he complained that the neighborhood was going to shit because of all the gangs and the punk kids loitering at all hours. When it was time to cook dinner, they put on their matching KISS THE COOK aprons and her grandfather showed her how to bake enchiladas and make his special molé sauce. He even let her listen to 93.7 KRQ, the radio station Rainbow's mother hated because it had thinly disguised songs about sex and DJs who openly flirted on the phone with lonely teenaged girls— I can't believe they broadcast that filth like they're PROUD, she grumbled every time Rainbow begged to listen to the Top 9 at 9.

Each evening, when Rainbow first arrived, her grandfather pointed to the mulberry tree growing in the backyard, reminding her it was hers, and told her to go play on it. She climbed it and carved pictures of flowers and stars and smiley faces into the bark with a steak knife, and her grandfather didn't even get angry when she sometimes ate mulberries and accidentally smeared the purple juice onto her clothing. It made her feel safe when she looked down from the tree, toward the back porch, and caught her grandfather looking up from his crossword puzzles, his ubiquitous Jack on the rocks in hand, smiling as he watched his granddaughter play outdoors.

Outside the back fence was a pomegranate tree Rainbow often wished she could climb. When the fruit fell into her grandfather's backyard she split them open with a rock and picked out the tiny bulbs full of red juice and squirted them into her mouth with a pinch of her two little fingers while she concocted recipes for pomegranate casseroles and cakes and juice drinks that she wanted to make when she was a full-grown princess with a husband and a home of her own.

Because they spent so much time together, Rainbow slowly began to prefer her grandfather to her mother. So on the nights when he went to bed with her, it made her happy to welcome him. If he didn't come to her within fifteen minutes of her scuffling off to bed in her nightie and fuzzy pink slippers, Rainbow sat up in a panic, clutching her bedclothes to her chest and listening for a sound, any sound, to tell her that her grandfather hadn't forgotten her and was still coming to visit, so she could sleep easily.

Thankfully, he always arrived. Wearing his ironed pajamas, her grandfather tapped lightly on the bedroom door twice with his wedding band—she thought it romantic that he still wore it even though her grandma had died of emphysema years earlier—and then opened the door and switched off her nightlight. In the darkness she heard him remove his glasses and set them on the dresser. Then she heard the rattle of ice in his glass when he took one last swallow and placed it on the nightstand. And then the rustling of the sheets on what had now become his side of the bed. It was at this point that her heart finally calmed, knowing she was going to allow her grandfather to love her. Knowing he would soon call her his little pomegranate and kiss her lightly, brush her hair away from her face, pull her to him in his warm, strong embrace. It made her feel safe, being beneath her grandfather. Nothing could get to her under there. And she knew how much he loved her. She could feel it when he gasped and quivered and held her extra tight for a few moments, his heart bucking in his chest, before letting out the breath of air he held in the entire time. It made her feel more loved than all the other girls in the world.

Rainbow preferred her grandfather's company because even though he always drank, like her mom, he was never actually *drunk*. He never passed out. He never raised his voice or hurt her. He didn't do crazy embarrassing things like the afternoon near the end of third grade, when her mother had shown up at her classroom unannounced and demanded through a slur that the teacher allow Marísol Delgado to leave class early, she needs to come home and clean the house with me. She NEEDS to come take care of me, her mother, Paloma Cynthia Alvarez Delgado, because she's all I have and I just need to take her home now, please. PLEASE. The teacher stood staring at Rainbow's mother, trying to identify the strange woman and decipher her drunken request, and finally remembered that this was exactly the kind of occasion for which they'd installed classroom intercoms. So the teacher backed away from Rainbow's sobbing mother and held out her chalk in front of her, the only object she had to defend herself with, and hit the intercom button, smashed her palm up against it over and over until finally the bored voice of the principal's secretary answered, and Rainbow wished she could just lift up the lid of her desk and crawl in there, among the pencil shavings and the gold stars she always peeled off her perfect spelling tests and lined up on the underside of her desk top, maybe hide between two of her textbooks, anywhere but here, where she was so ashamed of her mother Rainbow ended up peeing in her seat, right there in front of her classmates, who snickered and looked around to make sure everyone knew she'd just pissed herself. She could feel it soak the bottom of her dress and heard it drip over the rim of her chair and splash onto the floor, drop by humiliating drop.

But her grandfather never did anything like that. Instead he woke every morning, shuffled out to the front yard and to the pole where he raised the flag—the soothing clink of the chain against the flagpole was Rainbow's wakeup call—then shuffled into the kitchen, pouring his first glass of Jack for the day, and out to the back porch to do a crossword puzzle while she staggered sleepily toward the restroom to take a shower and ready herself for school.

On the day her grandfather died, two months and eleven days after Rainbow's fifteenth birthday, she found him lying in bed surrounded by rotting pomegranates. She'd always thought death was supposed to smell horrible. She'd assumed the decaying body would make her puke and pass out. But the smell was wonderful. She closed her eyes and breathed deeply and knew her grandfather loved her so much he had even made his death beautiful for her. Since her mother had already left—she always just dropped her off at the front gate and drove away without even waving goodbye, just a light tap on the horn—Rainbow crawled into bed with her grandfather one final time, and draped her arms over his chest and her legs over his waist, and breathed in the smell of pomegranates and grandfather until her mother arrived in the morning to pick her up for school.

After her mother called the police and dropped her off at home the next day, Rainbow locked herself in her room, lying in bed weeping and chewing on her pillow until it was little more than a soggy mass of feathers. She didn't leave her bed for three days, instead slipping the one rotten pomegranate she'd smuggled out of her grandfather's house into the pillowcase and pressing her face into it, breathing the smell she would forever associate with her grandfather. I was his little pomegranate.

The fourth day after his death, she emerged to find her mother gone and their home emptied of all the dishes and furniture and clothing. Rainbow wandered through her empty home in confusion, trying to see if maybe her mom had gone a little crazy with the cleaning, or taken all their belongings to another place so she could scour the entire home. Maybe her mom wanted to go buy all new things, or better yet, maybe she wanted to replace all of their old broken-down crap with the nice sturdy furniture in her grandfather's house. It made her happy, thinking maybe her grandfather's stuff will be here soon, and then I can sleep in our bed every night and feel safe because his smell is probably still in the mattress.

What Rainbow didn't know was that while she had been mourning, her mother had methodically packed the house, room by room, loaded the boxes into a U-haul, and driven to Bisbee to start a new life. She didn't leave a note. She didn't kiss her daughter goodbye. All she left was a fifty taped to the inside of the front door, where Rainbow would be sure to see it, and a house so clean and empty it appeared as though no one had ever lived in it. Rainbow didn't blame her mother for leaving, convinced she'd left with a broken heart, just like her own. So it was okay.

It took Rainbow two more days to realize that she had been abandoned. When she realized she was all alone, *really* all alone, she knew she had to leave and go to the only place where she had good memories—her grandfather's neighborhood by Reid Park.

The only things she took with her were her wedding plans envelope and the fifty.

———

When she first met Brightstar she was wandering the alleys behind her grandfather's house, where she returned because even though she couldn't live in his house, she could at least walk by it unnoticed. She enjoyed sneaking down the alley to the spot where the pomegranate tree grew, gathering pomegranates to eat until she found work or a place to live. After all, the fifty her mom left her wasn't enough to feed her for long, and it certainly wouldn't pay rent anywhere.

Wandering aimlessly in the days following her mother's disappearance, Rainbow often sought out shade, a place to nap in the shadows since she couldn't sleep at night. The neighborhood where her grandfather lived had, in fact, slowly been going to hell, as he had complained so many times—she heard gunshots frequently, saw the way men looked at her when she walked alone through the park, ignored the catcalls of the thugs hanging out in front of Torchy's yelling about her sweet ass and all the things they wanted to do to her.

When she suddenly realized just how vulnerable she was, alone in Tucson, fifteen years old with fifty dollars and an envelope of magazine clippings, Rainbow knew she had to act soon if she were to survive. She knew it was time to get rid of the wedding plans envelope. It wasn't realistic to wait on a man to come around. It was dangerous to keep up the charade of being a princess when there were no princes in the world. But before she threw it away forever, Rainbow decided she wanted to wear her lace and tissue dress one last time.

It was at that moment she stumbled upon the cement drainage tunnels beneath Park Mall. They were all dark and foreboding even in the blinding sunlight. And if anywhere in the city was likely to be neglected by the police and other adults, it was there. Still, the tunnels looked large enough to stand in, if she crouched a little, and wide enough to lie down, if that's what she needed to do. Rainbow slid down into the arroyo with her manila envelope because the dark and cool entryway to the tunnel was the perfect place to perform her imaginary wedding one last time, then bury Marísol Delgado forever.

She stood alone before the entrances to three drainage tunnels whose ceilings were roughly shoulder-level, trying to decipher the colorful graffiti that covered the entrance like a hieroglyphic welcome mat. There were letters that looked vaguely English or Spanish, but they were turned on their sides or upside-down, they were pointy in the wrong places or round and bubbly, or there were street names and numbers and crowns and grotesque nudes, and she stood admiring the variety and thinking that probably kids come down here to skip school or smoke cigarettes and drink, or maybe they come down here to hide from their moms driving by right when they are about to make out and touch each other, when they're supposed to be in the mall with their friends. Rainbow stood for the first time outside the tunnels, listening for any sound that might signal danger, wondering what might be inside. However, the potential of such a place and its privacy—how far in would regular kids venture, and for how long would they really risk staying?—made her decide to brave the tunnels.

Stepping inside, she walked a few feet into the shade and brushed a spot clear of broken glass with her foot. Then she knelt down, opened her envelope, and spread out all the clippings she'd been collecting for years. She lined up the cakes, the flowers, the tables full of smiling guests, the bridesmaids, the minister, the ice sculptures, and finally she removed the dress with all the tenderness of a bride handling an heirloom wedding gown. She gently pulled it over her head, arranged it lightly on her figure, and unfolded the paper with her wedding vows. She read them aloud and wept. Not imaginary tears as she had done so many times before, but an actual steady flow of tears. She wept for her grandfather. She wept for her mother. She wept for her missing father. She wept for the hard times ahead—the pangs of hunger she would suffer, the cruelty men would subject her to, the love she'd never know. She sobbed and collapsed to the floor, ready to call the whole thing off, to just give up now and grab one of the large chunks of broken glass and slit her wrists and lie down bleeding to death all over her wedding pictures and her paper wedding gown. She wept until she finally slept, beneath the parking lot of Park Mall, where Marísol Delgado died in her sleep and Rainbow fully emerged.

As the sun began to set, Brightstar shook her awake, having witnessed Rainbow's heartbreaking wedding performance from deeper within the tunnel. He didn't want to startle her, so he let her cry herself to sleep, resisting the temptation to reach out and pull her close. She looked as fragile as her paper dress. But now it was getting dark out, so he had to get the girl out of here before anyone came to take advantage of her.

When Rainbow awoke to a strange-smelling man crouching above her, she gasped, then remembered where she was and that she was still wearing the paper wedding dress, now soggy with tears. She ripped the dress from her body and crumpled it up, then gathered the rest of the clippings and tore them apart, flinging them to the floor while Brightstar watched in silence.

He asked where she had come from so he could escort her back to safety. When she answered with a growl—I'm from nowhere, I have nothing—he knew she'd been sent for him to watch over.

He kept his distance, but explained to her how the tunnels were dangerous. There's gangs and druggies down here all the time. Dangerous people. They stopped messing with me after I put them in their place. This one tunnel's mine and they know it. But you, you're young and all alone and they'll eat you alive.

Rainbow knew what Marísol Delgado hadn't fully seen was true. She recognized some of the symbols outside the tunnels, the same spray-painted crowns and curses covered the alley walls behind her grandfather's house. She knew who ran this part of town and the south side, so she asked Brightstar if she could stay with him. Just until I find some work and a place to live or something, you know? He nodded and walked her deep into the concrete tunnel to what he explained was the tunnel's halfway point, where he had a mattress laid on top of cardboard layered on top of plastic milk crates to protect it from snakes and scorpions and rain whenever a storm came and the water flowed through the

tunnels and out into the wash. He lit a candle and showed her their surroundings. There were many half-burnt candles, a battery-powered
radio, and a pile of clothes Brightstar had taken from the clotheslines of
nearby houses. Nothing else.

You can lay here, he told her. I'll sleep on the ground next to you,
and don't worry about anyone coming back here to mess with you. I'll
be here and I'll take care of you. She wondered if he was trustworthy.
She worried he might try to hurt her while she slept. But he didn't look
at her the same way other men did when they wanted to do bad things
to her. As she grew older, she had gradually become aware—acutely
aware—of men and how they looked at her when they wanted her for
sex. No, Brightstar wasn't one of those men, she decided. He's safe.

She lay down, her mind sluggish, and when Brightstar blew out the
candle, she whispered for him to come hold her. I just want to be held.
So he did. And they slept that way while above them the mall parking
lot emptied and outside the entrance to the tunnels shadows grew
longer and a few of the Kings climbed down into the arroyo to smoke
grass and spray graffiti atop the newly painted symbols of a rival gang.

It was the first night her nightmares began. While Rainbow slept in
Brightstar's arms, she bucked and kicked, breathing short, ragged
breaths and murmuring unintelligible sentences, which despite their
confusion, had a tone that filled Brightstar with sadness.

It was during these moments that Rainbow dreamed she was running, her breathing grew rapid and harried, her feet hurt as though they
were pounding the ground, rocks and cactus and animal bones cutting
into her soles as she ran faster and faster across the desert hardpan, and
then her feet left the ground and she flew above the earth, her body rising into the sky before she realized it, up an invisible spiral that took her
higher than the tallest buildings of Tucson, higher than the Catalinas
and the Tucson Mountains. She flew into the air until the grid of the
city lay beneath her and she was able to take it all in without moving her
eyes at all. And then her body stopped. She floated in the night sky,
among the stars, and watched as the city went about its business. Planes
flew beneath her and scuffed runways with their tires. Tucson's tallest
building towered above the landscape, its red aircraft warning lights

blinking and keeping watch over the city. Cars rumbled back and forth and in circles and inexplicable patterns until it made her dizzy. She squeezed her eyes shut, then opened them. When she focused again on the city below, her heart threatened to explode at the sight of the earth barreling toward her, and suddenly she was floating above a playground in some schoolyard where, under the cover of night, she watched two men pin a girl against a domed set of monkey bars while a third raped her. She levitated there, mere inches above them, and tried to kick at the men. To punch them. She cursed them and threw futile, underwater punches that made no impact and wouldn't have hurt if they had. She cried out and tried to look away, but the dream only became distorted and the men moved faster, took turns, pinned the poor girl harder against the bars—Rainbow heard the girl's back and ribs cracking from the pressure—and beat her and raped her and threw her to the ground and kicked her and ran off at breakneck speed, leaving her weeping and fumbling with the gravel, trying to find the torn clothing just beyond her reach. Rainbow tried to speak. To tell the girl everything would be okay because she was alive and Rainbow had seen everything and would help her back into her clothes and go with her to a police station.

Then she was flying again, away from the girl and the playground and the city. She was looking at the grid of lights and trying to keep her stomach from emptying itself onto her clothing and splashing to the earth like a bile-cursed rain until she was falling toward the city again. Rainbow kicked in her sleep and Brightstar held her tighter, shushing her and wiping the sweat from her face with his shirtsleeve. But Rainbow continued to dream. She couldn't stop it. There were mothers weeping and bodies strewn about the desert. Prayers sailed past her, desperate cries from the victims below. She flew into the city and watched as someone bled to death in a culvert behind an adult bookstore on Speedway. She was sucked into the living room of a young family just as a drunk driver smashed through the wall, throwing their newborn daughter from her crib, just past Rainbow—she felt the baby's nightgown brush the tips of her fingers—and she listened to the crunch of the baby's body slamming against the opposite wall and the last breath of air that escaped her body in a small and devastating puff. She flew out of that home and into another. She came upon a man who lay staring at the ceiling, trembling in his bed, terrified because he'd seen a much older version of himself downtown, completely by chance, and he knew that he would become a wino, lying passed out in his own piss and vomit in the doorway of an abandoned business, beaten by street punks and covered in pigeon shit and left to rot. Rainbow was forced to watch as a father of three children, on his way home from work, fell asleep at the wheel and slammed into the side of a train, and the car and the man were shredded while the train dragged them along the length of Tucson and out into the desert. Her heart broke again and again as the people of Tucson held vigils by the hospital beds of their loved ones succumbing to the final blows of cancer. She overheard the name of a stillborn child. A young woman lamented the loss of her first love. A child awoke screaming in an empty room.

She soared over the city, dipping in and out of various lives. Experiencing the losses and the tears and the dashed hopes. The lives scattered beneath her. She wished for it to stop but knew it wouldn't. She tried to wake up. She wished aloud to die along with, or in the place of, one of these people. She tried to pull the bloated infant body out of the half-empty pool of an abandoned motel by the interstate. The city dragged out its dead and left-for-dead and she had to watch and say nothing. And do nothing. She begged for it to stop, but the words couldn't form in her mouth. If only she could tell just one mother where her kidnapped child was buried. If she could tell the wife that her husband felt nothing when he was pulled beneath the train because a strip of the car's metal hood pierced his skull immediately upon impact, sparing the man from the torture of having his body strewn about the city of Tucson and eaten by the vultures and wild dogs.

Then she heard the unmistakable sound of water, and to the north an enormous wave came surging over the Tortolita Mountains, rushing toward the city and destroying everything in its path. It swept over the mountains, crashing into the Catalinas, burying the landscape in minutes, wiping out the entire population of Tucson. The city wailed and shrieked and then fell silent as the water rose higher.

Rainbow could turn away, but she couldn't ignore the terrible knowledge that something atrocious was going to happen just on the other side of her closed eyelids. She wanted to claw her eyes from their sockets but could only claw the air. She lifted her head and unleashed a scream that caught in her throat and lingered there, stewing and churning, refusing to leave her mouth, choking and gagging her as she coughed and tried to spit the scream out, but her mouth was too dry, and the scream scratched the roof of her mouth and scraped against her teeth and cut into her gums and caked her tongue, and she hacked and shook her head with such force that she finally freed herself from her nightmare and awoke in a dark concrete tunnel, in the arms of a stranger, sweating and shaking violently.

Brightstar brushed her hair back from her face. He blew on her to cool her forehead and said don't be afraid. I've been to the desert and I've seen how it can be. I know how humans are. Rainbow nodded, grateful to be alive and in Brightstar's strong arms. He smelled. He stunk like urine and rotten alcohol, but she was so happy to not be alone she let him hold her and whisper how she was safe with him because he'd been in war and seen awful things and yet he still came out of it alive. People thought he was crazy, but he was just realistic, because that's what it took to survive. When it had been life-or-death in the jungles of Nam, Brightstar had no problem putting a bullet through the forehead of a wandering child. Because children don't wander alone when there's a war. If they do, they're strapped with homemade bombs. He'd seen it himself, he told Rainbow. During his tour he once saw a terrified kid running toward a fellow soldier, crying, pointing toward a hut smoldering nearby and blabbering in Vietnamese, tears washing the mud down his cheeks, and the Marine knelt down and set his rifle on the ground beside him, holding out his arms to comfort the little boy—he had a kid at home roughly the same age—and the child ran to the Marine, who welcomed him to his chest, wrapping his arms around the little boy and palming the back of his head, pressing the tear-stained face into the crook of his neck, which was the last thing Brightstar saw before both bodies exploded and sprayed fleshy chunks and bony shrapnel into the faces of his battle buddies, most of whom gagged and cried out, not understanding what had caused the child and their fellow soldier to erupt into the bloody mess that was running down their faces and turning their vision red, and one of them spat a piece of the Marine out of his mouth and vomited into his cupped hands, unable to stop the retching and the convulsing as he tried to clear the metallic taste of his dead comrade from his tongue. So after that, every time Brightstar found a child wandering alone in the jungle, he didn't take chances. He shot each little fucker through the forehead and walked on before the body had slumped to the ground. It was like killing a mosquito. He put about that much thought into it. And that's what it takes to survive down here in the bowels of the city, he told her. So you're going to be okay. Because I have what it takes to survive. You just have to learn it too.

Rainbow shuddered at the thought of this man who now held her killing children to stay alive. She didn't want to think of him as a murderer. But she understood he'd had reasons to kill. It was necessary. So she told him her nightmares, how frightening and real they were, Brightstar, to watch everyone's misery. To see everything, even the private things. It was too much. I just wanted to die.

Brightstar shushed her softly and told her not to worry, that there were ways to survive. There were things she could do. And he would help her, he would protect her until she could take care of herself. Then he rose to head aboveground and called back to her that it was daylight now so it was safe to leave and wash up in the mall bathrooms. And then he was gone.

Rainbow decided she first wanted to investigate the rest of the tunnels, now that the danger seemed less real than it had the evening before. What she discovered was that the tunnels ran beneath the entire mall and its parking lot, all the way from Wilmot to the west end of the mall right next to the McDonald's on Broadway. They were immense and foreboding. It was so strange that the city above seemed to have no idea these tunnels existed. She left the tunnel where she and Brightstar had slept, and went back out into the wash. The sunlight warmed her skin and made last night's fears and nightmares seem foolish and girly.

She turned around and faced the entrance to the three tunnels. The middle one was where she'd slept. The other two were beckoning her to enter. She stepped inside the tunnel on the left, bending enough so that she wouldn't hit her head on the concrete ceiling, and walked forward, touching the ground lightly with the toe of her flip-flop before stepping with all her weight, unsure of what might be underfoot. She walked in this manner almost five minutes and then saw light in the distance and realized she'd almost made it through the first tunnel, which was far shorter than she had expected. That gave her a little more confidence, so she quickened her pace until she reached the end, where she emerged from the tunnel and looked around the wash, which ran down the middle of an alley, backyard walls lining both sides.

She climbed up to the edge of the wash and looked up and down the alley. There was more graffiti, but no one was in sight so she scrambled down into the wash and back to the tunnel. She went back inside and walked past bottles and empty spray-paint cans and a sock and a pair of panties and trash everywhere. She walked on at a steady pace, crouching sometimes to avoid hitting her head, and traveling more quickly than she had before until she arrived at the tunnel's end and stepped out. The first tunnel wasn't so bad. She felt a little uneasy, but much less so now that she saw there was nothing but trash and signs of people drinking or just relaxing. But there was one tunnel left. And this one scared her. There wasn't as much litter in this entrance, and the graffiti petered off a few feet into the tunnel. It was as if this one were off-limits, even to the people who dared enter the first two. But it didn't look nearly as terrifying in the daylight as it had the night before, so instead of leaving and going aboveground to freshen up, she walked into the final tunnel and felt her way along the walls, stepping lightly, kicking trash and old clothing and cardboard and a small dead animal, walking farther and farther into the tunnel until she lost track of time and distance, her skin getting sweaty with uncertainty and her fingers running along the wall more slowly, suddenly more aware, feeling every single grain of dirt in the cement walls, every crack and abnormality in the smooth surface, and her hearing grew more acute and she heard the silence of the earth, heard it shifting and trying to throw off the weight of the buildings overhead, and for a brief moment Rainbow began to panic, realizing she was beneath countless tons of cement, walking underneath a mall, and the whole thing could collapse, trapping her in the tunnel, crushed beneath the cement and the bricks and the graffiti, drowning underground in a heap of man-made material that would pulverize and smother her, but probably leave just enough space for her to breathe in agony for a few more seconds, maybe a couple minutes, and then she'd be gone. Just like that.

But then the panic subsided and Rainbow knew the structure was sound, even with a few superficial cracks, and despite not knowing what was in here, she knew that there was enough room down here for her and Brightstar to live comfortably. So she walked the rest of the way, forcing herself to breathe steadily, wondering when she would reach the end, but not particularly worried because the place was strangely beginning to feel like a home. No other people would bother her as long as she had Brightstar.

When she finally reached the end, she immediately turned around to go back the way she came. This far entrance had the same graffiti. The same bottles and trash. It was nothing to fear. Just some punk kids playing tough. So she walked back through the tunnel more confidently, observing the change in temperature the farther in she went, getting excited and like any new homeowner, she started figuring out the layout of the place so she could designate different areas for different purposes. She could scrounge a few dime books from the thrift store and a cheap flashlight for reading at night. Rainbow continued walking, considering the possibilities, pleased by the size and the privacy and the sturdiness of her new home.

Now, all these years later, Brightstar was gone and the tunnels stood empty. Except for the dead body she left lying behind her. Rainbow walked through the concrete drainage tunnel, feeling the walls with her hands, counting her steps until she neared the place where the tunnel turned abruptly, half the distance to the end where she and Brightstar had lived for what had been the happiest months of her life after her grandfather's death—something that actually resembled a normal life. And once again she wondered if this was her destiny—to die a lonely woman in a city teeming with bums, whores, and strip clubs. To fall over dead one day while crossing the street, only to get hit by a bus and then run over by a dump truck, some cars, another bus, bicycles, the feet of children, more cars, a motorcycle, a military truck from the base, some DUI driver's moped, tires and feet flattening her endlessly, until she blended with the street, dried by the sun, smashed paper thin, disintegrating piece by piece and ultimately washed away by rain.

Everywhere she had ever looked in her lifetime, all she had seen was loss and suffering. If it wasn't her grandfather's death, or her mom's alcoholism, then it was the day-to-day events she saw living all alone in Tucson.

With her three newfound dollars, Rainbow climbed out of the wash and made her way across the mall parking lot to the Sun-Tran bus stop on Broadway. She took the bus back downtown to her regular room at the Hotel Congress. Two years earlier, when she turned nineteen, she struck a deal with one of the hotel's managers, who, in exchange for some head in his office before she turned in each night after her last client, always kept the same room reserved for her, provided she paid cash daily and checked out each Friday afternoon. On weekends she took a room at a motel on the Mile and worked there.

But today was a weekday, so she got off the bus at the downtown depot and walked to the Congress and into the hotel's bar. She didn't need to order a drink; she'd been coming there for two years. The bartenders all knew her name and purpose there, and they treated her like any other well-paying customer. Cape Cod. That was her favorite drink. Heavy on the cape, honey, and easy on the cod cause there's always plenty of that to go around, aint there, the bartenders knew to joke, dumping twice as much vodka as normal into the glass before splashing a little cranberry juice and tossing in a lime wedge.

None of the bartenders had given her a free drink on her twenty-first birthday, as was the custom, because they assumed she was much older, the way Rainbow had been coming in there all confident and caustic for two years now, smoking cigarettes and telling dirty jokes with the other afternoon regulars before she went back up to her room and put on one of the nine sexy, semi-expensive outfits she'd saved up to buy. It takes money to make money, she knew that much. On her twenty-first birthday, just like today, she'd acted no different, as if nothing were particularly special about that one day above any other. So her birthday had gone unnoticed. The one day all teenagers and college students dream about. The day they finally get to go to bars without fear of getting in trouble.

Rainbow drank her Cape Cod, relishing the sting of vodka in the back of her throat because it made it nice and numb for the rest of the night. She bummed a cigarette and smoked it, then snuffed it out and ordered another drink. Then another.

By the fifth one she didn't so much mind being alone. By the fifth one she understood her mother's penchant for hitting the sauce, how it made her problems blurry and unimportant. By the fifth one she forgot about Brightstar being gone and the tunnels and the fact that she was still, these many years later, all alone in the world. By the fifth one she accepted that tonight would be just like any other—walking the downtown streets, switching her hips in an exaggerated fashion that told the businessmen she was for sale, that she'd be happy to keep them company for a little while before they had to go home to their wives or their lonely hotel rooms. She rarely had to do more than two or three blocks of walking before she snagged her first john, almost always a middle-aged man who tried to discreetly whisper under his breath how much, baby? but she always pretended not to hear, walked a little longer and made him follow her a few more feet, made him want her just that much more, so she had the upper hand, if only for those few moments before they agreed on a price as they walked down the sidewalk side by side, her telling him to meet her at the Congress bar, in the back corner, in a dark booth, *her* dark booth, where he should have a Cape Cod waiting for her and a couple of twenties. Three johns in one night paid for her room and left her thirty dollars. So the daytime was pure profit.

During the day she dressed in a more modest outfit and headed out into the bustling downtown district to give quick handjobs or blowjobs next to the dumpsters behind the parking garage. If the man was lucky enough to have a job where he had an actual hour to spare for lunch, she took him back to her room at the Congress and let him have a quickie for twenty-five or thirty bucks, then she showed him to the door and took a nap, happy to have money for more drinks before her night shift began.

So it went, every day. Rainbow waking in the morning, showering and making her bed, then down to the bar to toss back a few Cape Cods before the lunch crowd arrived, then rushing out to make money to pay off her tab, then a quick nap, then back to the bar, then back out on the street to find another man with the lonely look in his eyes making him an easy target. She knew better than to try demanding higher prices. She worked alone, and so she really considered it luck when the men paid her anything at all. How many times had they given her money, only to wrestle it out of her hands after she let them fuck her? How many times had a prosecutor or a judge or one of those asshole public defenders given her money, ridden her for ten or twenty minutes, then brandished a badge and taken the money back, telling her just be happy I'm not haulin your fuckin ass in. Too many to count. But most businessmen were too afraid to pull a fast one on her. After all, they walked into the hotel too ashamed to even consider bullying, knowing that the desk clerk and the bartender knew why they were there, which also meant they knew Rainbow, which meant they probably had her back if something went wrong.

Before all of this whoring-around-downtown nonsense, before the deal with the hotel manager and the hustling on the sidewalks of Miracle Mile, Rainbow had been more hopeful. There was Brightstar, with his ever-present Army surplus jacket and his long braided hair, trying to give her a push. Trying to help her out. Trying to inspire her.

He'd wake her in the mornings to go looking for work, giving her a pep talk, and then he rode the bus to the VA campus to check on his case file, leaving her to wash up in the mall bathrooms and greet the possibilities. But it quickly became obvious to Rainbow a job wasn't going to come anytime soon.

In the first few days she rose early, excited and hopeful to work at Orange Julius or maybe one of the other joints in the mall food court— the A&W stand, the Spaghetti Shoppe, Golden China Wok, Subway— but it was always the same response. Sorry, you're too young. Or, sorry, we don't have any jobs. The managers giving her a fake look of disappointment for being unable to help her out. She knew they weren't actually sad. She knew they looked at her and were either disgusted by her physical appearance, or they leered at her with man eyes that stared past her worn clothing to her young breasts, where their eyes lingered and caressed her skin—eye fucking her, as she'd heard other girls call it. She could feel them staring at her ass and watching her walk away to the next place, only to be given the same treatment there. And every afternoon she went back to the tunnels to wait on Brightstar, who returned a little later each evening, bitter because the VA just kept ignoring him. They don't give a shit about us vets, he muttered, then took her hand and led her into the tunnel, where he pulled out a bag from Eegee's or Whataburger and let her eat first, then ate whatever was left.

Sometimes he told her stories of being in the war. Sometimes he told her the methods he used to panhandle because it was so tough with the downtown streets overrun by war vets who came by the busload to wait for a handout from the VA, even though they owe it to us. His approach was to appeal to a person's sense of values, not their sense of guilt. With so many homeless in Tucson it was virtually impossible to play the guilt card. And on top of all that he continued waiting, day in and day out, for the VA to make a decision. Even though he knew one would never come. He told her nobody ever heard from the VA. Especially not poor people. And especially not Indians like me. They always say something like check back next week, we already sent your paperwork to Phoenix and should be hearing back soon. It's out of our hands here. We've done our job. Every vet including Brightstar had heard this, and most had nothing else to do except wander the city of Tucson, up and down south 4th, 5th, and 6th Avenues, Veteran's Boulevard, within walking distance of the Greyhound bus station, where they congregated at lunchtime to see what kind of handouts the Catholic soup kitchen had fixed up for the day, sleeping behind Southgate Shopping Center or bumming change from people at the greyhound racetrack and crashing for the night beneath overpasses, where eventually the TPD shook them out and forced them to wander half-drunk until they found an arroyo to sleep in for the night, one of the only places the cops rarely went. What happened below the city wasn't their concern. As long as the bums were out of sight, the TPD didn't stir up too much shit.

What is the point, Brighstar often asked Rainbow, of coming to Tucson, of staying in Tucson, of doing anything in Tucson, when the VA people only pretended to care or told him we filed the paperwork already. Keep checking back. And still the numbers of vets grew. Rainbow had seen it herself downtown every time she walked past the Greyhound station where disheveled men disembarked from the buses, army duffel bags thrown over their shoulders, visibly hopeful until they left the parking lot and rounded the corner and saw the others who had come before them filling the alleys and scattered on the sidewalks and passed out on the grass of Veinte de Agosto Park where they slept in groups beneath the trees until the cops came and moved them along.

What is the point, Brightstar said, and Rainbow wondered the same thing. She too had finally given up trying to find work at the mall. No one was hiring. That fifty from her mother ran out after two weeks, so she had to rely on Brightstar for food, which made her feel guilty. She expanded her search to the businesses on Broadway and on 22nd, only to be turned down again and again. She went to Food Giant and filled out an application, hoping they might remember her from the many shopping trips she had taken with her grandfather, then walked to the produce section and stole some fruit, knowing she couldn't jeopardize a job she'd never get anyway.

Every night, after she told Brightstar about her failed job search and he told her about his failure with the VA, she read to him until they fell asleep, and she dreamed the nightmares of her first night in the tunnels. It was always the same thing. The horrific deaths and the flood.

One night, three weeks after Rainbow's arrival at the tunnels, Brightstar returned with an outfit he had pieced together from the clotheslines in the neighborhood—a short denim skirt and a mauve halter top—plus a pair of cute strappy heels he'd bought at Payless on sale, telling her maybe this will help. If you dress a little older, maybe they'll give you a job. It's worth a try, right? You keep saying they say you're too young, so lie to them. Make yourself look older.

The next morning she took the new outfit into the mall and changed in the bathroom, washed her face with hand soap and ran her wet fingers through her hair, then brushed her teeth with a dab of soap on her finger. She posed in front of the mirror. Stuck out her breasts, pushed them up a little bit and bent over to look at her cleavage. She liked how it looked. Her breasts were so round and mysterious. Her shirt showed just enough to make people want to see more, like older girls' shirts. And the skirt was exactly what was in fashion right now. Rainbow had seen tons of high-school girls in the mall wearing this exact same skirt, and they had boys all over them. This was the perfect thing. Just what she needed to be taken seriously.

She decided she looked old enough to maybe get a job at Dillard's or Sears, who cares about the food court anymore? Who wants to get fry grease all over themselves and leave with the stench of burgers in her hair and all in her clothes? No. Brightstar was exactly right. This was going to work.

The first place she stopped in Dillard's was the makeup counter. It was blindingly white. It was as clean as her old house. And the girls who worked the counters looked like angels, all dressed up in white smocks, white panty hose, white pumps. All of them had their hair pulled back and had perfect posture. *These* are princesses, Rainbow thought. This is where I belong. But when she stepped up and asked for an application, the woman standing on the other side of the glass counter gave her a look of condescending pity and said oh honey you could *never* work here, I mean look at your *skin,* and she grabbed a well-lit magnifying mirror and shoved it in front of Rainbow's face and said your face is absolutely riddled with blackheads. Don't you ever exfoliate? Have you ever even once used an oatmeal mask to clear your pores? She snickered at Rainbow and then called some of the other women over and said *look* at this poor thing. She thinks she can work in the makeup section. Isn't that just the best? I mean, *look* at her hair. It's like someone grabbed a handful of dyed straw and glued it to her head—giggle, giggle.

Rainbow was mortified. She looked back at the mirror, at her face magnified three times its normal size, but she didn't see anything wrong. What was wrong with her face? What was a mask? Did the woman mean she should just cover her face? And her hair, she'd just combed through it with her wet fingers a few minutes ago. It wasn't as bad as straw. She stood looking at the four women who mocked her, telling her they hadn't seen pores that big and clogged in ages, that's where Aqua Net and a complete lack of hygiene will get you—giggle, giggle.

It was the giggling that finally drove Rainbow out of the store. She would put no applications in there. She couldn't even stomach the idea of ever seeing those women again. The giggles followed her out of the store and burrowed into her head, prodding her, mocking her. They grew louder and more piercing until Rainbow could hear nothing else and she wanted to bash her head into a wall or shove a pencil or screwdriver into her ears to rid her head of the sound. Instead she staggered back to the bathroom, chomping down hard on her tongue to distract herself from the burning clump of embarrassment growing in her chest.

Back in the bathroom she scrubbed her face repeatedly with hand soap. She pressed hard, pushing her skin against the bones of her face with all the strength she could muster, trying to dig really deep and get into the pores to clean out the blackheads she still couldn't see—how come I can't see them? How am I supposed to get rid of something I can't see? Rainbow ran water through her hair and massaged hand soap into a nice lather on her scalp and cursed the women who'd made fun of her for something she wasn't even aware was a problem. She'd seen a pimple or two on her face before, sure. But all she had to do was pop them and they were gone the next day. She was blessed with dark skin, that's what the girls at school told her when they started getting their first zits. Theirs lingered for days, sometimes even scarred. But hers were gone the next day. She always thought that's what made her so pretty. It was what made her different from other girls her age.

Rainbow forced herself not to cry, rinsing her hair and her face and ignoring the moms who came in with their young daughters and shot her looks of disgust. With her head beneath the hand dryer she couldn't hear what they were saying about her, but it wasn't difficult to imagine. That is exactly the kind of girl you don't want to become, Tracy, some girl with a face covered in blackheads and hair ratty beyond all hope.

Look closely, Tracy, and see where you'll be if you don't put oatmeal on your face. Embarrassing, isn't it?

When her hair was finally dry enough to manage, Rainbow pulled it back and tried to French-braid it, but it was impossible. There was no way to do it without an extra set of hands. So, she simply shook her hair out and then pulled it back into a tight ponytail and readjusted her clothing in the mirror—honestly, I look nice like this, what was their problem?—and went to apply at Sears.

This time she avoided the makeup counter, and the shoe department, and the Juniors and Misses departments, and the hair salon, and the photo lab. She purposely skirted each part of the store where attractive women or cute girls worked because they too would certainly notice her flaws that up until now she never knew she had. Which left menswear, the boys department, electronics, appliances, and car service. She thought she'd try her luck at the electronics department since it was probably the only place where she stood a chance, but when she walked up to a bank of TVs and VCRs and camcorders, she saw her image splashed across every screen in the whole department and realized the bitches at the makeup counter were right. She did look pathetic. She looked horrible. Her hair was frizzy and her face was all splotchy and plain. Rainbow knew at that moment she was a hideous mess, and she walked out of the store in shame.

Every store she passed sent a sting of failure into her stomach, reminding her she was not only all alone, but inadequate. Alone and ugly. That's what she was.

Maybe this place would be better off underwater. And she with it.

As Rainbow walked out the main entrance and across the parking lot, she noticed a car slowly following her. She walked faster, switched to a different aisle. She ignored the car but the driver kept up with her, and when she got to the end of the aisle, the car pulled up in front of her, blocking her path. The driver rolled down the window and motioned her toward him. He looked at her outfit, at her shoes and her legs and her cleavage, and said I've got some work for you if you want it. Twenty dollars for just a few minutes of your time. I'll even buy you some lunch. You're too damn cute. Whaddya say?

She said nothing. Instead she straightened her back, glanced around the parking lot, and got into the passenger side of the car. She cringed a little at the man's touch on her thigh, but she took the twenty and crumpled it in her hand, then steeled herself.

Just relax, baby. Like I said, this'll only take a few minutes, and then I don't have any problem running you by El Taco or something for a meal and bringing you back here.

His hand crept higher up her thigh, pushed her skirt up enough that her panties peeked out. She tried to pull it down a little bit, even though there was no point, but he gripped her thigh harder and said don't. He drove across Wilmot and pulled in behind the Buena Vista movie theater, parked the car beneath a row of paloverde trees, shut off the engine, and leaned over toward her, his thumb pulling her panties to the side while his fingers played with her little tuft of hair and tickled her, and his breath was warm on her neck, then he was kissing her and telling her how beautiful she was. He kissed her all over her face, on her forehead, like her grandfather used to, and he didn't seem to notice her blackheads or her bad hair. He just kept telling her how cute and sexy she was and how bad he wanted her, and then he grabbed her hand and put it on the crotch of his jeans. He was hard so he couldn't have been lying about being attracted to her. It made her feel like other girls were just jealous because here she was, walking all by herself, and a grown man wanted her, not the makeup counter girls, not the women working in the department stores, he wanted her and so she knew the other girls had been lying about the blackheads and she grabbed his dick through his jeans and squeezed it and he moaned and unzipped his pants, kissing her the whole time, muttering sweet things amid his heavy breathing, and Rainbow opened her legs to him, opened them all the way, as far as she could in the front seat of the car, and the itch returned that she'd felt years before, the itch that needed to be scratched, and he was going to scratch it for her, so she kissed him back, squeezed him harder, let him touch her however he wanted to, and when he told her to crawl over the console and onto his lap she did it happily, now that she felt beautiful again, and he pulled her close to him, lowered her down onto his dick, and laid his seat back, and they had sex, right there in broad daylight, that's how unashamed he is of me, she thought, he wouldn't want to be seen in daylight with me if he didn't mean those things he said because any minute someone who works at the theater could come out to smoke a cigarette or take out last night's trash before they opened up for the matinee, surely someone could drive back here, it's not like it's abandoned, and they kept going, the car rocking with their motion, until finally the man shuddered and held her close, and let out a long breath of air and kept saying goddam, baby, goddam, as his shudders subsided, and Rainbow was pleased that she made him so happy, pleased she had this ability to make grown men call her baby.

He didn't buy her lunch, though, which disappointed her. He looked in the rearview mirror, the side mirrors, then told her he was late for something, sorry, and opened his door and told her she had to get out fast. Then he was gone. But she still had the twenty. She had money and she felt whole once again, for the first time in a long while.

This time, when Brightstar returned to the tunnels, she had a bag of food waiting for him. His favorite: a chilidog and cheesy fries from Weinerschnitzel. He devoured the food and told her I just knew a new outfit was all you needed, Rainbow. You know, show a little skin and they assume you're older. So where'd you get a job?

It never crossed her mind that he would ask her where the money came from, she just thought he'd be grateful and excited when she found work. So Rainbow lied. She stuttered and told him she got a job waiting tables, didn't name a restaurant. Not that he'd care. Or maybe he would. She didn't know. Thankfully he didn't notice her pause.

The next morning she did it again. She scrambled out of the arroyo, then washed up in the mall bathroom, fiercely scrubbing her face with hand soap, trying to get at those pores she still couldn't see. She wet her hair and dried it beneath the hand dryer, happy she had finally figured out a way to make money. Happy she wasn't going to starve.

The makeup counter looked abandoned when Rainbow walked past the entrance to Dillard's, so she walked in quickly and swiped a tester bottle of Liz Claiborne perfume and walked out calmly. She sprayed a slight amount onto her wrists, rubbed them together, then rubbed them on her neck. Her chest got a spray as well. And when she was sure no one was looking, she lifted her skirt slightly and sprayed toward her panties, then squatted down quickly to catch the perfume mist before it fell to the ground.

Prepared for a new day, she walked around the mall trying hard to look like she belonged, like she was actually shopping. She browsed Spencer Gifts, laughing at the raunchy birthday cards with fat naked women on the covers, flipping through the posters of swimsuit models and famous bands and ripped boys wearing only jeans and standing by bales of hay.

Her first score of the day was just outside a jewelry store, where a man came out carrying a necklace for his wife's birthday, saw her slowly walking past, and offered her an Orange Julius. She accepted gladly because she hadn't eaten yet and the drink would fill her up. She licked the froth off the straw for him, putting on a show to let him know she was interested and okay with his come-on. He kept glancing over his shoulder, looking for security or maybe his wife or kids. Finally he asked her to leave with him, offering ten dollars if she came outside to his car and went for a ride, but she refused and told him it would take twenty. The man rolled his eyes, but he pulled a twenty out of his wallet and gave it to her, then he rose and gestured for her to follow. The look on his face told her to follow at a discrete distance. So she did.

He took her to Reid Park, since it was just a couple blocks away, and paid for a paddleboat ride on the lake. Once they were settled in the middle of the lake, he pulled out his dick and told her suck it nice and slow, I'll keep a lookout for trouble. And he paddled slowly in a circle while Rainbow went down on him, oh she was so good at this. He couldn't believe his luck. This hot little piece giving him a blowjob. Something he was sure would never happen again in his life, but here he was, sitting in a boat with a cute bitch he picked up at the mall for twenty dollars. And she sucked like a pro. Like she just loved being down there. He pushed her down. Made her take all of him in her throat, and she did, just slid down like it was nothing and then he closed his eyes and bit his lip while he came down the back of her throat and then whispered swallow, swallow, you little slut, like it's your last meal, and he saw white behind his eyelids, then opened them and the perfect Arizona afternoon greeted his eyes and he was happy, so goddam happy because it was the best twenty he'd ever spent in his life. He zipped up his pants and they paddled back to the shore in silence. Yes, she was good.

At Rainbow's request the man left her in the park, and she walked over to the water fountain and swished her mouth with the warm, stale water. It wasn't a big deal really, which actually surprised her because she'd never done that before. It wasn't like she could get a job doing anything else. And nobody had seen. No one else was paddling on the lake. The park wasn't full of people since it was a weekday. Twenty dollars was a good amount for ten minutes of work, plus a free Orange Julius.

She spent a couple hours at the park. Relaxing, strolling leisurely through the grass, lying down in the shade, smelling the roses in the garden, feeling beautiful and wanted. She swung on the swings for a little while too, listening to the children laughing and squealing in the sunlight. Yes, Rainbow, it looks like everything might just work out after all. It was such a pretty day and she walked back over to the mall to try her luck again.

Since she didn't want to be obvious, Rainbow spent a couple bucks on postcards of Arizona at one of those shops in the mall that sold tacky Southwestern-themed things like shirts printed with ARIZONA: IT'S A DRY HEAT; or little snow globes minus the snow, a carrot and two pieces of charcoal and a black top hat floating around inside the plastic water-filled dome with a plaque on the front saying ARIZONA SNOWMAN; or shot glasses in the shape of saguaro cactus. The postcards were a gift for Brightstar. She figured they could tape them up on the wall above their bed and make the place look a little more homey.

The rest of the day, she had no luck. Plenty of people leered at her or even made comments, but it got old walking around pretending to be shopping. And when the schoolkids got out and swarmed the mall, there was no point in staying. The good news was Brightstar loved his gift. He smiled as he watched her duct tape the postcards on the grimy cement walls above their bed. It made her feel better to look up at the pictures of the wide-open Arizona sky and the Saguaro National Forest and the Grand Canyon and the San Xavier Mission.

The mall routine worked out nicely for a while. Every morning Brightstar woke her gently and prodded her into getting up and going to work. Some days she made nothing, and once she made ninety dollars in one afternoon. It wasn't bad work, just embarrassing when sometimes mall employees recognized her and seemed to suspect what she was doing. Because of that, she expanded her workplace to other malls in the city—Tucson Mall, El Con Mall, Foothills Mall—taking the Sun-Tran across town. She finally broke down and got a bus pass, learning the layout of the city a little at a time. And the money was getting good enough that she hoped to be able to rent a place soon. She wanted more than anything to be able to mention this to Brightstar, to repay him for his kindness and protection. But she knew she shouldn't because she'd been lying to him all along about where her money was coming from.

The most important thing was that she wasn't starving, and fucking men in cars, in alleys, in parks, and the many other places they picked, well, that hardly bothered her at all. They scratched her itch too. It was a fair trade-off.

That was until one afternoon in Park Mall when, though she hadn't been there all week, someone realized that Rainbow was there to pick up men. Security was on to her, and they were waiting for her to reappear so they could ban her from the mall, plus call the cops to teach the whore a lesson.

Rainbow had no idea until she emerged from the bathroom and ran into the chest of a police officer blocking the doorway with his arms crossed. Mall security guards flanked him, sneering when he ordered Rainbow to come with him, I've got a few questions for you. She glared at the security guards, both of whom she'd seen many times, and flipped them off, following Officer Loudermilk out to his cruiser, where he opened the back door and motioned her inside, then got in the front and rattled some codes over his CB, then spoke to her in the rearview mirror, asking what is it, exactly, young lady, that you're doing here in the mall? Security tells me you've been spotted leaving with different men on several occasions.

Rainbow shrugged, trying to look cool, but her hands were shaking in her lap and her heart was beating faster, adrenaline coursing through her body. She looked away from the mirror, but Loudermilk kept talking.

You've got some options. You can admit to what you're doing and I can take you in and book you, or you can make it easier on yourself by taking a little ride with me.

She looked back up to the mirror, but couldn't see his eyes because he'd put on sunglasses. What's one more guy? she thought. What's a freebie if it keeps me out of jail? She knew the last place she wanted to go was jail, and she didn't want to have to explain it to Brightstar, so she relented. Let's take a drive, Rainbow said, settling into the leather seat and leaning her head back to stare out the rear window at the puffy white clouds passing overhead.

The car shifted into gear and Loudermilk crept out of the parking lot. He drove east, past the air force base and out into the desert, pulling off the road and spraying dust into the air. Once they were out of view from the road, he stopped the car and got out. He opened the door and pulled Rainbow out of the car, threw her up against the trunk, her back to him, and cuffed her hands. Even though Rainbow was scared, she rejected the idea of screaming for help, because she knew it would only make things worse. Instead she cooed oh you're a bad cop, aren't you? turning to look at him as he took off his belt and laid it on the ground, then unfastened his slacks and pulled them down to his knees. It looked to her as though he liked her taunting, so she continued, with more confidence, cmon officer, make me pay. Make me sorry for being such a bad girl.

He pushed her head down onto the trunk and lifted her skirt, and Rainbow winced at the heat coming from the metal. It burned her forehead but took her mind off the man grunting and gasping behind her. The wind picked up and blew dust in her face and her knees were bruising as they pounded up against the bumper—and she let Loudermilk fuck her as hard as he could, even told him harder, officer, you have to teach me a lesson, and he thrust at her harder, pulled on her bound wrists with one hand and wrapped the other one around her throat, squeezing harder with each thrust, until she couldn't breathe, her throat tickled as it closed up, and her vision went black and right when she actually thought he's going to kill me out here in the desert, he's going to choke me to death and leave my body to the coyotes and rattlesnakes and scorpions and tarantulas, why did I come with him? then he was finished and released her throat and she gasped for air, breathing in the sweet, sweet dusty desert air while Loudermilk collapsed on her, his legs shaky, resting his sweaty head on her back while she lay splayed out on the car, covered in dust and sweat and bruises, trying to catch her breath.

Then the handcuffs came off and he reached down to get his belt and for the briefest moment Rainbow thought I should just kick him right in the face while he's down there, take his gun and shoot him. Just unload the gun on him, bullet by bullet, while he lays in the dirt begging me to stop. I can leave him for dead. Give him a taste of his own medicine.

She got back into the car and lay down across the backseat, hugging her knees to her chest while she waited for Loudermilk to get back in and drive her home.

Man, you fuck like a CHAMP. Where'd you learn to take it like that? Who taught you those moves?

She wanted to say my grandfather, but decided otherwise. Instead Rainbow said thought you'd like to know, you just fucked a fifteen-year-old girl. How'd you like it?

She didn't expect him to laugh, but he did. He sat in the front seat of the cruiser, his face in front of the air-conditioning, and laughed and said you've GOT to be shittin me. Fifteen? You fuck like a grownass woman. I know just the place for you. Fifteen. I'll be godfuckindamned. The boys wouldn't believe me if I told em.

The entire ride back into the city he kept chuckling and saying fifteen. Sweet piece of fifteen-year-old ass. He flipped on his cherries and sped down the road back into Tucson, swerving past drivers who slowed down instead of pulling out of the way, turning onto I-10 and cutting a quick path through the city, then taking the Stone Avenue exit, where he finally turned off his lights and slowed down. Once he stopped the car he got out and opened the back door again, pulling Rainbow out and around to the front of the car, where they leaned side by side against the hood. He pointed at a rundown motel. It looked abandoned. But its sign said Mountain Top Motel—Vacancy, and it was lit, so she figured it was still in business.

Now this here's Miracle Mile. You ever heard of it? She shook her head, cringing at the way he was touching her, his hand wandering beneath her halter top, smoothing her skin, lingering on a mole on her right shoulder. What's your name, by the way? She told him. He laughed again. Rainbow, that's fuckin choice. I couldn't have picked a better name for you myself. Fresh as a goddam rainbow's exactly what you are. Little pot of gold is *exactly* what you've got down there, little girl, pinching her ass.

Well, here's what I'd do if I were you. He rubbed the mole in tiny circles with his thumb. I'd come work this strip, because anyone who knows anything comes here for tail at the end of the night. Right now it's dead, but in a few hours it'll be crawling with girls just like you—not nearly as hot, honey, don't you worry, you'll be a hit—and guys with money to spend. That mall shit you're doing is just small-time. You want the real deal, you gotta come here.

Rainbow wondered what the real deal meant. Would it mean she'd finally get a place to live? Would it mean she could sleep in an actual bed again, with electricity and a swamp cooler and a shower?

The problem is, you're fifteen. But that's actually more of a benefit. So here's how it's gonna work, Rainbow. He chuckled again. That name's fuckin great. I mean it. I'm not blowin you shit so don't get all uppity. He took off his shades and turned her face toward his. I'm serious. So what you're gonna do is work out here at night. You'll be solo. And there will be undercover cops. But I'm gonna let em know who you are, so you'll be taken care of. Only thing is anytime we want a piece, you're gonna drop everything and take care of us. Okay? I'll tell em what you look like, and we'll make sure you stay out of trouble. We can't go puttin a sexy little thing like you in jail with all them wetbacks and niggers. You're a free spirit, aintcha? Yep. You're gonna be just fine. Fifteen. Jesusfuckinchrist. That's too much.

Rainbow nodded and said okay. It sounded like a good deal to her. Nothing to worry about. Cops to protect her. Real money. Yeah. Things were getting better. And as gross as his compliments were, she kind of liked it when he told her she fucked like a grownass woman. She liked it when he promised to take care of her.

Rainbow gave up on malls altogether after Loudermilk took her to Miracle Mile. She returned to the tunnel and gathered her belongings, which by now included three cute tops and a pair of short-shorts. Plus the original outfit Brightstar had stolen for her.

Waiting on Brightstar to arrive, she glanced around the tunnel and felt guilty for leaving him here. But what else could she do? He couldn't take care of her forever, and she'd never make any real money sneaking around malls to pick up men. No, this was definitely the right thing to do. She waited and waited for him to return, frightened each time she heard a noise that could be him because she still hadn't figured out how to explain her situation.

It wasn't as hard as she thought. He seemed surprised when he arrived at their spot halfway down the tunnel to find Rainbow with her clothing folded neatly on her lap, staring at the walls, which were lit by a solitary candle beside her.

It was as if he'd known all along what she had been doing for money, because when she finally broke down and told him she was going to try her luck on Miracle Mile for a while, you know, I've got people who are going to help me and watch my back and everything, he simply nodded and told her well, I guess my work is done. I've done the best I could. You're still alive. You didn't starve to death. No one hurt you. Can't say I blame you for taking whatever you can get.

But she sensed the melancholy tone of his words and reached out for him, the two of them hugging, rocking back and forth, holding each other for some time until finally Brightstar broke their embrace and said I was thinking about going up to Phoenix anyway. The VA pricks here just won't budge. If I head to the source, maybe I can make some headway. I just can't stay here, waiting the rest of my life for some asshole to show me mercy. Rainbow nodded, happy Brightstar was finally fed up and ready to take action. She wanted to tell him she was going to miss him. She wanted to let him know how much it meant to her that he took better care of her than her own mother had. She wanted to let him know how greatly she appreciated feeling safe.

How she was scared she wasn't going to be safe without him. But there was no way to tell him without getting all sappy and weepy, so she just kissed his forehead, said thank you, Brightstar, and walked out of the tunnels and toward her new life.

———

Rainbow never saw Brightstar again, but even all these years later she often wondered where he'd gone, whether he'd had any success in Phoenix, or if he was slowly making his way across the country, hopping trains and begging for change at busy intersections until he ended up at his final destination, VA headquarters in DC.

On Miracle Mile Loudermilk had kept his promise. Not only did he visit her frequently, but he also sent other members of the TPD who were eager to get some action from the newest hooker on the Mile. A fifteen-year-old badass free for the taking. None of them could resist. She wished she could charge the bastards, since it seemed she was servicing them far more than real johns, but they never busted her, just as Loudermilk promised. And most of the time she felt safe on the Mile because cops were always present, whether in plain clothes or leaning against their squad cars in the liquor store parking lot, eyeballing the drunk men cruising for ass and obviously hoping one of them would get out of line so they could get in a little nightstick practice.

At the beginning it was kind of nice being the new girl on the strip. Word got out pretty quickly among the regulars, and everyone who worked the strip—whether bartenders or bouncers or strip club managers or the men who pimped some of the hookers, even one or two hookers themselves—wanted to try out Rainbow. Her age and her police protection gave her an allure that was simply too hard to pass up, and so her first few months were a whirlwind of clients, handfuls of cash, and one or two visits to the free clinic to get treated for itching or rashes or smelly discharge. But overall it was about what she expected, though she was often sore. However, when she closed the hotel door on her final john of the evening, she dug her cash out from under the flimsy mattress and laid it out on the bed, one bill at a time, savoring the sight of so many bills lying neatly in rows on the threadbare comforter.

At sixteen she started doing coke, which was all the rage on the strip. The first time a cop told her they wanted to give her a gummy she reeled in horror, unaware of what this deviant act might be. Since he was one of the plainclothes on the drug taskforce, his coke was top-notch. He licked his index finger, opened the baggy, and plunged his finger deep into the powder. Then he pulled her close to him and made her open her mouth, wiping the cocaine between her lips and gums, all around her jaw. It tasted like what she imagined baking soda would taste like. Kind of salty. Kind of metallic. A hint of tartness. But it numbed her mouth almost immediately, and then he cut two lines on the table next to the bed, the rickety particleboard table covered in cigarette burns, and handed her a rolled-up twenty and said do it just like this, showing her how he pushed one nostril closed with his left hand, holding a rolled-up bill in his other nostril with his right hand, and snorting the cater-pillar-sized line up in one second flat. She copied him. Her entire mouth was numb, and now so was her face, right behind her forehead it was like someone sprayed foam in there and it felt great and the feeling crept down her spine, down her chest, spreading all over her body and she hardly noticed when he took the twenty from her, tucked it behind his ear, and shoved his cock down her throat, holding the back of her head and slamming himself into her as hard as he could, and she thought thank god he gave me that gummy because my throat is prob-ably ripped to shreds, and she closed her eyes and enjoyed the foamy tingly feeling spreading throughout her body and waited for him to finish.

Once the undercovers knew she loved coke, they brought it to her all the time. And so did judges, prosecutors, defense lawyers, teachers, pro-fessors from the U of A, ministers, and priests. Everyone had coke when Rainbow was sixteen, and she hardly remembered doing anything but racing up and down the sidewalk, then into the hotel room, bang bang bang, out to the sidewalk, back to the room, a gummy, a throat fuck, bang bang bang, and on and on until one day she was seventeen and wondered where that year had gone.

Then she decided to lay off the coke, since there wasn't nearly as much of it around anyway, and she picked up drinking. It was far less intense, and it made her relax. It made her numb too, but in a fuzzy, comfortable way. Not the uptight way she'd reel around the Mile, night after night, pumped up on coke and pissing off the other whores because everyone liked her fresh meat better.

Hangovers were no good. And she found she could remember things better without the whirlwind blur of coke, so she started feeling the remorse of drinking too much when she rose the next afternoon, groggy and wondering whether she'd made any money or just drank it all away. She thought of Brightstar, hoping he was all right. She made it a point to take at least one night off a week and go out to dinner. She liked to pretend she was a girl just like any other. But when she saw kids cruising down the strip, hanging out of windows or standing up in the back of limos, their torsos peeking out from the roof of the car where they squealed drunkenly on their way to prom, so happy to be in love and the boys hoping their dates would give it up at the end of the night, she realized she would never know that kind of life.

She visited the tunnels every few months, but they weren't the same. With Brightstar gone, there was no reason to hang around. Besides, the city had only grown more violent since she'd moved to the Mile, so it wasn't wise to hang out there more than a few minutes. Maybe smoke a cigarette and walk a little ways into the tunnel. Nowhere near as far as where the two of them had lived because surely someone else had come to claim that prime piece of property by now.

Drinking on the Mile made things easier for her. If it was a slow night, she'd stand beneath a streetlight, or at the entrance to a parking lot, and share a bottle of vodka with one of the other girls looking to kill time until some business came along. The later it got and the more alcohol that was served, the more violent the men became, and they were pushed out the back doors of strip clubs by massive bouncers who stood by and watched, amused, as the drunk men went at each other's throats, punching and clawing until one of them managed to get the upper hand and began pummeling the other guy's face. These were the guys who didn't have enough money at the end of the night for a hooker, having spent too much on strippers, convinced they were getting somewhere and actually stood a chance at bringing one home.

Sometimes there were surprises, like the night she went into the alley to piss and found a man passed out, clutching a paper bag with a ring of silver around his mouth and nose. The man's half-open eyes were rolled back into his head, foamy spit slowly seeping from the corner of his mouth and streaming down his neck. She tried to rouse him, but he was dead weight. And the spray-paint can he'd been huffing was empty, so there was little she could do. She sat by him, holding his hand until his breathing stopped, staring at the buildings downtown and the ever-present red lights blinking atop the tallest one. Then, after she sifted through his pockets, she told one of the cops about him and went back to work.

The Mile was a ghost town in the daytime. But it transformed within minutes of sunset. Women stood in small clusters beneath streetlamps, some smoking cigarettes, some passing a joint, wearing next to nothing. The outfits were like bad Halloween costumes, like a group of ten-year-old girls playing dress-up in their older sisters' sluttiest clothing.

Sometimes the churchies came out and tried to witness to them. Of course many of them were customers themselves who thought they'd go unrecognized, but since the women wanted them to return and bring more business, they let them put on their little show for each other.

Rainbow's favorite night was when the pastor from one of Tucson's largest churches rolled up in his wheelchair and asked them if they knew what they were getting into, being out here on a street full of sin. One woman shot him a bored look and said just what the fuck ARE we doing out here, prick? If you're threatening us, you probably should reconsider before I splatter your Jesus brains into the dirt, you crazy fuck. She blew smoke in his face. He wasn't playing the game they were supposed to play. He was supposed to approach cautiously, pick one of them out as if he were picking out a greeting card, get a room at one of the dives, and climb on top of her for thirty minutes—or however many it took him to get off. Either they liked how she looked or they didn't. If not, move on to the next girl. It was as simple as that. But the preacher rolled closer and said look around here at your friends. She turned and asked so what's the big deal? They're fucking hookers? So that makes them what, criminals? Why? Cause we charge for what other dumb bitches give away for free? What else are we supposed to do? Can you see me bein some kinda goddam secretary? Managing a Denny's or Bob's Big Boy? Cmon man, you're not THAT fuckin stupid, are you? You really think I'm gonna look at my girls over there and that's gonna convince me to stop being out here? This is my life. And I'm good at it. If you gave me five bucks and stepped behind that dumpster over there, I'd have your jizz all over my hand in a second. Then you'd understand.

She bent over, lifted her skirt a little and revealed that she wasn't wearing underwear. Go back to the fuckin congregation with that shit.

When the preacher left, exasperated at his inability to shame the women into giving their lives to God, Rainbow told them about how he'd been to her room several times. How he was faking all along with that wheelchair, and they all had a good laugh. You sure told that small-dick motherfucker where to go. Haha.

—

Six weeks after Rainbow found the dead body inside the tunnels, she finally decided to go back again. It was nice to get away from downtown and hide out. She took a fifth of vodka with her for the bus ride and by the time she got off at Wilmot, the bottle was nearly finished. She had a good buzz going.

This time she was wearing her favorite outfit—a pair of skin-tight black stretch pants with black heels, and her silver glittery T-shirt—because when she finished her visit to the tunnel, she planned on treating herself to a nice dinner somewhere, then taking the night off to rest up, have a few drinks, maybe watch some TV back at the Congress.

She took off her heels to slide safely down the side of the wash, then stood up and dusted off the seat of her pants and walked toward the tunnel entrance. Nothing had changed. In all the years since she had first stumbled upon this place, it still seemed as though no one had figured out these tunnels were here, except for the neighborhood thugs who obviously saw it as a matter of pride to spray-paint at least every few days. But there were no signs of anyone else living here.

Just as she was about to step into the tunnel she and Brightstar had once shared, two boys came running out with a little pen flashlight, panting. Don't go in there, they gasped. There's DEFINITELY someone in there, probably someone crazy. We heard him. She pretended to be scared with them. Pretended she was grateful they'd spared her from something horrible roaming beneath the city, but when they were gone, she sat down in the entrance and cracked her bottle open and drained the rest of it in one chug. Then she leaned back against the wall and closed her eyes. Just for a minute. Just to rest them while she reminisced about Brightstar and wondered where she would have been without him.

Then she heard voices. Laughter. And suddenly she was yanked by her arm into the tunnel, her heels coming off as they dragged her inside just enough so no one in the wash or above it could see what was happening. The dark tunnel was crowded with bodies she could not distinguish. She tried to get to her knees but hands grabbed her from behind and pressed her to the tunnel floor, and she shook her head, trying to tell them she wasn't working right now but they could come visit her later and she'd give them a discount if they just let her go, but she couldn't make the words form and it didn't matter because the tunnel was spinning from her alcohol and she felt her new shirt being torn from her body as she curled up into a ball of tired drunk woman, and cold air hit her breasts and then her legs when they had her pants around her ankles and the guys gathered around her whooping and cheering at the naked body she futilely tried to cover up, and voices shouted it's that bitch from the Mile, what's she think she's doing here? this is King territory, and someone got on top of her and grabbed her breasts hard and more hands pried her legs open and searched her body, and someone grabbed a handful of her hair and said I guess you're ready to work now, you nasty bitch, and Rainbow cried and wished she were back aboveground, back in her bedroom all those years ago with her wedding plans envelope or safe in bed with her grandfather, and she tried to ignore the familiar and relieving feeling of a man inside her and sweating on top of her while he grunted and voices yelled hurry up so we can get a piece of that, and she tried to move but was too dizzy and her hands and feet were being held down anyway, and then the man was done and another climbed on top of her and grunted and laughed and pulled her hair and Rainbow tried to cry out but couldn't because a hand shoved a fistful of dirt into her mouth and covered it up so she could barely breathe, it was like trying to suck air through a stir stick, and tears streamed down her cheeks and her whole body felt like it was on fire and then the next guy was done and another climbed on top and then she felt warm blasts of come landing on her chest and in her hair and she wanted desperately to beg for them to let her go, please, I'll never come back, I swear, just let me go, but then another man was inside her and more sneering and more yelling and then the sounds faded away as Rainbow began to drift in and out of consciousness, and soon the entire tunnel was filled with unbearable heat and lust for Rainbow and the men circled around like dogs, waiting their turns and cheering for whoever was on top of her at the time, biting her and pulling her hair and choking her, Rainbow lying on the cold concrete floor, covered in scratches and blood and come, her sweaty body battered and bruised.

Then the hand on her mouth was gone, and she spit out the dirt. She couldn't tell if she had any cuts in her gums or nicks in her teeth, running her tongue around her mouth to check for damage. But then her mouth was stuffed full again, this time with someone's cock, and Rainbow chomped down on it as hard as she could.

His scream was so horrible everyone froze—even the man inside her—and he hovered there for a moment, his Adidas grinding a few granules of dirt into the cement floor, and before Rainbow had time to react, the guys realized what had happened, saw their boy holding his bleeding limp dick, and they swarmed around her. They pulled her to her knees and slammed her up against the wall of the tunnel. And she blacked out.

What woke her was the prodding of feet, kicking her slightly, enough to nudge her awake. She heard voices speaking excitedly. The sound of a pipe scraping against the tunnel floor. She tried to focus her eyes but saw nothing. It was getting dark out and there were too many bodies around her for light to get in from outside the tunnel. All she saw were the outlines of several men.

And then the brief flicker of light off the pipe swinging down toward her face.

This she noticed just in time to turn her head and take the pipe to the back of her skull, where it carved a gash and left a ringing so loud in her head that everything else took on a muffled sound. Like she was underwater. The muted sound of fists to the back of her neck. The hushed pop of the pipe cracking her ribs. The almost inaudible scraping of ground beneath her, cement tearing her flesh, the dirt mixing with her wounds, the side of her head repeatedly striking the cement as she was pulled by her feet into the wash, where her attackers circled her and unleashed a storm of kicks and pummeled her with fists, the one whose cock she'd almost bitten off stood above her with the pipe now, taking turns striking her with it and then pausing long enough to let someone else get a running start and kick her in the face as hard as he could, which went on forever, the kicking, then the muffled thump of the pipe, then the boot to the face, and so on, as the moon turned red behind the blood filling her eyes and she closed them and let them stay that way, ignoring the fists and the pipe, reminding herself that this wasn't the way she was supposed to die. This is what she thought as they raised her body up and tied her by the wrists to the guardrail protruding over the top of the wash, designed to keep cars from plummeting into the arroyo—this one having apparently worked, because despite being bent over the wash, it remained rooted firmly in the ground—perfect for stringing Rainbow up and stripping off the remains of her tattered clothing, leaving her battered and destroyed flesh exposed to the cold night air. A stone hit her in the face. Then another. Then in the crotch. One glanced off her kneecap, forming a strange kind of rhythm, like brutal raindrops, as the Kings picked up stones and hurled them at her, using their strongest pitches. The stoning continued and still Rainbow thought this isn't how I'm going to die. This isn't what I've been dreaming. Even after the stones and the cursing had stopped. Even after the last voice had died off and the men had had enough.

And so she hung, silent, swinging gently, like an ornament in a tree, bloody and shiny in the light of the moon where they left her for dead. The last image she saw through her swollen eyelids was the red lights downtown mocking her, forever blinking, witnessing the whole event but not helping her.

Rainbow awoke to see a tiled ceiling and herself reflected off the screen of the TV bolted to a stand in the room's upper corner, the TV looking down on her like the judgmental eye of God, a gray, shiny, non-blinking eye, and when she saw how vulnerable she was there, lying in her gown with tubes coming out of her arms and nose, she felt more alone than ever. No Brightstar. No family. Just her and the TV and the Demerol button. She vaguely remembered being told to tap it whenever her pain was higher than six on a scale of one to ten. She tapped it a few times. Then went back under.

They released her three weeks later, wheeling her out to the sidewalk, where no one waited to pick her up. She wore baggy jeans and a T-shirt that was way too big for her, clothing donated by the Salvation Army for situations just like hers. As she stood to leave she nearly collapsed, her muscles throbbing and her head foggy with the last dose of Demerol they'd given her a couple hours before her release. She gripped the handles of the wheelchair, waving off help from the nurse, pausing long enough to get her bearings, then standing and staggering out of the parking lot, heading toward the giant glass building downtown reflecting in the sunlight like a pillar of fire.

The doctor told her not to drink while taking the pills they prescribed her, but that was exactly what she intended to do. So when she got to the bar at the Congress, she slumped on a stool and told him to double em up, ignoring the jokes and then the questions about where she'd been and why her face was all bruised up. Just double up those Cape Cods, and don't ask me any fuckin questions. She slammed the first one, and the second sat waiting for her. After she slammed that one and the liquor began to mix with her medication, she no longer felt the dull, lingering pain. So she drank more. It felt so much better, the cushion of alcohol protecting her from her aching body. It was a miracle she'd lived, that much she knew, but she wondered why. Why let me live if I have to go back to the same thing? Really, thirty years from now, I'm going to be doing the same thing?

She drank more. She wondered about her mother and thought about how it felt to almost die and wake up alone in a hospital room. The cops had come to ask if she wanted to press charges. But when one of them recognized her, they left, figured if she had something to say, she'd tell them on the Mile. She could let Loudermilk know and he'd figure out what to do. They shook their heads when they left because she looked so fucked up there was no way she'd be able to work as a hooker anymore. Nobody would want to touch that. But at least she'd lived through the rape, poor bitch.

By the time she finished her fifth drink, the bar was cloudy and the conversation right next to her indecipherable and she liked it just like that. Rainbow settled into her little fog of numbness and let the vodka soak in. She lingered there on her stool, slumped over, teetering slightly, remembering the tunnel and the horror of it all, sad because now she could never go back. Now she only had hotels as homes. Now she was stuck bouncing between the Mile and the Congress. She no longer had a special secret place. They had made their point, those fuckin thugs, and so it wasn't hers anymore.

They made their point, she finally said to the bartender when he came to ask her if she wanted another. Those motherfuckers made their point, OKAY? He nodded and poured her another, then reached out and put his hand on hers, an act of kindness that Rainbow mistook for malice, like this guy wanted to fuck her right there when she had just been raped, couldn't he tell that she'd just been raped? She pulled her hand back and glared at him, then at the people in the bar enjoying their afternoon drinks and she said YES, okay, YES I just got fuckin raped in a wash by a bunch of gangsters.

It felt good to let it out. Her cushion of alcohol was strong and empowering. Yes, she said, I guess everyone wants a fuckin piece of Rainbow, huh? Getting louder and more confident as the liquor and painkillers mixed. Look at this sweet ass. She slapped it. People turned away, embarrassed. The bartender tried to calm her down. OH NO YOU DON'T. This is MY fuckin hotel. I'm the one who runs this place. I'm the girl who sucks the manager's dick every night and fucks your husbands, yes, you there, ma'am, I have probably fucked YOUR husband, he looks familiar—the couple got up to leave and the bartender came around the bar to calm her down—this is MY city, she yelled, raising her arms and almost falling off the stool, and I'm the sweetest piece of ass for miles. ME. RAINBOW. And she stood and lifted her T-shirt and showed her tits to the bar, yelling GO AHEAD AND STARE. YOU KNOW YOU WANT THESE, while the patrons whispered behind their hands, and Rainbow walked up to one of the booths as everybody watched and she grabbed a man's hand and stuck it on her tit and said go ahead and squeeze. Now you see what all the hype's about, huh? The bartender went back behind the bar and phoned the manager to tell him about Rainbow while she kept yelling at the bar, this is the BEST FUCKIN PUSSY IN THE SOUTHWEST, BITCHES, and she pulled her pants down and showed her bruised legs and then pulled down her panties and turned around so everyone could see. Get a good look, she said. This is it. This is what you came for, isn't it? The customers began to leave the bar, shaking their heads and averting their eyes from Rainbow, who now lay down on the floor, her legs splayed, yelling WHO WANTS IT FIRST? spreading herself open for anyone, everyone who wanted a piece of her sweet ass. She started crying. She couldn't see anyone but she knew there were more people in the bar, someone who would take her up on her offer and climb on top of her right there on the floor. Who wants it first? she mumbled. First come, first served she said through tears, and a couple more people walked out. They walked out of the bar and abandoned their drinks and their bar tabs and the bartender shouted RAINBOW, YOU'RE COSTING ME A FUCKIN FORTUNE, and the manager appeared and balked at the sight of Rainbow lying on the floor of his bar, is this little cunt fuckin crazy? he muttered to the bartender, and the two men reached down, apologizing loudly to the few male patrons who remained, unable to look away from the show Rainbow was giving them, too bad she's all fucked up and bruised otherwise we might've actually taken her up on her offer, and they silently groaned when the bartender and manager finally redressed Rainbow and dragged her out of the bar, her head lolling from one side to the other, and then carried her to the alley behind the hotel and left her there.

Rainbow blacked out. She knew that much had happened when she awoke in the alley behind the Congress, drunk and thirsty for more Cape

Cods. Her body was sore, but the drugs and alcohol still coursed through her. When she walked into the hotel to go up to her room, the manager stopped her and told her you've been evicted. We'll keep whatever shit you left in your room to pay for the bar tab and your room bill. And by the way, you're banned for life. So get the fuck out of here, you psycho, or I'll have you arrested. Rainbow tried to reason with him, but her logic was garbled. I suck your dick every night, man. Business comes because of me. I suck you and we have a deal. Hotel guests within earshot turned to look and the manager grabbed Rainbow by the arm, pulling her toward the door while he smiled for his guests and hissed to her between his teeth I'll fuckin kill you if you get me in trouble. I mean it. I'll take you out to the desert myself and put a bullet in your cuntass skull if you try to pull some shit like this ever again. Now here's twenty bucks. Get a meal and find someplace else to sleep from now on. Don't ever come back or you'll regret it. You think you're fucked up now? You have no idea.

It was laughable to her that this guy had the nerve to threaten *her*, Rainbow, the most protected and hottest piece of ass in all of Tucson. I'm the hottest ass in this town, she sneered. He laughed in her face. You may have been, Rainbow. But your Congress days are over. Good luck, hottest ass in town, and he shoved her out onto the sidewalk and ordered a security guard to keep that bitch out of here no matter what you have to do. Break her goddam legs if she won't leave. Take her to the fountain and drown her if you feel like it. I don't give a flying fuck what you do. But keep that bitch out of my hotel.

Rainbow stood and tried to gain her balance. Leaning against the front of the hotel, she couldn't focus on the people passing to see if any of them were looking for some action tonight. The looks she got were looks of pity or disgust, but she couldn't see clearly enough to notice. People went out of their way to avoid her when they walked past the front of the hotel where she wobbled, leaning against the wall, muttering how tonight only was the special, ten dollars, I just need a few bucks, I need to get a place to sleep, and people shook their heads and shared knowing glances with one another—this city is just going straight to hell, oh yes, I agree, nothin but whores and bums—and quickened their strides until Rainbow was out of their sight.

Using the wall for support, Rainbow made her way down the sidewalk, heading toward the Greyhound station, since someone just getting to Tucson on the bus might want a date for the night. Straightening her clothes with one arm and leaning on buildings with the other, she finally arrived at the bus station and stood by the entrance mumbling hottest ass in town, ten dollars, and the travelers pushed past Rainbow, who reached out for them, her head still foggy and confused, trying to come in contact with someone so he could feel how soft her skin was and want to take her home with him or to a hotel room or anywhere, just a couple bucks and I'll do anything, but they only walked past and left Rainbow standing all alone, bruised, wincing, the pain returning now that some of her alcohol was wearing off, so she took one of her pills and trudged to the liquor store and bought a plastic jug of vodka and a pack of generic smokes, which left her just under two dollars, and she opened the bottle before she even left the store and washed down another painkiller with a long pull that burned her mouth and throat and sinuses and chest but finally settled in nicely and the pain subsided and then Rainbow left the store, holding the jug in her arms like a proud parent holds a newborn baby, protectively, but with enough pride to attract the admiration of other people, she thought, yet the only looks she actually attracted were either curious, pitying, or disgusted, and so she walked the alleys and slowly made her way toward Miracle Mile, convinced she would be able to drum up a little business there.

She'd drunk vodka her entire walk and could barely stand by the time she arrived. The painkillers had kicked in and she stumbled onto the Mile just as the streetlights came on, stashing her vodka in a bush behind the Lone Star Lounge after taking one last swig, then making a drunken attempt to straighten her clothing and using all her concentration to go out onto the sidewalk, where she leaned against a streetlamp and tried to chat up men walking past. But no one responded. Every single person she propositioned ignored her. The streetlights made everything all smeary and distorted. The undercovers pretended they didn't know her. She looks like shit, they told each other, which was a shame because it meant no more free ass since now no one would take a piece of her even if she gave it to them for free. Which was precisely what she tried to do before the night was over, desperate for anyone to touch her, to tell her she was the hottest ass on the Mile. To call her beautiful or maybe just hold her and kiss her forehead. She managed to reach out and grab a man strolling past and told him just fuck me for free, and he looked at her, saw her bruises and her ill-fitting clothes and the cuts and stitches on her face, and a patch of hair shaved on the back of her head where a gash from the pipe had been sewn shut, and he told her you have to be kidding, right? You look like you were dragged through the desert by horses, and he squirmed out of her grasp and pushed her away from him and she collapsed on the ground and vomited onto the sidewalk, her body finally rejecting the mixture of painkillers and alcohol.

Everyone pretended not to see her. The other prostitutes couldn't have been happier to see that Rainbow's days on the Mile were obviously over, and they stepped over her as though she were a piece of dog shit and moved down the street in a group, away from the mess that was Rainbow, vomiting and crying on the sidewalk and begging for someone to just please fuck her, tugging at her pants, trying to take them off and just lie there with her legs spread so anyone who wanted a piece of her could come and take it. But no one stopped.

Finally Rainbow dragged herself back to her feet, then staggered to the Lone Star Lounge and retrieved her bottle, tipped it back and took a huge swig, then knelt down, her back against the dumpster, cradling her plastic jug on her lap and sipping for the rest of the night, whenever she remembered it was there.

By morning, when the Mile was quiet again and the jug was half gone, Rainbow realized she would be getting no business there, though she couldn't exactly understand why people used to practically line up to have her and now no one would even talk to her, and so she gathered what little strength she had and decided to find a shady place to sleep. She walked slowly, sipping the vodka, which was getting harder and harder to lift to her lips. She stopped often, resting and getting out of the sun whenever she could. Each time she found a place that looked safe enough for sleeping she passed out for a few moments, only to wake shaking and clawing at the air and covered in sweat, dreaming the flood more vividly and violently than ever before. After five attempts at sleep, each time having nightmares and grinding her teeth, she finally gave up and decided to keep drinking and walking. Something or someone would have to come along and save her. She just knew it.

It took her most of the day to make it to 4th Avenue, where she thought she might be able to beg some change or offer a homeless guy sex for a dollar or two. By the time she arrived most of the coffee shops and thrift stores were locking their doors and the bars and tattoo parlors were opening for the night's business. She sat on the stoop of a women's clothing boutique, her bottle between her legs, a solid buzz raging through her body, and looked at the beautiful dresses hanging in the window, wishing she could walk in and try one on, have the owner doting on her while trying desperately to make a sale. But the lights were off. The CLOSED sign was showing. And so she sat on the stoop, gazing at the colorful dresses and teetering back and forth. Smoking her last cigarettes. Waiting for the sun to go down. The red lights mocking her atop the tallest building downtown.

She ran out of cigarettes before midnight. Someone threw her the last of his own pack out of pity. Everyone else either laughed at her, collapsed there in the doorway of the boutique, in dumpy clothing, her eyes bloodshot and swollen, or they ignored her. She tried to talk, but nothing came out except for a grumbling hiccup. So she sat on the stoop, trying to focus on the dresses whose patterns were too complicated to make out because the vodka was swirling around in her empty stomach. She thought about food, but it didn't interest her. The only thing she could concentrate on was the jug and how it took the pain away and set her atop a cloud that kept her safe from the world and the evil eyes blinking at her from downtown. She nodded off and dreamed of floods. Above it all the evil eyes blinked and watched her worthless life. She woke up.

The vodka disappeared as the sun began to rise. Rainbow held the plastic jug above her mouth, eking out the last few drops and wondering whether she could scrounge enough change to get more. She felt around for her pills, for anything to keep her buzz going, but they were gone. She had nothing. No money. No drink. No food. She needed to keep drinking. Anything to keep from sleeping because she simply couldn't take the nightmares anymore. And nothing was worse than seeing the flood and the lights and all the horrors of her Tucson nightmares, only to wake and have the first thing she saw be the red lights on the tower downtown. There was no escaping them. They were driving her insane.

Rainbow knew the owner of the beautiful dress store could show up anytime, so she gathered herself and went to the only place she thought she might get lucky and get a scrap to eat or a couple bucks for a drink—downtown.

The piercing Arizona sun made her sweat. She wanted to rip off her clothing and go for a dip in the fountain downtown, but people were arriving for work and there were more cops patrolling the business district, keeping the money flowing, making sure none of the homeless got out of hand or bothered the shoppers and working people.

Rainbow knew she probably looked like death walking and she could feel her injuries beginning to ache again now that the alcohol was wearing off. Inside the buildings people looked up from their desks or from behind their registers as she walked past in such bad condition they couldn't believe she was capable of carrying her own weight, let alone managing to put one foot in front of the other. Her clothes were filthy, stained with vomit and dirt. At some point during her two-day binge she'd lost her shoes. To anyone who looked at her she seemed two or three times her age. Beaten, starving, half-drunk, Rainbow looked like she could go at any moment. Just fall over and expire right there on the sidewalk in front of them. That's what each person who looked up thought, and they waited until she had passed, watching her slow progress, almost disappointed—though they'd never admit this, even to themselves—when she was safely gone from view.

Because she hadn't had a drop since sunrise, when her jug had gone dry, Rainbow started to get desperate. She thought about going to the fountain and pulling out all the coins people threw in when casting for wishes. But the place was always being passed by cops on their way to the courthouse.

Opting not to bother with the fountain, Rainbow decided to relax on the grass of Veinte de Agosto Park. With all the other homeless there, she would blend in easily and not be bothered while she tried to think of a way to drum up some money and keep her buzz going. It was so close to gone. A headache was starting to move in. She needed a fucking drink. Just one Cape Cod and I'll be fine. Just pour the vodka right down my throat. Squirt some cranberry in there. No need to waste your glass.

Almost to the park, Rainbow passed the courthouse, where lawyers and jurors and the wives or mothers of men on trial avoided eye contact, walking an exaggerated arc around her, shaking their heads at her and elbowing each other and pointing with their heads at the waste of a human being right there, covered in puke and looking like some washed-up whore. Pathetic.

And that's exactly how Rainbow felt. Pathetic. But she stopped off to rest on the freshly watered courthouse lawn, and it felt so soft and so cool. Far superior to the concrete tunnels or an alley on Miracle Mile or a doorway on 4th Avenue. She never wanted to get up. She wanted to lie there until she died, to just fall asleep and wait for the flood to finally come and bury her, but she heard the unmistakable thump of a cop slapping his nightstick on his palm, making his way toward the lawn to run off the vagrants, so she rose to her knees, blocking the glare of the sun with her hand, until she located the source of the sound. Sure enough a cop was making a beeline toward her and the other homeless people relaxing on the grass, taking a break from the sun for a couple minutes, so she stood and shook her head and said I'm leaving, I'm leaving, stumbling in the opposite direction.

She crossed the street toward the UniSource Tower, skirting around the front of the building where people lounged in front of the fountain smoking cigarettes and eating their lunches, gossiping and pointing at her, glad to have something different to talk about, tired of the whole day in day out routine of eating lunch with the same people, going back inside, pushing paper around, making phone calls, and earning a paycheck. The water fountain was a little too crowded, but she walked toward it anyway, dipping her hands into the square pool of water, resisting the overwhelming urge to dive in and retrieve the thousands of pennies and nickels and the occasional dime or quarter that littered the bottom of the fountain's pool. Instead of diving in she dipped her hands in the water again and ran them through her hair, brushing it away from her forehead and tucking it behind her ears.

She looked around at the businessmen milling about, wondering how many of them she'd been with. Or if any of them recognized her. Maybe she could get one of them to help her out. Tell him how she undercharged all those times and can you just throw me a couple bucks for a drink? She thought she recognized one standing with a few other guys, holding a briefcase and smoking a cigarette and discussing some merger or something, so she crept up to him and asked if he remembered her. You know me, I'm Rainbow. Remember? We went to the Congress a few times on your lunch break and had a good time. The pain in her swollen eye when she tried to give him her best sexy face made her wince. The men looked at one another, not even attempting to mask their disdain, and the man she'd talked to flicked his cigarette at her feet and said listen, bitch, I'll be the first to admit I've fucked a hooker or two, even divorced one, hahaha, but you are one of the foulest women I've ever seen, and if you think I'd get anywhere near that bruised-up ass of yours, you have gone completely insane. Look in a mirror. I wouldn't fuck you with Jared's dick here— pointing at one of the guys, who started laughing uncontrollably then apologizing while he tried to get his laughter under control—would I, Jared? I'd rather fuck a pregnant black midget with one leg, videotape it, and show it at the office Christmas party than be caught dead with you. Now get the FUCK out of my face. All four men walked away, each of his friends slapping the loudmouth on the back.

She stood sobbing in front of the fountain, realizing that she'd never again feel the touch of a man, paid for or otherwise. If she was so hideous, what was the point? All she had ever had that made people want to be with her were her looks and her ability to drive men crazy. With all that gone there would be no money. There would be no food. There would be no more alcohol to make her pain go away. Her life had been rendered completely hopeless overnight, even more hopeless than before. She desperately wanted someone to call her his little pomegranate.

Any man would do, Rainbow thought, so when she walked across the street to Veinte de Agosto Park and saw the statue of Pancho Villa on his horse, looking grizzled and strong, she climbed the statue, collapsing when she reached the top and slid into the saddle, her head against Villa's back. She thought fuck it. I'm finished. They think I'm crazy. Let the cops come and take me away. I deserve to be locked up. There's nothing more I can do. Let them pull me down and drag me to jail forever.

When she saw the lightning break across the sky, all the childhood lessons about staying away from trees and metal objects came rushing back to her. And there she was, sitting atop a bronze statue, in the middle of a park, just waiting to get struck down.

Rainbow lifted her face and watched the lightning splay its ragged fingers across the afternoon sky. She looked for clouds. She turned in the saddle, first one way, then the other. But nothing. Not a cloud. Just heat lightning. Nothing out of the ordinary. She closed her eyes and breathed deeply, needing that freshly washed smell that sweeps in just before and right after a storm. The smell of cleansed air. The smell of new beginnings.

Rainbow waited. She sat behind Pancho Villa, admiring the handiwork of the sculptor who, despite the fact that normally no one would ever view Pancho Villa's back, and certainly never his sombrero or his hair peeking above his shirt collar, had gone through the painstaking effort of carving each individual hair, hair that looked so real Rainbow couldn't help but reach up and try to run her fingers through it. She stood up in the saddle and ran her fingers over the brim of Villa's sombrero, feeling the superb craftsmanship of the weave. A fine, quality hat. One fit for a warrior. And the bullets on his belt, they looked like perfect replicas of the six-shooter bullets that had tamed the Southwest, the same bullets Pancho Villa and his men used in their countryside uprising. She rubbed the bullets with her fingertips. So real. She could pull one out if she wanted to. Borrow Pancho Villa's weapon—I'll bring it right back, I promise—and walk around town shooting the gun up in the air. No, she could ride the horse through the streets of Tucson, shooting off the pistol and forcing people to love her, why didn't she think of that earlier? For the briefest moment, Rainbow knew what it would have been like be on the other end of the rape. The one forcing someone to have sex with her at gunpoint. She felt a puff of power fill her chest like the first breath of the day, that first beautiful breath that you breathe when you realize that you've woken and lived through the night, another glorious day outside waiting to meet you. Yes, she could have been powerful with a gun, forcing people to realize how attractive she was. She and Pancho Villa could ride together, starting right here where El Hoyo had once been, and working their way west, shooting off their pistols and galloping through the streets, the sun on their backs and the wind blowing dirt from their faces and their tangled hair, until they reached the ranches lying west of the city, and then they could turn south and head toward the mission, galloping up to people and forcing them to love her right there beneath the shadow of the cross, then returning to the streets of Tucson, the very streets the horse's shoes were tearing up beneath them, the same streets that would soon be overrun with rushing water and screaming people when the flood finally came and battered the city, chipping the plaster from the thousands of adobe homes dotting the cityscape, rain falling with such ferocity it whipped palm tree fronds down the street like clusters of plucked chicken feathers, the fountain overflowing and expelling the countless wishes cast into it in the form of pennies and nickels and dimes and quarters that spilled into the streets unnoticed by the people running in all directions seeking shelter from the storm, the sheets falling so thickly that people racing to safety would be nothing more than gray blurs passing at random, crashing into each other, tripping and splaying out on the sidewalks and being swept away from where they had fallen until they managed to grab onto a lamppost or a newspaper stand or a tree trunk or the bumper of a parked car, only to right themselves and then struggle against the wind and the rain even more, because in that brief amount of time it had grown even more powerful, thundering against the windows of Tucson's skyscrapers, seeping beneath doors that opened constantly, spewing forth more and more refugees who entered businesses shivering and shaking, some crying, but most angry that they would have to wait in a steamy room full of strangers until the storm cleared, Rainbow could ride past it all, shooting off her gun and never looking back at Tucson and those poor idiots, cowering beneath the dim lights of downtown lobbies, trapped by the flood and clutching at the arms of complete strangers for comfort, shivering and clustered in a mass of wet bodies and wide eyes trained on the river running through the streets.

While her arms were wrapped around Pancho Villa's torso, Rainbow felt the strength of the man, and she couldn't deny how much she wished this dead soldier in front of her were still alive. She wanted to be held by a strong man just one more time. She missed the way her grandfather had held her every night. The way Brightstar had held her in the tunnels.

And even though she hated every person who'd ignored her for the last two days, even though she absolutely despised the manager for banning her from the Congress and the bartender for turning her in, she still longed for someone to notice her and tell her she was beautiful. She would happily forgive any of the men who'd hurt her, right now, even the guy who had humiliated her in front of the fountain. Even him. If only one person would just utter the words my little pomegranate. But everyone had gone on about their day, returning to their offices and mumbling about that crazy drunk hooker out by the fountain who'd cracked up and convinced herself she was attractive enough to score businessmen in broad daylight, right in front of their coworkers.

She heard the crack of thunder and looked up. Off in the distance she was sure she saw storm clouds forming and she thought thank god. It's finally going to happen. Now. Just in time. But she didn't move from where she was, staring at the sky and thirsty for something to drink, sitting atop the statue of Pancho Villa, her arms wrapped around his body, high above the scurrying crowds of flustered people who jostled and shoved in an effort to return home as quickly as possible now that a storm was coming and the work day was finally over, worn out completely from a long day at the office, and now, looking up at the sky, Rainbow hugged the strong, thick torso of Pancho Villa and wished she could just leave too, that he would grab his horse's reins with both hands, turn his head to the side, and tell her to hold on as he spurred the horse and it leaped down from its pedestal and raced past Tucson's houses and barbershops and liquor stores, whose lines of patrons were just now beginning to form with men returning from laboring all day in the orchards east of the city or on the roofs of homes being erected in the foothills, the barbershops filled with men who weren't necessarily in need of a haircut but who simply didn't feel ready to return home to the wives and the children or the empty houses and the TVs and the same news they could get at the barbershop or the liquor store or the bar, she wanted to gallop full speed past the men returning from the fields who ducked into alleys and changed clothes, hoping to make it to the next job busing tables for the dinner rush downtown, changing their clothing as they walked, hopping on one leg while they pulled off dirty jeans and then on the other leg while they pulled on white slacks and then jogging up the block tying their apron strings behind them, too busy to take notice of her and Pancho Villa streaking past them down the road and out into the desert, past the homes where dinners sat waiting on the table and the kids played in the backyard, ignoring the food smells and knowing better than to ask for even a scrap before Dad got home because the cardinal rule of dinnertime is that there is no eating until Dad is seated at the head of the table and Mom has placed the pots on the potholders in the middle of the table and removed the lids, but since Rainbow had no meal waiting for her and only now remembered she hadn't eaten so much as a crust of bread in the past two days, she rested her head on the statue's back and wept—hoping for a miracle, praying she would open her eyes and they would be galloping through the desert, leaving behind Tucson's rancheros and whorehouses and bootleggers and drug smugglers and crooked cops, outrunning them all, the banks and the hotels and the courthouse, the parks and tunnels and Miracle Mile and the Congress, the red evil eyes of the tower that had tortured her for so long, though she could never articulate how, couldn't ever place the reason why each time she passed beneath the eyes resting atop Tucson's tallest structure she shivered and crossed herself, the eyes that never closed but watched over the city, burning bright even beneath the blinding light of the desert sun, blinking and mocking the people passing beneath them, eyes on all four corners, gazing out to the farthest reaches of Tucson—the San Xavier Mission to the south, Gate's Pass to the west, the resorts and ranches to the north, the forest of saguaros to the east—taking note of every action no matter how insignificant or how well hidden, even now the eyes watched as Rainbow wished fiercely for a new life, furrowing her brow and clenching her teeth with all of her strength, wishing it would all wash away, her short life that had been woeful and incomplete, the shunned Rainbow sitting atop the statue while crowds of people passed below, the very same people ignoring her as they always had, unless they had a sexual appetite they longed for her to quench, all of them ignored Rainbow, who only wanted the same things they did—a marriage, boundless love, children to rear, money to travel the world—clutching Pancho Villa with all of her strength, willing him to live again, willing him to rescue her, to race off into the desert and away from here, hugging herself to the bronze statue and surveying the land below, gazing at the awful beauty of the city that had been at once cruel and forgiving, the city that took her in when everyone else had abandoned her, peering past the homes and businesses and thinking my god, from here you can almost see the end of the desert, if only we could leave this place, looking to the west where the Santa Cruz ran the length of the city and thinking yes, we might head in that direction, toward the ocean and California, the land of dreams, yes, we could ride there in a matter of days and start all over, me and Pancho Villa, then staring south toward the interstate where semis sped by on their way to places she had never seen, towns she'd never visited, and over to the east she saw the Congress, her old home, not a door was open to her so why shouldn't she just leave and escape the flood up here on this horse, tall enough to keep her safe, to forage through the flooding streets of Tucson, because she refused to witness the end of a damned city, instead she clutched the statue and begged for it to take off running, but the only response was the gurgling of bile and liquor that had been eating into the lining of her empty stomach, and Rainbow suddenly grew nostalgic for her former home beneath the mall, which had housed her and Brightstar faithfully for those few months and sheltered her from the very people she now wanted to escape forever, she just had to get away, if only the horse would go, if only it would just hop down and run then we could go back to the tunnels and Pancho Villa could take care of me, avenge me with his six-shooter, show those gangs what a real man is like, and Rainbow felt oddly proud of this man in front of her, as if he had already avenged her, as if he too understood how badly she needed to escape and had agreed to it, that he would be her husband, yes, she'd finally found the perfect groom, she understood that this was her prince right here in front of her, a sombrero and some bullets, a strong horse, and the ability to survive in the desert, he had been here all along, oh how many times had she passed him by, ignoring the patient man who watched her come and go and yet still waited, Pancho Villa, who had always loved her and seen her beauty, patiently waiting for Rainbow to climb up behind him and join him as his wife, no paper gown needed, no wedding plans envelope, there would be no smiling guests and no need for a father to give her away, no ceremony was necessary because her entire life had been the ceremony, a slow walk down the aisle that began the day Rainbow was born, the day Marísol Delgado died in her sleep and began dreaming the end of Tucson, no ceremony was necessary because he too wanted to start a new life and raise a big healthy family, but even if he didn't want to start a family that would be okay, either way her life here was done, though she did want to perform one final task with Pancho Villa's gun, to shoot out the red lights that never stopped staring, to shoot out each one and blind the building once and for all, that's all she wanted to do and then they could leave for good, she and her husband, her Panchito—she stroked the hair cascading beneath the brim of his hat—we'll leave and the flood will come and one day years from now our great-great grandchildren can read all about this drowned city, and maybe people will come to visit the tunnels where she'd once lived, sheltered from the world above, all that spray-paint on cement, and if they deciphered it maybe it would tell the story of Tucson in its final days, and suddenly she grew ashamed of herself for not having written everything down, for not scratching the story of Tucson's demise into the walls of her underground home, a permanent parchment that would hold her words until some distant day centuries from now when scientists could analyze her scrawled tale of visions and the evil tower, years from now, when the floodwaters finally receded, leaving behind a muddy surface as pure and rejuvenated as the moon, a fresh start, another chance for humanity to start over—she sat behind her husband with a heavy heart, thinking if I just had a pen and some paper I'd jot down the essence of the story, the horrors in the desert and the wasteland of humanity, Miracle Mile, the underground tunnels, my dead grandfather, my missing mother, the children who played in the park, the gangs, the rape that almost killed me, the education I received from all of it, it all came together, the many lovers she'd had and the countless men she'd never had, the men who abused her, the men who proclaimed their love for her in the throes of passion on the sweat-soaked sheets of her bed on the Mile, the men who told her, in confidence, about the misery of their lives while they lay panting next to Rainbow after they'd mercilessly thrust themselves into her, pounding out their frustrations and disappointments between the welcoming legs of Rainbow, the men who ignored her in her final two days of living, she would gladly write their stories someday, then toss the sheets to the wind, if only Pancho Villa would grab those reins and ride, save me and take me away from here. Please, please, just spur your horse on. I want to feel the wind blowing through my hair. I want to be pretty again. I want to start over. Just jump down from this pedestal and let's ride. She whispered to his back, Pancho, my love, let's leave this horrible city. Let's make it happen. Yes, any minute now it would happen. It was only a matter of time. She could wait. It was okay.

So Rainbow waited.

COLOPHON

Drowning Tucson was designed at Coffee House Press, in the historic
Grain Belt Brewery's Bottling House near downtown Minneapolis.
The text is set in Caslon.

FUNDER ACKNOWLEDGMENTS

Publication of this book was made possible, in part, as a result of a project grant from
the Jerome Foundation, and from the National Endowment for the Arts, a federal
agency, because a great nation deserves great art. Coffee House Press receives major
operating support from the Bush Foundation, the McKnight Foundation, from Target,
and from the Minnesota State Arts Board, through an appropriation from the
Minnesota State Legislature and from the National Endowment for the Arts. Coffee
House also receives support from: three anonymous donors; Allan Appel; Around
Town Literary Media Guides; Bill Berkson; the James L. and Nancy J. Bildner
Foundation; the Patrick and Aimee Butler Family Foundation; the Buuck Family
Foundation; Dorsey & Whitney, LLP; Fredrikson & Byron, P.A.; Sally French; Jennifer
Haugh; Anselm Hollo and Jane Dalrymple-Hollo; Jeffrey Hom; Stephen and Isabel
Keating; Robert and Margaret Kinney; the Kenneth Koch Literary Estate; Allan &
Cinda Kornblum; the Lenfestey Family Foundation; Ethan J. Litman; Mary
McDermid; Rebecca Rand; Schwegman, Lundberg, Woessner, P.A.; John Sjoberg;
David Smith; Jeffrey Sugerman; Stu Wilson and Mel Barker; the Archie D. & Bertha
H. Walker Foundation; the Woessner Freeman Family Foundation in memory of
David Hilton; and many other generous individual donors.

This activity is made possible
in part by a grant from the
Minnesota State Arts Board,
through an appropriation by the
Minnesota State Legislature
and a grant from the National
Endowment for the Arts.

To you and our many readers across the country,
we send our thanks for your continuing support.

Good books are brewing at www.coffeehousepress.org